KU-247-323

Dear Reader,

Spring is on the way, and the Signature Select program offers lots of variety in the reading treats you've come to expect from some of your favorite Harlequin and Silhouette authors.

The second quarter of the year continues the excitement we began in January with a can't-miss drama from Vicki Hinze: *Her Perfect Life*. In it, a female military prisoner regains her freedom only to find that the life she left behind no longer exists. Myrna Mackenzie's *Angel Eyes* gives us the tale of a woman with an unnatural ability to find lost objects and people, and *Confessions of a Party Crasher*, by Holly Jacobs, is a humorous novel about finding happiness—even as an uninvited guest!

Our collections for April, May and June are themed around Mother's Day, matchmaking and time travel. Mothers and daughters are a focus in *From Here to Maternity*, by Tara Taylor Quinn, Karen Rose Smith and Inglath Cooper. You're in for a trio of imaginative time-travel stories by Julie Kenner, Nancy Warren and Jo Leigh in *Perfect Timing*. And a matchmaking New York cabbie is a delightful catalyst to romance in the three stories in *A Fare To Remember*, by Vicki Lewis Thompson, Julie Elizabeth Leto and Kate Hoffmann.

Spring also brings three more original sagas to the Signature Select program. *Hot Chocolate on a Cold Day* tells the story of a Coast Guard worker in Michigan who finds herself intrigued by her new downstairs neighbor. Jenna Mills's *Killing Me Softly* features a heroine who returns to the scene of her own death, and *You Made Me Love You*, by C.J. Carmichael, explores the shattering effects of the death of a charismatic woman on the friends who adored her.

And don't forget, there is original bonus material in every single Signature Select book to give you the inside scoop on the creative process of your favorite authors! Happy reading!

Marsha Zinberg

Marsha Zinberg
Executive Editor
The Signature Select Program

SAGA

JENNA MILLS

Killing Me
SOFTLY

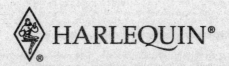

HARLEQUIN®

TORONTO • NEW YORK • LONDON
AMSTERDAM • PARIS • SYDNEY • HAMBURG
STOCKHOLM • ATHENS • TOKYO • MILAN • MADRID
PRAGUE • WARSAW • BUDAPEST • AUCKLAND

ISBN 0-373-83705-4

KILLING ME SOFTLY

This edition published by arrangement with Harlequin Books S.A.

® and TM are trademarks of the publisher. Trademarks indicated with ® are registered in the United States Patent and Trademark Office, the Canadian Trade Marks Office and in other countries.

www.eHarlequin.com

Printed in U.S.A.

AUTHOR NOTE

Killing Me Softly was written during the winter of 2004/2005, long before a hurricane named Katrina ever formed in the southeast Bahamas. As a native of south Louisiana, New Orleans holds a special place in my heart. The history. The spirit of the people. The dialect. The ambiance. The music. The food. The passion. The legends. These are the hallmarks of New Orleans that I set out to share with readers—the hallmarks that cannot be wiped away by any storm. Ever. Like so many others, I watched in horror during those chilling late August days when Katrina stormed ashore and wreaked her havoc, and I mourned for all that was lost. But in my heart I know the city of New Orleans will live on, and prosperity and vitality will return.

In the meantime let me tell you a story about a proud and passionate family named Robichaud, and a part of the country I love. South Louisiana.

Laissez les bon temps roulez!

Writing a book is a solitary experience...but creating one is not! So many people helped make this book possible: For my amazing partners in crime, Cathy, Linda, and Vickie, thank you for putting up with me! For my tremendous agent Roberta Brown, thank you for your unending faith. For my terrific editor Wanda Ottewell, thank you for believing, and for encouraging me to always dig deeper.

For my husband and daughter, thank you for your love, support, and patience.

And a special thanks to my father, for taking the picture that fired my imagination!

PROLOGUE

SHE WAS GONE.

New Orleans police detective Cain Robichaud tore through the dense undergrowth, but even as he came to the clearing, he knew he would find no trace of the woman to whom he'd made love less than forty-eight hours before.

She was gone.

After ten years on the force, he was intimately familiar with the taste and feel and smell of lies and deception. He'd become a master at illusion. No matter how viciously he wanted to believe otherwise, he knew the instructions were just a ruse.

Savannah Trahan was gone.

"It's after midnight!" he called anyway. "I did everything you asked, damn it. *Everything.*"

Come alone, the note had instructed. To the burned-out ruins. At midnight. Leave your service revolver at home.

"Where the hell is she?"

Memories pushed in on him, images he didn't want to see. The sheen of her eyes the first night they'd met. The lingering taste of wintergreen the first time they'd kissed. The feel of her blond hair tangled in his hands. The husky cry that had torn from her throat the first time they'd made love.

There had been no dimmed lights or soft music for them. No bed fitted with silk sheets. That would have been too trite, too tame.

There had never been anything tame about Savannah Trahan.

He'd tried, damn it. He'd done everything short of locking her away to keep her from stumbling too close to the truth. He'd warned her to quit poking around where she didn't belong. He'd made it clear what would happen if she didn't stop taking risks that didn't need to be taken. Graphically, he'd described the fate of others who hadn't known when to stop.

The memory of a single bullet hole dead center between a pair of open, lifeless blue eyes twisted through him.

Savannah hadn't listened. A hotshot investigative reporter, she'd been too drunk on the need for justice to turn away from the investigation that consumed her. And he…he'd been too drunk on *her* to see through her platitudes.

Now she was gone, and just as Cain expected, nothing but the screech of a lone owl answered his hoarse command. The creature sat high atop a skeletal cypress tree, its solitary form silhouetted by the wavery light of a crescent moon.

Dark urges ripped through him. He was a man of action—the blood of his Cajun ancestors ran hot in his veins. He wanted to be doing something, anything. Run. Punish. But all he could do was make sure he was heard.

"You're making a grave mistake!" he warned, surveying his surroundings. A row of crumbling columns jutted up toward the sky, solitary remnants of a once-grand plantation. No longer pristine white, the equally spaced columns had faded to ivory, scarred by the fire that claimed the manor they once embraced. The pillars stood as out of place among the sprawling oaks and towering cypress as Cain did among New Orleans society. Fingers were already being pointed. With every day that the darling of the Baton Rouge evening news remained missing, the whispers grew louder.

"You won't get away with this!" he vowed, striding toward what had been the front of the house. A set of wide rounded steps remained, rising from a tangle of ferns and leading to a verandah that no longer existed.

Cain mounted them. "Savannah!"

"R-Robi…"

The hoarse cry barely registered above the yammering of crickets, but it reverberated through Cain like a shout.

"Savannah!" Heart hammering, he leaped down and ran toward the trees.

"Vannah!" She was the only one who'd ever called him Robi, an abbreviation of his last name. They'd been in bed the first time she'd used it, their legs tangled, hands joined. She'd smiled down at him and said, "More…Robi. More."

Now the leafy canopy stole the light of the moon. The darkness grew deeper, thicker, but Cain never missed a step. This was Robichaud land. He'd grown up scrambling across the gnarled undergrowth and climbing the emaciated cypress trees. He knew every twist and turn. Every hidden trap. Every danger.

"Robi…" Louder. Closer. *"H-help me."*

"Hang on!" Low-hanging branches slapped his face. "I'm here." He tore at vines and stumbled on the knee of an old tree, shouting her name with each step he took. Until the gauzy light of the moon illuminated a flash of pink—and a puddle of red.

"Vannah!" He lunged toward the oak and dropped to his knees, violating everything he knew about proper crime-scene management. He grabbed the silk blouse and drew it to his face, not giving a damn about the blood.

"Robi…h-help me."

His heart kicked violently against his ribs. *"Cher,"* he breathed, twisting toward the voice.

The sight of the tape recorder embedded in a nest of Spanish moss at the base of a tree stopped him cold.

"Robi—please."

Deep inside, the hope he'd been harboring, as fragile as spun glass, shattered. She wasn't here. Had never been here.

"Cain!" The urgent, familiar male voice echoed through the wooded area.

"Where the hell are you?" came a second voice, this one older and strained. A creative stream of Cajun swearing echoed on the warm breeze. "Now is not the time for games!"

Two beams of light cut like knives through the gathering fog. "Cain! Answer me, damn it."

Numbly he balled his hands, still tangled in the mutilated silk blouse, into fists.

That's how they found him. On his knees. Holding her shirt. With blood staining his hands.

Detective Alec Prejean and Sheriff Edouard Robichaud tore through the moss and stopped abruptly, their flashlights aimed like weapons.

"Merde, mon neveu…what the hell have you done?"

CHAPTER ONE

Eighteen months later

THE SECLUDED BAYOU cottage Savannah Trahan had once used as a retreat from the cutthroat world of journalism still stood. There, away from prying eyes, she'd been able to relax and rejuvenate—and rendezvous with the darkly seductive police detective everyone had warned her to steer clear of.

Cannas bloomed in an untended rainbow of red and orange and yellow, guarding and inviting, hinting that once, someone had tended the overgrown grounds. Now waist-high weeds crowded out the walkway, the windows were dark, the door boarded shut.

A lone tire swung from a rope affixed to a stumpy old oak, the breeze easing it in and out of the gathering fog.

It's still there, after all this time.

Renee Fox drew a hand to her mouth and moved closer, careful not to step on a partially secluded anthill. There was a sadness to this remote corner of the swamp, an aura that extended beyond the stark fall day.

Here, in the farthest reaches of southern Louisiana, fall arrived with little of the orange-and-red fanfare northern climes enjoyed. Gray skies and cool damp winds slithered in and stripped the trees of their leaves, turning them from green to brown in the blink of an eye.

"This is private property, *cher.*"

The disembodied voice came from behind her. Dark and drugging, its innate masculinity struck a chord deep within her. And without even turning to look, she knew who stood behind her.

Her heart revved and stalled, her breath hitched. A protest hammered through her. She'd not meant for him to find her here. She'd not meant for him to find her at all.

The Robichauds didn't take kindly to deception.

Brutally aware of the crossroads she'd reached, she took a steadying breath and turned toward him.

He stood beyond the clearing, a shadowy specter lounging against a cypress tree. Fog licked at his long legs and swirled about his chest, making her question whether he existed at all. But the woman in her recognized this was no mere spirit watching her. No ghost, no phantom, no illusion. She recognized him in a heartbeat, the man who resided in the darkest corners of the need that pushed her from day to day. Now he stood dead center between her and the truth she'd come to claim.

Cain Robichaud. She would have known him anywhere, anytime. His picture had been splashed all over the press, even in Canada. The shadows about him were darker, but little else had changed since his days as an undercover detective in the city of sin. Not the midnight-black hair, nor the midnight eyes. Not the square jaw, nor the dark stubble covering it. Not the wide, forbidding shoulders. Not the predatory stance.

He started toward her, his purposeful steps trampling the tall brown grass. "Perhaps you didn't hear me the first time, ma'am, but this is private property."

"I heard you."

He stopped so close his six-foot-plus body crowded out the rest of the world. "Then that makes you a trespasser."

She'd always enjoyed a challenge, had never been one to back down. That trait had always been her greatest asset and, according to her brother, her greatest liability.

"And here I thought Bayou de Foi was a friendly town," she said with all the sugary Southern charm she could muster. "Is this the way you welcome all strangers, or just lucky ones like me?"

The lines of his face tightened. "If you're looking for hospitality, you should head on back to New Orleans, *belle amie.*"

Deep inside, she shivered. This man was not calling her pretty lady as a compliment.

"All a pretty lady like you has to do is name her price."

But not here, she knew instinctively. Not this man. He didn't play by others' rules. He sought to indulge or please no one but himself. "What I'm looking for can't be purchased."

"Everything has a price."

Even your soul? she wanted to ask, but the question jammed in her throat. "Then what's yours?" she surprised herself by asking.

She wasn't sure what she'd expected, but it wasn't laughter. The rough sound broke from his throat and echoed on the breeze. "My price is my penance," he said, then gestured toward the highway. "And like I said, this is private property. It's time for you to be going."

Time changed people. She knew that. So did loss and betrayal. After months of media notoriety, mentions of Cain Robichaud had trickled off to the point where recently there'd been nothing at all. Not even his photography Web site had been updated. It was as though the man had ceased to exist.

"I mean no harm," she said, realizing she had to backtrack. She'd been wrong to play footsy so quickly. "I was just…" Eventually, he would discover her real reason for being here, but the longer she kept him in the dark about her assignment, the safer she was. "Someone I knew used to come here."

Something sharp and volatile flashed through his eyes, but other than that he went unnaturally still. "There's no one here now but you and me."

Heat rushed through her, despite the cool fall breeze. He was right. There were just the two of them, a woman no one would look for and a man many believed belonged behind the steel bars of Angola State Penitentiary.

Vulnerable was not a word she liked, but she'd taken her safety for granted before, and it was not a mistake she would make again. "I can see that. I just—" had to come, to see what remained from that night in the not-so-distant past. "—needed to come here."

"Needed?" In that moment he sounded every bit the cop he'd once been, renowned for securing confessions. Coercion or seduction, the method hadn't mattered. "Trust me. A pretty thing like you, the only thing waiting for you out here is trouble."

That's where he was wrong. Remnants of a life gone by remained, a mystery begging to be solved. There were answers here. And truth.

But those words could not be said.

"I wanted to see if I could still feel her," she said, choosing her words carefully. "My friend who used to come here to clear her head." And to make love with the unorthodox detective who'd made her forget everything she knew about caution and survival.

His expression darkened. *"Who?"* For such a big man, he uttered the question in a deceptively soft voice. "Who is this friend?"

The urge to turn away was strong. Once she spoke the name, there would be no going back. She knew that. If she wanted to walk away, to pretend she'd not stood close enough to Cain Robichaud that she could scrape the whiskers darkening his jaw with her fingertips, she should do so now, before she waded into waters dark and deep. She had only to accept that some questions would never be answered, some needs never met.

She could accept neither.

"Savannah," she said, wincing at the way his eyes went cold and flat. "Savannah Trahan."

It was just a name, that's all she said, but the shadow that fell over Cain made it clear she might as well have cursed his soul to perdition and beyond. Because Savannah Trahan would never be just a name to this man, not when half the parish believed he'd murdered his former lover. Buried her on his land, some believed. Submerged her naked body in the swamp, others claimed. Burned her in a bonfire of her pictures, another said, and let her ashes scatter with the wind.

He stood there so horribly, brutally still, the planes of his face tight, his eyes like shrapnel. Even his mouth flattened, turning into a hard, uncompromising line, and in that instant, he looked frighteningly capable of the cold-blooded murder she'd read about in the newspapers.

Everything became sharper, more intense, carving out the afternoon in sharp relief—the screech of the egrets, the wind slashing through the skeletal trees, the fog soaking into her bones. Even the silence intensified.

He drew the moment out like a death sentence, then shattered it with his voice. *"Who the hell are you?"*

Relief flashed so profound she could taste it. He didn't recognize her. Then reason surfaced. Of course he didn't recognize her. There was no reason he should.

"I asked a question," he said in that same quiet voice. "Don't make me ask again."

An endless valley of lies lay ahead, but right here, right now, she chose to offer the truth. "A friend."

"A friend." He made the word sound like an offense. "Any friend of mine or Savannah's knows better than to come here."

The blade of pain nicked fast and deep. "If you're trying to frighten me," she said, "it's not working."

His smile was sardonic. "I suppose you're not trembling, either."

Refusing to give an inch, she hugged her arms around her middle. "It's cold."

"Maybe on the inside, but not on the out. Try again."

She angled her chin, said nothing. The man could see subtleties and nuances others couldn't. Once, the trait had made him a good cop. It also explained his success as a photographer. His work adorned the walls of galleries in New Orleans, as well as many a coffee-table book and calendar. His flair for shadows and light brought solitude to liveliness, sobriety to gaiety.

The quiet spun out between them, thick, pulsing. From the darkened copse beyond the clearing, dead leaves rustled and twigs snapped. It almost sounded as though—

He pivoted toward the cypress trees jutting up like a line of soldiers separating land from water. "Don't move." Slowly he edged forward. Each step, each movement, each breath still screamed the caution of the cop he used to be.

Renee's imagination sprinted along a dangerous path as she watched him go down on one knee.

"Beautiful."

Heart hammering, she turned to see a great blue heron perched atop the old swing.

"Perfect," Cain murmured as he angled a 35mm camera toward the tire. "Ah…that's ma girl. Me, I'm going to be very, very good to you…"

Until his big hands cradled the sleek metal outfit, Renee hadn't noticed the camera hanging from his shoulder. Easy mistake with a man like Cain. His intensity made it impossible to register anything but the man.

Seconds blurred into minutes, minutes into a searing intimacy. Cain inched closer to the bird while his drugging voice urged the heron to stay in place.

"Let me have you," he coaxed. "I won't hurt you… just want to make you mine."

The black-magic drawl did wicked things to Renee's immunity. How could he shift from suspicious detective to reverent photographer in the space of one broken heartbeat?

Somewhere close by, more twigs snapped. The bird reacted instinctively, lifting its magnificent wings and soaring into the gray sky. But Cain remained crouched, staring at the point where the heron had vanished.

What did he see? Renee wondered. Heavy storm clouds gathering beyond the cypress trees, like she did? Or something different, something no one else could envision.

"You're still here?"

She blinked, saw that he had turned and was moving toward her. "Either that or you're hallucinating."

"My ghosts are my business, Ms...." He destroyed what remained of her personal space. "I don't believe I caught your name."

"No, you were too busy playing big, bad wolf."

An odd light lit in his eyes. "Do I know you?"

Her heart gave a quick, cruel kick. "That's a question only you can answer," she said with a calm that pleased her. Then she took a leap of faith.

"Renee," she said. She'd known this man and all that he represented would be her greatest challenge, but nothing, not months of preparation, nor layers of scar tissue, had prepared her for the rush of being close to him. "Renee Fox."

"Well, then, Ms. Fox." His gaze flicked down the length of her body in a purely male gesture. He made the return journey slowly, thoroughly, leaving her warm and flushed, as though he'd touched her with those big hands of his. "Shall I walk you to your car?"

"I can manage on my own." Had for a long time. Without another word, she turned and strode toward the rental, refusing to let his less-than-enthusiastic greeting deter her.

"The highway's just a few miles down the road." The

falsely friendly words echoed on the breeze. "Don't look back and you'll be in New Orleans before sundown."

Renee ignored the sting and kept walking. No way was she going to give him the satisfaction of looking back. Coming to Bayou de Foi jeopardized the life she'd been quietly building, but she could no longer live without knowing what had really happened the night this man was found with his lover's blood on his hands. She would find out, and she would avenge.

Then, and only then, would she be free from the nightmares that made it impossible for her to sleep with the lights off.

CAIN WATCHED THE WOMAN slide into the nondescript white rental car and pull onto the narrow road, then grabbed his mobile phone and stabbed a series of numbers.

As always, his cousin answered on the second ring. "Damn, you've got to quit freaking me out like that."

Cain couldn't remember the last time Gabe had answered the phone with a simple hello. An assistant distract attorney, Gabe always got straight to business—unless he was playing poker. Then he could tap-dance with the best of them. "Like what?"

"I was about to call you. There's no way I'll be at Ruby's by six. The D.A. just called a quickie for the end of the day, but he doesn't know the meaning of the word."

An old pickup pulling a boat rumbled up the road and momentarily blocked Cain's view of the woman's car. When the truck had passed, the white sedan was gone. "Neither will I."

"Good," Gabe said, and Cain could see his cousin, who preferred T-shirts but had to wear suits, kicked back at his desk, folders scattered around him, dead coffee in his cup, an empty ash tray next to his laptop. "Then, we can just—"

"I'm coming."

"—meet later on…" A pause, then a muttered curse. "What do you mean you're not coming? We've been waiting months for *Oncle* to make a move. You can't bug out on me now."

Cain continued to stare at the scarcely traveled road leading to the back of his property. Almost two years had passed since his career with the NOPD crashed down around him, but the instincts that had made him a good cop remained razor sharp. His former partner called it his spider sense, the tingle at the base of his neck that warned danger lay near. The reaction was always the same, a buzz through his body, a disturbance, like a low-pressure system sweeping in fast. The white sedan could no longer be seen, but the hum remained. There was something off about Renee Fox, like a song played in the wrong key or a photograph taken in the wrong light.

Secrets. Half-truths and outright lies. They swirled around the woman like a shroud, reminding him of the mist that hovered above the stagnant waters of the Manchac Swamp.

"Something's come up in Bayou de Foi," he said. "Something I need to keep an eye on."

Someone.

He'd sensed her before he'd seen her. Someone on his land, someone who didn't belong. The locals knew better than to trespass on Robichaud property, and on the rare occasion he did find people, they wore ratty sneakers and carried fishing poles. He'd never run across a woman in a designer suit and high heels. For a long moment he'd just watched her standing there, long dark hair whipping in the breeze and a faraway gaze in her eyes.

It wasn't until she'd turned toward the swing that he'd realized she wasn't just another apparition, a figment of fantasy he'd indulged entirely too long.

Savannah wasn't coming back.

It didn't matter how many times he waited in the clearing or thought he heard her laughter or smelled her perfume. It didn't matter how many times they still made love during the long, dark hours of the night. He knew that now. He understood the evidence.

Savannah was gone.

Cain glanced back at the infestation of cannas surrounding the cottage. Damn things wouldn't go away. They just kept coming back, thicker and more vibrant with the passing of time. Maybe this year he'd try poison.

"Cain? You there?"

Frowning, he ripped himself from the past. "What?"

"That's what I want to know—what the hell is going on?"

He'd finally lost his mind, that's what. He'd found a beautiful woman alone, and instead of toying with her as he once would have, he'd deliberately growled her off his property.

"Nothing you need to worry about. Best case, I'm there tomorrow morning. Worst case, tomorrow night." He headed toward the trees, hoping to reach the remains of an old pier while the light was still right. "What's the word on the street?"

"Same. *Uncle*'s back, stronger than before and looking to make someone pay for what happened last time. D'Ambrosia's got his ear to the street but nothing specific yet."

"What about Prejean?" Seven weeks before, Cain's former partner, Alec Prejean, left his wife and turned in his badge, then dropped off the face of the planet. "Any word?"

"Nothing new."

The bad feeling in the pit of Cain's stomach drilled deeper. It wasn't like by-the-books Alec to just...disappear. Or to leave the wife to whom he'd been devoted. "Christ."

"No shit."

Cain reached up and slapped away a cluster of vines. "So much for being dead and buried," he muttered, then wound down the call and tromped into the woods.

Oncle was back. Prejean was missing. And now a secretive woman had appeared on his land. He'd be a fool to chalk it all up to coincidence.

ASSISTANT DISTRICT ATTORNEY Gabriel Fontenot hung up the phone and pressed his fingers to his temples. Didn't help. The pressure still pounded against his skull, blurring his vision to the point where he wondered why he'd thrown down two grand for Lasik surgery.

"Marjorie," he said, pressing the intercom button. "Tell Vince I'll be there in five."

Frowning, he loosened his tie and leaned back, wondering what in God's name was keeping Cain from New Orleans. His cousin had been itching to settle the score ever since he'd been railroaded out of town. But he couldn't settle it against a ghost, so he'd been forced to wait. And wait.

For months, there'd been nothing. No rumors, no chatter, no whispers. The mysterious *Oncle* had vanished the second Cain intercepted a sizable shipment of money on its way out of the country. It had been a crippling blow to *Oncle's* organization, but rather than receive credit and commendations, Cain had taken the fall right along with *Oncle*. Because of Savannah.

More than just a woman disappeared that night in the swamp. A vital part of his cousin had, as well.

Frowning, Gabe glanced across the stack of folders on his desk, past a snapshot of his mother and sister, to a framed black-and-white taken at Pat O'Brien's two years before. They'd been celebrating that night, high on life and love and the lead that promised to bring down *Oncle's* crime syndicate. Cain had never been one to smile casually, but even he'd been animated, brought to life by the break in the case and the woman sharing his bed. In the picture, he had Savannah tucked against his side while lifting a beer for a toast. Grinning, Gabe also had his mug extended, while keeping Val close to his side.

Val.

Gabe leaned back in his chair and closed his eyes, but he could still see Val as she'd been back then, laughing and vibrant and...happy. It was hard to believe how quickly things could change, how viciously the events in someone else's life could affect your own.

Val didn't deserve the fallout from Savannah's disappearance. She hadn't deserved to pay the price for actions and decisions that had nothing to do with her.

They'd drifted. Val had grown to resent Gabe's long hours, the endless meetings that he'd been unable to discuss with her. She'd accused him of being obsessed, and he'd had a damn hard time defending himself. She felt shut out, she told him. Alone. Left behind.

And she had been.

"Gabriel," came Marjorie's molasses-tinged, maternal voice from the intercom. "It's been five minutes."

He opened his eyes and glanced at the Rolex Val had given him for his thirtieth birthday three years before, then at the picture. "I'll be right there."

But Val might not be. She'd made that clear.

THE HOTEL ROOM looked as if it belonged in a pre-Civil War plantation home, not a sleepy bayou town southwest of New Orleans. The furniture alone, a massive mahogany bedroom suite, must have cost a small fortune. It wouldn't be hard to imagine a Southern belle sleeping in the big poster bed or primping at the dainty vanity. "This is gorgeous."

The hotel manager breezed in beside Renee. "Isn't it though?" Millie Comeaux, a petite Creole woman with dark hair and dark eyes, had bustled to life the second Renee walked through the door and hadn't stopped chattering since. "When the Robichauds do something, they do it right."

Renee stripped the surprise from her face before turning toward the armoire. When opportunity knocked… "The Robichauds?"

Millie threw open the doors, revealing a television and DVD player. "Oh, I just assumed you knew the Robichauds—everyone does. This is their town, you know. Their parish, really."

Their everything. "Yes, I—"

"When they bought the hotel, they tore it down and rebuilt from scratch. Didn't want a run-of-the-mill hotel, said people had a certain expectation of the Deep South, and it was their duty to give it to them."

Duty and expectation. They were odd words in conjunction with former police detective Cain Robichaud, but with his Uncle Etienne serving in the United States senate, Renee guessed the family was trying to scrub their image clean.

The hotel was impressive. If any of the senator's cronies chose to visit and didn't want to stay in the Big Easy, they could stay in style in Bayou de Foi. The hotel's facade resembled a Greek Revival plantation, complete with Corinthian columns, a wraparound porch and an upstairs verandah. Bushy ferns hung from the exterior rafters, while overflowing barrels of petunias flanked the front door. Inside, the reception area spilled into a foyer, where a curved staircase led to the second level. A massive crystal chandelier oversaw it all.

Millie crossed the room to fiddle with the heavy brocade curtains, drawing Renee's attention from the furniture to the walls. The pale salmon color complemented the bedding and offset the black-and-white artwork. Three gilded silver frames embraced photographs of Louisiana sunsets, stark, haunting images accentuating the play of shadows and light.

One featured a bayou, with two small children in baggy overalls standing with their backs to the camera, looking at the sleepy canal of water, fishing poles at the ready.

There was a shot of the marsh, with a skeletal cypress

tree in focus and everything else artistically blurred, while the sun sat low on the horizon.

But it was the third photo that stole Renee's breath.

In a palette of grays, a row of crumbling columns stretched toward the hazy sky. A cluster of graceful oaks stood in the background. The perfect symmetry of the columns made it clear they'd once flanked a home, but the brick and mortar were no longer there.

"Breathtaking, isn't it?" Millie asked with a sigh. "They were taken by a local."

"He certainly makes an impression."

"Keeps a gallery down on Pecan Street, he does, if you'd like to take any of his work back with you."

Renee found a polite smile, but knew Cain's gallery was the last place she belonged. It was bad enough she'd had to step into his world. His intensity bled into his photographs, even without the use of color. Through the lens of a man who'd once frequented grisly crime scenes, even birds and trees and sunsets looked stark and uncompromising.

"Thanks," she said, because it was the right thing to do. "I may have to take a look, though I'm pretty sure I'm the last person he wants to see."

"What on earth makes you say that?" Millie asked, turning. "Pretty girl like you, I'd think Cain would be more than happy to show you his work."

Showing her the highway was more likely. "Somehow I doubt that. I ran into him out by the old cottage and when I mentioned Savannah—"

The hotel manager sucked in a sharp breath. *"Savannah?"*

Renee chose her words carefully. As deep as the hunger

for information ran, the need for discretion ran even deeper. "I was trying to explain why I'd come to town."

"Ah, child." Millie's voice was thick, tense. Sad. "That explains it then. Nobody speaks that girl's name to Cain. For all intents and purposes, Savannah Trahan never existed."

Renee had known coming here would be hard. She'd realized she might learn things she didn't want to know. But the matter-of-fact words landed like a quick punch to the stomach.

"Has he come to hate her that much?"

"It has nothing to do with hate, nothing at all." Millie glanced at the door before continuing. She almost looked...nervous. "Their affair was the talk of the town. Everyone knew they were carrying on in that cottage at the back of his property."

"Then why doesn't Cain want her name spoken?"

Millie's eyes went dark as she did a quick, shaky sign of the cross. "Because he killed her."

CHAPTER TWO

THERE WAS A VASE OF roses sitting atop a white lace doily. Renee stared at the crimson-tinged yellow petals and the dark green leaves, the long, thorn-lined stems dipping into the blown glass. A quick glance in the mirror revealed her expression to be one of careful, practiced indifference, revealing not one trace of the chill seeping through her.

Because he killed her.

Four words. That's all they were. Cold, clinical, to the point. Words Renee had heard before, insidious claims largely responsible for drawing her to Bayou de Foi.

The media had an appetite for scandal, the darker, the juicier, the better. When one of their own was involved—believed murdered by her cop lover—the fascination escalated into a feeding frenzy. Everywhere Renee looked, she'd been confronted by the rumors and allegations and so-called exposés, but the black, typeset words had never quite seemed real. It had been like reading a disturbing story. But here now, hearing the words spoken aloud, by someone who'd lived through the ordeal, stripped away the bandage of denial.

"Killed her? Are you sure?"

The hotel manager frowned. "They say he was just fooling around with her to keep tabs on her investigation. Even Eddy—that's his uncle—said their affair was just a physical kind of thing. Lust."

Lust. The word sounded so dirty. "Is that what Cain said?"

"As far as I know, he never said one way or the other."

"So no one really knows. It could have been more."

"*Could haves* don't matter," Millie shot back. "All that matters is that girl vanished and Cain was found with her blood on his hands."

The image chilled. "You really think he did it?"

Millie closed her eyes, opened them a long moment later. "I've known that boy since he was knee-high to a nutria. I saw him grow up. He gave me this job. He's always been good to me. It's hard to accept that he could kill in cold blood…"

But all the evidence indicated that he had. Notes from Savannah's apartment indicated her investigation into corruption within the New Orleans Police Department was pointing at her lover. Then she vanished. Seven weeks later her car was found submerged in Manchac Swamp.

Savannah Trahan was never seen again.

Renee turned toward the photograph of the solitary columns and felt the ache deep in her bones.

"You never really know what's beneath the surface." And that was the rub. Everyone had their secrets, buried deep, little half-truths and lies that shaped them into who they were—and the mirage they wanted the world to see. "You might think you know, hope you know, but at the end of the day, the only person you ever really know is yourself."

Millie sighed. "Cain's not someone you want to cross, hon. That boy has never been one to forgive."

"Forgive?" Renee twisted toward her. "Forgive who?"

The widening of Millie's eyes was the only warning she got. "I'd say that's between my nephew and Father Voissin," came a low masculine voice, and on a rush of adrenaline Renee turned to find a tall man dominating the doorway, broad of shoulder and long legged, without a trace of middle-aged spread at his waist. Silver dominated his hair, but enough dark remained to hint at its original color.

Cain's uncle was far more attractive in person than in the angry photos that had once filled the press.

"Ed—Sheriff…" Millie's voice wobbled on the word. "I didn't realize you were stopping by."

"Non?" he drawled, and though his eyes glimmered with potent sexuality, he sounded more like a parent indulging a forgetful child. "Weren't you the one who told Becca we have a visitor?"

Renee realized her mistake immediately, the foolishness of thinking she could make a single move without a Robichaud breathing down her neck.

"Well, yes," Millie was saying. Flushing, she glanced from Renee to the sheriff. "I'm sorry, I didn't realize—"

"Obviously not," he said quietly.

"But she mentioned Savannah, and I thought I should let her know why that's not a good thing to do around here…"

"Very kind of you, too, sugar." The sheriff stepped toward her and put a hand to her waist, steered her toward the hall. "Now be a sweetheart and give me a few minutes with our visitor. If I discover you've left anything out, I'll be sure to fill in the blanks."

"Of course." With a slightly awed look at Edouard, Millie hurried off, leaving Renee alone with Cain's uncle. He turned toward her with the cool, assessing eyes of a cop—but his easy smile was pure Southern gentleman.

"Ms. Fox," he said in a slow molasses drawl. "As sheriff, I like to personally welcome all visitors."

Especially those he wanted gone. "I appreciate it," she said with a forced smile. Now was not the time to provoke. "It's a lovely little town you've got here, almost picture-book perfect."

Unless you looked too close. Then it was neither picture book. Nor perfect.

"It's no secret we've had our trouble," he said, "but we've done a damn fine job of putting all that behind us. Folks around here know I don't tolerate shenanigans." His eyes bored into hers. "They also know not to talk about Savannah."

Her throat went tight. "I'm not here to cause trouble, if that's what you're worried about."

"Not worried at all," he said mildly. They might have been discussing antiques. "Just curious. Bayou de Foi is hardly on the beaten path. It's not often a lady like you comes to our little backwater—unless, of course, she's one of Cain's."

The insinuation scraped. So did the truth. There were very few legitimate reasons for her presence. Soon, she'd have to throw them a bone. "Just passing through," she said.

His gaze slipped to her two suitcases. "Traveling alone?"

Instinctively she glanced at her purse lying on the bed, was relieved she'd snapped it shut and nothing could spill out. "For now."

"Anyone know where you are?"

She stiffened. "Excuse me?"

"Law enforcement isn't pretty," he drawled. "I've seen things I don't like to think about, much less discuss with a lady. I know the danger that comes from being alone. Something happens…it can be a long damned time before anyone realizes it."

The chill was immediate. "I appreciate your concern, *Sheriff,* but I assure you I can take care of myself."

"Glad to hear it," he said, and his eyes were on hers again. "But know that if you need anything—*anything at all*—I'm never too far away."

SHERIFF EDOUARD ROBICHAUD had been in law enforcement long enough to recognize a bluff from a parish away—they didn't call him the Silver Fox simply because he'd returned from Vietnam a twenty-two-year-old with hair the color of his grandfather's.

Frowning, he strode down Main, sparing an occasional nod for the good folk who waved his way. For over twenty-five years he'd kept the parish on an even keel, even during his brother Etienne's senatorial campaign. Things got dicey when Eti won, with a few reporters slipping into town, determined to prove the charming senator who spoke fluent Cajun French had skeletons in his closet.

He did, they all did, but the Robichauds were a

fiercely private family, and folks in the parish knew better than to jabber with strangers. Even Millie and her husband had kept their mouths shut back then. The media went home empty-handed.

Everything had been quiet in the eleven years since, just an occasional mention when a hurricane hit the coast or the Saints made the playoffs—neither of which happened all that often.

Quiet, that was, until the night eighteen months before when a tip had sent Edouard running through the woods only to find his nephew kneeling with his lover's torn blouse balled in his hands, covered in her blood. The murder weapon—a knife—had been found a few feet away.

The memory galled him. He glanced at his watch and picked up his pace, didn't want to be late. Cain said it was important.

He'd warned his nephew not to get involved with that woman. A reporter, for crissakes. But Cain hadn't listened. He'd been too blinded by lust, something else Edouard had warned his nephew against. Not that he didn't enjoy sex, because he did. But Robichauds and intense relationships had a bad track record. Early on Ed had taught himself the importance of keeping a clear head and staying in control, not letting a lady cloud his judgment. Kind of like a priest—but with certain fringe benefits Father Voissin was forbidden to enjoy.

Zydeco music blasted from the open front door of the honky-tonk side of Le Bon Temps. Ed did a cursory check to make sure the early-evening party wasn't out of hand, then stepped into the lobby of the restaurant. Lily greeted him and led him through the crowded dining area, toward the booth at the back of the room, where the Robichauds always dined. Cain sat there, staring at what looked to be a photograph.

The restaurant grew quieter, out of respect Millie always said, but Edouard knew it was salacious curiosity. Everyone loved a scandal, and over the years the Robichauds had provided not just the financing on which the town was built, but the gossip upon which the town thrived. In the days following Cain's arrest, the once sleepy town had again been thrust into the national spotlight. The media had converged on Bayou de Foi hungry to revel in the scandal. Sex and murder. It was a juicy combination no reporter could resist. The press had gotten downright drunk on its witch hunt.

Edouard and Etienne had quieted things down, working hard to keep their deathbed promise to their brother, Cain's father, to keep the boy out of trouble.

But now this woman was here, and Edouard would bet his last dollar that Renee Fox was up to no good. His nephew knew it, too, but Edouard worried that after so many months of living like a monk, Cain might be thinking with the wrong part of his body.

CAIN SLIPPED THE PHOTOGRAPH into his leather portfolio and picked up his beer, took a long, slow drag. He didn't need to glance around to know his uncle was coming. The silence announced that. It always did.

Where Edouard Robichaud walked, the folks of Bayou de Foi stared. Whether it was love, hate or outright fear was debatable, but the citizenry kept putting Edouard back into office, and in turn, Edouard made sure the town ran like a well-oiled machine. There was nothing the man didn't know, no lengths he wouldn't take to ensure he was always, always in control.

Which is why Cain knew Edouard not only knew about the Fox woman's sudden appearance in town, but also that she'd driven south when Cain had told her to drive north, and that she was now ensconced in Bayou de Foi's only hotel.

Like his uncle, Cain made a point of knowing everything there was to know about everything that affected him.

And the lady with the sleek body that made a man think of tangled, sweaty sheets definitely affected him.

Joining him, Edouard wasted little time on pleasantries. "She wants something," he said, signaling the waitress for a drink. An Old Dixie. His usual. "Something from you."

The words *want* and *from you* triggered images Cain knew better than to indulge. He could still see the photographs he'd developed only a few hours before, the image of the reporter materializing like a ghost taking form. Her sudden appearance was so damn dead wrong he couldn't let it go.

"I've got T'Roy on it." Some would say it was a premature to have a private investigator digging into the life of a woman whose only crime was sending off bad vibes—but Cain's instincts were never wrong. And the woman most definitely was.

"He's decent." Edouard paused as the waitress set his bottle of beer on the table. "But it's a dog-damn shame that other gal never surfaced."

Femme de la Nuit. Lady of the Night. Over the four years she'd catered to New Orleans elite, she'd developed a reputation for giving her clientele exactly what they wanted. Information. Cain had started working with her after his cousin Gabe had sung her praises, and the private investigator had never failed to deliver. She'd never revealed her real name, either—or her face. That had been part of her allure.

The slice of regret was quick and brutal, the knowledge that he was as responsible for her death as he was for Savannah's.

"If she's got a skeleton or an agenda, T'Roy will find it," Cain said.

Edouard took a long swig of his beer. "My money's on *Oncle*."

The possibility that the brutal crime organization responsible for taking Savannah from him might now be responsible for delivering the Fox woman sent something dark and primal twisting through Cain. Corruption was to New Orleans what a whore was to a weak-willed man. Everyone knew about the corruption, but few people talked. And virtually no one tried to stop it. Because the payoff was too damn good. One, quite literally, thrived off the other. No one got hurt, and everyone looked the other way.

With *Oncle,* people had gotten more than hurt. They'd died.

Now sources alleged that the Russian Mafia's link into the city was active again, ready to slip from the shadows and finish what Cain had interfered with two years before.

"A man can hope," he said as the waitress returned with two plates of blackened redfish.

There were those who believed Savannah had been

his downfall. That his desire for her had blinded him, made him weak. And maybe they were right. But the heinous way in which she'd been taken from him had made him strong. He'd surrendered his badge, but not his determination to take down *Oncle*.

"But if someone thinks resurrecting Savannah's ghost is all it takes to neutralize me, I look forward to showing him just how wrong he is."

Edouard's eyes took on a gleam. "Well, well. Speak of the devil."

Cain glanced toward the front of the restaurant, where Lily was handing a menu to none other than Renee Fox. She'd abandoned her fashion-magazine suit in favor of black pants and a sweater in muted tones that screamed *expensive* even from across the room. Moss, he noted, the same shade as her eyes.

She took the menu and smiled, then visibly stilled, reminding Cain of the young doe looking up from a watering hole that his Uncle Etienne had wanted a ten-year-old Cain to shoot. As a rite of passage. Cain had lifted the rifle, shot wide.

His preference for film had begun that very day.

Now Renee's gaze went straight to his, and held. The flicker of recognition was dark and immediate, but she neither smiled nor waved.

The urge to penetrate that untouchable aura and make the folly of playing with a Robichaud explicitly and unforgettably clear was strong.

"She's testing you," Edouard said as she lifted her chin and pretended he wasn't there.

"Let her." He'd been lying in wait too long. "She won't win."

THEY WERE WATCHING HER. Renee could feel the glare of the nonexistent spotlight in every pore of her body. The slow burn of Cain's stare had seared her before she'd even turned to find him dining with his uncle. The message in his gaze had been unmistakable—*I'm watching you.*

The warning in his uncle's perusal had been equally chilling—*you've been warned.*

She had. That was true. But too much lay on the line for her to turn back. She'd taken the critical first step. Now she had to keep her eye on the prize and anesthetize herself against the disturbing undercurrent that hummed like a prelude in her blood.

Five minutes dragged into ten, ten into forty. Renee quietly finished her meal and glanced across the restaurant, found Cain lounging in the booth with one arm slung across the back, his long legs jutting out from the table and crossed at the ankles. His message remained clear—*I won't warn you again.*

With equal insolence, she picked up the water glass the waitress had just refilled, lifted it toward him and smiled, then drank deeply.

His gaze darkened, but he didn't move a muscle.

Renee fished out a twenty-dollar bill and smacked it on the table, then stood and walked toward the door with the grace that had been drilled into her by her Southern belle grandmother.

A quiet buzz rippled through the restaurant as she neared the exit, making her realize that just as the sights of countless rifles would track a single mallard across the marsh, the people of Bayou de Foi were tracking her as well. Heart pounding, she glanced at the vacant-eyed birds and game mounted on the walls, and reminded herself Cain was not the only one who would frown upon her presence.

The cool breeze greeted her as she stepped outside. She inhaled deeply of the earthy scent of southern Louisiana, an odd combination of decay and life, and headed down Main Street.

Far from the glare of New Orleans and obscured by trees that had stood for over a century, the sleepy bayou town had a simplicity that seduced almost as completely as the man she'd been warned about. The quiet song of the crickets and the rhythmic refrain of the toads, the occasional splash from the bayou across the street, were all different and yet hauntingly similar to the quiet nights she'd left behind in Nova Scotia.

Confident she was alone, she fished her mobile phone from her purse and punched a series of numbers.

"It's me," she said when the answering machine picked up after the fourth ring. "I'm here…I've made contact."

One week. That's all she had. One week in Cain's fallen world to find the truth, and expose the lies. One week to mete out a justice too long denied.

Seven days hadn't seemed like a long time before she'd stepped off the plane, but now that the clock was ticking, she realized the naïveté of her plan. One week was an eternity. A lot could happen. Lives could change. Hopes could shatter. And the best-laid plans could blow up in her face.

A man like Cain Robichaud only needed one day—*one tiny minute*—to compromise everything.

"Don't worry," she added at the end of her message.

"I'm being careful." She knew better than to play chicken with a wounded animal—and yet, she couldn't suppress the tiny rush of accomplishment. It was the most primitive female victory, the thrill of being able to knock a male off balance. To know that even though he claimed to want her gone, he couldn't stop watching her.

And that's where the danger lay. No matter how seductive she found the cat-and-mouse game, she would have been far safer if she'd never aroused Cain Robichaud's curiosity.

She could still turn back. She'd caught Cain's attention, but he didn't yet think of her as the enemy. There was still time to abandon the plan her grandmother called foolhardy.

Picking up the pieces of a dead woman's life ain't like pickin' up toys, she'd said, and Renee knew it was true. Especially a woman who'd been the victim of a violent crime. Whose attacker remained free.

There was only a finite amount of time she could poke around before curiosity turned to suspicion. Then danger. When a cornered animal was afraid, he didn't run for cover. He attacked.

Biting down on her lip, Renee slipped her phone into her purse. Soon, she would have to give Cain Robichaud a plausible reason for her interest in a warm May night from what seemed like another lifetime, and the questions that had never been fully answered.

What had really happened the night he'd lost his lover? Why was her blood on his hands? There'd never been a body or an indictment, but he'd been forced to give up his badge anyway.

"You're Savannah's friend."

The quiet words stopped her. Pulse jumping, she turned toward the alley between the florist and the coffee shop, saw two men standing in the shadows. Every scrap of self-defense training she'd ever received said to run.

Curiosity wouldn't let her move.

"Don be 'fraid," the taller of the two said. He had to be at least six foot. The gray in his hair placed him somewhere near fifty. "We ain't gonna hurt ya."

Slipping a hand into her purse, she curled her fingers around the butt of the .22 she'd tucked inside, just in case. "How do you know who I am?"

He glanced beyond her, toward the restaurant. "Pretty lady," he said, his eyes sharper, more focused. Alert. "Nice clothes, never seen you before—who else could you be? We don't get many like you here."

"We was at the restaurant," the second man added, this one shorter, with a deeply receding hairline. Younger, Renee guessed. "Saw the Robichauds watching you like a drake on opening day of hunting season."

The analogy didn't sit well. Renee swallowed and studied them closer, found the memory. They had been at Le Bon Ton, a few tables away from her booth. And they had definitely been watching her. "What do you want?"

The taller man shifted his gaze back to her. "The name is Travis," he said, then gestured toward the second man. "This here is Lem."

The smell of liquor that came to her on the breeze explained a lot.

"We mean you no harm," Travis was saying. "We just wanted to tell you to be careful. Folks around here don't like questions."

Instinctively Renee glanced down the quiet street, lined by trees and flanked by buildings, saw the hotel four blocks away. "Thanks. I appreciate the warning—"

"But if you're serious about exposing the truth, I kin tell you things nobody else will."

Renee's breath caught. "About Savannah?"

"About who killed her."

"You know?"

Travis shoved his hands into his pockets. "I've got it narrowed down pretty close."

She knew better than to believe him. He was clearly drunk—or at least he wanted everyone to think that. And yet, something in his eyes got to her—a stark light she immediately recognized as fear. "Then why haven't you gone to the police?"

Lem shifted uneasily, shot a quick look to Travis. "That's enough—"

"Got a wife and a kid," Travis muttered, and the urgency to his voice betrayed the fear the big grizzled man was trying to hide. "A couple of grandkids."

In other words, he was scared spitless.

"Push me."

Mind spinning, she blinked. "What?"

He put a big sweaty hand to her arm and slid it down to her wrist. "Push me away," he practically snapped. "Pretend like I'm annoying you!"

Lem pushed closer.

Renee jerked back. "What—"

"Just do it!" Travis commanded. Then, "Such a sweet thang…"

Someone was watching. Catching on, she shoved him away from her. "I'm not interested," she said extra loudly, to which Travis laughed and staggered back into the alley, Lem hot on his heels.

Only then did Renee allow herself to glance behind her, where she saw a tall woman with long hair standing stiffly outside the restaurant.

THERE WERE MANY WAYS to kill someone—and many more ways to die. Some deaths were visible and public, garishly smeared all over the evening news for the whole world to gawk at. Others were more peaceful and private, quiet almost.

Some people died surrounded by family. For others, it was strangers who stood by them as they drew their last breath. The lucky ones passed alone.

Some deaths were of the body. Others were of the soul.

Cain turned from a photograph of a butterfly hovering over a honeysuckle. He strode away from the exhibit, stared into the darkness. He'd received more than a few horrified looks when he'd announced his plans to renovate the old abandoned church, turn it into his gallery. Even his sister had tried to talk him out of it. The building was cursed, legend said. Had been for almost a century, since someone broke in and desecrated the altar, stole the crucifix and statue of the Virgin Mary. Only a few weeks later a fever hit the town, and no matter how much time locals spent kneeling in prayer, a substantial portion of the town perished.

Cain curled his hands around the porch rail and listened to the crickets and the toads, the bayou gurgling nearby, just as he'd done as a kid, when he and Gabe had concocted increasingly creative dares pertaining to

·the old church. Go inside. Kneel at the altar. Sleep beneath the spot where the crucifix once hung.

The building should have been torched long ago, the locals claimed, but no one dared make the first move. So the town had let the church fall into decay, allowing wild roses to ramble up the sides and the windows, while bougainvillea and camellias consumed the porch railings. Weeds hid the rest.

He couldn't imagine a more perfect place to display his work.

He stood there now, as he had so many other nights, and stared out at the oaks sprawling down the grassy slope toward the water. The shadows danced uneasily, swaying and violating in ways that made his hands curl even more tightly around the wood rail.

Because of the woman.

He turned toward her slowly, found her standing in the shadow of an overgrown white oleander at the far side of the porch. Unnaturally still. Unnaturally pale.

"Hasn't anyone told you," he drawled, and felt the slow burn spread like poison through his body, "it's not smart to be alone with me in the dark?"

CHAPTER THREE

DETECTIVE JOHN D'AMBROSIA emerged from the swarm of tourists crowding historic Jackson Square. He walked with purpose, his expression hard and unreadable. Despite the fact the sun had already gone down, dark aviator glasses concealed his eyes…however Gabe knew the detective saw everything.

The two had been working together for over a year, but Gabe still didn't know much about the man who'd taken over Cain's investigation. He was the son of a Texas oil heiress and New Orleans cop killed in the line of duty. D'Ambrosia kept to himself, never discussed his personal life, always declined invitations for Thursday-night poker. Not even his partner, Alec Prejean, knew much more. D'Ambrosia was rumored to be thorough and efficient, brutal when necessary, always uncompromising.

In a word, the perfect man to replace Cain. With his dark hair, dark eyes and rough edges, all he had to do was slip into a ratty black T-shirt and jeans and he fit in with the city's underbelly with remarkable ease.

"You said it was important," Gabe said when D'Ambrosia approached. "What's going down?"

D'Ambrosia motioned for Gabe to walk with him.

"A body was found in the warehouse district earlier this afternoon. Male. Caucasian. Probably twenty, twenty-five tops."

"Cause of death?"

"Single gunshot to the temple."

"ID?"

"None."

Gabe tensed. "Black fleur-de-lis on his ankle?"

"You got it." The two men stopped at Decatur Street and waited for the light to turn as a horse-drawn carriage packed with tourists ambled past. Nearby, a street performer belted out "Somewhere Over The Rainbow" on his sax.

Gabe chewed on the information, acutely aware eighteen months had passed since the last murder victim had turned up with the mark of a fleur-de-lis. It had been a commercial pilot, and the son of a bitch had been in jail. Cain had made the arrest. *"Oncle."*

D'Ambrosia started walking a second before the light turned green. "Probably a courier."

Gabe reached the sidewalk and the two men turned left.

"There's more," D'Ambrosia said, and his pace quickened. Never once did he look at Gabe. "It's about Prejean."

Alec Prejean was not just Cain's former partner, but also he'd been a friend. Gabe and Val had spent numerous evenings with Prejean and his wife, Tara.

Val. Christ. He'd forgotten to call her, to tell her he'd be late. She'd talked about a special dinner…

"We've made a positive ID on the body," D'Ambrosia said, and his grim tone sent Gabe reeling.

"Oh, Christ, it's not—"

"Not yet." D'Ambrosia wasted no words, not on details, not on compassion. "Prejean was spotted leaving the scene."

CAIN'S IMAGINATION HAD ALWAYS served him well. As a boy he'd frequently left the stuffiness of the Robichaud estate and ventured out into the swamp, where fallen trees and tangled vines created his own personal sanctuary. Later, as a cop, his ability to conjure possibility out of nothingness had kept his solve rate among the highest in the state. As a photographer, his penchant for seeing beauty where others saw only waste had earned him national acclaim and an impressive income. As a man, his proclivity for experimentation brought great pleasure.

But now his imagination betrayed him. He looked at Renee Fox standing not ten feet away, at the shadows playing across her face and the fire burning in her eyes, at the curves bared by her clingy sweater and slim-fitting pants, and knew he needed to see a threat, not a woman who made him itch to touch. And taste.

For a long moment she just stood there, watching him as though she'd come face-to-face with one of the ghosts rumored to inhabit the old church.

Then she stepped toward him and smiled. It was a slow smile, almost mocking. "Tell me something," she said in a voice so rough and smoky his blood ran even hotter. "Do you personally try to run off every visitor to Bayou de Foi?"

He curved his mouth into a slow smile. "Not *every* visitor."

"I see," she said, shoving her hair behind her ears.

"Just us unfortunate souls who innocently stumble across your land?"

"Innocently?" The word practically shot out of him. "There's no such thing as innocence, *cher.*" He pushed away from the porch rail and strolled toward her, didn't stop until he stood so close she had to look up to see him. "Everyone is guilty of something."

The wind blowing off the bayou pushed the hair back into her face, but this time she made no move to brush the strands away. A few lodged against her mouth, a soft pink with the slightest trace of gloss.

Ever since he'd arrived at the gallery the crickets had been carrying on, but as he watched her, he no longer heard them, heard only the sound of her breathing, maybe even her heart if he listened closely enough. He definitely heard her sigh.

Slowly, her gaze locked onto his. "What are *you* guilty of?"

The urge to slide the hair from her face was strong. The curiosity streamed through him like an aphrodisiac. What would she feel like? What would she taste like?

"That's the question, isn't it?" And from what his uncle had said, she hadn't wasted any time asking it. "And while I'm sure the fate of my soul must make intriguing conversation, I assure you it's also quite pointless."

"Tell me, though, which of my alleged sins would you like to know more about. Burning Savannah's pictures?" He'd stood on a warm spring evening with a small bonfire before him, and he'd fed it all he had to give. "That has to make me guilty, right?"

Her eyes almost seemed to glow. "I don't know, does it?"

"What about vanishing for six weeks after the grand jury failed to return an indictment?" He'd never told a soul where he'd gone, what he'd done. Not his uncle, not his cousin, not even his sister. "Does that titillate you?"

The question dangled between them on the cool breeze, but Renee said nothing.

"Or maybe," he said hoarsely, and took a deliberate step closer, violating the proper space between strangers, "you're more interested in how women come and go from my bed faster than I can develop the film of what happens there…"

She lifted her chin. "If that's the truth, yes."

Not many people went toe to toe with him. Even fewer questioned him. He was a man who'd learned to use his size to his advantage: Step a little too close, stare a little too long, and he could send even a jaded punk into a skid. Size and proximity. They were the most reliable weapons he possessed.

Renee Fox responded to neither. She just…looked at him. Sweet Mary, he would have sworn she looked *through* him.

"Why are you still here?" he asked. "What do you want from me?"

"The truth," she said, point-blank. "About Savannah." Her voice was quiet but laced with steel. "After all the rumors, it's only natural I'd want to understand what really happened to her."

"Natural. Now there's an interesting word." A word that had nothing to do with the way her voice flowed through him like the moonshine he and Gabe had sneaked from Uncle Edouard's liquor cabinet in honor of their thirteenth birthdays. "Tell me, *cher*. Does this really feel natural to you?"

Her eyes darkened, answering his question without words. "Completely."

Like hell. On a hot stream of adrenaline, he lifted his hands to his eyes like a camera and framed her face, noted the way the shadows played across her eyes, like Spanish moss shimmying against the night sky. Her irises were dark olive, earthy like the swamp, with the same combination of mystery and beauty and danger.

She went very still. "What are you doing?"

He shifted the angle of his hands, focused on her mouth. Her top lip had a rounded bow, the bottom was full. "Studying," he murmured, knowing he was making her uncomfortable. "Imagining."

The lines of her face went hard as she turned from him and headed for the steps so quickly the curtain of dark hair swung like a shield against her face. "I was wrong to come here."

"Yes, you were." He stepped into her path, not about to let her go. "But you came anyway, and now here we are." Alone. In the dark. "Don't you want to know what I see when I look at you?"

Her shrug was artful. "Not especially."

"I see something wrong," he said anyway. Something that bothered him. "And the cop in me wants to know why."

"That's what this is about? The cop in you?"

"And the photographer," he conceded. "But mostly the man. When he sees you, he sees beauty on the outside, but something darker on the inside. Something…lost and alone. Broken."

That was it. She seemed broken.

Her skin reminded him of the petals of a magnolia, far lighter than the majority of the residents of south Louisiana. It fascinated him to discover there in the faint moonlight that her cheeks could go even paler, creating the kind of stark, washed-out image of a black-and-white photograph, making her look…lost, like a woman out of time and place, who just didn't…belong.

"And I want to know why." The admission surprised him. "Did he do this to you?" he asked, watching closer for flickers of recognition or flares of guilt. "Is that how he controls you?"

Confusion flitted through her eyes. "What are you talking about?"

He was a trained interrogator. He knew the signs of deception. Sometimes they were obvious, such as a twitch. Other times they were more subtle, revelation coming only through pupils going wide or a change in the rhythm of the breath.

Renee gave away nothing.

"The man who sent you here," he clarified, hating the words even as he spoke them. "The man who thinks he can use a woman to break me."

Again.

Her eyes darkened. "No one sent me here to break you," she said, then moved toward one of the windows he cleaned every morning. Light glowed from inside, illuminating the pictures visible from the porch. Dead center hung a photograph of an old oak, its trunk more than three times the size of his waist, its branches so thick that those dipping to the ground made perfect benches. "I just needed to feel closer to Savannah."

"Then you've come to the wrong place." There was nothing of Savannah left here. He'd seen to that.

She turned toward a second picture, this one smaller, more obscure, not in his usual palette of blacks and whites and grays, but with a splash of yellow. A butterfly. It hovered over a honeysuckle, starkly visible against the curve of a woman's shadow thrown across the ground.

Slowly, her hand came to rest against the glass. "You're very talented," she whispered, and the words stabbed deep.

Renee Fox was not the first woman to remark on his talent.

Cain stared at the butterfly, but saw a woman stretched out among tangled black sheets, thick blond hair flirting with her shoulders, a gleam to her slumberous blue eyes, her body nude save for the sheen of perspiration.

You, Robi, are a man of excruciating talent...

Savannah had not been talking about his photographs.

With a fierce shove, Cain stalked to the door of the gallery, reached inside and flicked off the light. "I didn't take that picture."

"Then why is it hanging in your gallery?"

He pulled the door closed and stabbed his key into the lock. "Because it's mine."

Out of the corner of his eye he saw her move toward him. "How much for it?"

"It's not for sale."

She stopped so close he could feel the warmth of her body swirl against the night. "Everything has a price, isn't that what you said?"

The burn started low, spread fast. He turned to see

her standing suspended between shadow and light, and realized the slow burn came from neither anger nor mistrust. "Sweet Mary, I may live to regret this, but I've decided you can stay."

THE FAINT LIGHT of the moon played across Cain's wide cheekbones and emphasized the whiskers shading his jaw, somehow making him look soft when Renee knew without doubt everything about Cain Robichaud was unmistakably hard.

He'd decided? To let her stay? An irritated retort burned through her, but she bit it back, knowing he was right. Whether out of fear or respect, the people of Bayou de Foi jumped when the man many believed guilty of murder barked an order.

If Cain Robichaud wanted her gone, she didn't stand a chance.

If…Cain…wanted…her.

Hearing the words strung together, even if only in her own mind, sent a shiver whispering deep.

"It's been a long time since I've had someone to play with," he added thickly, and the words wound like silken threads around her heart. "Most people are too afraid I'm going to kill them."

Renee just stared. She told herself to say something. Knew she should say something. But her throat had gone tight, and whatever words he deserved, jammed there.

"So tell me, *cher,* just so we're clear. What kind of game are we playing? What kind of rules shall we play by?"

There were no rules. No boundaries. Not when the game was one of life and death.

"Why the frown? Isn't this what you wanted?"

What…she…wanted. Oh, she wanted, all right. A lot. "Are you always this suspicious of people you don't know?"

"Not just people I don't know. Only the naive think knowing someone means you can trust them."

"Once a cop, always a cop," she murmured. He'd said as much.

His laugh was dark. "Ah, *cher*. My instincts have nothing to do with a badge."

"And what are your instincts telling you?"

"That beneath all that bravado, you're hiding something. You stroll onto my land like you have every right to be there, then defy me as though you haven't a clue as to what I'm capable of."

She knew what he was capable of. That was the problem. It was also the draw. She knew she should have gone back to the hotel after her encounter with Travis. She should never have walked deeper into the night, directly toward the oak-shrouded church where people had once come to pray…and mourn.

But the second she'd seen the glow from within, she'd been drawn to move closer, look inside. What she'd seen there had chilled her, even as a warm rush had whispered through her. He'd looked so alone standing in the shadows among photographs that said far more about the man he was, than the places he'd visited.

The butterfly…

Angling her chin, she shoved the unwanted emotion aside and focused on an equally unwanted possibility. "I suppose your instincts are why you arranged for my little welcoming committee?"

His eyes narrowed. *"Pardon?"*

"The two men who so gallantly wanted to warn me this evening after I left the restaurant." On more of a fishing expedition than a crucifixion, she held back their names. It disturbed her to realize how badly she wanted his denial. "How much did you pay them to prove your point and scare me off?"

The rumble started low in his chest. "You think I paid someone to scare you off?"

She lifted a single eyebrow. "Didn't you?"

He stepped closer, crowding her against the side of the old church. "You really think I'm the kind of man who pays others to do his dirty work?"

Her breath quickened. No. She didn't think that at all. If Cain Robichaud had dirty work to do, he took great pleasure in doing it himself.

"I have to consider the possibility," she whispered.

His thighs brushed her hips. "But you don't want to." His voice was quiet, hoarse. "I can see that in the way you're looking at me."

The night pulsed around them, thick, intimate, reducing the world to just the two of them. She eased the hair from her face and reminded herself to breathe, but only succeeded in drawing the scent of patchouli and clove deep within her.

The urge to step away was strong, but he stood too close, wedging her between his big body and the wall. "How is that?" she asked. "Like you've lost your mind?"

His smile was slow, purely carnal. *"Non,* like I'm the only man in the world." Shadows played across the planes of his face, emphasizing the glow to his eyes, the heavy whiskers at his jaw. "The mistrust and the fascination, the curiosity, like you're looking at something you want to touch, but aren't sure if you put your hand out whether you'll be kissed—or bitten."

Her heart kicked hard. Every instinct for survival told her to break the contact between them, look away, focus on the statue of a woman seated on a park bench overlooking the bayou, waiting for a lover who never returned. But she didn't move. "All that just from my eyes?"

"I'm a photographer." He raised a hand to her face, but rather than touching, he traced the outline through the smoky air. "You can look for my secrets all you want, but know that before all is said and done, I'll have yours, too."

Because God help her, she would give it to him.

"Be careful what you wish for," she shot back with a silkiness that pleased her. Refusing to give an inch, she slipped under his arm and let a slow smile of her own curve her lips. "Some secrets are best left buried."

Without waiting for a reply, she crossed the porch, went down the steps and headed for her hotel.

Cain caught up with her near the statue. His hand found her wrist, his fingers closed around flesh and bone—gently. She turned slowly, felt her pulse jump when she saw the glitter in his eyes.

"A pretty lady like you in the middle of the night—" his fingers moved with the words, slid to skim the inside of her palm "—maybe you should let me take you back to your hotel room."

The words shimmied through her like an intimate caress, leaving warmth everywhere they touched. She felt herself lean into him, reach up to him, forget every damning reason she had for staying away from this man.

His gaze slipped down her body, then returned to her face with equal leisure, revealing the glow of invitation—and the burn of warning. "Be very sure...."

CHAPTER FOUR

THE DESIRE TO TASTE and feel and discover stunned her. Renee looked up into his brutally handsome face and felt her breath catch, her heart race. The night pulsed in perfect rhythm with the dance of his fingers against her hand, creating an intimacy that could tempt even a nun.

Renee was not a nun—but nor was she naive.

Women come and go from my bed faster than I can develop the film of what happens there....

One week was all she had. One day was already gone. Six remained—at most. In only a few hours Cain had blurred the lines between them. He was good at that. He knew how to manipulate any situation to get what he wanted, how to use size and strength, even his reputation, to twist circumstances to his advantage. He wasn't above using sex to intimidate and control.

Nor was she—but tonight was not the time to carelessly toss down gauntlets he was sure to pick up.

"Not necessary," she said, twisting her wrist from his hand.

He made no move to stop her, just watched her with a dark light in his eyes. "Maybe not tonight, *cher.* But soon."

It was the *soon* that fed the ache deep inside. But she

ignored the temptation and kept her face blank as she turned. This time she had no problem walking away.

THE SUN WAS BARELY UP when she arrived at the library. She sat quietly on a bench, sipping coffee from the shop across the street and jotting in a notebook. The steady breeze blowing in from the bayou whipped her hair against her face, but she made no move to brush it away.

Intrigued, Edouard leaned back in his chair and watched her through his office window.

"I can be on the next plane to New Orleans," Etienne said from the Hart Office Building in Washington.

"No." The word came without hesitation. "There's no need to feed a fire." Etienne's abrupt return would accomplish nothing except extra publicity, which Edouard categorically did not need. "Everything's under control."

Sometimes it still amazed Edouard that someone as excitable as his brother had gotten himself elected to the highest echelons of government.

But then, that's what smooth talking and an easy smile could do for you.

"You'll take care of it then?"

Edouard glanced toward the library and frowned. Of course he would take care of it. That's what he did, what he'd done since the time they were boys and Etienne had come home dead drunk for the first time. Just because Edouard didn't have a fancy office and a face that had been on the cover of national news magazines didn't mean he wasn't capable.

Family came first. The town second. There wasn't time for a third.

"I've got someone looking into her," he told his

brother. Cain had T'Roy, but Edouard preferred to do his own dirty work. "If she's got a hidden agenda, I'll find it."

The call wound down, and Edouard swiveled in his chair to review the contents of the folder open on his desk—the desk his grand-daddy had occupied until his death at the age of eighty-four. The articles clipped from various newspapers stared back at him, nasty reminders of how fast a man could go from hero to goat. His nephew had been doing his job, leading the investigation against a dangerous criminal organization. But in the blink of an eye—

Not the blink of an eye, he corrected. The stroke of a pen. Cain's investigation had been going fine until his informants started turning up dead and critical evidence went missing, whipping the media into a frenzy. Stories about a cop turned dirty had been splashed all over the front pages.

Then Cain had been found with Savannah's blood on his hands, and the suspicions had turned into an unholy witch hunt. With the heat turned up, illegal activities had conveniently dried up, leaving his nephew with a burning thirst for vengeance but no more than a phantom to follow.

Someone had gone to great lengths to frame Cain for a crime he did not commit.

Edouard had gone to even greater lengths to clear him.

Yanking open his desk drawer, he looked for a cigarette that wasn't there. Some said his thirst for justice was his downfall. At least, *someone* had said that. But she hadn't understood. To her the world was a simple place. A friendly place. Pretty and untarnished. She believed in white picket fences and rainbows, fairy tales and promises that lasted forever.

Vietnam had taught him otherwise. He'd learned the truth about the dark side of human nature there: a man with his head in the clouds was doomed to stumble and fall.

A man needed a purpose. Goals. That's what kept him strong. Kept him focused.

It was why he'd come home from 'Nam with nothing worse than a head full of silver hair, whereas so many of his buddies had come home in body bags.

Frowning, Edouard leaned down and opened the bottom drawer of his desk, fumbled under a stack of reports and pulled out an old wooden frame. The black-and-white picture had weathered, but they were all still there, young and innocent and drunk on the promise of the future. He couldn't believe how young they looked—couldn't believe he'd ever been that young.

Or that naive.

Only a week later, three of them had landed in 'Nam.

Two tours later, only two of them had come home.

Holding the photo, Edouard leaned back in his chair and turned toward Renee Fox. She'd stopped writing in the notebook, now just looked toward Main Street with the oddest expression on her face.

He wasn't nearly as uneasy about her presence as he wanted everyone to think. The criminal, after all, always returned to the scene of the crime.

It just took time.

And while he was pretty dog damn sure Renee Fox was not responsible for hanging Cain out to dry, maybe,

62 KILLING ME SOFTLY

just maybe, she would lead Edouard straight to the bastard who was.

The buzz of his intercom broke his thoughts. "What's up, Becca? I told you not to interrupt unless it was urgent."

"It is urgent," his secretary said. "It's about Travis."

"Comeaux?" he asked, frustrated. Travis Comeaux and Lem Lemoine had a habit of showing up in the strangest of places. "Where's he passed out this time?"

"That's just it," Becca said. "His wife says he didn't come home last night."

"That's nothing—"

"His car is there. Keys are in the ignition, and Millie swears there's blood on the seat. But she can't find Travis anywhere."

GONE. IT WAS ALL GONE. Every article, every piece of microfiche, every magazine—everything with the slightest reference to Cain and Savannah was gone.

"How can it be gone?" Renee asked the librarian. "Are you sure it's not somewhere else?"

The research librarian, Lena Mae Lamont, closed the file cabinet. "I'm sorry, but there's nowhere else it would be."

"Maybe in a local collection section?"

Lena Mae shook her head. "I've already looked there."

Someone had beat Renee here. She knew it as surely as she knew she was being stonewalled. Maybe last night, or maybe days or weeks before, but someone had deliberately scrubbed information about Cain and Savannah from the public domain.

Frustration tightened her chest, followed quickly by

a punishing stab of disappointment. She'd researched the case as much as she could from afar, using the Internet to secure articles from the *New Orleans Times-Picayune* and the *Baton Rouge Advocate,* but instinct insisted that the payoff would come here in Bayou de Foi, from the accounts and opinions of the locals.

Accounts and opinions that were now missing.

Renee had a feeling she knew just who to thank for that little stumbling block, too.

"Maybe you can help me with this," she said, handing Lena Mae a slip of paper. "It's a book. *Louisiana Lore and Legends.*" It had come up when she'd done an Internet search on Robichaud and murder. "I couldn't find it either."

Lena Mae, an attractive dark-haired woman with light brown eyes and olive skin, accessed the card catalog and checked the Dewey Decimal number, then led Renee to a section on Louisiana history—a section Renee had already checked.

"I'm sorry," Lena Mae said after scanning every shelf. "It seems to be missing, as well."

"Could someone have checked it out?"

A search in the library's surprisingly elaborate computer system refuted that possibility.

"But why?" Renee took a deep breath, reminded herself to stay calm. "I understand why someone might take the files pertaining to the murder investigation, but what does this book have to do with anything? It was published in *1954.*"

Lena Mae frowned. "Because of the legend, I suppose."

Renee blinked. "Legend?"

The lines remained carved in Lena Mae's face, but

she forced a laugh. "You know us Louisianans. We've got legends about everything."

"I wasn't aware of one pertaining to the Robichauds," Renee said.

"And I'm afraid I can't tell you what it is, either." Lena Mae glanced nervously toward the front door. "The Robichauds fund this library, and with Etienne in the senate, they're real cautious of what information gets released. If you want to know, you'll have to talk to one of them."

It was starting. Less than twenty-four hours after her arrival, the town was shutting its doors and barring its windows. The stream of information was already drying up.

But Renee *had* learned something—Cain was not the first Robichaud to tango with murder.

"NEVER HEARD…her," Gabe said above the garble of static coming across the mobile phone. "You…me to run…through NICS?"

"Not yet," Cain bit out as the hotel came into view through the lingering rain. Almost an hour had passed since T'Roy's phone call, but the P.I.'s revelations still burned like a hot poker to the gut. "I want to see what I can get out of her first."

He looked forward to it, actually.

"Let…know if…change your…ind."

"Will do." Scowling at the lame connection, Cain swung into the parking lot. Damn phone company didn't seem to understand that the Robichauds hadn't forked over big bucks for the substandard cellular service to continue.

"Cain…Prejean's…spotted."

He killed the ignition. "Where?"

"…murder…"

Reaching for the door, Cain went very still. "Repeat that."

"…courier murdered…" Gabe's voice broke in and out of the crackle. "Prej…running from…scene."

Cain squeezed his eyes shut, opened them a moment later. His former partner had been one of the few to stand by Cain during the Grand Jury trial, even though he'd been there that night, had seen Cain kneeling with Renee's blood on his hands. "No." He shoved open the door and stepped into the drizzle. "I don't give a rat's ass what it looks like, Alec did not kill that courier."

"…just thought…should know."

"I'll be there tonight," he said, striding toward the town's signature hotel. Once, he'd found great pride in the massive columns that flanked it. Now, he couldn't look at them without seeing the ruins south of town. "We'll talk then."

Without breaking pace, Cain wound down the call and pushed through the doors, shoved the damp hair from his face and took the curving stairs two at a time.

The door at the end of the hall served as a flimsy barrier to a former undercover cop accustomed to infiltrating ironclad criminal organizations. He could knock it down with a shove, but something he didn't understand kept him from just barging in.

He knocked loudly and placed his finger over the peephole.

"Yes?" Her voice rasped with the roughness of sleep.

He wondered if he had visited hers, as she had visited his. "Can I help you?"

Despite his anger, his body responded. "You better believe you can." In ways that could easily destroy them both. "Open up and I'll show you how."

Silence. Absolute, deafening silence.

"Don't make me use my key," he warned, sliding his hand into the front pocket of his suddenly tight jeans.

A sigh. He heard it through the two-inch layer of wood, as provocative and damning as though it brushed his neck. "Cain."

"Don't pretend you're surprised. This is what you wanted, *non?*"

More silence, followed by another sigh. *"Non."*

Sweet Mary Mother of God. Her voice flowed like honey when she spoke in English, but when she used it to caress a word in French, even one simple syllable, it conjured images of sin and—

"Don't test me." To prove his point, he jingled his keys.

A chain rattled, followed by the click of the dead bolt. Slowly, the wood eased from between them to reveal her leaning against the door frame. She didn't look frightened, as Millie had. She looked resigned.

"Far be it for me to test one of the mighty Robichauds."

The words, the tone, had the effect she no doubt intended. For a second, a damning fraction of a second, shame taunted him.

Do you make it a point of personally trying to run off every visitor to Bayou de Foi?

He pushed the question aside and strode into her room. The bed caught his eye first, the tangled sheets and indentation on one of the feather pillows. Then he noticed the heap of damp clothes on the floor near the bathroom, the stylish, slightly muddy boots. And despite everything, the thought of this buttoned-up woman getting caught in the rain fired through him. He turned toward her, took in the bulky hotel-provided robe wrapped around her body and gaping at the chest. Her damp hair was still tangled and pushed back from her face. She wore no makeup. Water slid down her legs.

"What in God's name are you doing answering the door dressed like that?" he demanded.

A smile flirted with her pale lips. "You didn't give me much of a choice, did you?" She moved from the door, leaving it open. "Had I taken the time to get dressed, you would have barged in using your key." She arched an eyebrow. "Care to tell me which would have been more indecent?"

The image formed before he could stop it, of walking in to find her sliding out of the terry robe and into something more…appropriate.

"Do they train you to deceive?" he asked in a deliberately quiet voice. "Or does that just come naturally?"

At first he thought she would say nothing, sidestepping his demand as she'd done the day before. But she angled her chin. "You know."

"You didn't really think I wouldn't find out, did you?" It hadn't even taken that much effort. "A quick Internet search and there you are, *True Crime*'s newest addition, acclaimed for your ability to dig up secrets and hang them out to dry." As far as smut TV went, *True Crime* ranked right up there with the most offensive. "Is that how you get your kicks?" When her eyes flared, he took a deliberate step closer. "Telling lies and exploiting scandal, no matter who you screw in the process?"

"I'm here to do a job, Cain. A job I take very seriously. Screwing you has nothing to do with it."

"Your job is snooping into my life?"

Defiance flashed through her eyes. "At the moment, yes."

The tightening started in his gut and shot out through his body. There was anger, yes, a cold feeling he'd lived with day in and day out during the weeks after Savannah vanished, but damn it, it was the disappointment that punished. He'd wanted to believe her. He'd wanted to believe she was just a woman passing through town.

Now the truth burned. Renee Fox had come to Bayou de Foi to resurrect Savannah—and nail him to the wall—all in the name of journalism. "You stood there on the porch last night, smiling, when all along you knew you were here to crucify me?"

The first trace of nervousness flitted across her face. "I'm not here to crucify you."

"Then what would you call it?"

"Research," she said with that stubborn tilt to her chin. "I'm here to see if there's a story to tell."

"A story?" The word, the simplicity it implied, sickened. He'd seen the show, after all, and he knew there was nothing simple or innocent about the scandals it exploited. "This is my life you're talking about, not some sordid little it-was-a-dark-and-stormy-night tale."

"I'd think an innocent man would welcome the opportunity to clear his name."

"Trust me, *cher*," he said very quietly, with absolutely no emotion to his voice. "You can't clear my name."

She staggered back from his words, as though he'd pummeled her with fists and not the truth. "No?" Determination glowed in her eyes. "Why not?"

He stared down at her, at the way her hair tumbled from her face, revealing skin ridiculously beautiful and flawless for a woman her age. The blast of lust was obscene—and dangerous as hell. He had no business being attracted to this woman, not when she was out to destroy his life.

"I don't owe you any explanations."

"Is that what you'll say when I have a camera trained on you?" she asked with equal directness, sounding exactly like the reporter he now knew her to be.

"Rest assured," he said. "There will be no cameras."

They stood that way a long moment, locked in a fierce battle neither wanted to lose. Now, at last, he understood why she'd disturbed him upon sight, why he'd been unable to quit thinking about her.

"Was it all a lie?" he asked harshly. "Did you even know Savannah?"

Her mouth trembled slightly before she answered. "I would never lie about that." Emotion flooded her expression. "That's why I'm here," she said in an oddly thick voice. "Because of Savannah—I know enough to make me want to know more."

He stepped closer. "Reporters aren't welcome in my town."

Finally she backed away from him, but the massive mahogany armoire stopped her retreat. "I'm not a reporter."

He reached toward her, his hands framing, but not touching, her flushed cheeks. "Then what would you call it?"

"A researcher."

"And just what, goddamn it, is the difference?"

"A reporter reports the news. A researcher explores the unknown."

The heat radiating from her robe seared through him, bringing the unwanted temptation to press her against the armoire and teach her firsthand about exploring the unknown.

"So somebody else can report it," he said instead, his hands settling against the warmth of her cheeks.

She flinched, didn't twist away. "Not report. Share. Milton Leonard is a respected journalist. He treats each story with care and respect."

"Care and respect?" He almost choked on the words. "I've seen the show, *cher*. The more sex, violence and scandal, the better."

Her eyes flared. "Like you said, your life."

The burn started low, spread fast. "And I intend to keep it that way—*my* life is not for public consumption."

"I don't want to consume anything, Cain. I just want the truth. Does that really frighten you so much?"

He stared at her a long moment before answering. He should be furious. This woman wanted to tear apart his life, and yet there was something about the way she stared at him, that ridiculous glint in her eyes and the slight part to her lips, that overrode the darker emotions, replaced them with something even more dangerous.

"You really want to know what frightens me?" he asked with a slow, lethal smile.

"Yes."

The spurt of enjoyment was so damn wrong. "You,"

he said in a rough, quiet voice. "You frighten me." The shock on her face felt better than it should have. "The fact that despite everything you've told me, all I can think about is what it would feel like to put my mouth to yours." He leaned closer, until just a fraction of an inch separated them.

"Would you taste like lies?" he murmured, "or like sin?"

She sucked in a sharp little breath and lifted her eyes to his. "The truth," she whispered, then stunned him by lifting her hands to his chest and giving him a good solid shove. "I would taste like the truth."

God help him, he laughed. "We'll see about that," he drawled. Then because he didn't trust himself to stay, he turned and walked to the door, pivoting before leaving. She stood with her back against the armoire, its dark finish highlighting the lack of color in her cheeks. A swing of dark hair curtained her face.

Cain steeled himself against the stirring deep within. "A word to the wise. Little girls who play with fire get burned."

She didn't so much as flinch. "I haven't been a little girl for a long time."

He refused to let himself smile. *"Touché"* was all he said, then he walked away.

RENEE STOOD THAT way for a long time, with her back to the armoire, staring at the empty hallway. Her heart thrummed a painful rhythm. Shock seared her throat. Cain had been gone for fifteen minutes, but she could still feel the heat radiating from his body, like the first blast of summer air after a long cold winter.

She had to be more careful. She could not let the man realize how deeply she responded to him. Falling under Cain's spell invited consequences more dangerous than she was willing to risk.

Swallowing hard, she turned toward the armoire and looked into the mirror, searching for any trace of the woman she'd once been. The woman who'd loved blindly, foolishly, without reason or caution. The woman who'd been confronted with evidence that shattered her world.

The woman whose life had ended one hot, sticky night eighteen months before.

Shaking, she crossed the room and slammed the door, then grabbed the phone from her purse and punched a familiar number.

"Gran," she said when the cherished voice answered, the voice of the woman who had loved and protected and healed her. Slowly, she sucked in a deep breath, then let it out. "It's me…Savannah."

CHAPTER FIVE

New Orleans
Two years earlier

HE WARNED ME TO LEAVE him alone. He warned me to mind my own business. He warned me to stay away.

The good detective might as well have thrown open his doors and invited me in, spread out his secrets like gourmet chocolates on a fine silver serving tray.

I, in turn, warned *him* to watch *his* back. Savannah Trahan doesn't run scared, I informed him, and I don't take no for an answer. Unless, of course, no is the answer I want.

There is no faster way to lure me in, than to try to shut me out. My brother calls me nosy. My editor calls me a Pulitzer prize in the waiting. The police detective who thinks I'm trying to sabotage his investigation calls me dangerous.

They're all right.

With the hour pushing toward midnight, I work my way down Royal Street, toward an antique shop where an informant waits. I dressed with care, making sure I look neither like the reporter I am, nor the call girls who come out to play after the sun goes down. In jeans, a black turtleneck and my brother's old bomber jacket, I blend in perfectly.

Of course, in a town like New Orleans, that's easy to do. Anything goes here, and usually does. Sometimes being here, working for one of the local affiliates, still feels like a dream.

And to think it all started because of my fascination with urban legends.

At first the wild claims that kept appearing in my e-mail box seemed about as likely as syringes found in movie theater seats or identity theft through hotel key-cards. God knows every time I opened e-mail, my inbox overflowed with scams and hoaxes.

The Russian Mafia in New Orleans? As if.

But the e-mails kept coming, and along with them details. Very, very specific details.

Reporters love details.

Organized crime targeting the Big Easy is nothing all that startling. This is Louisiana, after all. Greased palms are practically a way of life here.

What caught my attention—and my imagination—were the references to the gaming industry, an electronic device, code named the Goose, small enough to fit into the palm of a child's hand. Slap it to the side of a random slot machine, and ta-da! Payoff city.

Once I started digging, rumors had come out of the woodwork like cockroaches—more often than not dismissed as propaganda—of unusually large payouts at local casinos, sometimes as many as twenty per night.

The allegations of extortion are different. No one

wants to talk about those. At least not in public and on record.

But I'd found notes in the strangest places, claims of casino owners being backed against the wall, demands of huge sums of blackmail money in exchange for never using the device again.

That's why I'm here. A note. From an informant. He's ready to talk.

And I'm ready to listen.

It's the part of my job I thrive on, gathering facts, sifting through the pieces, seeing how they fit together. And, when necessary, butting heads with those who try to block my path, even cops. Make that *especially* cops, particularly one who gets off playing games with—

Footsteps. Someone less trained would never notice them. They're not that loud. Not heavy. But they are in perfect cadence with my own.

Heart hammering, I slow my steps.

The soft thudding behind me slows, as well.

On a nasty rush of adrenaline, I pick up my pace.

The rhythm behind me increases.

Two blocks from my target, I slip my hand inside my purse and curl my fingers around the butt of my .22. My station manager would be furious if he knew I'd defied his orders and carry a gun instead of Mace, but self-protection isn't something I take lightly. Neither are risks.

I am so not ending up a statistic.

My heart races so hard it hurts to breathe, but with the determination that comes from growing up a little sister, I slide my finger onto the trigger. And spin.

Nothing. Just Royal Street, its sleepy collection of antique shops and restaurants. On the opposite sidewalk, a young couple is walking away from me hand in hand, so lost in each other I doubt they're aware the rest of the world exists. Farther down, two well-dressed older women stand in front of a shop window, pointing at something inside.

But no one is on my side of the street.

The rush of relief is intense. But so is the frustration. I'm not crazy. Someone *is* following me.

Frowning, I turn back toward my destination.

He's on me so fast there's no time to scream. I pull my hand from my purse, but he's faster, stronger, and the gun slips from my fingers. His hand clamps around my wrist. His pelvis bumps up against mine. And in a lightning-quick move he's backed me into an alley and up against a wall of damp bricks.

"Well, well, well," he murmurs, and my heart, beating hard and fast only seconds before, slams to a cruel halt. "Isn't it past your bedtime, *cher?*"

Viciously I lift my eyes to his. "Detective." The word bursts out of me. "You have precisely five seconds to take your hands off me before I scream."

He doesn't move. "Rule number one," he says in that slow, black-molasses voice of his, the one I want to despise but don't. "When issuing a threat, make sure it's something the other party fears." His eyes go dark. "Not something they've been craving for weeks."

The words sear through me like a shot of bourbon. "I've always heard rule number one is to keep your cards close to your chest, not splay them on the table for the world to see."

His mouth, normally a hard, uncompromising line,

curves into a carnal smile. "That depends upon what it is you want," he says, leaning closer.

My throat goes dry. "And what is it you want?" I ask against every scrap of better judgment I possess. The draw is too strong. The curiosity.

Detective Cain Robichaud still has my wrist in his hand. He draws it higher, positions it against the wall near my face. All the while his eyes smolder. "You," he says, and I feel the hardness of his body push into mine.

Then, with an abruptness that stuns me, he pulls back and looks me dead in the eye. "Out of my town."

It's a bald-faced lie and we both know it.

"I suppose that's why you can't keep your hands off me?" We've been playing this game for weeks, shadow-dancing around each other, baiting, taunting, stepping close then pulling away. He doesn't like me stepping too close to his investigation—which makes me wonder why. What is he afraid of? What does he not want me to find?

"Just what is it you're trying to do, Detective? Scare me off…or seduce me?"

"Whatever works," he murmurs. "I'd enjoy both just fine."

The ache starts low, spreads fast. "How about answering a few questions?"

"Isn't that what I'm doing?"

"About *Oncle*—and the Goose—"

The gleam in his eyes is the only warning I get. "You sure you want to play this game?" he asks, stepping closer.

I smile. My heart rate surges. "Quite."

"Let her go or you're a dead man." A different voice. Eerily quiet. Wholly lethal. It rips through the intimacy and jars me back into reality.

"Adrian—"

My brother emerges from the right and plows into Detective Robichaud, sending them both sprawling to the ground.

"You son of a bitch!" he shouts, rolling on top of the detective and rearing back with his right fist.

Robichaud catches it. "Be very sure, Trahan." Despite the darkness, I can see the lethal glint to his eyes. My brother isn't a small man, but the detective has a good five inches and fifty pounds on him. He could crush Adrian without breaking a sweat. "Assaulting an officer carries jail time."

Adrian glares down at him. "What about assaulting a woman? Police brutality? What do they carry?"

Robichaud glances at me through those hypnotic eyes of his. "Did I hurt you, sugar?"

Something as simple as a voice shouldn't be able to heat my blood.

"Did I touch you in any way that you found offensive or inappropriate?"

Slowly, I take the wrist he held into my other hand, and gently caress the flesh. "Adrian, it wasn't what it looked like." But even as I say the words, uncertainty nags at me. "We were just—" I stop mid-sentence and stare at the two of them.

New Orleans isn't a huge city, but big enough that I should be able to walk down a street without running into the cop trying to halt my investigation and my brother, unless—

"There was no informant," I breathe, and the truth twists deep. One of these two men arranged the midnight meeting for God only knows what reason. "This was all some kind of twisted test."

A shadow crosses my brother's face, and I have my answer—and my culprit.

"Vannah—"

"Don't bother." Adrian, general manager of New Orleans's biggest and newest casino, has been trying to derail my investigation for weeks. There's nothing going on, he insists. Everything's fine. The rumors about a new breed of organized crime are just that. Rumors. Stories.

There's no such thing as a Goose.

There haven't been payoffs.

No one has gone missing.

The airline pilot who committed suicide after being arrested had a drinking problem—not one with organized crime.

Right. Math may not be my thing, but I can add two and two. I know when four smells like trouble.

"Kill each other if you want," I say, glaring down at the two of them. "But know this. I'll have the truth one way or another." I pause, look Cain Robichaud dead in the eye. "You can play big bad wolf all you want, Detective. You can try to scare me off, run me off, even seduce me if that's how you get off. But in the end—you…will… fail."

With that I turn and walk away.

CHAPTER SIX

Bayou de Foi
Present day

RENEE CLOSED HER EYES, refused to yield to the emotion searing her throat. Her past with Cain seemed like another lifetime, an intense story she'd read long, long ago. But with every minute she spent in Bayou de Foi, every scorching look Cain sent her way, every touch, every threat, the memories rushed back, hotter and deeper than before.

Opening her eyes, she looked into the mirror and lifted a hand to her face, traced the line of her reconstructed cheekbone.

He didn't recognize her. The realization should not have stung. Anonymity was what she wanted, after all, what she'd planned. What she needed. But nothing had prepared her for the gleam of raw desire in Cain's eyes…a gleam that had haunted her during the months spent recovering from a brutal attack.

A gleam now directed at a woman he'd just met.

The twist of jealousy was ridiculous, but the want in Cain's eyes felt like a betrayal of everything they'd once shared.

But then, if the arrest reports were accurate, they'd never shared anything more than mind-blowing sex.

It galled her that she no longer knew. It wasn't that she didn't remember. She did. In excruciating detail. But everything she'd once believed, everything she'd valued, died that steamy night eighteen months before. The doctors may have restored her physical body, but no one could touch the damage inside.

No one.

That's why she was here, despite her grandmother's pleadings to leave well enough alone. She couldn't do that. Couldn't waltz forward with her life while so many loose ends dangled. The only way to get on with the business of living was to return to the town, the night, where everything had ended.

Answers. That's what she needed, once and for all. Justice.

Sometimes she felt like a ghost, walking anonymously among the living, knowing their secrets while they knew nothing of her. To the people of Bayou de Foi, she was a stranger. But she knew them intimately. She knew their wants, hopes and dreams. Their desires. She knew Millie had gotten married when she was sixteen and that Lem and Travis fancied themselves amateur detectives. She knew the reason for the sadness in Lena Mae's eyes.

And she knew why Cain didn't want her asking questions.

It shouldn't scrape that no one, in turn, recognized her.

The people of Bayou de Foi thought she was dead. Their lives had gone on. During the year and a half she'd spent recovering, her friends had lived and laughed and loved. Seasons had come and gone. Babies had been born. Couples married. Dreams pursued.

And all the while, a murderer walked among them.

The reality, the memory, turned everything inside Renee stone cold. She glanced at a picture from her research file, a snapshot taken days before her investigation blew up in her face. Cain stared up at her, his eyes secretive, his mouth an uncompromising line. He had his arm around her, holding her close. Val had always said they made a stunning couple, her fair, Germanic complexion the perfect complement to Cain's dark Cajun features. Her brightness the perfect balm to offset his shadows.

Val.

What had happened to her in the ensuing months? Renee didn't think Val and Gabe had married, but she didn't know why. The night before Savannah went missing, Gabe had asked her opinion about engagement rings. He'd wanted something special…

Savannah had brought him to a small jeweler in the Quarter and straight to a stunning emerald-cut diamond flanked by two tapered baguettes in an exquisite platinum setting.

Frowning at the memory, she lifted her eyes to the mirror. It still jarred her to find a stranger looking back at her, but she recognized the rare opportunity she'd been given. She'd worked hard to create her alibi, had sold *True Crime* on the proposed segment and constructed an elaborate, albeit phony, professional Web site. Now, courtesy of a new face and a new voice, a borrowed name, she was poised to undertake the ultimate undercover assignment—solve her own murder.

"Heard you got some trouble down your way, Ed."

The late-afternoon sun glinted through the dense canopy of oaks, falling in little slivers along the highway much the way it had cut against the jungle floor back in 'Nam. Edouard squinted against it, wondered if there'd ever come a time when the slightest thing didn't throw him back.

Of course, a phone call from Nathan Lambert didn't help.

"Then you must be listening to the wrong people again," he said, steering the cruiser off the main highway and onto a small country road.

"Oh?" the celebrated importer/exporter asked. As kids, he and his brother had attended the same boarding school as the Robichauds. As adults, the whole state of Louisiana was barely big enough for both families. "You mean there's not a pretty little reporter down there digging up your secrets?"

Edouard swerved around a fallen branch alongside the road. "You mean Renee?" He let his voice thicken with fondness on her name. "That sweet thing wouldn't hurt a fly."

Nathan laughed. "Is that a fact?"

"That it is."

"Glad to hear it," Nathan said, and Edouard could almost see him in his St. Charles Avenue mansion, leaning back in his desk chair with a glass of brandy in his hands. "Sure would have been a shame if history had to repeat itself."

Down the driveway, the Acadian style frame house came into view. "That's not going to happen."

"I mean, if a second woman were to come sniffing

around Cain—wouldn't be too good if something were to happen to her, too, would it? Wouldn't look too good for any of you."

Edouard braked suddenly. "Stay away from my family, Lambert. We don't need your kind of help."

"I mean, what if people started asking questions… wondering just what that reporter was getting close to—and who was running scared." Nathan hesitated. *"Again."*

Nathan was enjoying this a little too much. Edouard lifted a hand to his chest and rubbed, reminded himself now was not the time to lose control.

Never was the time.

A man had to keep himself focused.

"No one's going to be asking questions," he said, his voice low and forceful, "because nothing's going to happen to anyone."

But sweet God have mercy—he didn't know why he hadn't realized it before. No matter who Renee Fox was or who she worked for, what her intent was, her very presence jeopardized them all.

If someone wanted to launch a killing blow to his family—a political enemy of Etienne's or a nuisance with an ax to grind—Renee Fox presented the perfect weapon.

"If that's what you want to believe," Nathan said mildly. "But you should know, regardless of how you got your nephew out of that last jam, this time rumor has it he's going to fry."

The line went dead.

Edouard yanked the earpiece from his face and let it fall to the seat, stared at the thin black cord lying on the seat next to a plate of cookies. He'd known all along the

Fox woman's presence left them vulnerable. He just hadn't realize *how* vulnerable. Even if the killing blow didn't come from her, it would come from someone.

Lambert was right. All someone had to do was off the reporter and make sure there was a body, and this time Cain *would* fry.

Swearing softly, he reached for a cookie, ended up shoving the whole plate to the floorboard. Damn things had been arriving like clockwork every other Monday for the past several years. No one claimed to know where they came from. As sheriff, he didn't much like unsolved mysteries, but as a man, he rather found it flattering.

And hell. He liked chocolate-chip cookies.

Swearing under his breath, he yanked open the glovebox and pulled out a cigarette, jabbed in the lighter.

Renee Fox didn't need to be run out of town.

She needed to be protected.

It was a damn strange irony.

Refusing to let his hands shake, he grabbed the lighter and lit the cigarette, brought it to his mouth.

But did not take a drag.

He hadn't in over twelve years.

On a low growl he threw the car door open and strode toward the house he'd built forts behind as a child. He found Millie standing on the wide porch. Her surprisingly long dark hair fell from the ponytail and blew in the cool breeze, reminding him of so many other times he'd stopped by to say hello and check in on things, just like Jesse had asked.

Jesse. Hard to believe it had been a quarter of a

century since he'd held his best friend's hand as he took his last breath in some godforsaken field hospital on the outskirts of Saigon.

Throwing the cigarette to the ground, he crushed it with his boot.

"Ed." Millie started toward him. "Oh, my God, no—"

He caught her as her knees went out from her. "No," he said, hating that for so many folks, his presence meant bad news. But that was the way of it, he knew. The role of law enforcement. His job wasn't to make nicey-nice. It was to keep the peace, no matter what that entailed.

"We don't know anything more," he quickly explained, and the color came back to Millie's cheeks. He could still see her as she'd been the day she married Travis, when he'd stood as best man to his best friend's little brother. Jesse would have wanted that. "I do have some questions, though."

She swiped the hair from her face. "Yes, yes, of course. Come on in." She disentangled herself and turned briskly toward the house, ushered him into the darkly paneled front room.

"Let me get you something to drink," she said, and before he could protest, she was gone.

The furniture was all old, original pieces from Travis and Jesse's parents, who'd passed on within two months of each other five years back. Edouard glanced from the heavily curtained window to the old piano, then back toward the fireplace.

The portrait was new.

He moved closer, drawn by the luminescent quality to the oil painting of two young girls in crisp white dresses, juxtaposed against the plantation ruins just outside of town.

"Isn't it lovely?" Millie said from behind him.

He turned to find her approaching with a glass of iced tea in her hands and a smile on her face. "Lena Mae did that for me last spring."

"Lena Mae?" He took the tea and stepped closer, stared at the innocence in the faces of the girls.

Of course. *Lena.*

"Those are Amy's girls," Millie said, referring to her daughter who lived over in Arizona. "They were here for Easter."

"They're beautiful," he said. Lena had captured them perfectly—why the hell hadn't he known she painted?

Forcing himself to look away, Edouard abruptly returned the conversation to Travis. Damn renegade. Edouard had warned him countless times to mind his own business, but Travis never had.

"I need you to tell me everything you can about Travis's activities the past few weeks. Anything unusual?" Fisherman by day, conspiracy theorist by night, Travis had never learned where not to poke his nose. Edouard's deputies had already confiscated his computer, but so far, nothing.

"What was he working on?" he asked.

Millie frowned. "He didn't talk to me about that kind of thing."

Actually, Edouard was pretty sure Travis and Millie hadn't talked about much. Catholic down to their toes, divorce wasn't an option, despite the drinking he knew Millie despised. "Think. It's important. To help him, I have to know in what direction to look." Giving her a minute, he looked away, saw the old oak secretary. And the photograph.

The same one he kept in his bottom desk drawer.

They all looked too dog damn young—Jesse, Travis and Edouard, Millie and Lena and his sister Julia. They'd just graduated. War lay around the corner. But down by the old burned-out bridge, the lazy summer day had been perfect.

"There's nothing," Millie said, drawing his attention back to Travis. "The last time I saw him was when I got home from work yesterday."

Edouard pounced. "Did you tell him anything about that Fox woman?"

"Just a little. Nothing about that scene with you." Millie narrowed her eyes and glowered at him. "What in the world were you trying to do, anyway? Scare her half to death?"

He took another sip of tea. "If we're lucky."

"You're a piece of work, Edouard Robichaud, you know that?"

The exasperated tone warmed him. But there was no time for sentiment. "This is my town, Millie. I'm not going to let another reporter come around and stir up trouble."

Just like that the light drained from her eyes. "You think her being here has something to do with the blood in Travis's car?"

"Too soon to know," he said, setting the now-empty glass in a coaster on the coffee table. "Him and Lem been known to tie one on in the past, go sleep it off somewhere."

"But the blood—"

The tears in her eyes got him. "I know, hon," he said, pulling her into his arms. "I know."

CHAPTER SEVEN

VALERIE HOPKINS SQUINTED at the antique mantel clock. The Roman numerals were faint, but she knew not much time had passed since the Westminster chimes announced Gabe was over three hours late.

She refused to cry. There'd been enough tears. After three years together she knew the more emotional she became, the more Gabe withdrew. He was a man who dealt in facts not emotions. He saw the world in black or white. There was no gray.

In the beginning, her insecurity had baffled him. Then, later, after they'd become lovers, it had alarmed. Now, it frustrated. He'd told her he loved her, and that meant he did.

To him, it was as simple as that.

But as Val lay in the darkness, listening to his keys jingle in the door, uncertainty streamed through her. Gone were the easy times, the fun times, when they would stay up till all hours, drinking expensive wine and sharing secrets, making love until the sun came up. Gone was the laughter. The innocence.

They'd died right along with Savannah.

The front door opened and closed. She heard him move through the house, his footsteps as quiet as his touch had once been gentle. He wasn't rough now; that wasn't the problem. A little roughness would have been a welcome change. He just wasn't—there.

"Honey, that you?" The words were sleep-roughened, tinged with more emotion than she'd intended.

He crossed to the sofa and went down on one knee. "Thought you'd be in bed," he whispered, lifting a hand to her face. "I didn't mean to wake you."

His touch, painfully tentative for a lover of three years, sent an ache through her. "Couldn't sleep." Not after how they'd left things that morning, when she'd stormed out without even saying goodbye. "I'm sorry about this morning."

"Don't worry about it," he said as he always did. "You were right to be upset with me."

"Your job is important, I know that. I was silly to expect you to play hooky just because my client never showed." A real-estate agent, Val enjoyed a schedule much more flexible than Gabe's.

"It was a sweet thought. Maybe when things slow down—"

She put her index finger to his mouth. "Shh," she said. "Don't say it, okay?" They both knew it wasn't true. Things at the district attorney's office never slowed down.

Gabe wouldn't let them.

He moved relentlessly from case to case, pursuing justice like a phantom that could never be caught. Because of his dad.

"Dinner's in the fridge." The candles were in the trash.

"Thanks, babe, but I'm not really hungry."

The twist of disappointment made no sense. "Vince

called a couple of hours ago." She'd sat in the bathtub, surrounded by fading bubbles, not aware of how cold the water had become until the district attorney's phone call had blown Gabe's story about working late.

Gabe's expression, a poker face that helped him rack up at local tournaments, gave away absolutely nothing. "He reached my mobile."

Questions burned the back of her throat, but she refused to voice them, didn't want to let herself become that needy, clingy person her mother had always been.

"I was with Cain," he offered, but said no more.

When it came to his cousin, he rarely did. The more Cain called, the more distant Gabe became. For a while there, after Savannah died, Gabe hadn't had much contact with Cain. No one had. After the Grand Jury failed to come back with an indictment, he'd all but dropped off the face of the planet. There had been the occasional rumor of a sighting, but never from Gabe.

Instinct warned he knew more than he was saying. And that made her uncomfortable.

"It's late." With a soft smile, she lifted a hand to the whiskers at his jaw. "We should get to bed."

"Christ, you're amazing," he murmured, and there was unspoken gratitude in his voice for not pressing him further.

"Not really." She paused, loving the feel of his hand sliding down her throat. "I just…" The second his fingers eased back the silk of her pajama top and brushed her breast, her mind went blank. Sensation flooded her, the quick rush of anticipation, and eagerly she drew his face down to hers.

The bourbon on his breath was like a slap to the face.

Gabe had not initiated lovemaking in weeks. Maybe months. He was always too tired or too stressed, too distracted. The hour was too late or he had to get up too early.

That it took the influence of alcohol to have him reaching for her, wanting her, added insult to injury.

"Let me show you how amazing," she whispered despite the disappointment. Driven by needs that ran deeper than pride ever could, she drew him closer and arched into him, gave herself to him as completely as she could.

But feared it would never be complete enough.

RENEE JERKED AWAKE to the shadowy light of night and tried to breathe, but the weight of memory pushed down on her like the dark slimy water that had almost ended her life. That's what she needed to remember. The night of the attack. The devastating evidence she'd uncovered the day before. The horror of seeing a knife flash in the darkness, of feeling it slice into her flesh. The screaming and the blood. The running. The crash.

With a hand to her mouth, she slipped from bed and pulled on the bulky robe the hotel had provided. Nothing made sense. Nothing. She was a smart woman. Perceptive. Thorough.

How could she have been so wrong?

The soft ring of the bedside phone halted the unsettling line of thought. Exhaling, she reached for the receiver. "Gran?"

"I'm sorry," the caller said, and though her voice was rough and tough, she sounded frightened. "I must have the wrong room. I was trying to reach Renee Fox."

"That's me," she said. "I'm Renee. Who's this?"

"The name doesn't matter," the woman said. "But you need to know that you're looking in the wrong place."

CAIN STEPPED BACK FROM the pool table in the back of Leroy's and studied the last three balls on the green felt. One stripe, the eight and the cue. "Did they find her?"

D'Ambrosia took a beer from the waitress and handed her a stack of ones, then waited until she was out of earshot before answering. "Some teenagers stumbled across her car at the old Windmere factory in Algiers. She was in the trunk."

Cain swore softly. Violence he understood, even accepted. Retribution came with the territory. But it was the car that got him, the car that sneaked in like a sucker punch to his gut.

Savannah's car had vanished.

Savannah's car had been found submerged in the murky waters of Manchac Swamp.

Sometimes he still awoke at night, as cold and wet as he'd been that June evening when he'd watched a nameless, faceless cop take a crowbar to Savannah's trunk. Cain had stood in the drizzle like a man facing his execution squad, jaw set, arms at his sides, watching but unable to stop, unable to do anything or feel anything—not the rain, not the horror that seeped through the canvas of his jacket and into his skin. There'd been only the agonizing weight of each second that dragged by, slower and slower until each mocking riff of his heart felt like a broken lifetime.

Until the trunk popped open.

And then he'd gone to his knees.

"It's your shot," D'Ambrosia said, and only then did

Cain realize he'd violated his own personal rule and let himself go back.

"*Merde*," he muttered, leaning over the table to check an angle. They weren't talking about Savannah. They were talking about the sixty-seven-year-old mother of a casino manager who'd gone to the cops with what he knew. "How's Fenton taking it?"

D'Ambrosia rolled the bottle of beer in his hands. "Like he's supposed to—as a warning."

"What condition was the body in?"

"Alive." D'Ambrosia squatted to study Cain's shot. "Bound and gagged and roughed up, but alive."

Cain wasn't proud of the quick rush of envy. "*Oncle* has other plans for him then." Otherwise, Keith Fenton would be planning a funeral, not lining up insurance coverage.

"What about the woman?" D'Ambrosia finished off his beer. "You think she's involved?"

The question sounded casual enough, part of the give and take between men on opposite sides of the law, but the same side of justice. D'Ambrosia could lose his badge for conspiring with Cain and both men knew it.

Cain rocked back on his heels and studied his shot, then rolled forward and slid the cue he'd been using for the past fifteen years between his fingers. "Eight ball in the back right pocket," he called as he sent the white ball spinning across the worn felt. It slammed into D'Ambrosia's striped ten, which nudged the adjacent black ball straight into the back right pocket.

"Son of a bitch," D'Ambrosia swore, pulling out his wallet. "I'm done."

"You were done before we ever started," Cain

pointed out. D'Ambrosia's finesse with darts did not carry to the pool table. But it did extend to interrogations. "Leave the woman to me."

The detective forked over his last fifty. "She could be a plant."

Cain shoved the wrinkled bill into his pocket. "She could."

"Pretty lady sent in to distract you," D'Ambrosia went on, voicing the very thoughts that taunted Cain as he'd driven from Bayou de Foi to New Orleans. "Gets you all hot and bothered while *Oncle* moves in for the kill."

Cain looked up at his friend and pierced him with the same look he'd given the airline pilot he'd busted trying to ferry dirty money out of the country. "She can try."

D'Ambrosia understood what he didn't say. "And you'll enjoy every minute of it?"

The woman was thirty-five miles away, tucked safe and sound in the big poster bed of her hotel room, under surveillance, and yet the heat of anticipation rushed through him.

"Funny thing about playing games." With a dark smile, he tossed his cue stick onto the table. "A smart man only falls into the same trap once."

TWENTY MINUTES LATER, Cain maneuvered his car into a tight spot along St. Charles Avenue. During the day, the street was lined with tourists and locals, out for sight-seeing or a walk, catching a ride on one of the streetcars that rumbled through a tunnel of oaks stretching from Audubon Park to the Quarter.

But at this time of night, most of the activity had died down, leaving only the occasional college kids crowding into a late night café or drunks looking for the mansion that belonged to the vampire writer.

Cain took it all in as he strolled up a sidewalk, lined by bloodred mums, to a welcoming front porch dripping with colorful bougainvillea even in November.

A single light burned beside the screen door.

He didn't have to knock. The door swung open and the woman stepped into the night. The white silk robe he'd picked out for her shimmered in the darkness as she opened her arms. "You're late."

CHAPTER EIGHT

"YOU CAN CALL ME ANGEL."

Frowning, Renee studied the woman who'd called her the night before. Actually, woman was a stretch. The thin blonde seemed more like a girl. Early twenties, tops. Long blond hair framed a delicately featured face, and for a fractured moment Renee felt as though she were looking at herself in a mirror.

Then reality slashed in, reminding her that she no longer wore her hair blond. Among other things.

They sat at a small table across from the cathedral in Jackson Square, normally occupied by a palm reader named Magdalene—the perfect cover for a chance meeting that would not arouse suspicion.

In the mornings, while the rest of the Vieux Carré slept off the excesses of the night before, the pedestrian mall bustled with tourists and locals, merchants and street artists. The rich scent of coffee drifted in from across Decatur. Even the horn player already stood in place, loitering outside Café du Monde and playing "When The Saints Come Marching In," despite the frigid wind blowing across the river.

"Angel?" Renee asked.

"That's what he calls me."

"He?"

"Cain," the girl said, the one who looked so very much like Renee had. Once.

Renee braced herself. "I take it you know him."

"I do," Angel said, but her smile, an unsettling combination of fascination and bone-chilling fear, said so much more. It was a contrast Renee knew well, the way a recovering alcoholic gazes at a glass of scotch just before he falls off the wagon.

"You know him, too," Angel said. Understanding stripped away pretenses and heaved the truth between them. "But I bet you never took his money."

It took every ounce of willpower Renee had not to jerk back from the table—and the images trying to form in her mind.

"They think that just because they got more money than God, they can buy whatever they want. Women. A good time. Fast cars or judges or juries. Doesn't matter. They own it all."

"You're saying the Robichauds bought Cain's acquittal?"

"His cousin is with the D.A.'s office. You do the math."

Renee already had. "Gabe removed himself from the case."

"So they say," Angel said, lifting a hand to fiddle with the small gold hoop at her eyebrow. "Whether you believe them or not is another story. People like them say *what* they want to, *when* they want to. If someone gets hurt in the process, too flipping bad, right?"

Renee stilled. "Did someone hurt you, honey? Cain? Is that what this is about?"

Angel shook her head, sending stringy hair flinging into her face. "He never hurt me, not physically, anyway."

"Then how?"

Blue eyes closed, opened a heartbeat later. "You got any idea what it feels like to go to bed with a man but wake up with a stack of hundred-dollar bills?"

Something dark and cold tightened through Renee. "Cain Robichaud paid you for sex?"

The girl looked down, said nothing.

"Angel." Renee squeezed the palm she still held in her hand. "Talk to me."

Angel brought her index finger to her palm, where she slowly traced the curve of her lifeline. "Let's just say when Cain was a cop, he had a fondness for mixing business and pleasure. I…obliged him on both fronts."

Everything inside Renee went brutally still. She sat there staring at the girl she now realized was a prostitute, but saw only a tall man in a dark jacket, a pair of dark hypnotic eyes and an insolent smile.

Just mixin' business and pleasure, belle amie. *Nothing wrong with that.*

Depends upon how you do the mixing.

I think you'll like it…like it a lot.

She had. But now she shoved hard against the unwanted memory. There had never been any commitment between her and Cain, no promises, but hearing a hooker parrot Cain's words shredded her in ways she'd never imagined possible.

"And just how did you oblige him?" she forced herself to ask. She'd come here for information, after all. The truth.

No matter how badly it hurt.

Angel looked up, startled. "You want details?"

The image formed all by itself, of Cain and this girl, together, hot and naked and sweaty, rolling and twisting, thrashing, bringing each other to the brink and back.

Clenching her jaw, she pretended to study Angel's fate line. "Facts."

"I gave him what he wanted," Angel said. "He made it worth my while to watch that casino owner who was carrying on with his sister. Adrian Trahan. There was bad blood between those two."

Bad blood was an understatement. Cain and her brother hated each other. Renee didn't want to ask the question but had to. "You think he killed him?"

Angel's hand twitched. "Can't say for sure but when he came to me the night they found Trahan's body, he was…different. I mean, he was never a man for chitchat or foreplay, but that night he was all over me the second I opened the door. Before he left he told me he didn't need me to watch Trahan anymore. Things had taken a different…direction."

Renee sat back. "He came to you the night they found the body?" That, she knew, was a bald-faced lie.

"Not really the night, it was more like the morning. It was just starting to get light when Cain showed up."

The coldness spread deeper. Renee wanted to deny the girl's words but couldn't. The simple truth was she had no idea where Cain had gone after he left her town house just before dawn.

The feeling of devastation came back to her, wound like a silk scarf around her neck.

Angel stuck her left arm across the table. "You want

to see my other hand—it can't look like we're just chitchatting."

Renee stared at the girl's hand, her pale flesh and long, elegant fingers full of silver rings. She wanted to hate her, this deceptively fey prostitute with the huge lost eyes and the compromised soul. But all she felt was pity…and the sobering realization that the two of them weren't that different.

Cain hadn't paid Savannah with money, but with the currency of illusion and hope, dreams she'd wanted desperately to believe could come true.

Swallowing, she watched a tattered maple leaf fluttering around on the breeze. "How often did Cain come to you?"

Angel shrugged. "Three or four times a week…most every night he wasn't with that reporter."

Renee leaned closer over Angel's palm, focusing on her heart line. "Savannah Trahan."

"Poor woman had no idea she was sleeping with the man she was trying to nail. It was hardly a surprise what happened to her."

"Why not?"

"Cain's thorough," Angel said, watching the maple leaf settle next to her hand. "Once he realized he'd never get that woman to quit snooping around by sleeping with her, he had no choice but to silence her."

CAIN TWISTED AGAINST the sheets and cracked open an eye, cursed the quiet trill of his mobile phone. He didn't want to be interrupted, didn't want to leave her hot and flushed and eager for more. It had been so damn long—

The phone kept ringing.

Swearing, he reached for the damn thing and stabbed the talk button. Then he swore more creatively.

"What do you mean not there?" he demanded, and just like that the last vestiges of the dream shattered, leaving him tangled in the sheets, ready and naked, but alone. "Where the hell is she?"

Millie's explanation didn't come close to satisfying him.

"What about her suitcases? Are they in her room?"

His chest tightened when the hotel manager said no. "Did you hear anything?" Images formed before he could stop them, a disturbing sense of dread that made no sense. He wanted her gone, after all. He wanted her out of his town and his parish.

But he didn't want her to end up like Savannah.

He slammed his feet against the soft Oriental rug and stood, welcomed the slap of cool air against flesh still hot from the dream. "Was there any sign of a struggle?"

The need to get back to Bayou de Foi ground through him, but before he could pull on his jeans, his uncle's voice came across the phone. "Looks like she took your advice after all, son. There's nothing out of place here, no sign of forced entry or anything untoward. Hell, the bed is even made."

"Looks like Ms. Fox just packed up and left in the middle of the night, ran out on her bill."

"I don't like it." It was one thing having Renee Fox around and knowing where she was. But having her unaccounted for disturbed him in ways he understood only too well. "Let me know the second something changes. If anyone sees her, hears from her—"

"Don't you worry about Bayou de Foi. I've got everything covered. You just take care of finding Alec."

Cain wound down the call and took a quick shower, dressed and picked up his Glock, headed out the door. To find Alec. Before whatever game he was playing backfired on them both.

No one had talked to his former partner in almost three months, not even the wife he'd supposedly adored. He'd turned in his badge and dropped his wedding ring on the bathroom counter, walked out the door and into the shadows. Since then the rumor mill had been in overdrive, implicating Alec for everything from obstruction of justice, extortion to selling information to the highest bidder, scare tactics, excessive force—and murder.

Of Savannah.

Slamming the door behind him, Cain took the stairs two at a time. Rumor had it that Alec would be at the race track in less than an hour. That something big was going down.

His former partner would be there to greet him. Guilty or innocent. One way or another, Cain would find out for sure.

REVULSION SWEPT THROUGH Renee, but she refused to let it show. Angel's revelation was consistent with police speculation, a sordid claim that had run in all the local papers and a few of the cable networks. It was what her own brother had believed.

Despite all of that—the warnings and the evidence, the cold hard logic—there was still a place deep inside Renee that rebelled at the allegation.

How did a woman accept that the man she'd been falling in love with was a pathological liar?

"You think their relationship was just a tactic?" she asked with a detached calm she didn't come close to feeling.

Angel flicked away the maple leaf. "What man in love leaves his woman's bed to come to mine?" Her mouth curved into a cynical smile. "Not a satisfied one, that's for sure."

Despite the fair skin and blond hair she'd been born with, Cajun blood ran through Renee's veins. Her father's mother and mother's father were both full-blooded. She'd grown up adoring them, enchanted by the rich cadence of their voices and the hot passion that guided their actions. As a child, she hadn't known the flashes of temper and bursts of happiness were passion, she'd just known her grandparents were bright, vibrant people.

Knowledge of passion had come later, when she'd discovered she'd inherited that same intensity. When things were good, she could ride the wave and savor every moment.

When things were bad… It was hard to explain to anyone who didn't share her blood, hard to make them understand urges that were dark and punishing, capable of frightening even herself.

And Cain. She could still see him at the plantation ruins, standing in the incessant drizzle, begging her to abandon her investigation into her brother's death.

Calm down, cher. *You're scaring me.*

A big bad police detective like you? Aren't you the one who told me fear wasn't in your vocabulary?

That was before, belle amie. *Before I met you.*

He'd kissed her then, hard, deep, and by the time he was done, she'd believed every word he told her.

Now, sitting in the French Quarter on a chilly fall morning, pretending to be a palm reader while listening to skanky details of her ex-lover's secret life, Renee's heart pounded so fast she could barely breathe. Her blood thrummed in perfect, erratic rhythm, just as it had that sticky night when the rookie cop had revealed her brother's dying words.

"Why should I believe you?" It took effort, but she feigned fascination with the young prostitute's palm, when all she really wanted to do was shove away from the table and get out of town as fast as she could, go back to Nova Scotia and never come back, start over again and forget about justice. "Do you have proof?"

Angel's hand twitched. "Nothing concrete."

Renee didn't know whether she felt disappointment—or relief. "Then why did you call me?"

Angel lifted her eyes. "Because history has a habit of repeating itself, over and over again."

SUNLIGHT GLINTED THROUGH the tunnel of old oaks that lined St. Charles Avenue. Renee sat in her rental car, across the street from the bed-and-breakfast whose address Angel had given her, watching and waiting. Even in the dredges of fall, the house looked vibrant, with red mums lining the walkway and bougainvillea dripping from the wrought-iron porch, huge baskets of bushy ferns swaying in the breeze.

Sipping on her coffee, Renee smiled when the streetcar rumbled by and momentarily obscured her view. When it was gone, Cain was there—holding another woman.

After what seemed like forever he pulled back and took her hand and kissed the back of it, a foolishly gallant gesture that unsettled Renee in ways she didn't want to analyze too closely.

Then he turned and walked away.

Renee watched him slip inside a black Mercedes convertible—the car he'd always talked about purchasing—and merge with traffic. She could feel the woman's sadness from across the boulevard, and though part of her wanted to cross the street and find answers to the questions twisting through her, she pulled into the stream of traffic.

Four cars ahead, at the next intersection, she saw the Mercedes turn right, and gunned her engine in pursuit.

The fabled Fair Grounds came into view twenty minutes later. In the springtime, the sprawling park hosted the world-renowned New Orleans Jazz and Heritage festival, a raucous outdoor party featuring the best of both music and food. She and Cain had attended just weeks before their world came crashing down. Vividly she remembered how it had felt to stand in the curve of his arm as they listened to a New Orleans favorite sing the blues.

Now, she followed him into the half-full parking lot and maneuvered her car into a spot two rows from his.

During the winter months the Fair Grounds hosted a party of a different kind—horse racing. People from all over south Louisiana congregated on a daily basis to wager on the horses, eat, drink and escape. She doubted Cain had any of those pleasures in mind.

Sliding from the car, she sank deeper into her jacket and hurried against the wind, merging with a group of what looked to be college kids as she made her way toward the entrance.

Inside, the throng of racing fans swallowed her. She'd never understood how a man of Cain's height could blend in with a crowd, but it was a skill he'd honed through years of undercover work. She squeezed through the crowd and made her way toward the betting windows, but it was as though the man had simply vanished.

"Me, I'm thinking you look lost, little lady," came a heavily accented Cajun voice from behind her. Turning, she found an elderly man in a worn, rust-colored suit and tie smiling at her. "Can I help you?"

She smiled, gave him a quick nod. "Thanks, but I don't think so. I'm looking for someone."

"My loss," he said, then gestured toward a closed door. "If you smile purty enough, you might be able to get Rusty to make an announcement over the big system."

"I'll keep that in mind," she said, feigning interest in the door. "Thanks—" Out of the corner of her eye a movement caught her attention, and her heart thrummed hard in recognition. "I think I see him now," she said, then pivoted and worked her way toward the side of the concession stand.

Cain stood with his back to her, his tall, dark form looming like a specter against a dirty white wall. He had an arm lifted to his face, and as she approached, she saw the phone clenched in his hand. The drone of the crowd prevented her from making out words, but the tension in his body told her all she needed to know.

The red pinhole made her blink. It was just a small spot, a little red dot against his left shoulder blade.

But her heart flat out stopped.

She spun around but immediately realized the crowd was too thick. Then she found the stairwell and looked up.

Through a blur of movement she saw first the high-powered rifle, then the man. Recognition horrified.

She didn't stop to think. She didn't stop to plan. She simply reacted. On a violent rush of adrenaline she lunged forward and shouted Cain's name.

He turned as she neared him.

Vaguely she was aware of his arms reaching for her, but she kept right on going, launching herself at him and knocking him backward. Together, they slammed against the concrete wall, his big body absorbing the shock of impact.

"What the hell—" he started, but at the same moment she looked up. And their eyes met.

Everything around them blurred. She was aware of the people swarming around them and cutting off the shooter's line of shot, but she could put no faces to the curious throng of men and women. A voice boomed over the public-address system, but she couldn't make out the words. There was only sensation, the feel of Cain's body pressed to hers, his hands against her back.

Just as quickly the moment crystallized, leaving her staring up at Cain, a man with dangerously hypnotic eyes and a mouth capable of sin—and salvation. Standing in the circle of his arms, with the heat of his body soaking into hers, her mind screamed caution, but her heart mourned. And her body craved.

The ribbon of longing unfurled through her like a

spool of shrapnel-lined silk, unbearably soft but devastatingly sharp, seducing and slicing at the same time.

Before she could stop herself, not even sure she wanted to, she pushed up on her toes and lifted her mouth to his.

CHAPTER NINE

New Orleans
Twenty-two months earlier

I LOVE GAMES. I'm good at them. I enjoy the nuances and the strategy. I adore the cunning. Laying traps and luring my opponent in, smiling as I do so, it's all part of the fun.

Defeat is not an option.

From behind a contorted modern-art sculpture, I watch Detective Cain Robichaud pull his mobile phone from his pocket and bring it to his face. I watch his body tense, his expression darken. I can tell he's protesting. I see him frown. And I smile.

Because in the end he mutters under his breath and walks away, abandoning the rendezvous he'd arranged to coincide with the warehouse district's monthly street festival.

The good detective cuts his way through the crowd of art shoppers and club hoppers, but it's not until he rounds a corner that I lose sight of him. Courtesy of an emergency that does not exist, he's gone. Soon he'll realize the diversion, but I should have enough time to milk his informant.

Tensions are escalating. Another casino owner has gone missing. Some say a Goose has been stolen. That someone is fighting back…

…that someone else is about to be taught a lesson.

I recognize the informant immediately and make my way toward Mimi's, the eclectic art gallery specializing in pink poodles and purple monkeys. He's got a to-go cup in his hand and a cigarette hanging from his mouth. He's nervous. That's what gives him away.

A smile, some small talk, and soon I've got him in my pocket. I suggest we go somewhere more private, and with a nauseating gleam in his eyes, the man who calls himself Manuel agrees.

Once we're alone behind a renovated warehouse, the dark-skinned man with long dreadlocks leans against the brick wall. "He's going to own this town," he brags. "A pretty woman like you, he might enjoying owning you, too."

I grit my teeth. "I'm not for sale."

"That's what they all say," he says, then drags on his cigarette. "But *Oncle* has ways of changing people's minds."

So I've heard. "Why do they call him the Goose?" I ask, pretending ignorance.

Manuel laughs. "The Goose isn't a person, *mais non*. The Goose is *Oncle's* trump card. It's how he's going to own the city."

I know that much. Just two days before, I overheard my brother vowing to gets his hands on one. He said it was the only way to beat them.

Of course, when he saw me, he clammed up.

I want to know why. "I don't understand."

Manuel takes a last drag on his cigarette and drops it. "People think computers are where it's at, that all that modern who-ha makes them better, stronger. But all you gotta do is go to the movies to know computers are going to be the undoing of society. All it takes is something the size of a nickel to—"

I see his eyes go wide and, without turning to look, I know.

"To what, Manuel? Something the size of a nickel can do what?"

The deceptively quiet challenge jump-starts my pulse. I spin toward the voice, not at all prepared for the sight of him standing so close, or the awareness in his eyes. He knows.

"Detective."

He looks over me, toward Manuel. "I thought you'd see things my way."

And by the time I look over my shoulder, the other man has vanished around the corner.

"Well, well," Cain says, as he almost always does. "Why am I not surprised?"

The rush is intense as I lift my eyes to his. Accepting the inevitable, I let a slow smile curve my lips. *"Parce que,"* I say in an oddly hoarse voice, "the two of us are getting very good at playing this game."

He steps closer. "Is that what you think?"

I don't want to step back, but the reaction is instinctive. The second I feel the cool brick wall against my shoulders I realize his intent. "It's what I know."

Dressed in all black, he comes close to blending with the night. "It's what you *think,*" he corrects, and his voice is so quiet I have to concentrate to hear him. "And

it's also where you're wrong. I'm not playing, *belle
amie*. I'm trying to keep you from making a mistake you
will not live to regret."

My throat goes dry. "Is that a threat?"

"Take it any way you will."

"And if I don't?"

The planes of his face tighten. "Damn it, woman…"

And I know. Despite what he says, despite what he
does, all I have to do is look up into his eyes, normally
so cool and in control, and I know. There's a ferocity
there. An urgency. A desperation unlike anything I've
ever seen, and as I stand there in the alley behind Mimi's,
something deep inside me comes to life. "My God."

He brings his hands to the wall, splaying them on
either side of my face. "Praying won't help, *belle amie*."

Zydeco music drifts in from the street festival, but
my body stills in anticipation. "Do it," I challenge.

He leans closer. "Do what?"

I tilt my face to look at him, feel the breath catch in
my throat. The need roars in my blood. "What you want
to do…what I see in your eyes."

He tries to hide it, but I see the flare of surprise. "Why?"
The word is unusually rough. "So you can cry foul and
have me arrested like the dirty cop you want me to be?"

"They won't arrest you," I say as I go up on my toes
and slide my arms around his neck, "if I'm willing."

Still he doesn't move. "What kind of game are you
playing?"

It's a damn good question. "The same one you are,"
I say. "The one you deny." Pushing closer, I feather my
mouth to his. "You want me."

His mouth is hard against mine, unmoving. "You really do have a death wish, don't you?"

His control staggers me, the way he won't reach out and take what he very clearly wants—and what I want to give. I feel him against my abdomen, after all. I know.

"What's the matter?" I purr. "Don't tell me the big bad detective is scared?"

A hard sound breaks from his throat. "I'm not scared."

I slide my body against his, loving the feel of all that power, all that control. "Then prove it."

Sometimes during the spring, when the rains come to Louisiana and overstay their welcome, when the sky stays gray and the heavens dump too many inches of rain for a bowl-shaped city to hold, the civil engineers are forced to open the spillway, allowing the trapped waters of Lake Pontchartrain to pour into the low-lying marshland, viciously consuming everything in their path. When I was twelve, my grandfather took me to watch. I remember standing there, marveling at the power of the water, the fierce surge, wondering what it would feel like to be in its path.

Now I know. In history I learned that surrender is a sign of defeat, but there is no defeat in Cain as he hauls me to him and crushes his mouth to mine. There's only strength. And need. So very, very much need it rampages through me much like the water surging through the spillway.

I'm not a wallflower. I've known other men. But nothing has prepared me for the feel of Cain's mouth taking my own, kissing me, possessing with a raw intensity, a driving urgency beyond anything I ever imagined—and I have a very good imagination.

His hands find my face and cradle with a tenderness

that rocks me. Dizzily I bring my own hands higher, stab them into his hair. It's softer than I anticipated.

Then on a harsh breath he's pulling back and staring at me, doing something no man ever has: he makes love to me with nothing more than the look in his eyes.

"Wintergreen," he murmurs, and I remember the roll of candy I sucked on while watching him wait for his informant.

The surprise in his voice tells me more about this big, bad, untouchable police detective than any rumor ever could.

"You like?" I ask with a vulnerability that stuns me.

His smile is slow, easy, purely carnal. "My favorite," he says, then comes in for more.

Somehow, I know there will never be enough.

CHAPTER TEN

New Orleans
Present day

"CAIN?" In the City Hall cafeteria miles from the race-track, Gabe pulled his mobile phone from his face to make sure the call had not dropped. It hadn't.

He brought the handset to his ear and tried to make sense of the distorted rumble coming from the Gentilly Oval. His cousin had been telling him about a lead on Alec when he stopped abruptly. Then there'd been a loud crash, as though Cain dropped the phone. "You there? What the hell is going on?"

Nothing.

"Damn it, cuz—"

He heard it then, the sound of murmured voices, one belonging to Cain, the other to a woman, and his concern melted into a combination of aggravation and amusement.

"Call me later," he barked even though he knew his cousin wasn't listening. Stabbing the end button, he stalked to the coffee machine, where the charred remains of the late-morning brew smoldered against the bottom of the pot.

Needing the caffeine kick, Gabe carried the pot to the sink and cleaned it, then ripped open a pouch of dark roast and prepared a fresh batch.

One of these days, he'd sleep for more than four hours at a stretch. He and Val had gone to bed early last night, and though he'd watched her slide the nightgown from her body, he'd fallen fast and deep before she made it between the sheets. Vaguely, as he sank further into sleep, he was aware of the sound of her crying, but he hadn't been able to pull himself back.

Hadn't wanted to face reality.

He'd been awake three hours later, and that had been that. He'd read, worked at his computer, surfed the Net, then given up and headed for the office before the sun had a chance to rise.

Val was right. There were things he wasn't telling her, little pieces of his life that had spiraled away from him. He told himself he was protecting her. He just needed time. He'd gotten in over his head, but he'd find a way out, and everything would be okay again.

Deep inside, he knew he was full of crap. There was no way to turn a foul into a flush.

"It helps if you turn the machine on."

Absently he turned toward the unfamiliar voice, worked damn hard to keep his jaw from dropping open. She wasn't a bombshell, it wasn't that. She wasn't classically beautiful. Her eyes were a little too far apart, her nose a little too crooked, as though it had been broken long ago and not set properly. But the way she looked at him, with a confident knowing in her brown eyes, a bemused smile curving her wide mouth, rattled his cage.

The jolt of familiarity made no sense. Tall and athletically built, with glossy shoulder-length hair the color of chestnuts and that I've-got-a-secret smile, she was not the kind of woman a man forgot. But he couldn't place her.

"Unless, of course," she added as she sized him up, "you're practicing your telekinetic skills."

Now there was a thought. "I can think of far more… *interesting* ways to practice those," he said.

She laughed. "Maybe I should introduce myself before you go too far down that path." She reached around him and pushed the brew button, then stuck out her hand. "Evangeline Marceau."

Gabe put his palm to hers and made a mental note to let the D.A. have it for not warning him. "The new kid on the block." New A.D.A. starting today, Vince had told him. A real shark. But Gabe's mentor had left out the fact that the killer fish was a woman, and a knockout. "Welcome to Sin City."

Her lips curved. "I thought that was Vegas."

The small mole just above her top lip caught his eye. "Maybe. But the way I see it, there's plenty to go around."

"I see," she said, releasing his hand. "Good thing I already know my way around then, isn't it?"

Sin and the city. It sounded like one of those chick movies. "Well then," he said, refusing to let the prosecutor in him go one step further and query as to just what she knew her way around. The city? Or sin? "Care for some coffee?"

"I'd love some."

He was handing her a foam cup when the district attorney took command of the cafeteria. It was like that wherever Vincent Arceneaux went, whether it was a courtroom, the men's room or the poker room at the back of Bubba's. Whatever was happening stopped. People sat or stood a little straighter. Held their cards closer.

Gabe found it all quite amusing.

The change came over Evangeline immediately, the transformation from confident young attorney to wet-behind-the-ears recruit. She smiled anyway, hid her nerves with a disarming curve of her mouth.

"Good, good," Vince said, approaching them. "I see you two have met." He grabbed the pot despite the fact the coffee was still brewing and filled his ancient mug. "Gabe, I want you to show Evie here around, teach her the ropes."

Evie. Gabe watched her cringe, wondered why.

"My pleasure," he said as coffee splattered on the burner.

"Rumor has it she's a mean card shark," Vince added. "Maybe you should bring her round to Bubba's, let her give you a run for your money."

The visceral reaction made no sense. Gabe wasn't a chauvinist. Not by any stretch of anyone's imagination. So it wasn't that she was a woman and no woman had ever joined their card games before. But Thursday-night poker had always been a rite of passage. And a refuge.

Newcomers didn't belong. Especially newcomers with killer legs and smoky eyes.

And he, damn it, had no business caring one way or the other. "I doubt I'll be going this week, but maybe next time."

"Good enough." Vince shoved the pot back under the stream. "Just don't let me hear any more about you being seen in back alleys with that cousin of yours. The last thing I need is the newspaper running a story about my rising star running around with a criminal."

Gabe felt his fingers tighten around the white cup, crush it into something unusable. "The grand jury acquitted him."

"Doesn't mean he isn't guilty," Vince said, "just that he was smart enough to hide the body where no one could find it."

And then he was gone, leaving Gabe and Evangeline standing like naked strangers in the awkward silence.

HER MOUTH MOVED against his with a hunger that stunned him.

Peripherally Cain was aware of the fact that this was Renee Fox, the reporter who wanted to wring him out, but his body didn't flat give a damn. There was only the feel of her in his arms, all soft and fluid, the taste of her on his mouth, the need and the greed and the urgency, the fresh tingle of wintergreen.

That alone should have stopped him.

Instead he hauled her closer. His hands found her hair and fisted, urging her head back for a better angle. She didn't fight him when he tugged, just opened and kissed him with an urgency that fired his blood and numbed his mind. It was the way a woman kissed a man she'd spent weeks and months and years longing for, the kind of frenzied kiss reserved for those plucked from the arms of death.

It was the way he kissed Savannah in his dreams.

That did stop him.

The realization slammed into him, etching reality

into sharp focus. He tore his mouth from hers and took her shoulders in his hands, plied her from his body. She staggered and stared up at him, her mouth swollen and her face flushed, her hair tangled. But it was her eyes that got him, the glassy, stricken, incoherent gaze commonly associated with shock.

The urge to pull her back to him, not to his mouth but to his chest, to run his hands along her spine and *comfort* her for crissakes, seared through him more brutally than the way she'd kissed him.

For a man used to being in control, it was not a feeling he could tolerate.

"Not that having you pressed up against me isn't a damn fine sensation," he drawled, and though it took effort, he resisted the urge to slide his hand up her neck and rub his thumb over her bruised lower lip, "but after the last time we spoke that's hardly the greeting I expected. Mind telling me what in sweet Mary's name you're doing?"

For a moment she said nothing, just kept staring at him as if she expected him to vaporize right before her eyes. Then she blinked. "Cain."

She almost sounded surprised.

"Who else—" he started to ask, but stopped when she twisted from his arms and spun toward the stairwell.

"He's gone," she whispered.

Cain squinted, watching the flow of men and women between the racing area and concession stands. "Who's gone?"

She grabbed his wrist and looked up at him, her eyes no longer glazed with passion but hard with resolve. "The man who was about to shoot you."

And then Cain knew. He knew what had triggered Renee's kiss, what her distraction had cost him.

Swearing hotly, he pulled the Glock from inside his sport coat. "Stay put," he ordered. Then he ran.

A CAUTIOUS WOMAN would have turned and walked away, gotten in her car and out of New Orleans as fast as she could.

The woman she'd once been would have charged after him, determined to be in the thick of the action.

Renee did neither. She stood there with the sea of oblivious racetrack patrons ebbing and flowing around her, staring at the stairwell where a gunman had stood, and Cain had vanished.

God.

It hit her then, the enormity of what she'd done, and deep inside she started to shake. Slowly her hand found her mouth, and her fingers skimmed the flesh that still burned from Cain's kiss.

She'd known coming back would be hard, but she'd trained herself and steeled herself, tested herself without mercy, day after day, night after night, until she was sure she could return to New Orleans and flirt with the life she'd once lived. Walk the same streets. Talk to the same people. Challenge the same man.

All without feeling a thing.

She might as well have convinced herself she could hold up her hands to fend off a hurricane.

She'd just been so sure, damn it. So sure she could remain objective, that all the days and nights recovering from the attack and reading every crumb of information she could find about the investigation had fortified her, stripped away emotion and vulnerability, longing and sorrow, hardening her into a near robotic woman who felt nothing but the burning need to find the truth, and avenge.

Then she'd seen Cain standing in the clearing, the same in so many ways, but horribly changed in other ways, scarred in ways that plastic surgery could never correct, and the illusion had started to crumble. All the pain and betrayal, the heartache and the longing, all those seething emotions she'd buried simmered closer to the surface, lurking and waiting, dangerously close to breaking free.

This morning, they had.

She'd sat there listening to Angel, feeling colder and dirtier with each word the prostitute spoke. She should have gone straight for a shower, stood under the long hot spray and scrubbed hard, for as long as it took to feel clean again. To feel warm.

Instead, she'd gone straight for Cain. And kissed him. Hard.

When he kissed her back, when his mouth opened to hers and invited her in, she'd died a thousand little deaths.

Need. That's what he'd tasted like. Need and hunger and chicory coffee, all swirling in a kiss that had the power to curl her toes. Still. After everything.

Two days in, and the game had changed, the rules shifted. To survive, she was going to have to be a lot more careful.

Because now she realized the truth, and it sobered. All this time she'd convinced herself she was returning for answers. For justice. She'd never thought beyond that, never realized that answers and justice were merely a means to an end.

What she really wanted was what she'd lost.

Her life.

"Well, well," he said a heartbeat later, and she turned to find him emerging from the thinning crowd. The horses were in the paddock. The race was about to begin. "You're still here."

She ignored the little jolt of relief that he was back unharmed. "You sound surprised."

He slid his gun back into his sport coat. "Up until now obedience hasn't exactly been your strong suit."

The smile formed by itself, slow and overly sweet. "If you're interested in obedience, maybe you should get a dog."

"I'll keep that in mind." He stepped closer, urging her back against the concrete wall. "But first I'd like some answers."

Her throat tightened. She could keep her face blank, but there was nothing she could do about the dangerous desire to feel him step even closer. "Did you find him, the man who was about to—"

"Do you have any idea," he asked, and his voice was so ominously quiet her breath caught, "any idea at all what could have happened to you?"

The question did cruel things to her heart. Memory bled through, bringing with it the illusion of concern. For a fractured moment the past eighteen months were gone, and Renee Fox did not exist. She was Savannah again, and this was Cain, coldly furious with her for taking chances that did not need to be taken.

"I thought we already covered that," she said with a bluntness that pleased her. "I was trying to stop someone from shooting you."

"Did it ever occur to you that I welcomed that shot?" he asked, his fingers fumbling with the buttons of his dark gray shirt. "That I was ready?"

She stared at the bulky Kevlar vest, wondered why she hadn't felt it before. "I don't understand."

"There's no reason you should," he shot right back. "My reasons for being here are my business, Renee. Not yours."

All too quickly she realized what she'd walked in on. "You were trying to lure someone into the open."

The planes of his face tightened. "And you, my dear curious reporter, damn near walked into the crossfire."

The reality of that punched. "And would that have been such a bad thing, Detective?" The question came out hoarser than she intended. "Isn't that what you've wanted since the moment we met? Me? Out of the picture?"

The gleam in his eyes went dark. "I'm not a detective anymore, *belle amie,* and there's a difference between out of the picture and dead."

"My point exactly." She lifted her chin. "How could I steal your secrets if you wind up on the wrong side of a bullet?"

From across the public-address system, an excited voice announced that the horses had moved into the gates, but Cain didn't so much as flinch. "And just how do you plan to steal them with me on the right side?" he asked in that same low, hypnotic voice he'd used on the heron in the clearing. "I think that's the better question."

He had no idea. "I'm not worried about that."

Very deliberately, he lifted a hand to her face and rubbed his thumb along her lower lip. "Are you going to kiss them out of me? Is that what this is about?"

A hundred thousand alarms went off simultaneously inside of her, but she made no move to stop the equally slow, equally deliberate smile that curved her mouth. "Would that work?"

"It never has in the past, but if that's what you've got in mind, you're more than welcome to try."

The invitation should not have hurt. Should not have scraped like a betrayal of all they'd once shared. But it did.

She'd spent close to two years mourning this man, even as she read newspaper articles incriminating him in her death. She'd always known he was dangerous, but there was a difference between knowing that and accepting that he could make love to her by morning, only to try and end her life by night.

"You have no idea what I have in mind," she said as the horses broke from the gate.

Cain abandoned her face and bracketed his arms on either side of her. "Don't be so sure about that."

She narrowed her eyes, felt the reinforcement of steel clear down to her toes. Without saying a word, she twisted under his arm and headed for the exit.

"Why didn't you scream?"

The question stopped her cold. She didn't want to turn around, had no intention of turning around, but before she could so much as breathe Cain was by her side, taking her wrist with his hand and urging her to face him.

But she didn't look at him, just stared at an empty, greasy carton that once held French fries, discarded near the turnstiles.

"Answer me." The seduction was gone from his voice, replaced by the razor-sharp edge of the detective hungry for information. "Most women would have screamed when they saw the gun, or shouted for security."

True enough—but Renee hadn't enjoyed that luxury.

Slowly, she lifted her eyes to his. "It takes more than a gun to make me scream."

His mouth curved into a purely carnal smile. "Challenge accepted," he said, and his thumb began to rub the inside of her wrist. "But for now, I want the truth."

She swallowed hard, saw the danger in continuing the game. "I didn't want him to know I saw him!" she said, and yanked her arm from his hand. "There, does that make you happy?"

"You saw him?" The roar of thousands of racing fans filled the track, but there was no mistaking the thunder in Cain's voice. "Did you recognize him? Have you seen him before?"

Renee went very still. She stared up at Cain, but saw only a tall lanky man with sandy-brown hair and moody blue eyes, crouched down with his partner beside a beaten up old sedan they used to cruise the Ninth Ward, ambling along Bourbon as he tried to blend in with tourists, kicked back at Pat O'Brien's with a beer in hand as he joked exactly what was inside the little room reserved for men at the infertility clinic.

"Tell me," Cain urged, taking her shoulders in his hands. "Who did you see? What did he look like?"

Alec.

Dear God, she'd seen Alec. Cain's partner. The man he'd served with for over ten years, trusted with his life, loved like a brother. The man who'd turned his back on his family's wealth to serve the public good, who'd adored his wife and stood by his friends. The man who'd found her hurt and bleeding in an alley and held her as he waited for Cain to arrive.

The man who'd recently turned in his badge and walked out on his wife.

But Renee Fox, producer for *True Crime* and stranger to the area, had no way of knowing any of that.

"Tall," she said against a painfully tight throat. "Dark blond hair. A goatee."

Cain tensed. "Eyes?"

"Behind sunglasses."

"What kind of sunglasses?"

"I couldn't tell."

Against her shoulders, Cain's hands tightened. "Anything else? Any kind of distinguishing marks? Clothes?"

She looked into his eyes, felt the desperation blazing there clear down to her toes. He deserved to know, even if the betrayal would destroy him.

"A tattoo," she whispered, despite the fact Alec had worn long sleeves to the track, and as soon as she said the word, she felt the change in Cain, the way he braced himself for the killing blow.

Which she gave him. "On his left forearm."

CAIN RELEASED HER and felt everything inside of him go very tight. He hadn't wanted to believe it, damn it. Had been so sure his informant had been wrong. That coming to the track would turn out to be a wild-goose chase. "Son of a bitch."

Out of the corner of his eye he saw Renee lift her hand, felt his blood pump a little harder. She was going to reach out in concern. And he wanted her to, he realized. He wanted to feel her again, craved the human contact in a way that disturbed him. After Savannah died he'd shut himself off and out, trained himself not to want, not to need.

The fact this reporter who wanted to crucify him one day but kissed him the next could make him do both rocked him.

"Does that mean something to you?" she asked, but rather than touching, she reached into her purse and pulled out her keys.

Because he wanted to take her wrist anyway, he shoved his hands into the pockets of his jeans. "My partner—" he started to say, but stopped before he went too far. "A lot of people have tattoos."

She frowned. "I wish I could have been more help," she said, and sounded like she meant it.

But he couldn't let himself believe, couldn't afford the illusion offered by white flags, no matter how pretty, how soft. "Is that why you followed me?" He let some of his anger show with the question. "In case I needed your help?"

Her eyes flared and he could tell the question caught her off guard. "You think I followed you here?"

He smiled, broad and sure. "I'm sure of it."

"Then I hate to disappoint you, big guy, but I was here to meet an informant."

As far as recoveries went, he'd give her a B+. "Really?"

"Really."

"Then where is he, this informant?"

"Long gone, I'm sure," she said with a contrived look around. "You seem to have that effect on people."

She had no idea. "And just what juicy tidbit did you hope to learn?"

Her shrug was a thing of beauty. "Hard to say since he didn't show."

She was a piece of work, all right, far more intriguing than he'd first realized. In the space of twenty-four hours she'd turned the tables on him, transformed herself from hunted to hunter. It was a bold move, risky, and it made him curious to see what kind of game she was playing.

"Tell you what. I'm going to be at the Golden Pelican tonight." He paused, let a slow smile curve his lips. "You really want to see me in action, join me. I'll be there at nine."

Then without giving her a chance to respond, he turned and walked through the turnstiles. Long strides brought him to his Mercedes. Minutes later, as he cruised down Elysian Fields, two thoughts consumed him: finding Alec, and playing with Renee.

If everything went according to plan, tonight he would achieve both.

WITH SUNSET Renee stood in the crowded lobby of the ornate casino her brother had once managed and took it all in—the French Quarter-themed artwork he himself had picked out, the entrance to the museum chronicling the history of Mardi Gras, the stunning statues of Dionysius, Bacchus and an eclectic mix of other Greek and Roman gods celebrating excess. From the buffet the scent of fried fish, oysters and shrimp called to her. It was like coming home, with two very cruel exceptions.

Her brother no longer roamed the gaming area, and

someone was following her. The prickle of awareness crawled down her spine like a trail of ants, much as it had from the second she left the Fair Grounds.

Slipping her hand into her purse, she closed her fingers around the butt of the .22 she'd bought to replace the one she'd lost the night her life almost ended, and slowly turned around.

CHAPTER ELEVEN

A GROUP OF COLLEGE students swarmed by her en route to the gaming room. There had to be at least ten of them, all big and raucous and excited. Clearly their party had already begun. Heart hammering, she worked her way through them, catching glimpses of a man across the lobby as the casino patrons ebbed and flowed around him.

Tall, she noted on a wicked rush. Dark haired. Pretending like hell to read the newspaper in his hands.

The sunglasses were a nice touch.

She released the .22 and slid her hand from her purse, merged with the crowd and squeezed by a cluster of men in business suits. Anticipation zipped through her, just like so many times in the past. He wanted to play? Well, fine. She could play.

But then she stepped around several oversize, overheated tourists and found the spot where her target had stood empty.

Gritting her teeth, she pushed up on her toes and scanned the lobby, saw him moving toward the men's room. She acted fast, not about to let him think he'd gotten away with his little charade.

She caught him just outside the door, reached around

a woman in front of her and grabbed the back of his sport coat. "Enjoying yourself?" she asked as the woman scampered away, leaving her pressed against his back.

He went very still. He turned slowly, stared down at her from behind dark, dark sunglasses. His expression was hard, forbidding. His voice was silky. "Should I be?"

She felt the chill immediately, low and slippery like an icy ribbon twisting through her stomach. "You're not—" *Cain.* "I'm sorry," she said with a forced smile. "I thought you were someone else."

He looked down at her hand, still clenched in the fabric of his sport coat. "Would you like me to be?"

The husky words stunned her. They were so…Cain. Everything about this stranger screamed of the same intensity, the same dangerously seductive undercurrent.

"My mistake," she said, releasing the tweed and stepping back.

"My loss."

Her instinct. He wasn't Cain—but something deep inside whispered that he wasn't a stranger, either. That even though she didn't know who he was, he knew damn well who she was.

"We'll see," she said, then flashed an overly bright smile as she turned and slipped into the crowd, confident he watched her every step—it was a cat-and-mouse game Cain had taught her well.

"AH, *CHER,* GET OUT! You were da friend of Adrian's?"

Renee let the thick accent role over her as she smiled at Jean Paul Bourgeois, her brother's assistant manager who'd taken over running the casino after Adrian's death. She had forty-five minutes before Cain arrived, and intended to use them well.

"*Mais,* yeah," she said, slipping back into the cadence of her youth. "Me and Adrian, we grew up together. Our *grand-mères* were friends." True enough. Her mother's mother and father's mother had been as close as two women could be. "I loved him like a brother," she said on a bittersweet crest of emotion.

Standing near one of three elaborate bars, Jean Paul frowned. "Ah, *cher,*" he said. "We all miss him."

"He talked fondly of you," she said, baiting the hook. "Said you were a good friend."

Jean Paul stood shorter than her brother had. As a kid, he'd probably been called husky. He had one of those ruddy complexions that likely made it impossible for him to play poker—or keep secrets. "So was he."

"He'd be so proud to see how well the casino is doing," she said, glancing around at the press of men and women filling the semilit gaming room, the crowd around the poker tables, the filled stools in front of row after row of slots.

Casually, Renee went fishing. "I was hoping to visit with Evan and Lynn, too, while I'm here," she said, and hoped her voice didn't catch on the names. She'd recited them in her mind so many times. When she lay alone in the still of the night, she could still hear them on the young cop's voice, echoing over and over. Evan…Lynn. "Are they around?"

Jean Paul watched one of his scantily clad cocktail waitresses stroll toward a cluster of tables on one side of the gaming area. "Come again?" he asked. "Who dat?"

"Evan," she repeated. "And Lynn. Are they here?"

Her brother's friend brought a hand to his graying beard and rubbed. "Can't say dose names mean anything to me."

"Adrian talked about dem all the time," she pushed on, trying to keep the desperation from her voice. The names had been among his last words. Find them, and answers would follow. "I figured dey worked here with him."

"'Fraid not."

Disappointment punched deep.

"Sorry I couldn't help," Jean Paul said.

Not ready to give up, she found a tentative smile. "Dey said such awful things about him in Baton Rouge, that his death was a mob hit, that the Russian Mafia took him out to punish him for stealing from them…" She let the words, the bait, dangle.

She'd expected Jean Paul's skin tone to give him away, but it was his eyes that betrayed him. They went dark. "It's best not to be repeating things like that, *cher*," he said as the cocktail waitress returned and handed him a folded napkin. "Adrian was a good man, even if he did have his secrets."

Adrenaline kicked through her.

Jean Paul looked up from the napkin. "What did you say your name was?"

"I didn't," she said, "But it's Renee."

His ruddy features darkened. "I should throw you out of here," he growled, shoving the napkin into her hand. "I din understand how people like you live with yourself."

Then he was gone.

Even before she looked down at the damp napkin and saw the handwriting, she knew what the neatly printed words said.

Be careful. She's a reporter. Renee Fox. True Crime.

On a wave of frustration she looked toward the tables and saw the trio. Gabe sat with his arm around Val's shoulders, and though she leaned into him, the intimate pose looked strained.

There was nothing strained about Cain. He sat with his long legs stretched out, rolling a tumbler between his hands as he watched her. The second their eyes met, he lifted his empty glass to her.

He still enjoyed playing every bit as much as she did.

The realization should not have scraped like the blade of a dull razor, but deep inside she bled anyway. People talked about life going on as though it was a good thing, a panacea for every ache and pain and bruise. But no one ever talked about the corollary, when life going on was a betrayal, the desecration of the hopes and promises that were all she had left.

But that was ridiculous, and she knew it. She was the one who'd come back to this town. She was the one trying to reclaim a life everyone else thought was over. She was the who would not allow herself to believe in, to trust, the fractured hopes and dreams that grew more vivid with every second she spent in Cain Robichaud's presence.

She watched him lounging there, the way his big body dwarfed the club chair, and felt the draw clear down to her bones. Refusing to concede the match, she did the only thing she could.

She dropped the napkin and accepted his challenge.

"How many guesses do I get?"

"Guesses?" Gabe watched his cousin walk toward the leggy brunette. "For what?"

Val didn't know whether to laugh or cry. After the tension of the night before, she'd been surprised when Gabe suggested they spend the evening at the casino. His voice had been warm, almost flirtatious as he'd encouraged her to buy a new dress, something pretty. Something special.

She'd done just that, gone to her favorite boutique and let them deck her out in sequins. When Gabe had seen her, she'd felt as jittery as a sixteen-year-old on her first date with the starting quarterback, a completely ridiculous response considering she and Gabe had been lovers for years. It's not that he didn't excite her anymore. He did. But there was very little about him she didn't know, and vice versa. And though she loved the familiarity, she hated the way it tended to dull the excitement.

At the casino they found Cain waiting and she'd realized Gabe had not asked her out to pop the question she was longing to hear. And yet he'd mentioned a surprise, and his eyes had smoldered as he'd reached into his sport coat.

Cain had picked that moment to laugh softly, then roll to his feet and stroll toward the woman. And for some reason Gabe was riveted on the sight of the two of them squaring off in the middle of the casino.

"My surprise," Val said, careful to keep the uncertainty from her voice. In a move designed to look casual, she trailed her index finger along the rim of her wineglass. "You know what being left in the dark does to me."

More than anything, she hoped the words didn't sound as desperate as she felt. Sometimes she hated how clingy she'd become and tried to pull back, to let the Fates take care of things. Gabe loved her. She knew that.

But then she'd see the secrets in his eyes, feel the tension in his touch, and the blades of panic would nick all over again. Savannah had assured her that if she would just focus on her relationship with Gabe, everything else would work itself out. But sometimes it was hard not to worry. If she lost Gabe—

Slowly, as though coming out of a trance, he turned to look at her. The transformation was immediate, from brooding watcher to charming companion in less than two seconds. "I'm sorry, hon," he said, and the warmth in his eyes went a long way toward chasing away her doubts. "Just trying to see how much trouble Cain's getting himself into this time."

Val glanced toward the brunette. "Who is she?"

"That producer I was telling you about."

Val took in the way Cain stood deep into the woman's personal space, watching her as if she was a piece of filet mignon and he was famished. "I thought you said he wanted her gone."

Gabe laughed. "My cousin doesn't know what he wants."

"Doesn't look that way to me," Val said, bringing her wineglass to her face. She sipped. "Looks to me like he knows *exactly* what he wants."

Gabe practically growled. "That's what I'm afraid of."

"Pretty," Val commented, practically feeling the heat from where she sat. "I can see—"

"Shh," Gabe said, stunning her, and before she could even turn to look at him, he was pulling her closer and holding her hand in his. "I didn't invite you here to watch Cain."

The jolt, the long-forgotten rush, was immediate. "No?" She smiled up at him. "Then why did you?"

With his free hand he reached into the inside pocket of his sport coat and pulled out a small bundle. "I stopped by the travel agent this afternoon."

Val stared down at the brochures he spread across the small table, hardly able to believe what she was seeing— or hearing. He'd been so distracted lately, barely listening when she talked, barely there when they made love. "I thought you said you were too busy to get away."

He drew her hand to his mouth and brushed a kiss across her knuckles. "I am."

"But—"

"I won't be forever. And when the air clears, I'm taking you away from here, just like you've been suggesting for weeks. Anywhere you want to go. Aruba, Antigua, Barbados…"

That schoolgirl feeling grew stronger, giddier, and as she looked into his eyes and saw the contrition glowing there, she realized how skilled she'd become at torturing herself. There'd been no need to cry when he left that morning, before the sun had risen. No reason to curl into a ball and wonder how she would survive if she lost him. No reason to run into the bathroom and do something she'd sworn she would never do.

"Gabe," she whispered, looking up at him. "I'm sorry."

He took her face in his hands, making her feel small and delicate and fragile, even though she was none of those things. "You have nothing to be sorry for. I'm the one who's been a horse's ass."

"I'm sorry for doubting you. Doubting us."

"Don't—" he started to say, but then abruptly turned from her and stared off toward the cashier's cage.

Val followed his gaze, expecting to see Cain and that woman, but found no one she recognized. "What is it?"

"Nothing, I just…" He brought his fingers to his temple and pressed hard. "I thought I saw the new A.D.A."

Val frowned, realizing what he'd been hiding from her all evening. "Headache?" she asked, reaching for her purse. The migraines had been plaguing him for years, since shortly before Savannah went missing.

He nodded. "Must not have been her, though."

Her. Val shook off the grab of panic, reminded herself that Gabe worked with a lot of women. But he always came home to her.

"Here you go," she said, handing him two prescription tablets from the little box she always carried for him, all the while refusing to dwell on the other pills she'd handled that day, the little beige ones she'd flushed down the toilet.

She'd stood in the bathroom for a long time, under the accusing glare of the fluorescent lights, staring in the mirror but barely recognizing the woman staring back at her. It certainly wasn't the international ballet star she'd dreamed of as a shy young girl. But life had a way of changing people, shaping them. Loss and fear and desperation could harden even the softest places into lethal edges. She couldn't lose Gabe, no matter how high the cost. He was her everything. Without him—

Without him didn't bear considering.

"Thanks." He threw them back with whiskey. Then he stood. "Be right back."

Then he walked toward the cashier's cage.

"WANT TO PLAY?"

Renee lifted a hand and twirled a long strand of dark hair around her index finger, a hauntingly familiar gesture that fired Cain's blood and slayed what remained of his moral compass. "Depends upon who I'm playing with."

He watched her standing there in her killer little black dress, the way her glossy hair played with her shoulders and the slinky fabric draped over her curves, just like he'd watched her weaving magic on poor Jean Paul. The fool hadn't stood a chance.

"Is that how you do your job?" he asked, enjoying the way her eyes darkened. "Is that how you do your—" he plucked two stems of red wine from a passing waitress and handed her one "—what did you call it?" He let a beat of silence build. "Research?"

She brought the glass to her mouth, rubbed the rim against her bottom lip. "If that's what it takes."

Cain wasn't quite sure how he stayed standing, how he kept himself from grabbing her shoulders and pulling her to him—grabbing her shoulders and shoving her away. He wanted to do both. He wanted—

That was the problem. He wanted. For eighteen months he'd been living in a self-imposed exile, giving himself to his photography the way he'd once given himself to police work, and to Savannah. After he'd lost both, photography had been all that kept him going. Sometimes he'd stayed gone for days, weeks even, alone in the swamp, the marsh, along the bayous, staking out sunrises the way he'd once staked out crack houses, craving sunsets the way he'd always, always craved Savannah.

In the weeks and months since then, he'd felt nothing. Not rage for all he'd lost, not desire to fill the empty spots deep inside of him. He'd gone from day to day, using his lens to stay on the periphery of life.

But now here was this woman, this *reporter* despite what she called herself, who wanted nothing more than to tear his life to shreds. He should be moving hell and high water to stop her, but all he could think about was how she'd feel underneath him, soft and warm and naked—how she'd tasted just that afternoon, when she'd kissed him like there was no tomorrow.

Wintergreen, for crissakes. *Wintergreen.*

"You're good," he told her, reminding himself that the coincidences really weren't that surprising after all. "You've obviously had a lot of practice." Renee had known Savannah. They grew up together. Lots of childhood friends shared quirks like favorite candies. "I especially liked your move this afternoon."

Renee lowered the wineglass, but her lips remained parted, and the slight flare to her eyes told him that she was remembering, too.

"You surprised me," he said. And that wasn't easy to do. "Is that why you're in the Big Easy? To follow me?"

Her smile was immediate. Too immediate. "I had a few leads I wanted to follow up on."

"And did you find anything?"

"Nothing you don't already know."

He sipped his wine. "Tell me anyway."

For a second he thought she was going to dodge his request, but then she lifted her hand and once again began twirling a strand of hair. "I'd much rather you tell me something. What went really down between you and

Adrian Trahan? Why did you hate Savannah's brother so much?"

"Who says I did?"

"It's common knowledge," she shot back. "You two were constantly seen arguing. Just days before his death someone overheard you threaten him if he didn't start cooperating."

Cain lifted an eyebrow, surprised by how much she'd learned in such a short time. Someone had a loose tongue, he realized. Someone had forgotten the lessons of the past.

Instinctively he scanned the semidarkened gaming room, much as he'd been doing since the moment he arrived. It would be easy to attribute the hum in his blood to Renee, but Cain had never been one to take the easy way. Instinct wouldn't let him. The swarm of gamblers looked innocuous, the press of the elderly and the impoverished, those who had no business trading hard-earned money—or social security checks—for the lure of chance…or the hunger of the Russian Mafia.

"There's a difference between knowledge and rumor." And the bridge between the two was illusion. During his days on the force, he'd worked hard to make people believe what he wanted them to believe, see what he'd wanted them to see. And it had worked. Not even his sister, Saura, had realized the truth. "If your intent is to uncover all my dirty secrets, you're going to have to dig harder."

"He was dating your sister," Renee pointed out.

This time Cain laughed. "I'm not sure which one of them wanted to piss me off more." Older by eleven months, Saura once thrived on doing the exact opposite of what was expected. She'd taken rebellion to new heights…until the day a bullet had killed two for the price of one.

Cain lifted the glass to his mouth. "Is that all you've got?"

She released the strand of hair, let it fall against her cheek. "You really think I'm going to lay all my cards on the table for you to analyze?"

"Analysis isn't what I have in mind." He wasn't sure what he expected when he stepped closer, but it wasn't for her to go deadly still, to stare beyond him as though he'd neither spoken nor moved. Intrigued, he slipped his hand between her arm and her waist and let it settle against her lower back. "Maybe I just want to help."

The sharp intake of air felt better than it should have. So did the shock coloring her eyes. Since the moment he'd caught her trespassing by the cottage, she'd been in control, remote almost, untouchable, as though she had some preordained right to do whatever she wanted, ask whatever she wanted, all else be damned. The only falter had been at the racetrack, when she'd thrown herself at him and pretended to kiss him—

Pretended, like hell.

There'd been nothing pretend about the way she'd greedily slanted her mouth against his.

To see her here, now, like this, rattled and unsteady, finally responding to his nearness, his touch, told him she wasn't as immune to him as she wanted him to think.

"Just relax," he murmured, loving the feel of her, the smell of her. "Just let it happen."

"My God." Her voice was low, hoarse. "That's him!"

Cain blinked and the scene changed, shattered. Renee wasn't mesmerized with desire. She was frozen in horror.

And he knew.

"Who, honey?" he asked anyway. "Who do you see?"

Her eyes met his. "The man from the racetrack. The one who tried to shoot you."

"Does he know you've seen him?"

She shook her head. "I don't think so. He's just beyond the poker tables. He's on his mobile phone."

"Good girl." Slowly, he slid his hands up her back and tangled them in her hair. "Just follow my lead," he said, and dipped his face toward hers. Their mouths met and opened, slanted against each other. Deepening the kiss, he moved with her, walked her toward the slots as he scanned the casino—and saw the lanky man standing where she'd described, with the phone to his face.

Betrayal ran like ice through his blood.

Fighting the darkness, he urged Renee to safety and pulled back, took her face in his hands. "Get Gabe," he instructed. "Tell him what's going on."

"But—"

"Just do it," he said with a quick kiss to her forehead. Then he turned and went after the man he'd once trusted with his life.

CHAPTER TWELVE

"YOU SAID THERE would be more time."

The softly spoken words lured Gabe closer. She stood with her back to him and a mobile phone to her ear, adjacent to a statue of the god Dionysius just beyond the entrance to the gaming room. A long leather jacket concealed much of her body, but he could tell her shoulders were rigid.

"I know," she said. "I'm trying."

Gabe told himself to turn and walk away, go back to Val. Evangeline Marceau was none of his concern. The district attorney's request to show her the ropes did not extend beyond the courthouse.

"Okay." Her voice was a little harder. A lot more resigned. "I understand," she said. "I—"

There wasn't time to move. She glanced over her shoulder so suddenly that Gabe didn't have a snowball's chance south of New Orleans of bluffing.

So he grinned.

"—have to go," Evangeline said, never stripping her gaze from Gabe's. She flipped the phone shut and slid it into the small purse hanging from her shoulder. "Gabe."

The way she said his name, low and throaty and more like an accusation than a greeting, socked him somewhere near the gut. She looked pale, he noted, a sweep of hair falling against eyes uncomfortably dark. It was a look he'd seen countless times before, from scared witnesses and distraught victims.

It was not a look he'd anticipated seeing form the cool, refined, confident A.D.A. he'd met earlier in the day.

"Are you okay?" The question shot out of him before he could pull it back.

Her mouth tumbled open for a brief heartbeat before she clamped it shut. "Of course."

But that was a lie, and he was pretty sure they both knew it. If he didn't know better, he'd swear she looked ready to bolt. "Look," he said, stepping closer and lowering his voice, "if something's wrong—"

If someone is trying to hurt you—

"Nothing's wrong." She smiled, widely and brilliantly, and his breath damn near jammed in his throat. But his attorney's instincts did not relax. At least he told himself they were his attorney's instincts.

The instincts of the man had no relevance with this woman.

"Just…stuff," she said breezily, and he could literally see the smoke screen forming right before his eyes. Something was wrong. That he knew for a fact. He knew spooked when he saw it, and Evangeline was textbook.

He also knew he had no business pressing her further, despite the shady possibilities that automatically surged through him. One thing about being a prosecutor in a city like New Orleans.

Worst-case scenario became a way of life.

"If you're sure—" he started to say, and if possible, her smile widened.

"Are you here alone?" She put a hand to his arm. "I'd love to see if everything I've heard about—"

"Gabe!"

They twisted around simultaneously to see Renee Fox racing from the gaming area.

VAL SHOVED AT THE fire exit and burst into the alley.

"Wait!" Renee darted through the door before it closed and absorbed the bite of the wind, felt the chill penetrate the leather of her jacket and soak into her blood.

Breathing hard, Val braced her hands against her knees, revealing a tear at the back of her tight dress. "Damn him."

The men had come this way, first Alec just seconds before Cain had reached him, then about ten seconds behind them, Gabe.

Now the alley stood dark and deserted, quiet save for a collection of newspapers and leaves twirling in a mini tornado.

Frustrated, Renee watched Val, resisting the urge to go to her friend and throw her arms around her. Despite the fact they'd once been close, she had to pretend to be nothing more than a polite stranger, ignoring the shopping escapades and lattes they'd once shared, the pedicures and the dreams. Back then they'd seen a different future than the one fate had delivered—a future of weddings and babies, play dates and joint family vacations.

"Try not to worry." The pain and fear in her friend's eyes made her wish she could promise her everything was going to be okay. "Cain can take care of himself."

Jerkily, Val pivoted toward her. "I've seen how the man takes care of things. That's what worries me."

Renee winced, the venom in Val's voice driving home the fact that while Renee's life had stood still, the lives of everyone she loved had moved on, and changed.

"Gabe's got a blind spot when it comes to his cousin," Val said, wrapping her arms around her middle. "Thinks he can do no wrong."

Renee stepped toward her. "And you disagree?"

Val shook her head. "I just don't know anymore." She looked up, her smile so brittle it could only come from a broken heart. "Have you ever felt like you're losing something precious, something that you love, but the tighter you hold on, the faster it slips away?"

The question pierced deeper than it should have. Renee looked at Val standing there in a torn dress and smeared makeup, and felt the ache weave around her heart, and tighten. "I have."

Val pushed back the hair that had fallen from her stylish twist. "I'm sorry. I don't know why I said that. It's just…" She stared down the alley a long moment before turning back to Renee. "Look, I know who you are, why you're here. And from the way you were looking at Cain earlier, I can tell you think he's some sort of fallen hero."

She was going to have to be more careful. "He's a complicated man."

Val surprised her by laughing. "You don't know the half of it," she said. "Don't get me wrong. I don't think he's evil. But I don't think he's a saint, either. All I know is that whenever people get tangled in his life, bad things happen."

"Like Savannah…"

"And Gabe, and me," Val went on. "If it weren't for

Cain and what happened with the Trahans, we'd be married by now. Gabe would never have…" Her voice trailed off and she shook her head. "I suppose it doesn't matter anymore. What's done is done."

The breeze kept blowing in from the river, bringing with it a damp chill and the muted sounds of traffic and music, the razor sharp edge of realization—and resolve.

More lives had been shattered on that warm night eighteen months before than Renee had ever let herself realize. With a little luck, the truth would heal them all.

"Take the alley!" Cain instructed doing a quick sweep of the deserted street. "I'll take the warehouse."

"Got it." Gabe caught the .22 Cain tossed to him. "Be careful."

The words burned, but Cain nodded and ran toward the condemned building. They were talking about Alec, damn it. *Alec.* Cain should not have to be careful around the man who'd muscled Cain out of harm's way on more than one occasion.

But his cousin was right. Alec was no longer the man Cain used to know—the man who'd once broken down and cried about his inability to give his wife the one thing she wanted most. A baby.

The memory twisted through Cain as he ran. Alec Prejean, the cool, debonair detective who always had a smooth comeback, who unblinkingly walked the streets of the Ninth Ward, who'd somehow held it together when he'd pulled up to a crime scene only to discover his own brother in a pool of blood, had broken down behind an old warehouse and sobbed.

Cain had a lot of experience comforting women, but

he hadn't had a clue how to comfort a man. In the end he'd squatted beside his partner and put a hand to his back. Somehow, that had been enough.

Neither of them had ever spoken of the incident.

But now that man no longer existed. Alec had become the human equivalent of a crapshoot, and if Renee was right, he'd almost become an assassin.

Floorboards creaked as he climbed through a broken window and took in the gloom. The stench hit him immediately, the rancid combination of stale food and cigarette smoke and sex. He knew if he had a flashlight it would reveal other trophies littering the floor, leftovers from the all-night parties that attracted teens from parishes across southern Louisiana.

"Damn it, Alec!" he roared into the cavernous building. "What the hell are you doing?"

Movement to his right caught Cain's attention. He turned, the faint light oozing through the windows revealing a man in a doorway, and the semiautomatic in his hands. "God damn you, Cain."

Instinct kicked in, kicked hard. "Maybe," Cain conceded, "but what the hell has he done to you?"

Alec emerged from the shadows, revealing scraggly hair falling against his face and a scar at the corner of his eye. "You just don't know when to stop, do you?" he asked in a voice Cain instantly recognized, the one Alec used when closing in on a suspect, a low snarl that promised no mercy or reprieve. "You're so freaking *saison de pluie* to atone for your sins that you cannot see when to leave well enough alone. The world doesn't need another hero, *partenaire*, and neither do I."

"This isn't about playing hero," Cain said point-blank. "I think you know that."

"Allez vous faire voir," Alec hissed.

"I saw Tara last night." It was a cheap shot and Cain knew it. "She's worried about you."

Alec jabbed the gun toward Cain. "Stay away from her."

"Why?" His Glock waited under his sport coat, but instead of reaching for it, he dropped his arms and opened his palms, wagged his fingers in invitation. "She's dead to you, isn't that what you told her? Sounds to me like that makes her fair game." He let a slow smile curve his lips. "You never told me how pretty she looks when she—"

Alec moved so fast Cain barely had a second to brace himself. The impact of man to man sent him staggering into the steel-reinforced wall. "That's it," he taunted, deflecting a blow to his jaw and catching Alec's other wrist, holding the gun away from them both. "If you're so hot to take me out, I'm not going to let you do it like a—" he recoiled on a blow to his gut "—coward," he spat, with a hard open palm to Alec's nose.

Alec staggered, swiped the blood from his upper lip.

Cain snarled at the sight of his former partner standing there, blood on his face, gun dangling from his hand. "You're going to have to look me in the eye when you pull the trigger."

Alec swayed on his feet, lifted the gun. "Be careful what you ask for, *partenaire.*"

"Why?" Cain pushed. Two and two were not adding to four, and he didn't like it one damn bit. "If you really wanted me dead we both know I'd be that way by now."

Wincing against a pain in his ribs, he stepped closer. "You're playing vigilante, aren't you? That's what's going on. Tell me. Let me help."

The lines of Alec's face tightened. "Didn't you learn anything two years ago? Didn't you learn what happens when you quit minding your own business?"

"You know me," Cain said on a deliberately glib shrug. "I've always been a slow learner."

Alec's eyes flashed. "*Merde,* Cain, he knows what you're doing! He knows you're on to him!"

Oncle. "Damn it, Alec, you don't have to do this alone—"

Alec was on him before he could finish, the butt of his gun slamming against Cain's temple. Pain blasted him, but it was nothing compared to the shock. He felt himself sway, felt himself fall, felt his head smack against the cold concrete. As the edges of his vision went black, he saw Alec move to stand over him, saw the barrel of the gun pointed at his temple, but couldn't do a damn thing to stop him.

"And he has ways to make you stop," Alec vowed, and the world went dark.

THE QUARTER welcomed her like an old friend. Renee walked along Royal Street, the warmth growing inside her with each step she took, despite the breeze blowing off the river. So much had changed since she'd been gone—people, relationships, hopes and dreams. And desires. Just outside town there were roads where wetlands had sprawled, shops and fast-food restaurants where she'd once gone on a photo shoot with Cain. But in the Quarter, life ambled on as it had two years before, two decades before. The more the world at large expanded, the more technology invaded everyday life, the more stubbornly the Vieux Carré clung to the old ways.

Lost in the blur of past and present, it took a moment for the sound to register. She stopped abruptly and fumbled for the .22. Then she spun. And laughed.

The street was deserted, devoid even of window shoppers or tourists reeling back to their hotels, college kids roaming from bar to bar. The sound had come from memory, the night two years before when Cain had sneaked up on her.

Cain. She'd stayed at the casino for over two hours, but he'd never returned. Neither had Gabe. She'd tried to convince Val not to worry, but with each second that passed the other woman had grown more agitated. Renee had tried to soothe her, but she was supposed to be a stranger, and there'd been little she could do.

Finally Gabe had reached Val on her mobile phone and she'd left, telling Renee Gabe didn't know what had become of Cain.

That's why he was on her mind. That's why she imagined the noise behind her. It would be so like him to wait outside the casino, to follow her and—

The attack came without warning. Renee thrashed as the man caught her from behind and dragged her toward a darkened courtyard. "This is getting old!" she hissed, realizing she'd been right after all. "You can't just sneak up on—"

The blade to her throat stunned her. "Shut up," the man snapped, slapping his free hand to her mouth. The voice was—wrong. Not low and drugging. Not hoarse and thick and seductive. Not…Cain.

CHAPTER THIRTEEN

New Orleans
Twenty months earlier

"YOU REPORTER TYPES don't learn, do you? You juz keep sticking your pretty little neck where it don't belong."

I hate being backed into corners. I hate being trapped. But as I scan the sunny courtyard, with its inoperable fountain and clay pots spilling over with colorful impatiens, I realize my options are limited. *Oncle*'s man is too big. Too strong. And he has a knife. "Look, I didn't think—"

"That's your problem," he says, tracking me deeper into the courtyard.

The step back is automatic. So is the glance at my purse, lying next to a statue of the Virgin Mary near the iron fence that separates the patio from Toulouse Street. My gun is inside my purse. If I can reach it…

I dart to the side and run toward the statue, but the man grabs my hair and yanks me toward him. My head snaps back and my eyes burn. "You don't want to do this!" I warn.

He laughs. "Speak for yourself," he snarls as he shoves me into the disabled patio fountain.

I go down hard, slamming first against concrete, then into cold stagnant water.

"Words don't work with people like you," he says, and then he's diving in after me, straddling my body with his own.

On a low growl I slam my head forward and smash it against his nose. He yowls in pain and jerks away, backhands me across my cheek. "You little bitch!"

Pain explodes through me, but I keep twisting, thrashing.

Snarling, he reveals the blood between his teeth and comes at me again. I ram a knee into his gut and try to lever myself out of the water, but he's like one of those movie creatures that just keeps coming. He grabs my wrists and yanks them over my head, wedges me against the side of the fountain and rips at my shirt.

"You so don't want to do that."

The voice is low and steely, one-hundred-percent lethal. My hair is wet and falling into my face, but I don't need to look to know who's just entered the court-yard.

The sound of a gunshot brings the man on top of me rearing back.

"Next time it will be at the base of your skull," the newcomer promises, and with a vicious oath, *Oncle*'s man rolls from my body and runs.

Alec Prejean charges after him, but just as quickly he's back, helping me out of the water and kneeling beside me, running his hands along my arms. "Jesus, God, Vannah. Are you...? Did he...?"

Cain's partner has seen the worst life has to offer, just like Cain has. He's witnessed depravity. He's knelt beside fallen officers and cradled victims of gang shootings, embraced grieving parents. I know that. I've seen it, heard about it. Alec is legendary for his calm. He has this rare ability to shut off every ounce of emotion and do what needs to be done.

That's why the stammer in his voice, the hesitation in his touch, surprises me. "I'm okay," I manage, but the wince gives me away.

"The hell you are—where does it hurt?"

I start to say nowhere, but then I breathe. And the stabbing pain in the right side of my rib cage make me wince.

"Christ." Dark spots push against the edges of my vision as he takes my hand and squeezes. "Help's on the way."

"But how...?"

"Your brother got worried when you didn't show up."

"I wasn't that late," I manage.

Alec shrugs out of his big leather jacket and drapes it over my damp blouse. "You know your brother."

I do, but—

"And Cain," he adds.

The longing is sharp, deep. The realization stuns. I do know Cain, better with each passing day. And despite the dangerous game we can't stop playing, it's him I want kneeling beside me, holding my hand. Because I know. I know the games are just a smoke screen, a protective device. *A prelude.* We keep dancing around each other, because the second we stop, we'll be left confronting a truth, a passion, that could destroy us both.

I'm supposed to be investigating him, for God's sake. My boss has warned me—

But then Cain is there, barging into the courtyard and stopping abruptly, swearing viciously and running toward me. I have no idea how much time has passed. Ten seconds. Ten minutes. I only know he's here, dropping to my side and leaning over me, scooping me into his arms and murmuring desperate words that feed some vulnerable place deep inside.

"Cain…"

"I'm here," he whispers, running his hands over my body. The juxtaposition between the gentleness in his voice and the ferocity in his eyes devastates me. "I'm here."

For the moment, that's all that matters.

CHAPTER FOURTEEN

New Orleans
Present day

"OH, *MON DIEU,* are you okay?"

Standing in a puddle of yellow porch light, Renee brought a hand to her throat and felt the sticky warmth of blood against her fingertips. "I—I need to see Cain."

The pretty blonde peering from behind a partially open door wearing a soft pink chenille robe and fuzzy slippers eyed Renee. A small sign proclaimed the old Victorian to be a bed-and-breakfast, but the innkeeper's stare inspired neither welcome nor refuge.

It was the cool, assessing look of a cop.

"Mon Dieu," the woman muttered again, then stunned Renee by fumbling with the chain and opening the door, practically dragging her inside. "You're that *True Crime* producer right?" she asked, shutting the door and turning the dead bolt, sliding the chain in place. "Renee…"

"Fox," she supplied. "How do you know—"

"Let's get a look at this." Briskly, the innkeeper urged Renee's fingers from her neck and made a soft clucking sound. "*Mon Dieu,* who did this to you? Are you hurt anywhere else?"

Renee shook her head. "I need to talk to Cain."

Need. There was that word again.

"Of course you do," the woman said, gently inspecting Renee's neck. "But he's not here yet. I swear, I never know when he's going to show up. I've given up trying to figure him out."

The laissez-faire tone struck Renee as odd. Clearly the woman expected Cain, but there was no possession or jealousy in her voice, nothing remotely close to the way a woman feels when her lover is late and another woman comes looking for him.

"But you do expect him...." She let her voice trickle off and flashed a tentative smile. "I'm sorry. I've barged into your home in the middle of the night, but I don't even know your name."

The woman pulled back and lifted a hand to her face, left a smear of blood against her cheek. "Oh, I just assumed since you're here..." Her eyes warmed. "I'm Tara. Cain and my husb—ex-husband were partners." She reached for Renee's wrist. "Now let's get this cleaned up."

Tara. Surprise came hard and fast. Trying to hide it, Renee let the woman she'd heard so much about lead her into a spacious room with rich jade walls. They passed a formal dining table and moved through a butler's pantry before entering the kitchen. A flick of a switch bathed the room in light.

Tara directed her to a bulky farmhouse table. "Go ahead and have a seat while I get a bandage from my bathroom." All business, she bustled out of the kitchen, leaving Renee sitting alone in the big kitchen that looked cold, but wasn't.

Slowly she lifted a hand to her neck and traced her fingers along the shallow cut.

Tara. She'd heard so much about her, from Alec, from Cain, but the two women had never met. Tara had been working as a consultant back then, spending weeks on assignment in Scotland. Alec had missed her desperately, talked about her incessantly. They were trying to start a family. Had been for a while. Alec joked about how tough all the practice was, but the anguish in his eyes, his voice, had been impossible to miss. Only toward the end had he mentioned his concern for his wife, the worry that their inability to conceive was taking a toll on her.

Renee closed her eyes and brought her hands to her face, felt the ache tighten through her chest. So much had changed. Alec had seemed deeply in love with his wife, that love evident in every word he spoke. But time had moved on for them, too. Moved on for Alec. He wasn't the man she remembered.

Maybe he never had been. It was hard to know anymore, hard to separate the lies from the truth, the sins from the penance.

"I'm glad you came here," Tara said when she returned. Going down on a knee, she lifted a piece of damp gauze to Renee's neck. "Thank God you weren't hurt worse."

Antiseptic came next, and it stung. "It was a warning." Just like so many others she'd received during her career as an investigative reporter. "Someone's scared of what I might find out."

"And rightfully so." Tara pressed a clean gauze to Renee's throat. "But there's got to be more to it than that. Mercy is not his calling card. If he left you alive, my bet is he wants something he thinks only you can provide."

Renee tensed. Maybe Alec had moved out, but clearly his wife still had her ear to the ground. "You sound like you know who did this to me."

Tara's eyes met hers. "Don't you?"

The question hung there between them, wicked in its simplicity. Like a bright, glaring searchlight, it exposed the shattering uncertainty Renee had been living with every day and night for the past eighteen months.

The answer should have been easy. Yes. She knew who was responsible for the attack. Tonight—and before. *Oncle. Oncle* was responsible. *Oncle* was the one who'd tried to silence her. *Oncle* was the one who'd ordered a knife to her throat.

But *Oncle* was a shadowy figure. No one knew who he was or where to find him, only that his payroll was extensive. There were cops on that payroll. Cops who carried out his bidding.

And that's where everything tangled. Because while that dark, wounded place within her refused to believe Cain could be involved, the facts said otherwise. So she'd walled that place off, tacked up every scrap of brick and concrete and plywood she could find, done whatever she could, whatever she had to, to drown out the chorus that refused to die.

"I'm not sure what I know anymore," she whispered, and God help her, it was the truth.

Tara frowned. "It's a crazy, mixed-up world—"

They saw it at the same time, the shadow moving across the bay window. Tara reeled back and Renee's heart kicked hard, but before either woman could move, the back door slammed open and he burst into the kitchen.

"Where the hell is she—" He stopped abruptly, as though he'd run smack into an invisible wall, and murder exploded in his eyes.

FOR A MOMENT Cain couldn't move. Couldn't think. Could barely breathe. Like a deaf, dumb, mute paraplegic, he could only stand and drink in the sight of her sitting at the table, alive.

Sweet God, for over two hours he'd been looking for her, scouring the streets of the Quarter, the alleys and vacant buildings. He'd found her rental car at a small hotel, but her room had been empty. An overstuffed garbage bag at the back of the parking lot had shut him down inside. Each Dumpster had thrown him further into the past.

Then Tara had called, said Renee was with her…

She was hurt. That was his first realization. There was blood on her neck, a bruise on her cheek.

She was safe. That was his second thought. She'd made it to Tara's. She was conscious, able to sit. Her clothes were intact. She wasn't crying or shivering or incoherent.

She was scared. That was his third thought, and it damn near slayed him. From the moment they'd met, she'd taken everything he'd dished out with aplomb and a courage that infuriated even as it seduced. Except at the casino. There she'd been rattled, nervous. Because the game had turned, and they both knew it.

But now there was no game, no strategy or carefully

calculated move. The glitter to her eyes, the clash of terror and hope, ran far deeper than mere nerves.

Four seconds, maybe six, that's all it took for the thoughts to register, and then the moment released him and he lunged toward her, dropped to his knees. "Sweet Mary."

"I'll leave you two for a minute," Tara said, and left them alone.

With a gentleness that stunned him, Cain lifted his hands to Renee's neck and found her flesh cold. Too cold. "Who did this to you?"

She looked away, down toward the ridiculously clean white ceramic tile. "You didn't come back." Her voice sounded robotic, stripped of emotion, and the change rocked him even further. Until that moment he hadn't realized how much he'd come to crave her fire.

"I…waited," she went on as he squeezed antibiotic cream onto a bandage and pressed it to her throat, "but you didn't come back. I was walking—"

His hands stilled. "You were what?"

She looked up, met his eyes. "Walking back to my hotel."

Alone. At night. In the Quarter. Just like— "Christ." The edges of his vision blurred and he saw her, sprawled and broken in his partner's arms, bruised, battered, bleeding. "You're just like her," he bit out, and the re-alization gutted him. "She never listened, always thought she knew best, that she could handle anything, that she wouldn't get hurt."

Gutsy and vibrant, he'd always thought, like a big beautiful magnolia, defying wind and rain to revel in the aftermath. Afraid of nothing or no one, even when she should have been.

In the end, that's what had gotten her killed.

On a hot rush of adrenaline, he narrowed his eyes and brought the room back into focus, saw Renee, her eyes huge and devastated, her hair tangled and falling against skin paler than before, staring at him as though he'd suddenly started speaking in the language of the damned.

"God damn it." There was no other way to explain it. "Do you really want to find out what happened to Savannah?" he asked in the deceptively quiet voice he used when fighting for control. "Or end up just like her?"

Renee winced. "That's what he said."

"Who?" The need to know, to punish, gripped him. "Tell me who, damn it."

Nothing had prepared him for what she did next, what she said. The gleam that fed some place deep inside him returned to her eyes, the steel to her voice. "That's what I came here to find out."

He went very still. Because in that one fractured instant, he knew. He saw the truth, the accusation, in every hard line of her body, the fierce angle of her chin, the cold glitter of her gaze, and it burned. "You came looking for me."

"To tell you to call off the scare tactics."

The ragged words slapped, not because she'd said them, but because he'd given her every reason imaginable to say them. He'd tried to run her out of town. He'd threatened and bullied and cajoled. And when words hadn't worked, he'd tried to scare her off through seduction.

"You think I'm responsible for what happened to you." It was more a statement than a question, and the words scraped on the way out.

She didn't flinch, didn't wince, didn't try to deny. "Can you blame me?"

No. He couldn't. That was the problem. He was a man who went to great lengths to get what he wanted. Limits were not in his nature. He loved the chase, the anticipation. He savored the taste of success, the high it always brought. Whether he'd been pursuing a suspect for weeks or crouched in the foggy swamp for hours waiting for just the right light didn't matter. The means were just a road along the way.

The end, the victory, was all that mattered.

But here, now, on his knees in Tara's kitchen, the high eluded him.

"Are you out of your mind?" The fury came over him in a wave and had him reaching for her, taking her shoulders in his hands and fighting the urge to pull her out of the chair. "If you think I did this to you, then what the hell are you doing here?" Something dark and unfathomable flashed through her eyes—alarm? fear?— and it ripped at him. But it didn't stop him. "Don't you get it? Don't you understand? If I'm the man you think I am, then you should be sitting in a police station right now, telling a detective everything you know."

There was a clock in the kitchen, a whimsical black cat with big animated eyes that Alec had bought Tara years ago. Its tail wagged with each second.

Cain counted twelve long, slow ticks before Renee answered. During that time she never looked away, never moved, just looked at him as if he was both antichrist and savior.

"The police can't give me what I want," she said.

It was a large kitchen, bright, spacious. But in that heartbeat the walls pushed in. "And I can?"

She stunned him by lifting a hand to his face. "You did." Her fingers were soft against his cheeks, cool and affirming. Dangerous. "The second I saw your eyes," she whispered, and her voice thickened, "I knew you weren't responsible."

The quiet admission should have brought relief. Instead it rocked. Cain released her abruptly and stood, backed away from her, her touch. Her confession. He didn't want it, not any of it, but especially not the way she kept looking at him, as though she could consume him with her eyes. Christ, he didn't want anyone looking at him like that, not ever, ever again. Only one person had ever looked at him like that—

No. He killed the thought, the comparison, immediately. He was so not going there.

"Why does that bother you, Cain?" Renee stood and moved toward him. "Why are you more comfortable with people thinking you're the bad guy?"

He turned away from her, moved to the window and stared out into the night. It was all he knew, damn it.

"Cain—" she said, and he saw her reflection, felt her moving closer.

"Don't psychoanalyze me."

"What about care?" Her hand touched his arm. "Can I do that?"

He spun toward her. "You have no idea—"

"Then give me one," she whispered, and before he realized her intent, she put a hand to the back of his head and urged him toward her, brushed her lips across his.

The kiss was soft and quick, so gentle it damn near sent him back to his knees.

With a sad smile, she feathered her thumb along his cheekbone. "Why do you want me to hate you?"

For one of the few times in his life he acted without thinking, without strategy or tactic. He acted on pure blind instinct and dark driving need. A hard sound ripped from his throat as he pulled her into his arms and crushed her against his body, took her mouth with his own.

There was nothing soft or gentle about this kiss, nothing quick. He held her face in his hands and slanted his mouth over hers, needing to taste her, claim her, with an urgency that stunned him. For two hours black thoughts had punished him, taunting him with horrible, cruel images. He'd shoved them aside, remained objective, but all that objectivity fled now, crumbled, leaving just the woman in his arms, alive and beautiful and dangerous as hell.

"Cain," she whispered, and as her mouth opened he went in for more, went deeper, wanted to touch and take every part of her, every inch. She pressed into him, held on to him with the same intensity that fired through him. She had a hand at the small of his back, the other shoved into his hair, holding, pulling. Demanding.

Lost in her, the moment, he backed her across the kitchen and into a wall. "No more chances," he murmured, reaching for her leg and hiking it up around his waist. "No more—"

The pain lanced through him like the bright punishing light of a laser.

CHAPTER FIFTEEN

RENEE RIPPED HER mouth from Cain's and stared up at
him. "What happened? Are you okay?"

Wincing, he put a hand to her face and traced his
thumb along her swollen lip. "I will be just as soon as—"

"Don't!" She struggled out of his arms and reached
for his shirt, tugged it out of his jeans and yanked it up.
"Mon Dieu."

"It's nothing—"

But she was already there, leaning over the nasty
purple bruise courtesy of Alec's boot. Her hands were
soft, devastating. "Who did this to you?"

The simple question stung more than the bruise. She
was the one who'd been attacked. She was the one
who'd had a knife to her throat, who was hurt, who'd
scraped together the courage to come to Tara's house
and confront the man most believed to be a monster, but
who she, for some godforsaken reason, did not fear.

And now she was the one angrily demanding to
know who'd kicked him in the ribs.

"It was him, wasn't it?" She looked up at him
through narrow, hurting eyes. "The man from the racetrack, the one who tried to kill you."

Cain looked away.

Renee lifted a hand to his face, and again stunned him with the gentleness in her touch, her gaze. It was a side she kept carefully hidden.

God help him, he wanted to know why.

He'd been right all along, he realized. She'd been hurt. Not just tonight, but before she'd ever stepped into the residue of Savannah's life. The remnants of devastation lingered in her eyes. Someone or something had come close to destroying her, forcing her to mask the pain with the hard edges she showed the world.

It was ridiculous, but in that moment the need to know who, or what, grew inside him like a beast. It didn't matter that he could have no future with this woman, that he wanted no future with anyone. It only mattered that she was a woman, and she'd been hurt. He had not been able to save Savannah, to avenge her, but fate had just handed him the second chance he'd never expected to receive.

"Tell me," she said. "What happened?"

That was a damn good question. He'd been convinced Alec had grown disillusioned with the politics and strings of the force and had decided to take justice into his own hands. But then he'd looked into Alec's eyes…and seen a stranger about to pistol whip him.

"He got away." The reality galled Cain. He'd come to on the floor of the warehouse almost thirty minutes later, alone.

"You know him, don't you?"

The question came at him like another booted foot. "Not anymore."

A sound from the butler's pantry had them turning to see Tara still in her robe, her hair tangled around her face. The color had drained from her cheeks. "It was Alec, wasn't it?"

Cain swore softly. "Tara." Renee's hand fell away and he crossed the kitchen, reached for the woman he loved like a sister. The urge to protect was strong, to concoct a neat-and-tidy story that cleared Alec of any involvement. But she was a smart woman and she'd been already been deceived too much. "I tried to get through to him. I tried to pull him back."

Tara Monroe had taken the debutante scene by storm. With a bright smile, an infectious laugh and delicate, porcelain-doll features, she'd left a string of broken hearts wherever she went.

But it was *her* heart that was broken now. Her expression, normally warm and vibrant, was wiped clean.

Robotically, she lifted his shirt. "He hurt you." Her fingers were soft and gentle like Renee's, but her touch did not bring the same warmth, only the chill of sorrow. "He did this to you."

Cain took her hands and pulled them from his body. "He's not himself right now, Tara." But he'd smelled no alcohol on Alec's breath, observed no evidence of substance abuse in his eyes or diction. "But I promise you I'm going to get to the bottom of this."

If Cain didn't, one of them was going to end up very dead.

"I don't think he really wanted to hurt me," he added. If Alec had, Cain would have left the warehouse in a body bag.

Tara glanced at the counter, where limp rose petals lay scattered beneath a crystal vase. "I wish I understood."

"You and me both."

"How did he loo—" There was an edge of desperation to her voice, but she aborted the question and reached for the red petals, brushed them into her palm and closed them in her fist. "It's late." Jerkily she looked beyond him to Renee. "I've readied a room for you upstairs. The River Road suite. It's the third door on the right."

Renee's smile was warm and unaffected, and it damn near knocked the breath from Cain's lungs.

"You're very kind, but you didn't have to do that." She glanced at her purse lying on the kitchen table. "I've got a room—"

Cain didn't let her finish. "*Non.* You're not going back there tonight."

THE FIRST PINKISH rays of morning streaked up from the horizon, visible through the naked branches of an old oak outside Renee's room. She stood at the window, much as she had the majority of the time she should have been sleeping, and tried not to think about how little separated her from Cain.

A wide hall, a locked door and one life-altering lie.

They could all be breached. It wouldn't take much. A few strides across the hall, a good solid kick to the door, another touch, another kiss. She'd been so sure, damn it. So sure she could return to New Orleans and pick up the threads of the investigation without falling back into the remains of her life. That she hadn't even wanted to pick up those threads. In becoming Renee Fox, she'd wanted to believe she'd become a new woman, someone whose existence was not inexorably tangled with Cain's.

But last night had proved just how wrong she'd been.

Impossibly cold, she wrapped the bulky robe tighter and hugged her arms around her middle, told herself if she concentrated hard enough, she could ignore the sound of water from across the hall. But she was wrong about that, too. Because the sound came from the room where Cain had stayed, and too easily she could see him standing under the spray of the shower. He was a big man—the average shower hit him just beneath his shoulders. With a slow smile she remembered how he would turn into the water and throw his head back, let the water stream down his chest.

Renee turned from the window and ran a hand through her hair, but the memory, the sudden warmth, kept streaming through her.

Something had to give.

Everything had seemed methodically straightforward from the relative safety of Nova Scotia. Like an animal in captivity, she'd forgotten the thrill of living in the wild. Confronted only with what could be found in newspapers or on the Internet, the punishing memory of Adrian's last words, she'd forced herself to strip every droplet of emotion from her body. Allowing herself to feel anything—sorrow, longing, even anger— would only compromise her ability to conduct a thorough, objective investigation. She'd convinced herself the past wouldn't matter. Didn't matter.

Then she'd stepped off the plane...and gone straight to Cain.

That was the fatal flaw in her plan. Emotion could not be scraped away like toxic residue. Emotion could not be discarded or ignored. Emotion was real and powerful and like a tree in the path of a hurricane, it had a way of surviving, enduring, against every single odd that predicted otherwise.

From the moment she'd stepped into the past, she'd walked through the remnants of her life like a crumbling old movie set. Everywhere she went, she saw people, places and things she recognized. She saw memories. She saw dreams. Fractured now, but there all the same.

She had a new face, she knew that. New hair color. New eye color. A new voice, a new name. Even a new way of walking. She'd worked tirelessly to make sure no one connected her with the woman she'd been. It was the only way to guarantee her safety, but the longer the charade went on, the more unsettling it became.

The water stopped, and in her mind's eye she could see Cain stepping from the shower and reaching for a towel...

Stay away. That's what the reporter in her demanded. Stay away from Cain. But that was one command the woman didn't know how to follow, not when simply being in the same room with him brought a song to her blood. It was like spontaneous springtime, everything inside her bursting into full, desperate bloom at the same time. The craving was still there, the need and the desire.

Because there was another truth she'd overlooked.

Life had gone on for the people of Bayou de Foi. But not for her. For her, it was all just yesterday. Her love affair with Cain. Her brother's murder. The attack. In coming to New Orleans, it was like stepping into a life trapped almost two years in the past, and though she knew the danger, every chance she got, she found herself seeking out Cain.

Throat tight, she crossed to the small bathroom and

turned on the cold water, splashed it against her face. She was still standing there when her mobile phone rang.

Grabbing a towel, she ran it over her face and hurried into the bedroom, picked up the flip-phone. "Talk to me." The wince was automatic. She'd not answered a call with those three words since the afternoon the nervous rookie cop had called, promising her explosive information about her brother's death.

"You that gal with *True Crime?*"

She tensed. "This is Renee Fox. Who am I speaking with?"

"Dey're after me," the man said. "Saw me talking with you in the alley, scared I told you something I wasn't supposed to."

"Travis?" Her mind raced. She'd slipped him her mobile phone number, but the last she'd heard he and his sidekick were still missing. "Who's after you?"

"No," he whispered away from the phone. "I know what I'm doing." Then he said to her, "The same people who killed yer friend."

Renee noticed the difference immediately: the maniacal, drunken slur to his voice was gone, replaced by an edge of urgency. "And now you think they're after you?"

"I know dey are," he said. "The sheriff warned us this would happen if we said anything, but I can't keep living like this. I cain't hold quiet when I know what happened to Savannah."

Her grip on the phone tightened. "Travis, what are you talking about?"

"Someone needs to know," he said, and his voice slipped on the words. "Before dey get me, too."

"No one's going to get you."

"There's a fishing camp a couple of miles off the highway. You'll pass a gas station—Al's, he closed up years ago but there's still a sign out front, an old pump—you'll want to turn three-quarters of a mile later. Take that road until it dead-ends, then go right. That'll take you straight to the cabin."

She knew the spot. Cain had taken her there one afternoon for a so-called fishing lesson—they'd done very little fishing.

"Come alone," he said. "Make sure no one follows you."

The line went dead.

Renee tilted her head and took a deep breath, let it out slowly. Travis wasn't someone she'd known before. She had no experience to call on other than their encounter a few nights ago. Now she had to wonder. He'd sounded oddly…sincere. And he was clearly scared spitless.

Class clowns and town drunks, she'd learned, were often gold mines of information. While no one took them seriously, they watched and heard everything. Decision made, she untied the robe and headed for the bathroom.

The loud knock stopped her. "Open up, Renee."

She absorbed the voice, the cadence, let it wash through her like an infusion of hot moonlight. "I'll be downstairs in a few minutes."

"The door, *belle amie*. Open it."

Her heart kicked, hard. In the beginning she'd bristled when Cain barked out commands, but then the shadow dance had slowed and she'd glimpsed the man behind the hard-ass detective, the passion that fired his blood, and the bristle had smoothed into a flood of anticipation. Because she'd discovered a secret.

The belligerence wasn't a form of control, but of fear. And it seduced like nothing else ever had.

"This better be good," she protested as she opened the door.

The sight of him was almost unbearable. His dark hair was damp and wavy, his shirt unbuttoned, his jaw unshaved. He looked exactly like he had after the last time they'd made love, when they'd woken up together, dressed together, gone back to bed. When they'd gone their separate ways an hour later, she'd never imagined it was forever.

His gaze dropped from her face to her chest, down to her waist, where the robe was slipping open. "You do have a way of opening doors," he muttered with slow appreciation.

She grabbed the sash and yanked the ends into a quick knot. "Somehow I don't think you banged on my door to steal a peek."

He laughed. "*Mais, cher.* You never know what a man like me might try to steal."

Her lips wanted to twitch. She didn't let them.

"*Mais non,*" he conceded. "No matter what the sight of you in that robe does to my imagination, that isn't why I'm here." He moved into the room and closed the door. "I'm here because I want to know what Travis told you."

CAIN EASED OFF the gas and glanced at Renee, saw that she'd barely moved in the fifteen minutes since he'd left his Mercedes behind the old gas station and climbed into the driver's seat of the rental. Like a statue she sat ramrod straight, her face angled away from him, her hands clenched in her lap. He knew that if he touched them, they would be cold.

She hadn't wanted to tell him about the phone call. She hadn't wanted him to come with her, either. But in the end, he'd given her little choice.

The road curved, seeming to vanish into a wall of live oaks. He took the bend faster than he should have, then abruptly slowed. "We're here."

Mechanically Renee turned toward the fishing camp barely visible through the skeletal cypress trees. The wood was weathered, the windows dark with grime. "Good."

He killed the engine, scanned the perimeter. The day was still, quiet save for the incessant caw of blackbirds filling the trees.

The spider tingle down the back of his neck was immediate, the tightening in his gut. As a cop, he'd learned to trust instinct above all else. As a refugee from that life, he still did. "Something doesn't feel right," he said, reaching for his gun.

Renee swung toward him. "They're hiding."

He pulled his Glock from its holster and pushed open the driver's-side door.

"Cain!" she started, but he didn't stop. He'd already made up his mind. From the time he was a small boy, his father and uncles had taught him and Gabe and their other cousins the way of the land, the way of the woods. He'd learned the nuances of the wind, the air pressure. He'd learned how the birds were supposed to sound— and how they weren't.

He'd learned how to smell a trap from a mile away.

"You can't do this," Renee said from behind him.

He slowed at the porch, took the two steps quietly. "I'm sorry, *cher*," he said without turning to her, "but you can't stop me."

At the door she grabbed his arm. "You lied."

The words shouldn't have stung. No promises bound them. "Not intentionally," he surprised himself by saying. Then he turned to her. "I need you to stay here while I check things out."

"Travis called *me*."

"But I have the gun." And that should have been all that mattered. But he hesitated, disturbed by the way she was looking at him, the piercing combination of betrayal and longing. "Not now," he said, and the words sounded more like a growl. Then he surprised himself again by pressing a kiss to her mouth. Hard. "Please." He pulled back to look at her. "Stay."

IT WAS THE *please* that got her. Instincts Renee had honed as a reporter urged her to charge after Cain, but the volatility she'd seen in his eyes, the pleading, held her in place. He'd seemed scared, not of what he might find inside, but for her.

Lifting a hand to her face, she touched where he'd touched and stared off at the trees, wondering what had triggered his alarm. He'd always had the ability, a sixth sense that had kept him alive when conventional wisdom guaranteed otherwise.

Restless, she put her ear to the door and strained to hear what was happening, voices, a struggle, something—anything—but heard only the whisper of the wind and the incessant drone of the birds. Then she saw the blood.

On a broken breath she squatted and stared at the partial footprint, the dark red smears beside it, the trickle leading down the steps to the dusty dirt path.

The sound of a door opening had her swinging around to find Cain emerging from the darkness with death in his eyes.

CHAPTER SIXTEEN

New Orleans
Nineteen months earlier

IT'S LATE. I should be tired. Normally I'm in bed by midnight, but tonight I can't stop pacing. It's been hours since my last cup of coffee, but the jittery high still jumps through me. Maybe that's why I can't stand still.

Maybe not.

Cain should have been here hours ago. Things have been different since the attack. Something changed between us as he'd cradled me in the damp darkness. Words had been said. Touches shared. Truths exposed.

At first we'd both tried to deny, to go back to the way things had been, the comfort of antagonism and sparring, the ironic safety of focusing on *Oncle*. But that was impossible. Neither of us could forget. Pretending didn't work. The want was too strong.

But being together is new, different. Awkward. We don't know how to have a relationship. Neither of us is pure as the driven snow, but somehow we still act like teenagers drunk on the discovery of raw physical attraction, the desperate, chaotic *need* to be with each other.

I thought tonight was going to be that night. Cain

invited himself over, said there were things we needed to talk about. That he was tired of playing games. The words had washed through me on a delicious wave, sending me shopping for new lingerie.

I notice the slash of headlights first. Then the rumble of an engine above the wail of Leroy's sax two blocks away. I brace myself as the car slows, stops. A door opens, closes.

Slowly, I look toward the front of the house, where I see Cain open the iron gate and move up the walkway.

The anticipation is intense, the way my heart starts to pound and my palms go moist. I hate that he can do this to me, reduce me to waiting around for him like I haven't anything better to do.

Bracing myself, I wait for the knock.

Long moments pass. I'm not sure how many. Thirty seconds. Maybe forty. Far too many for the short distance he has to cross. Ready for this to be over with, I stalk to the front door and yank it open—go completely still.

His eyes. God. They're always gleaming with the dark light of a predator, capable of slaying one moment, seducing the next. They do neither now. They're vacant almost, dull…like death.

The dread is immediate, a tight fist squeezing my throat. The cold comes next, sharp, debilitating, bleeding from the inside out. Because I know. It's the middle of the night. And Cain is a cop. On my doorstep. Stoic. Somber.

And my world tilts.

"Adrian." His name breaks on the way out. I see

Cain wince, see his mouth form words, but hear nothing beyond the brutal roaring in my ears.

"No—" Vaguely I'm aware of my knees buckling, the floor rushing up to meet me.

But then Cain is there, reaching for me, pulling me into his arms. "S'okay," he murmurs, and somehow I'm in his lap, and he's rocking, just rocking. His hands are all over me, running along my arms and my back, tangling in my hair, gathering me as close to him as possible.

"I've got you," he whispers over and over. "I'm here now. You're okay."

Everything around me is spinning, but Cain is there and he's solid, and I feel my hands digging into the fabric of his shirt. The temptation to sink into him is strong, to surrender to the darkness and trust him to guide me to the light. No one has ever held me like this before, infusing me with the heat of his body, his strength.

"No," I whisper but don't even recognize my voice. Then I'm fighting him, yanking out of his arms and grabbing the collar of his shirt, shaking him. "No, God damn you. No!"

He doesn't try to stop me. "There now," he says in that low, black magic voice of his. "That's a girl. Just let it out."

My fists curl and I shove at him. "Shake me back, damn it." Shove me. Hit me. "Make me wake up!"

His eyes gentle. "You know I can't do that."

"Yes, you can!" There's a ripping deep inside, starting low in my gut and working its way up through my chest. I feel the tremor tear through my throat and rush for my eyes. "You're a cop, damn you. You're supposed to protect people."

With devastating gentleness he gathers me to him again and holds me against his chest, buries his face in my hair and murmurs in French. I don't know what he's saying, but I hear the sorrow, the compassion. I feel the humanity in his touch.

Time passes. I don't know how much. I'm only aware of sensation, the thrumming of Cain's heart and the possession of his embrace, the cool breeze drifting through a door still open. My cat Esmerelda joins us, circling us, rubbing against my arm, stroking me with her sandpapery tongue.

Gradually the fog subsides and the need to know overrides the safety of Cain's arms. On a deep breath I pull back and meet his eyes. "Tell me."

"Not now, *cher*—"

"Now." There's no room for negotiation in my voice.

Frowning, he lets out a rough breath and lifts a hand to my face, slides the hair behind my ears. "He didn't suffer."

Moisture burns my eyes. I want to rage at him, scream that he can't possibly know how Adrian felt in those last moments. But the words don't form. "Was he…alone?"

"Looks that way."

I swallow. "Where?"

"His body was—" He squeezes his eyes shut, opens them a heartbeat later. "He was found south of Bayou de Foi."

Tears well. My throat burns. "What was he doing there?"

With his thumb, Cain wipes the moisture beneath my lashes. "Waiting for me."

The words jolt through me. "You? Why? You hate each other."

He shakes his head. "Things are not always as they seem, *cher.* Adrian called, said we needed to talk."

I struggle to take it all in, but the thoughts gridlock in my mind. "About what?" I manage, but Cain doesn't answer, just pulls me closer and holds me tight.

"We'll talk more later."

I want to protest, but then Cain is scooping me into his arms and striding toward the back of the house. In my bedroom he yanks back the covers and sets me on the mattress, then eases down beside me, pulling me into his arms. Esmerelda joins us.

The darkness is coming in waves now, punishing, jerky, and though surrender is not in my nature, for once in my life, I simply let go, knowing that no matter how far I fall, Cain will be there to catch me.

Sometime later I open my eyes. The sun has not yet risen. Esmy is curled on the pillow around my head, purring. Beside me, the mattress is empty.

Disoriented, I prop myself up and squint against the night, see Cain strapping on his shoulder holster. "Cain?"

He turns toward me and frowns. "Go back to sleep."

"But—"

He moves toward me. "I have something to take care of." The words are soft. "*Mais* I'll be back as soon as I can."

The disappointment is acute. "Don't go."

I've never said those words to another human being.

He leans down and eases the hair from my face, skims a kiss to my forehead. "I have to."

I reach for his face, savor the rough feel of whiskers beneath my thumbs. "Hurry back."

I've never said those words, either.

"I promise." The dark light is back in his eyes, the one that feeds some place deep inside of me. But then he's gone, leaving me alone in the bed with a pillow clenched to my chest. The tears start then, deep, gut-wrenching. For my brother. For myself.

And the man who stands between us.

CHAPTER SEVENTEEN

New Orleans
Present day

SLOWLY, RENEE STOOD. She knew the look in Cain's eyes. And without even having to ask, she knew what he'd found inside.

"No." Her voice broke on the word, just as it had that dark night a lifetime ago, the one that had catapulted them down a path unimaginable at the time. Unimaginable even now. "Cain—"

"I need your phone." His voice was tight. So were the lines of his face. "Mine's in the car."

Heart pounding, she reached into her purse. "Something bad happened, didn't it?" It seemed a gross understatement.

Cain jabbed seven numbers and looked beyond her, toward the trees. His body blocked the door. "Get to the old Comeaux place." The muscle in the hollow of his cheek thumped. "I've found Travis." On a rough breath, he met Renee's gaze. "Get the coroner."

Horror coiled through her, and squeezed. A week ago she could have passed Travis on the street and the encounter would have meant nothing to her. But now he lay dead, murdered, because he'd dared to tell her what no one else would.

"God, it's happening again." The vertigo whipped hard, fast. "It's got to stop," she murmured, pushing past Cain and shoving at the door, stumbling inside.

Everyone said Adrian hadn't suffered, that his death had been quick and clean, painless. But the second Renee's eyes adjusted to the shadowy room, she knew the same could not be said for Travis. The broken chairs told her that he'd fought. The blood against the wall told her it hadn't been fast. The unnatural position of his body told her that he'd suffered.

"Don't look," Cain said, turning her from the grisly scene and pulling her into his arms. On some distant plane she knew she should fight him, should not accept his comfort. But his body felt so good against hers, and the low thrum of his heart steadied her like nothing else ever had. Just for a moment, she bargained with herself. She could allow herself just this one moment. It didn't mean anything. Didn't change anything. It was just a time-out.

Every game had them.

CAIN'S IMAGINATION betrayed him, throwing him back in time to another night, another woman. He could still see the devastation in her eyes when she'd realized what he hadn't known how to tell her. He could still hear her voice break. And though it was Renee in his arms, it was Savannah he felt sag against him and hold on tight, Savannah he held with a savagery that stunned even him.

It was time to let go. He knew that. He just didn't know how.

Squeezing his eyes shut, he savored the feel of her soft body molded to his, breathing of her, wanting more. This time it would be different. This time he wouldn't fail. This time he would be there for her—

Her.

Abruptly he opened his eyes and stared down at her hair. Brown. Not blond. With a sharp twist to his gut he pushed back from her and put his hands to her arms, looked down into a face so flawlessly beautiful it defied logic. Mossy eyes, not crystalline blue. A thin nose, not sloped. A soft mouth, not challenging.

"Mon Dieu." The truth appalled.

He had no idea who he'd just been fantasizing about—the woman who still haunted his dreams, or the one looking up at him as if he'd just broken her heart.

He wanted to be angry with her. Furious, actually. Her arrival had kicked events into motion, as he'd predicted. Travis would not be the only casualty.

But as he looked at her, he could find no anger. Only fear. Like an icy fist, it reached into his gut and twisted.

"I told you to stay away," he bit out. Not trusting himself to look at her one second longer, he turned and strode outside, grabbed the porch rail and stared at the trees standing like emaciated soldiers against a dreary autumn sky.

Her voice came from behind him, so quiet he could barely hear the words above the crows. "I didn't mean for anyone to get hurt."

"We don't mean for a lot of things to happen, but that never seems to stop them."

"You're talking about Savannah," she whispered.

Beyond the trees, he watched a torn plastic grocery

bag flail against a chicken-wire fence. "She didn't listen, either." His voice was thick, and he hated it. "She thought she was invincible, that she could walk through fire and not get burned."

"Maybe she was scared, didn't know who trust."

A hard sound broke from deep in Cain's throat. The temptation to turn to her was strong, but he wasn't interested in looking into Renee's eyes and seeing another woman staring back at him. "The first time I saw her was on the news. She was covering a story about medical malpractice, and I remember sitting in this dive in Baton Rouge, watching this pathetic little black-and-white TV, thinking 'Now that is one fine woman.'

"Six months later I'd just busted an airline pilot trying to smuggle money out of the country, and the press is hounding me, wanting to know why we think this is a major bust, and I hear this voice from behind me. I turn, and there she is."

"Sounds like fate," Renee whispered.

"I used to lie awake and watch her sleep, wonder what the hell I'd done to deserve her. She was so beautiful sometimes I couldn't even breathe. Sometimes I'd touch her face and she'd smile. Sometimes I'd kiss her and she'd whimper." He closed his eyes, let the memory wash over him. "She started having bad dreams after her brother died. She tried to be so tough when she was awake, but in her sleep she would cry." The first time he'd heard the sound it had slayed him. "I've never felt so helpless in my life."

Renee let out a shaky breath. "What did you do?"

"The only thing I could," he said, not sure why he was saying anything at all. "Hold her, tell her everything was going to be okay."

Behind him, the porch creaked with movement. "Why didn't you make those promises when she was awake?"

The question scored a direct hit. He turned, found her standing close enough to touch. "Who says I didn't?"

Her eyes, awash with an inner light, met his. "You," she whispered. "I hear it in your voice. The regret. You wonder if saying those words would have made a difference."

That wasn't true. He didn't wonder. He knew, had spent too many nights alone in bed, rewriting the script, changing the ending. "I didn't want to spook her."

The wind whipped up, sending long strands of dark brown hair against Renee's face. "Sounds like you were the one who was spooked."

His fingers itched to ease the hair from her eyes. "Maybe," he said, but did not let himself move. They were at a crime scene, for God's sake. Two men lay dead inside with the mark of the fleur-de-lis. But all he could think about was what it would feel like to taste her again.

From the direction of the road the sound of an engine shattered the moment before he could do something stupid. He turned and saw his uncle's squad car pull into the driveway, realized maybe there was such a thing as salvation, after all.

"Wait here," he said, and if the command came out a little too rough, he refused to let himself care.

"Cain—"

His booted foot coming down on dusty gravel, he turned back to her. "Leave it alone," he said. "I have."

He walked away from her then, refused to look back.

RENEE DIDN'T TRUST herself to move. She stood on the old porch with her hand curled around the railing, absolutely certain if the wind blew so much as one more strand of hair against her face, she would shatter like the Limoges porcelain swan her grandmother had given her for her tenth birthday.

Just breathing hurt. Remembering destroyed.

Slowly, carefully, she uncurled the fingers of one hand and brought her palm to her chest, wondered how her heart could still pound while everything inside her bled. It wasn't fair that he could still touch her like that, way down deep, without so much as lifting a hand. She wanted to hate him for that. She wanted to condemn him. Black magic, she remembered thinking all those months ago. Voodoo. Some kind of strange spell he could cast to coerce those leery of him into doing his bidding.

But as she watched him talk to his uncle, she could find no hate, no condemnation. Not for him, anyway. She'd been wrong, she realized. So horribly wrong. With absolutely certainty she realized she'd not returned to Bayou de Foi to punish.

She'd come home to heal.

"THIS ISN'T THE WAY to the hotel," Renee said fifteen minutes later. She'd been staring out the passenger window and watching the blur of pine and cypress, searching for something benign to say—anything to break the silence.

Words seemed as inadequate as taking a water gun to an inferno.

Something had happened with his uncle. She'd watched them talking, seen the agitation in the movement of Cain's body, heard the edges of their voices carry on the wind. Then he'd turned and strode back to the house, taken her hand, and all but dragged her to the car. But that was it. No words after that. No explanations.

Then she'd noticed the gas station where Cain had left his car. But rather than turning left, he'd turned right.

Now she looked at the hard line of his jaw and the casual way he had a hand draped over the steering wheel, the way he stared straight ahead as if she'd not said a word.

"Cain." She spoke calmly, despite the drumming of her heart. "What's going on? What did your uncle say to you?"

The muscle in the hollow of his cheek thumped.

She'd seen him like this before, knew the brutal control was a protective mechanism. When something pushed him to the edge, he shut down to stop himself from going over. "It's been a long morning," she said, and let her voice gentle. "I'd really like to go back to the hotel and take a shower, get cleaned up." Wash away the stench of death.

He moved so fast she winced, swerving to the side of the road and slamming on the brakes. Then he turned to look at her.

"An hour and a half ago Millie let herself into your room to freshen the linens. She found the bed unmade, the sheets shredded and smeared with red. On the bathroom mirror she found four words, also written in red. *Will-you-be-next?*" He paused, let out a hot breath. "Still want to go back there?"

Trying not to shake, she sat back and stared straight ahead, watched a hawk circle above the treetops.

"It's happening," Cain rolled on. "Just like I said it would. You've knocked too many stones into motion. There's no stopping them now, not until they destroy everything in their path."

She swallowed hard and forced herself to look at him, felt the breath jam in her throat. Because of his eyes. They weren't victorious, weren't hot and accusing. They were…edgy and volatile, and for a shattering moment they dredged up memories of the night *Oncle*'s man attacked her, when Cain had run into the alley and found her in his partner's arms. She'd never forget the way he'd gone to his knees and touched her with a gentleness so excruciating it had seared into her flesh like a brand.

Until that moment she'd perceived fear as a weakness. But like everything else he did, Cain Robichaud wore it like a badge of honor. He hadn't cared what anyone thought of him. He hadn't cared about danger or consequences. He'd only cared about…her.

Fear, she'd realized, wasn't a weakness, but the source of strength and the consequence of emotion, the reflection of humanity. In its absence, there was nothing.

In its presence, there was…everything.

"Does that scare you?" she asked, and her heart slammed hard on the question. She wanted—God, how she wanted.

Slowly his gaze met hers, and scorched clear down to her soul. "Only for you."

His voice chilled. "Cain—"

"Don't." The word sounded torn from somewhere deep and broken and painful. Jaw set, he turned back to the road and jerked the car into Drive, veered back onto the narrow highway.

Within seconds, the trees once again blurred.

Travis was dead. She'd been threatened. And Cain was pulling back by the second. She tried to weave the three together, integrate them with the fabric of all the other information she'd gleaned over the past four days. She was getting closer, she knew.

Someone was running scared.

She wanted to feel victory. And maybe somewhere inside she did. But it didn't resonate with triumph like she'd anticipated. There was only the sinking hollow feeling, the realization that the life she'd walked back into was rapidly coming to an end.

At a narrow, unmarked road, Cain slowed the car and turned back in time. The oak and cypress and pine crowded the bumpy road like an adoring mob shoving and elbowing for the best position. The live oaks, their ancient, weathered canopies stretching across the road to create a tunnel, blotted out the sun. Only slashes and whispers of light fell, dancing with the sway of the Spanish moss.

The ethereal beauty fed Renee, even as it drove home the reality that she really was a dead woman walking.

She knew this road. More than knew it, she'd traveled its twists and turns before. With Cain. She knew what awaited her at the end of a narrow driveway up ahead.

"You didn't answer my question," she said anyway, because that's what a stranger would say. Renee Fox would have no idea what lay ahead. Everything inside of her would not be bracing for the blow. "Where are you taking me?"

Cain's hand tightened around the steering wheel. "Home," he said without inflection or feeling. "With me."

CHAPTER EIGHTEEN

New Orleans
Nineteen months earlier

IT WASN'T SUPPOSED to be beautiful. The breeze shouldn't be whispering like a warm caress against the side of my face. And the sun shouldn't be shining like a spotlight against a sky so impossibly azure that the whole world seems bright.

And the flowers... They're everywhere, all my favorites—azaleas and dogwood and bougainvillea—lifting their faces to the sun in an explosion of color, like a living rainbow shrouding the glowing white of the crypt.

The perfect juxtaposition of life and death.

Slowly, I lift my hand to the cool marble. "Adrian." My voice breaks on his name. He was my brother, my best friend. Sure we fought as kids, and as adults, but only because we loved each other. It is a longstanding theory of mine: Passionate people can't coexist in a static world. There has to be rain. There have to be storms.

But not this. Damn it, not this.

The pain is intense, coiling through me like a python,

choking off one organ at a time. "You promised," I whisper. "You promised you'd be careful. You promised you'd never leave me."

Moisture stings the backs of my eyes, but I won't let the tears fall. "You were supposed to protect him," I admonish a crumbling statue of the Virgin Mary. Dropping to my knees, I run my fingers along the wilted daisies at her feet. "Damn it, you were supposed to take care of him."

"What about you?" came a quiet voice from behind me, and the rhythm of my heart changed. Deepened. "Who's supposed to take care of you?"

Vulnerable isn't a word I like, but there's no other word to describe the way I feel kneeling beside my brother's grave, with devastation in my voice and tears in my eyes. Once, I would have hidden this from Cain. The hard-nosed reporter who came to New Orleans to find the link between the controversial police detective and the Russian Mafia would never, ever have let him, let anyone, see a weakness.

But there's only the woman now, the one who saw the terror in his eyes when he found me in the alley, who felt his arms cradle me when he told me about Adrian. Who'd fallen asleep to the low thrum of his heart. Who'd absorbed his warmth.

Who wants to absorb it now.

There's only me, and I'm so tired of the games.

And so I twist toward him and feel the rush move through me, even here among the dead. My body hums with life as I take in the sight of him, so tall and dark and battered against the blue, blue sky. As usual he's wearing all black. In his hand is a paper bag.

My eyes meet his—it would be so easy to drown. "What are you doing?"

"I was worried when you didn't answer the phone."

The words pour through me in a way the sunshine wasn't able to. "How did you find me?"

He goes down on one knee and hands me the bag. "I'm a detective," he dismisses. "It wasn't hard."

I take the wrinkled brown paper and look inside, see the wilted tulips. White. The color of salvation.

The tears burn hotter, but still, I don't let them fall. "Thank you."

"You're welcome."

It seems so simple.

He settles behind me and pulls me between his legs, holds me while the sun grows hotter. I tell myself not to do it, but I lean against his chest anyway and close my eyes.

The sense of rightness is terrifying.

"Promise me," he whispers. "Promise me you won't do anything stupid."

I want to. God, I want to. "He knew." I can't keep that truth inside anymore. "Adrian knew this was going to happen."

Cain eases the hair from my face. "Did he tell you that?"

"He called." My brother's uncharacteristically urgent voice still haunts me from my answering machine. "Late that afternoon. He called me, told me he loved me. Asked me to feed his cat."

Playing in my hair, Cain's hands still, but he says nothing.

I twist in his arms, look into his eyes. "He doesn't have a cat."

Now Cain's expression darkens.

"He was trying to tell me goodbye," I say. "I see it so clearly now, but didn't see it then."

"There's no way you could have."

"But you would have," I point out. "If my brother had called you and asked you to feed his cat, you would have known he was communicating in code, that something weird was happening."

"Maybe…assuming I knew he didn't have a cat."

"If *I* called then." The need to prove my point is strong. "If I called out of the blue and asked you to feed my dog, you would know, right? You would know I was in trouble, that I was trying to tell you something."

The scorched look in his eyes, somehow it reaches inside of me and wraps around my heart. "Don't do this to yourself, *cher.*"

"Please," I say. "Answer my question."

He lets out a rough breath. "I would know." Then his hands find my face and his thumbs skim my lower lip. "But that's one phone call I don't ever want to receive, you understand me?"

I do.

But it's a promise I cannot make. Because there is a vow I have made. To find my brother's killer, make him pay.

CHAPTER NINETEEN

New Orleans
Present day

PHONE CRADLED between his face and shoulder, Gabe picked up the microcassette recorder and clicked the rewind button, listened to the whir of the tape as it raced backward. Eleven seconds later, he hit Play for the fourth time.

And for the fourth time, Alec Prejean's distinctive voice filled the office.

"...not gonna stop me. No one will."

"How can you be so sure?" a second man asked.

"Because Robichaud thinks he knows me. I could put this gun to his temple, and he wouldn't believe his days are up until I pull the trigger."

"*Oncle* doesn't believe it either."

"People thought what I wanted them to," Prejean corrected. "What I needed them to."

Somewhere nearby, a freighter wailed. "And now?"

Gabe tightened his jaw at the sound of familiar laughter. "And now I can do anything," the man he'd called friend said. "*Anything at all,* and the good ol' boys in blue will insist I'm still on their side—just like before."

Gabe jabbed the Off button and stared at the series of photographs on his desk, all taken less than two hours before. "Son of a bitch."

D'Ambrosia's dangerously quiet voice sounded through the handset. "Still think he's innocent?"

"Where the hell did you get these?"

"Where doesn't matter." D'Ambrosia had couriered the cassettes over just after lunch. "All that's important is what's on this tape, in these pictures."

Gabe pressed his fingers to his temples. He'd known Alec for over ten years. He'd called the man friend. He'd stood up at his wedding. He'd helped renovate the St. Charles Avenue mansion into an in-demand bed-and-breakfast. He'd even fed the man's dog when Alec and Tara took their dream vacation to Kauai.

The possibility that Alec had been playing both sides all along burned. They'd been counting on the man to have a lingering trace of loyalty, if not to Cain or the force, then to his wife. If the only loyalty he had, had ever had, was to himself, then he was exponentially more dangerous.

Chewing on the implications, he picked up one of the glossy eight-by-tens. "You think he set Cain up?"

"He had the means and the access."

All along, even before Savannah was murdered, they'd been looking for a leak in the force. A dirty cop. Someone responsible for ciphering information about informants and evidence to *Oncle*. Gabe had pulled strings to land himself on the task force, kept up with the investigation as a representative for the district attorney's office. He knew Alec had never once been suspected.

Five weeks into the formation of the task force, suspicion had fallen on Cain; and Gabe, his cousin, had been asked to step down. Suddenly on the outside looking in, Gabe had been forced to resort to alternate methods to stay abreast of developments.

Setting down the picture, Gabe glanced across the hall to the door Evangeline Rousseau usually kept open but today had closed. Shortly before seven he'd run into her at the coffeepot. She'd had bags under her eyes, said she'd been working late. The D.A. had assigned the newcomer to the task force which he'd thrown together when feelers indicated *Oncle* was again planning something. Gabe had wanted on that task force himself. He'd *needed* on that task force. But the D.A. had insisted fresh eyes could see what tired eyes could not.

Gabe thought he was full of *merde.*

But Evangeline didn't know that, didn't know the history. So while they'd waited for the coffee to brew, Gabe had stoked up the charm and lulled her into a conversation. If he'd felt a pang of guilt, he'd ignored that. And if he'd found his hands itching to settle against her rigid shoulders and rub away the tension, well, he'd ignored that, too.

And if he'd found himself wondering if the tension he felt radiating from her really had to do with the task force—or with something else, something related to the phone call he'd overheard the other night—he'd most definitely ignored that.

"What's this I'm hearing about a shipment?" he asked. Evie had been vague, her tone distracted as she mentioned a boat they were waiting to arrive. From Bulgaria.

Christ. When the hell had he started thinking of her as *Evie?*

"A freighter due in tomorrow?"

"A shipment?" D'Ambrosia asked.

Either he didn't know anything, or wasn't about to give up what he did.

"Probably just a rumor," Gabe dismissed. He picked up the recorder and hit Rewind, then once again hit Play to the voice of the man he'd called friend.

Alec Prejean had to be stopped.

Movement from the hall beyond his office caught his eye, and he looked up to see Evie's door opening. She ran her hands over her pantsuit that reminded him of the plums he and Cain had once found growing wild at the back of the Robichaud property, then glanced up at him with a strained smile.

"Gotta go," he told D'Ambrosia, then dropped the phone back to the receiver.

Evangeline put a hand to his doorjamb and leaned into his office. "Everything okay?"

The smile was automatic. "That's what I was about to ask you," he drawled, and a little of the light returned to her eyes.

Curtain of dark hair swinging against her face, she strolled into the office. "I just—I had a weird feeling after this morning."

So she'd felt it, too. Watching her—unable to look away, actually—he lifted a hand to the back of his neck and squeezed. "Just a lot going on."

Normally she stopped at his desk. This time she kept right on coming, not stopping until she stood behind his chair. And put her hands on his shoulders. "Here," she said. "Let me."

He tensed. It was a damn stupid reaction and he knew

it. He'd had colleagues rub his back before. Marjorie could give a killer neck rub. He could close his eyes and enjoy feeling the muscles relax, not feel himself drowning in a scent that reminded him of brownies and musk.

"You're tight," Evangeline murmured, her fingers moving sadistically against his shoulders.

Instead of getting looser, his whole body began to harden.

"That your family?" Exerting every ounce of control to ensure he didn't do something stupid, it took Gabe a moment to realize Evangeline was referring to the picture on his desk.

"Mom and sister," he said, appalled at the hoarseness to his voice.

"She's a good bit younger than you then, isn't she?" Gabe focused on the picture, used it to ignore the feel of Evangeline's hands kneading his upper back.

Camille. It was the last picture he had of her.

She wasn't dead. At least he didn't think so. But no one knew for sure. She could be. There was always that possibility. But Gabe preferred to think of her living somewhere far away, maybe in a small fishing village along the Pacific seaboard, with a new name, where no one knew about her past. No one knew that she'd once been called Crazy Cami.

No one knew that she'd seen her father die in cold blood.

Suicide, the coroner said.

Murder, Cami said.

"Gabe?" Evangeline's voice was warm. Concerned. And it drew him in a way he had no business being drawn. Blinking, he tore his gaze from the faded picture and focused on another one, this one of Val.

"I've got to go." He stood abruptly and pivoted toward Evangeline, saw her standing beside his big desk chair with her arms hanging by her side and confusion in her eyes. "I—I've got an appointment," he explained.

And he so categorically did not need her hands on his body.

She glanced from him to the picture of Val, then back at him. And flushed. "I—I didn't know."

Because he hadn't told her.

Gabe told himself it wasn't disappointment that wound through his chest as he watched her walk away. And it sure wasn't regret he felt when the door to her office closed.

With one last look at the pictures on his desk—the montage of a life that seemed more fantasy than reality—he grabbed his keys and walked away from it all.

THE FIRST ROBICHAUD estate burned to the ground. According to legend, the owner torched it himself after returning from the Civil War to find his wife gone, the house he'd built for her ransacked, stained by dirt and blood and betrayal.

To this day, the ruins remained.

Sometime later another house rose from the ashes, big and grand and breathtaking just as the original manor house had been. But shadowed somehow. Remote, forlorn, isolated. More Gothic than Greek Revival, with pillars and spires and dark, heavy stone.

Cypress trees remained like sentinels around the

property, sheltering and protecting, separating the family from the town that flourished twenty minutes down the narrow road. Over the years the big house had witnessed birth and death, laughter and tears, love and lies.

People came and went, but the house stood. And the house watched. On some level, Renee felt as if the house knew.

The sensation slid through her the second Cain led her into the spacious foyer, with wood at her feet and a heavy chandelier hanging from above. The only natural light filtered in through a massive stained-glass dome, casting an odd fall of shadows against the floor and the wall.

Standing there, Renee could feel them all, generation after generation of Robichaud, watching her. Knowing her secret. Ready to defend. She'd been to this house before, after all, stood in this very spot. Then, Cain had held her hand gently, and his family's legacy had intrigued.

Now he would barely look at her, and his family's legacy alienated.

"I've got some calls to make," he said, leading her through the gorgeously furnished sitting room to a set of double doors. He pushed through them, ushered her into a sprawling paneled room. The achingly familiar scent of leather and patchouli seduced her before she even stepped inside.

Cain's study. Little had changed in the starkly masculine room since the last time she'd been there, when they'd made love on top of his desk. A fireplace dominated one wall, floor-to-ceiling bookcases another, windows a third. The room was dim, cozy, meticulously well ordered. The furniture was large. The feel was intimate.

"Make yourself at home," he said from behind her, but the words carried no warmth. She turned to see him unlock a beautifully carved cabinet and withdraw a thick folder. "This will keep you busy until I'm back," he added, handing it to her.

She took the file and watched him leave, reminded herself of the opportunity she had to seize.

One week. That's what she'd given herself. One week to shatter the lies and expose the truth. No alibi lasted forever, after all, and despite the extensive legwork she'd done to reinforce her alias, Cain was a thorough man. Very. Thorough.

In every way that mattered.

She harbored no doubt that he had a team of investigators scurrying around, checking every entry on her carefully constructed Web site, every source. Every lie. Death made a great disguise, but already the edges were crumbling. She saw it in Cain's eyes, felt it in his touch.

He recognized her. Maybe not on the conscious level, maybe not in any way he allowed himself to admit, but on some deep, intrinsic level, he recognized her. Responded *to* her. It was only a matter of time before that place figured out what his logical, analytical mind could not accept.

She'd known better than to reenter his life. She'd warned herself to steer clear. But being near him and not reengaging with him would be like knocking the stars out of the night sky.

It just wasn't going to happen.

And now she was again in his house. Once the sprawling old house had excited her. Now it condemned. Conventional wisdom cautioned that stepping foot inside Cain's ancestral home was like slipping into bed with the enemy, but as time dwindled, so did options. She could spend what time she had left with people who wanted to believe Cain was guilty, or she could grab every second possible with the man she'd never stopped loving.

If her heart was wrong, she was in big trouble closing her eyes in his house. But if someone else made a move, nowhere or no one offered more sanctuary than the secluded mansion.

Throat tight, she moved through his space, touching and feeling and smelling. Remembering. Until she saw the tree.

The chill was stupid. She knew that. It was just a photograph, one she'd already seen displayed in Cain's gallery. But she crossed to the wooden frame anyway and lifted her hand, traced a finger along the trunk of the sprawling oak. Light slanted through the branches and made the moss glow. Toward the bottom, a thick branch that should have been truncated when the tree was young dipped low to create a bench, the kind of place where you could curl up and lose yourself.

Where she had once lost herself.

She knew that tree, standing so proudly in a remote area over forty miles from Bayou de Foi. Adrian had stumbled across it while hunting. Romantic that he was, he'd said it reminded him of the tragic Longfellow poem *Evangeline*.

Hot moisture surged against the backs of her eyes. Blinking it away, she looked at the file Cain had handed to her. And felt her breath catch all over again.

The more things fell apart, they more they fell together.

There was just one word written on the plain manila folder, in a bold, neat hand.

Savannah.

The paneled room closed in on her, and through the silence she could almost hear the chant of his ancestors. Liar. Fraud. *Judas.*

And her hands wanted to shake.

Her life. The one she'd lost, the one she wanted back. It was in this folder. Through Cain's eyes. Pictures, maybe. Articles. Police reports. Maybe notes. She knew he'd kept them on all his cases. Personal thoughts and speculation, motivations. Strategy.

Why, then, had he just handed it all to a stranger?

THROUGH THE closed-circuit television, he watched her. She'd crossed to his desk and now knelt in his big chair, flipping open the contents of the folder and spreading them against the glass top of his desk.

He knew the exact moment she saw the second file.

Everything about her froze. He'd given her access to everything she claimed to want—but she couldn't take her eyes off the plain manila folder with one word written on the outside: *Fox.*

He wanted her to open it. That's why he'd left it in plain view. He wanted to see how she reacted to the fact that he was as interested in her secrets as she was his.

Slowly, he lifted a hand to the screen.

From the start he'd sensed something off about her. A coldness. Maybe even ruthlessness. But now he realized there was nothing cold about the woman who disturbed him on too many levels to count. Emotion consumed her. Drove her. Tortured her to the point where she'd tried to scrape it all away. But somewhere along the line she'd surrendered to it.

He wanted to know why.

Just as he'd known she would, she reached for the second file and opened it, skimmed through the three-page report inside. The relief that washed over her face was almost palpable. She closed her eyes for a long moment, then opened them and returned the file to its original position.

Then she returned her attention to Savannah.

It didn't escape Cain which file had concerned her more.

Frowning, he watched her reach for a scrap of newspaper and draw it closer, and though the monitor was black-and-white, he saw her expression cloud over. Curious, he glanced at the paper in her hand, saw the picture of him and Savannah.

Swearing softly, he picked up the phone and stabbed a series of numbers, waited impatiently. Not that long ago, he would have had answers by now. *Femme de la Nuit* had always come through.

When the harried female voice answered, he demanded to speak with T'Roy, who'd never quite measured up to his predecessor.

"Then find him," he instructed when the assistant insisted she didn't know where T'Roy was. "Tell him he's had enough time. I'll expect my report first thing in the morning."

He was tired of waiting. Tired of wanting. He needed the truth about Renee Fox, and he needed it before she slipped deeper into his blood. With one last glance at

the monitor, he walked out of the surveillance room and
headed downstairs.

He found her at the far side of the study again
fondling the photograph in the wood frame. Through
the monitor her movements had tantalized him. In
person, they fired his blood.

"It's an odd thing," he said in a deliberately low
voice, "when a man wonders what it would feel like to
be a sheet of glass."

She went completely still.

"Don't stop on my account," he said, moving to stand
beside her. He paused and breathed of her, the subtle
scent of vanilla mingling with that of leather. "It's not
every day a man finds a woman making love to a picture
of a tree."

He saw her throat work, watched her hand fall from
the frame. "I didn't take you for a man who liked to
watch," she said, and he could tell the words cost her.

He moved closer, let his body brush hers. "Why not?
I see something I like, where's the crime in enjoying?"

For a moment she just stood there, as though absorbing his words. Their meaning. Then she rallied. "No
crime," she said, and stepped away from his touch. "But
I pegged you as more of an active participant."

"I do that, too." God help him, he wanted to laugh.

She didn't seem to share the mood. "I'll bet."

He stuck out his hand. *"Mais oui."*

Narrowing her eyes, she swatted away his arm and
returned her attention to the photograph. "This
picture. It's—"

"All wrong," he finished for her. He'd staked out the
tree as though it were an elusive criminal, but had never

been satisfied with the result. He'd yet to capture the ethereal quality.

"I was going to say beautiful."

Her praise affected him more than it should have. "Adrian Trahan showed me that tree," he surprised himself by saying. The memory washed through him, the damp spring morning, the two-mile walk through a boggy swamp basin. "Said it deserved to be remembered."

Slowly, Renee turned toward him. "Adrian?" Her voice was low, thick. "Why would he do that? You two hated each other."

Her surprise confirmed his suspicions. Renee's digging had not yet unearthed the truth. "Things aren't always what they seem," he said, curious to see what she would do with the new information. "Just because the gossip mill says Trahan and I were enemies doesn't mean I didn't know he didn't have a cat."

Cain wasn't sure what he expected, but it wasn't for her eyes to go dark. "Wh-what?"

"Inside jo—" he started to say, but stopped abruptly. Not a joke, not for damn sure. "Suffice it to say Trahan and I were on better terms than anyone knew. We spoke the same language."

Her gaze met his. "Then why pretend otherwise?"

"Cleaner that way. Less chance of Savannah or Saura getting caught in the crossfire." His gut winced on the faulty logic. "Or so we thought."

Renee studied him a moment longer, as though the lines of his face would somehow tell her if he was lying. When he didn't so much as blink or flinch, she frowned and wandered back to his desk, ran her hand over the book *Louisiana Lore and Legends*. He wondered if she'd noticed the library stamp inside the cover.

Pushing it aside, she reached for a yellowed newspaper clipping. "So who do you think did it?"

Cain indulged the little blade of satisfaction. Crossing toward Renee, he wondered if she realized this was the first time she'd asked him personally about the night Savannah disappeared. "Can I assume by your question that you no longer think I did?"

Abruptly, she looked up. "I never said that I did."

"Not with words, no. But actions, *cher,* speak so much louder."

"Someone once told me the only way to stay one step ahead was to let myself go to the darkest place first. To envision the absolute worst. To let myself feel and smell and taste it. Let myself live it. Then, I'd be prepared for whatever happened."

Cain went very still. "This someone, he was a cop?" Even as he asked the question, he knew the answer. The motto she'd just described was the lifeblood of every good police officer.

She nodded. "Yes."

There was something pained about her voice, her expression. Something sad. "You were in love with him."

The newspaper article fell from her hand, and he had his answer. "Yes."

The study was a large room, warm and cozy. But the way Renee kept looking at him brought the walls closer and the temperature dropping low. "He broke your heart."

She looked away from him, toward his desk, where the picture of him and Savannah lay facedown. "I thought so."

Her voice was so soft and brittle Cain barely heard the words. "And now? You no longer think so?"

"I'm starting to think I might have broken his."

The urge to reach out to her was strong, to pull her to his chest and comfort her. But he wasn't a man for seconds. When he and Renee Fox came together, there would be no ghosts between them—not hers, not his.

"Then maybe you should go to him," he suggested, hating the damn stupid words even as he said them. "Explain things."

Her lips curved, but the gesture was too sad to be a smile. "Some things can't be undone," she said. "Can't be fixed. Sometimes there's too much damage."

Broken, he thought once again. But this time he no longer knew who he was describing—Renee, or himself. "And so you came here," he said. "To Bayou de Foi to sink your teeth into a meaty story and find a way to forget your demons." It was a strategy he knew well. "Is it working?"

"Not like I'd planned," she said, and her voice was quiet.

Fragile, he amended. For all her fire and strength, she suddenly looked as fragile as spun glass. If he so much as touched her, there was a damn fine chance she would simply shatter. "That's why you kissed me like that."

Her eyes met his. "Like how?"

"Like you knew me," he answered without hesitation, and her eyes clouded.

As a cop, he'd learned to state theories as facts rather than questions. The unexpected made liars stumble. Like standing naked in a spotlight, unrehearsed reactions left nowhere to hide.

"You think in my mind I was kissing someone else?" she asked.

He moved closer. "You tell me, *cher.*"

It was a challenge and they both knew it. He expected her to pull back or turn away, to shutter her eyes and attack his ego. Instead she tilted her chin, assaulting him with a smile so slow, so mesmerizing, his chest locked up.

"It would be easier that way, if none of this was real. If that kiss was for another man. If this," she said, lifting his hand to her chest, where her heart strummed hard and fast, "was for someone else."

And Cain could no more stop himself than he could stop the shadows starting to fall across the room. He dragged her to him and stabbed his hands into her hair, tilted her head and took her mouth with his own.

CHAPTER TWENTY

HE NEEDED TO GO. He needed to get to his feet and get in his car, drive back into town. His people needed him. They were uneasy. Scared. Two of their own had been killed.

On his watch.

Just like Jesse.

He'd promised to protect him. He'd promised to get him to the field hospital. He'd hacked his way through the hot, mosquito-infested jungle across sunset and sunrise, with his best friend slung over his shoulder in a firefighter's hold. He'd given him his water. He'd given him his rations.

Jesse had died anyway.

The memory slammed down on Edouard like a hunter's tarp, and squeezed. Dropping to his knees, he rested his head against the crypt and opened his mouth, tried to breathe.

I'm sorry. The words squeezed through him, but they wouldn't form. *So dog-damn sorry.*

He'd promised, damn it. He'd promised Jesse. His best friend. He'd promised him that he would take care of his brother, Travis. That he would look out for him. Keep him out of trouble.

Christ God have mercy, he'd made that same promise to so many other people over the years—his parents, Cain's father, Gabe's father, countless others who looked to the sheriff to be a demigod and make everything okay.

But Savannah had died anyway, damn near taking Cain with her. For a time he'd been sure the Lambert brothers had sicced her on his nephew, that while she warmed his bed at night, she plotted his downfall by day.

In the end, though, in one of those bitter, unforeseen ironies, it had been her death that had nearly destroyed his nephew.

Now Travis.

He'd had to tell Millie. The drive to the old Acadian house had been excruciating. The look on her face when she'd walked out onto the porch, with her silver-streaked hair falling against her cheeks and a dish-cloth in her hand—

She'd collapsed before Edouard could get to her.

Jerking back from the tomb, he shoved a hand into his pocket and pulled out a cigarette, tried hard not to let his hands shake as he fumbled for his lighter.

"Eddy."

The soft voice exploded through him like a hand grenade. Everything inside of him jerked. But on the outside, he went totally still.

"I thought I might find you here."

He could hear the leaves beneath her feet, but he didn't turn to look. Didn't want to see her walking through the old cemetery.

Didn't want her to see him.

Hands then. Soft. Strong. On his shoulder.

And then he smelled lavender and roses and vanilla, and the moisture he'd been holding back squeezed to the front of his eyes.

"It's not your fault." Quietly, as though she had every damn right to be there, she settled down behind him and slid her arms around his middle. Her face close to his, she held him. Ran a hand along his arm.

She was so soft, damn it. So sweet.

"Sometimes bad things happen to good people," she said in that soft melodic way of hers that he still dreamed of at night. After nearly twenty-five years. Sliding her hand to his, she plucked the cigarette from his fingers. "You can't stop them all."

The moisture leaked from his eyes.

"Eddy, listen to me—"

"Stop it." He couldn't do this. He couldn't sit on the damp ground of the cemetery and let Lena Mae comfort him. If he let go, even for one little minute…

He didn't know what would happen. That was the problem. But he knew it wouldn't be good.

On a low growl he stood and stepped away from her, turned toward the parking lot and walked away.

THE KISS WAS HARD and deep and demanding, and with all that Renee gave, Cain's only thought was that he wanted more. She tasted of need and desperation and, heaven help him, wintergreen.

That should have stopped him. But this time he embraced the punch of familiarity and lifted her against the desk. Need blotted out everything he didn't want to think of, all the secrets and the lies, leaving only the near-violent desire to possess. He didn't know how she did it, how she tied him into knots by simply walking into a room, but at that moment he flat didn't give a damn. He just wanted…her.

She opened for him, curling her legs around his thighs and pushing her hip against his erection, leaving little doubt that she wanted him every bit as much. He yanked her blouse from her pants and put his hand to her flesh, loved the feel of her skin, all hot and smooth. She moaned as he slid higher, toward her bra, where his fingers itched to slide beneath silk and to cup. Where his mouth wanted to taste. And suck.

"Good Lord, it's true."

The voice, low and overly dripping with disapproval, came from behind them. Cain felt Savannah go very still—

Then felt himself jerk back as if she'd taken a hot poker to his heart.

Renee. Sweet Lord have mercy on his pathetic soul. The sight of Renee standing there with her hair tangled and her mouth bruised, her clothes half-off, hit him like a bucket of ice water.

He stumbled away from her, just barely kept himself from making a sign of the cross.

"It's not like you to think with the wrong head, brother," Saura said from the doorway. "Can I assume by the look on your face that you forgot who you were about to maul on your desk?"

The question scored a direct hit. Swearing under his breath, Cain glared at his sister. "What the hell are you doing here?"

Her smile was overly sweet. "Last I checked it was my home, too," she drawled, then looked from him to his desk. "It's a darn good thing Uncle Eddy called me or I might not have stopped you in time. And to think I practically ran in here expecting blood…when it turns out you and I must have very different definitions of what it means to crucify someone."

He didn't need his last conversation with his sister thrown into his face. "I have my way, you have yours," he drawled, refusing to yield to that dark place inside, the one that knew he was being a son of a bitch. "It's a matter of technique."

Out of the corner of his eye he saw Renee shove her shirt into her waistband and step forward, and before she even spoke, he felt the hurt. "And I have mine," she said with a cutting smile, and once again Cain had to wonder just who was the hunter, and who was the hunted.

Saura's eyes flashed. "Apparently so." Strolling closer, she glanced at the police reports scattered across his desk. "What kind of game is this, brother? Show and fee—I mean tell?"

He heard the censure in her voice but refused to let himself react. The last thing Saura needed was anger, from him or anyone, even if that's exactly what she continuously went in search of.

"Always my favorite," he said to her, then looked at Renee and felt the punch deep in his gut. Saura was right. He'd almost taken Renee right there on the desk. "Next time, you might want to stick with words, *belle amie*. They're safer."

THE FIRST ROBICHAUDS arrived in Bayou de Foi in 1852. They brought with them great wealth, and even greater controversy.

There was something not quite right about Cora, the locals said. She had that look to her, the way she could see right through people. And she knew things she shouldn't know. Did things that shouldn't be possible.

After a visit to Cora, little Sarah Aucoin, blind since the day she was born, suddenly could see.

Old man Guidry, wasting away before his wife's eyes, was suddenly out working the fields again.

And exactly nine months after an afternoon visit for tea, the long-suffering and chronically barren Laura Leigh Melancon gave her husband twin sons.

The locals grew wary. The church investigated. A voodoo queen felt threatened. Rumors of a mysterious stained-glass window in Cora's possession, smuggled out of France, circulated. But no proof was ever found.

Sitting cross-legged on the guest bed, Renee blinked and reread the last paragraph for the tenth time, then blinked again, but the words kept blurring. No matter how fascinating she found the legend of lovers separated by war and condemned by a curse, the scene in the study kept playing in her mind. The odd revelation about Adrian. The risk she'd taken in parroting Cain's own words back to him. The way he'd torn himself away from her, then walked away.

It didn't fit. Like all the Robichauds before him, Cain was a man of confrontation. He met his opponents head-on. He didn't run or hide, didn't turn the other cheek. When riled, he attacked.

But today he'd done none of that. He'd just… walked away.

She hadn't seen him since. He'd been absent at dinner, absent during the evening, leaving her alone with his sister. Once, the two had been friends. Renee had been one-hundred-percent certain one day Saura would become her sister-in-law. The two had even joked about the dark-haired children Saura and Adrian were fated to have, with their father's penchant for adventure and their mother's flare for rebellion.

Though Saura tried to hide it, Renee and Adrian had both discovered what a tender heart she had. Tender, and bruised. It was so easy to understand why she did everything she could to be the anti-Robichaud. Hers was a patriarchal family. Male children were the prize, the concrete assurance that the family name would live on. Females were expendable. So while Saura was technically the oldest, Cain's birth eleven short months later rendered her practically invisible to her father.

Her mother's death from leukemia two years later stripped away any chance she had to feel valued.

Saura grew up a second-class citizen in her own family, despite the close relationship she shared with her brother. As a teenager, she began to act out. She drank too much. Lost her virginity too early. Went places she shouldn't go. Experimented with things she had no business even knowing about. Anything, and everything, to prove to her family she was not invisible.

Then she met Adrian. The spark had been immediate and intense, transforming Saura from a prickly hellion into a woman in the full bloom of love.

Then Adrian was killed.

And from the look of things, Saura right along with him. Renee had barely recognized the shell of a woman who'd charged into the study. No longer bright and

JENNA MILLS 223

vibrant and daring, but faded, like a camellia left out too long in the hot summer sun. Her curves were gone. Her skin was too pale, her eyes too dull.

Closing the book, Renee drew her knees to her chest and hugged them. If conventional wisdom was to be believed, Cain was responsible for destroying his own sister. He'd allegedly killed Adrian, after all.

But they were wrong. All of them. The cops. The newspapers. The gossipmongers who thrived on scandal.

Cain Robichaud was an innocent man.

Renee knew that in every corner of her soul. Deep inside, she'd known it all along. She'd tried to convince herself otherwise, tried to strip away all trace of emotion and entertain the possibility that maybe Cain had been the one.

He'd been the one, all right. But not the one who tried to kill her.

Whoever wanted her dead would have never found her in Nova Scotia. She could have stayed there, built a new life. But she didn't want a new life. She wanted her old life.

She wanted Cain.

Two more days, three tops. That's how long she had left. Then, God, she didn't know what then. Take Cain's hand and look him in the eye, tell him that the hell his life had become could have been prevented, if only she'd picked up the phone and told him the truth? He would never understand. Sometimes she wasn't sure she did. So many pieces still refused to fall together.

Renee closed her eyes to the soft light of the bedside lamp, but found no relief in the darkness of her own mind. Only Cain. She didn't understand what she'd seen in his eyes that afternoon after he'd damn near kissed her into oblivion. He'd looked at her as though he'd never seen her before. Or worse, as though he had.

On a deep inhale, she looked up and opened her eyes. Cain thought she was dead. If he saw, for so much as one second, any resemblance between her and the woman she'd once been, he'd fight the comparison with every ounce of strength he had. But no alibi lasted forever. One more memory, one more kiss, maybe just a sigh. The more time they spent together, the closer the noose became.

"*Non!*"

Renee released her knees and twisted toward the door.

"*Revenez a moi…*"

The low, tortured words knocked the breath from her lungs. She bolted off the bed and ran from the room, down the hall and toward the closed door. Heart pounding, she pushed it open and rushed inside, stopped the second she saw the big sleigh bed.

"*Je suis désolé,*" Cain rasped. He lay tangled in the sheets, clutching a pillow and shredding what remained of Renee's heart.

She didn't stop to think. She didn't stop to plan. She crossed the massive room and climbed onto the big bed, reached for him. "*C'est moi,*" she whispered, putting her hand to his cheek. The sandpapery feel of whiskers she expected. The dampness of tears she did not. "*Je suis ici.*"

"*Non!*" he rasped again, this time harsher. And then his arms shot out and closed around her, pulled her to his body. She went willingly, fit against him just as she always had. With his hands tangled in her hair and cradling her head to his chest, she could hear the rapid thrumming of his heart. Feel the moist heat of his skin. Her hands reached for him, clutched him.

"I'm here," she whispered, this time in English. "I'm here."

On a low sound he brought his hands to her face and dragged her toward him, took her mouth with his own. No time was wasted on preliminaries. He pushed his way inside and took immediate possession of all that she was. She kissed him with the same urgency, the same reckless abandon for all that stood between them. The pain, the denial, the betrayal. The inevitability.

He knew. On some level, in some place he tried to deny, he knew the truth.

Twisting beneath him, she scraped a hand down his back and cupped his buttocks, loved the feel of his erection straining against her. Only the silk of her pajamas separated them.

Sliding over her, Cain took one of her hands and dragged it over her head, laced their fingers together. To hold her in place, she thought in some hazy corner of her mind, so that she would never slip through his fingers. Like Savannah had.

"Yes," she whispered. "Yes." Her body hummed and burned and begged, responding on a primal level, tired of fighting the draw. The bond they'd begun to forge a lifetime ago flared stronger and tighter, and Renee realized she no longer gave a damn about consequences.

CHAPTER TWENTY-ONE

New Orleans
Nineteen months earlier

IT'S LATE. The night is dark, unusually still. My grand-daddy would have said a storm was prowling around offshore, sucking the oxygen from the city, waiting for the right moment to attack. He had an imagination like that. A way with words. A flair for melodrama.

There are those who say the trait runs in the family.

But Granddaddy's been gone for five years, since the morning he woke up before dawn to go fishing. We found him that night, slumped in his pirogue, both him and the fish trapped on his line as still as the night now enveloping me. He'd died a happy man.

Unlike my brother.

I've been walking for hours. I can't seem to stop. I just keep walking. No destination in mind. Just…away. Anywhere but the Palace Café, where Cain and I were to meet for dinner. I don't know whether he showed or not. I never did.

Everything inside me is jittery, unsettled, like the Gulf on a stormy morning. I can feel the whitecaps cresting, shattering.

It's been like this since Cain found me in the cemetery and held me, rocked me. He's a man of hard-driving passion. That I can handle. But the tenderness…

The tenderness can only lead one place.

All my life I've had a thirst for adventure. My *grand-mère* called me her *petite explorateur.* She worried that I had no fear. From the time I could walk, Adrian was dragging me through the swamps. The haunted ones were my favorites. We'd search for the lost stained glass and catch crawdads.

As I got older, my taste for the unknown intensified. The higher the risk, the higher the reward. There was no surer way to get me to do something than to dare me not to. Once, I spent the night in the abandoned morgue of the old Lady of the Lake Hospital. The teenage guys did it all the time. As far as anyone knew, I was the only girl who'd ever lasted more than twenty-two-and-a-half minutes.

I've always, always thrived on fear. It's never stymied me. Never stopped me. Until Cain.

He's just a man, I know that. He's got a reputation, that's true. But rumors have never frightened me. They make me want to know more, to find the truth. That's how it started with him. The more I heard about the un-touchable police detective, the more I wanted to touch. The more my brother said stay away, the closer I wanted to step. The more Cain himself tried to stop me, the more I wanted…

The more I want. That's the problem.

I've never wanted like this. It's not just hunger or a thirst, but more of a necessity. Like breathing. Except when I'm around him I can't do that. Everything inside of me riots. And for the first time in my life, I'm scared.

Because of the tenderness.

Because of the knowledge, the realization, that for the first time in my life, someone has the power to hurt me. *Destroy* me. If I let him touch me one more time, kiss me, take what I so desperately want to give, deep inside I know it will be like putting a brand to my flesh. There will be no turning back.

Even if it comes out everyone was right about him after all.

That's why I stood him up.

My instincts are razor sharp, always have been. But with Cain...I don't know anymore. The hum in my blood drowns out everything else, the caution, the instincts. When I look at him, I don't see the suspected dirty cop everyone else sees. When I touch him, I don't feel a ruthless monster. When I kiss him, I don't taste a man without conscience.

And that scares me.

After walking so many hours, I should be relaxed, but as I step onto my front porch, the pinball game inside me shifts into high gear. Inhaling the scent of jasmine twined around my porch rail, I lift my key to the lock.

The door is ajar.

Slowly, I reach for my mobile phone. Call 911. That's the smart thing to do.

On a rush, I kick open the door, feel my heart stall in my chest.

Moonlight slants through the shutters, revealing Cain sitting across the room in Granddaddy's old recliner. The shadows playing against his face do nothing to mute the hard glint to his eyes. Esmerelda is sprawled in his lap, arched into the curve of his hand. Even from across the room, I can hear the purring.

The survivor in me, the one who for the first time in my life fears the fire, demands that I turn and walk away.

Slowly, I step into my house and close the door.

Cain eases the cat from his lap, and stands.

I go to him.

He does not meet me halfway.

I don't care. The move is mine. I know that, see it in his eyes. He's furious with me. But it's not a fury born in anger or violence, but some place deeper. The place that has seen fear, knows its taste and feel and power.

The same fear that's shredding me from the inside out.

No words are spoken. No words are necessary. I step up against him and push up on my toes, press my mouth to his.

For a moment, there's nothing. No response. And I know it's taking every ounce of strength he has to restrain himself. But then the storm breaks and a sound tears from his throat, low and primal, and with the stealth of a lightning strike his arms close around me and he takes control of the kiss, his hands fisting in my hair, his mouth crushing mine in urgent demand.

His body is like a rock, hard and unyielding, and as I press myself to him, I feel his erection straining against my abdomen, and everything inside me turns wet and wanting.

And he knows. Without another word he lifts me from my feet and I wrap my legs around his waist. The world falls away, but I don't care. There's only Cain, the way he makes me feel, the way he makes me want.

Mouths locked in both battle and surrender, he carries me from the living room to my bedroom.

Life will never be the same.

CHAPTER TWENTY-TWO

Bayou de Foi
Present day

DURING THE LONG hours of the day, Renee had learned to push the memories aside. But at night, when she lay in exhaustion, that's when the memories attacked.

He'd come to her then, in the brutal quiet of her dreams, as demanding as he'd once come to her in her bed. Hours later she would awaken, nightgown damp and tangled, sometimes torn, body slick and heart racing, trembling from the aftermath. Imaginary, she'd always told herself.

But never quite believed.

Now she realized what had seemed devastatingly intense and real during the nighttime visits had been nothing more than tattered shadows, muted echoes of what she'd once shared with this man. She arched into him, loved the feel of his body pressing down against hers. He was hot and hard and slick, and everywhere he touched, she burned.

This, she realized. This is what she'd forced herself to forget. Because to remember would have destroyed.

"I'm here," she whispered again. Her legs fell open

and she could feel him between her thighs, heavy and straining. Her body hummed and begged, as though she'd been holding her breath for eighteen months, her body shutting down one cell at a time.

But now oxygen flooded her, and even as she wept, she rejoiced.

He ripped his mouth from hers so fast her heart never had a chance to prepare. Breathing hard, he pushed up on his arms and glared down at her, exposing her to eyes more decimated than should be humanly possible. Damp hair fell against his forehead, but did nothing to soften the lines of his face. His shoulders rose and fell with each choppy breath, as though he'd been sprinting for his life through the swamp, mile after mile after mile. And abruptly stopped.

"I can't." The words sounded dredged from a tortured place. "Not like this."

Her body screamed from the sudden loss, demanded that she bring him back. All of him. She could still feel him between her legs, his erection pushing against her, and despite the struggle vibrating through his taut muscles, she knew he wanted her, too.

"It's okay," she whispered, lifting a hand to his face. "I'm not some fragile—"

"Non!" He grabbed her wrist, pulled her hand away. "You deserve better."

She swallowed hard, tried to breathe. He was a man rumored to be amoral, without conscience. And yet here he was, denying himself what he so obviously wanted, because *she* deserved better.

The tarnished nobility, the cutting knowledge that she alone possessed the ability to put an end to his private hell, shredded her.

"This is what I want," she said with the ferocity screaming through her blood.

Propped over her, he held himself very still. "Don't cheapen yourself, Renee."

The words stung. "I'm not."

For a moment he said nothing, just stared down at her as if he didn't know whether to push her away or pull her in for more. Moonlight whispered in from a crack in the heavy curtains, revealing the sheen of perspiration against his nude body. She could feel the strength of him, longed to return her hand to his back and slide it along his flesh, feel the curve of his buttocks, pull him closer. But the way he looked at her held her motionless.

The silence worked between them, broken only by the hard thrum of her heart. His heart.

Then he swore softly and released her wrist, lowered his hand to her face and cupped her cheek. Again, it was the gentleness that stole her breath.

"Do you have any idea what you do to me?" he asked in that black-magic voice of his, and she would have sworn she felt the question whisper through her. "How you make me feel? Make me want?"

Everything inside of her went painfully still.

"I look at you lying here," he said on a rough breath, "all soft and warm and willing, some kind of twisted deliverance I don't come close to deserving, and I'm half out of my mind with the need to tear your pajamas off and be inside you…"

Her heart slammed hard against her ribs. "Cain—"

"But I can't," he said hoarsely. *"I can't."*

Shadows flitted across his face, but in a blinding

second of mercurial light, she saw the truth that punished, the moisture in his eyes. And she knew.

"It's her, isn't it?" she said, and her heart, her voice, broke on the question. "Savannah."

He winced as though she'd struck him, rolled from her and swung his feet to the floor, sat hunched over on the side of the bed. The urge to go to him was strong, to press against his back and drape herself around him, hold on tight.

Tell him the truth.

She put a single hand to his back, felt his muscles convulse.

"She's here," he ground out, "like a fucking cosmic joke. Hell, I don't know, maybe it's some perverted payback, retribution for how badly I screwed up, but, damn it, every time you so much as walk into the room, every time I kiss you, touch you…it's her. Her I taste. Her I feel."

Her, he wanted.

Her, Savannah.

Her, Renee.

The backs of her eyes burned and her mouth twisted. As some broken voice deep inside demanded that she walk away now, while she still could, she curved her arms around his waist and pressed her face to his back, absorbing the feel of him, the heat and the strength and the pain.

"It's been almost two years," she said into the deathly quiet. She hadn't thought it possible for words to form when her heart didn't even beat. "Surely there's been someone else since then."

His body tightened on the words, and with her palm

splayed against his stomach, she could tell that for a moment he didn't even breathe. Then, slowly, he turned toward her and took her hand, drew it to the slick warmth of his chest.

"Not here," he said holding her open palm against the wiry hairs above his left nipple. She could feel the thrumming beneath the flesh, hard and fierce and erratic. "Here there's been nothing." He'd been living on autopilot. He didn't say it, but she could see the darkness. "Until you walked into my life."

The admission crested through her, scalding like sweet poison.

"I don't know what's real anymore," he went on, and his voice was ravaged. "What's imagined. What's cursed."

Yes, he did. Trying not to shake, Renee lifted a hand and felt the telltale wetness beneath his eyes. "Because when you look at me—"

"My heart sees Savannah."

The words came at her through a vacuum of time and space, and for a moment everything fell away. She was kneeling on his bed. He was naked, his body twisted to hers. His hands were on her face. Hers were on his. And for that one fraction of a moment, time disintegrated and they were lovers again, drunk on each other and the insatiable need that kept bringing them back for more. Always more.

But then the moment shifted and reality poured in, and deep, deep inside, she started to bleed. "You resent me for that."

His eyes met hers. "Nowhere near as much as I resent myself."

"And you feel you're betraying her." The irony twisted deep.

Cain took her hands and pulled them from his face. *"Mais oui,"* he bit out, standing. Gruffly he reached for his sweatpants and jerked them up his legs. "And I just can't do it."

The room tilted. She wanted to reach for him, reached instead for his pillow and hugged it to her chest, watched him pace to the adjoining bathroom and splash water on his face.

"What about Angel?" she asked with near militant defiance, and even as the question left her mouth, she didn't know what she wanted more. Admission—or denial.

Admission meant Angel had told her the truth, that the agony she'd just heard in his voice and seen in his eyes was an act, an illusion designed to manipulate her.

But denial…denial meant Angel had lied, and that the agony was real.

He looked at her through the mirror. "Angel?"

"I met with her in the Quarter." She stood, grateful for familiar, solid territory. "A prostitute. She knew things about you, said you used to be one of her regulars."

"And you believed her?"

She lifted her chin, let the silence speak for her.

His eyes glittered. "The dark place, *cher,*" he said turning toward her, and almost sounded amused. "It can get you in trouble."

A tremor ran through her. She refused to call it hope. "You haven't been with Angel since—"

"Jamais." Never.

"What about while Savannah—"

Through the darkness, his eyes met hers. "There was never anyone else. Savannah knew that."

"You two hadn't been lovers for long."

"The intensity of a relationship cannot be measured by time," he said, then swung toward the closet and narrowed his eyes. She heard it then, the faint scratching coming from behind the door.

"Mon bebette," he muttered, striding from the bathroom toward the door. He opened it and went down on one knee. "How did you get in there, girl?" he asked.

She stood there staring, trying to breathe, as she felt the punch clear down to her soul.

Cain rose, bringing the big calico with the unmistakable green eyes up with him. "Does it really feel like," he asked, turning toward her, "you've known me less than a week?"

Esmerelda. Her heart swelled at the sight of the big cat cradled in Cain's arms. She'd wondered. She'd wondered what had become of the cat she'd found as a kitten abandoned along the side of I-10. She'd tortured herself with thoughts of Esmy left alone in her house, starving to death. Or worse, turned out on the street or surrendered to the fate of an animal shelter.

Never once had she imagined Cain—

The sight of them—Cain, tall and battle scarred, bare chested and barefoot; her cat, fat and happy and perfectly cared for—did cruel, cruel things to her heart. It thrummed low and deep, and in that one instant everything crystallized, the lies and the truth, the deceit and the hope.

"Her body was never found," she whispered, and even as she saw him stiffen, even as the voice of the survivor warned her to stop, now, while she still could, the risk taker she'd once been refused to cower. "What if she's still alive? Injured, maybe. *Broken.*" Just saying the words hurt. But she had to know. "Waiting to come back to you."

"That's not going to happen," he practically growled, and the cat began to squirm.

She stepped toward him. "How do you know that?" she asked, hating the desperation in her voice, and only when she saw the condemnation move back into his eyes, did she realize how the question must have sounded.

"Unless I killed her." The quiet words blasted like a shout. "Is that what this is about, *cher?* Another game, another trap, bait me with memories and see if I slip?"

"No!" The word shot out of her. She crossed the room and reached for him, froze when he stepped back.

"You said it yourself," he ground out. "It's been almost two years. Eighteen months, three weeks and two days to be exact. Without one word." He paused, pierced her with his gaze. "If Vannah was alive, she would have found some way to contact me. Even if she was hurt. She would never have stayed away, not as long as she had a single breath left in her body."

Silently, Renee brought a fist to her mouth, felt everything inside of her go cold.

"And if by some miracle she survived," he went on in that brutally quiet voice of his, "but never let me know, if she stayed away when one phone call would have cleared my name…then she is dead to me anyway."

Denial shouted through her, but words wouldn't form. Because deep inside, she knew he was right. She *was* dead to him, dead to herself, had been from the moment she'd come to in a small clinic in Mississippi, bandaged and broken, scared and confused, and chosen to call her grandmother, and not Cain.

"I was wrong to come here," she whispered through the tightness in her throat. Not trusting herself to look at him one second longer, she did the only thing she could.

She turned and walked away.

ACROSS THE HALL, a door closed. Saura Robichaud pushed aside her laptop and slipped from bed, went to investigate. She opened her door and looked both ways, saw nothing but the big calico cat slinking from her brother's room.

Relief washed hard and fast. She hurried downstairs to Cain's study and looked for any signs that the reporter had been poking around while she thought the house slept.

Satisfied all was secure, Saura made her way back upstairs, but paused outside the guest room. At first there was nothing, just silence, but then she heard the sound of running water from the adjacent bathroom. Only then did she return to her bedroom—and the Internet database awaiting on her laptop.

A long-forgotten hum buzzed through her. She climbed into her big canopy bed and crossed her legs, pulled the computer into her lap and let her fingers fly across the keys. It all came back to her, the routines that had once been so familiar. Once she'd thrived on the high, fed on the adrenaline. Adrian had always teased her, said she was like a woman possessed.

Adrian.

Her heart clenched on the memory, and deep inside,

she cried. Not on the outside, though. Those tears were gone. Dried up like a sunbaked riverbed.

Sometimes it all seemed like a dream. After a lifetime of being invisible, Adrian had seen her. And not just seen her, he'd *loved* her. Wholly and unabashedly. It had startled her at first, then frightened. No one had ever loved her like that. Other than Cain, she wasn't sure anyone else had ever loved her, period.

She'd tested Adrian, pushed him away as hard as she could, and when he refused to go away, she'd resorted to throwing dragons in his path. But like water working against rock, he'd worn her down, and gradually she'd begun to trust. Him. Her heart. The future. He'd known her as no one else ever had—her hopes, her dreams, her secrets, even the one she'd never confided in Cain.

It was that secret which drove her now. That secret which seduced her back to the world she'd abandoned…that of *Femme de la nuit*.

Her brother was a smart man. Cautious. Intuitive. But he was also fractured in ways only someone else who was broken could realize. And he'd been alone for so very long. That kind of solitude could warp a person, lead them to imagine things, see what they wanted— such as truth where there was none.

Renee Fox was a beautiful woman, but there was something about her, an air, an aura, that had assaulted Saura the moment she laid her eyes on her. Cain felt it, too. Saura knew that, could see it in his eyes when he looked at the woman. But she also knew he thought it was purely sexual, a base primal attraction.

But Saura was a woman, and she felt it, too. And while she'd tried many things in her life, she'd never been sexually attracted to another woman. So she knew whatever odd, disturbing energy swirled around Renee Fox came from somewhere else.

Saura wouldn't rest until she found out where.

CHAPTER TWENTY-THREE

THE COLUMNS ROSE up from the early-morning mist, solitary remnants of one man's great love for his wife. Where a plantation had once stood, weeds and gnarled shrubbery now fought back the encroaching swamp. *Grand-père* Robichaud had claimed the wind still carried Samuel's agonized pleas for his wife to come back to him.

Revenez à moi, ma petite. Notre amour ne va jamais mourir. Come back to me, little one. Our love will never die.

Going down on one knee, Cain lifted his 35 mm and zoomed in on the truncated staircase, shrouded in wild ivy. Clouds had rolled in after midnight, and now they fought with the struggling rays of the morning sun, granting him the haze he favored.

Cain snapped the picture, felt the immediate kiss of satisfaction. As a young boy he'd been intrigued with nature—doodle bugs and lizards and crawdads, love bugs, but most especially, butterflies. Their fragility had fascinated him, their beauty had seduced. When he was seven he'd coaxed a showy black-and-yellow monarch onto his hand, then secured it in a mason jar for safe-keeping.

The next morning he'd been devastated to find it dead.

That's why he switched to the camera. On film, he could capture and preserve, tucking away the images for his enjoyment without the risk of his trophies dying on him.

Or so he thought.

Frowning, he pulled out the picture of Renee he'd developed a couple of hours earlier, taken without her knowledge the day he'd found her by the cottage. Her tailored suit struck a stark contrast against the overgrown clearing, but it was her eyes that grabbed his attention, her eyes that haunted. They were as shrouded as his heart. Secrets, he remembered thinking. They festered in her soul.

It was the same way she'd looked last night, stoic, wounded, that had made it impossible for him to sleep. She'd stood there in those damn gold pajamas, the ones he'd burned to tear off her body, dark hair tangled and mouth swollen. Like a fallen goddess, he remembered thinking, drenched in moonlight and atonement and... pain. Someone had hurt her—Cain wanted to know who. And why.

And then, he wanted to punish.

The protective instincts staggered him. Fighting it, denying what the dangerous urges meant, he stomped across the clearing toward the ruins. But in his mind he saw her there, weaving with the mist among the columns.

Clenching his jaw, he blinked, and the image transformed, and it was no longer Renee taunting him, but Savannah. He could see her, just as she'd been the day a few weeks before she vanished, when he'd brought her here. He'd wanted to see her here, had known instinctively that somehow, she belonged.

He'd never been a man for self-torture, but he pulled out his wallet anyway, flipped it open and shoved his finger into a slot he'd not touched in eighteen months, and pulled out the picture.

His gut tightened. There she was, just as beautiful as he remembered, with her blond hair and daring blue eyes, dressed in a white poet's shirt, faded jeans and leather sandals, embracing one of the columns like a long-lost pagan lover. Her smile—

The sound of a twig snapping had him spinning, half expecting to see her emerging from the woods. At the sight of his sister, he didn't know whether to curse perdition, or laugh out loud.

With her hair pulled into a ponytail, she sauntered toward him as though out for a morning stroll, which Cain knew was ridiculous. Saura was neither a morning person, nor did she stroll. She walked with the catlike grace she'd perfected around the time she turned thirteen. The black top and tight-fitting jeans added to the image.

"What do you think they would say?" she asked as she approached.

Cain zeroed in on the envelope in her hand. "Who?"

"The columns. Just think of the stories they could tell."

A hard sound broke from his throat. He *had* thought of those stories. There'd been a time when he'd thought of little else. Had Savannah's abductors brought her here? Had they hurt her here? Had they kill—

He aborted the thought and turned to look at the row of columns standing like an eternal, forsaken doorway to all that Robichaud land had witnessed—love and loss, beauty and brutality, betrayal.

"They'd say it's going to rain." He glanced up, noticed the clouds winning the battle with the sun. "And that there's a very good chance you're going to get wet."

Saura shrugged. "I'm not worried about that."

He knew that was true. Saura hadn't concerned herself with much of anything since Adrian died, especially not her appearance or well-being. "What are you worried about?" he asked. He saw it in her eyes, the forgotten swirl of apprehension and excitement.

She lifted her chin, extended her hand. "This."

The envelope was blank, no markings, no stamp, no writing. "What is it?"

"Something you need to see."

RENEE HEARD the trilling as she stepped out of the shower. Wrapped in a towel, she hurried across the room and grabbed her mobile phone, listened to the apprehensive voice on the other end.

"I can't keep quiet anymore," the librarian—Lena Mae Lamont—was saying. "Not after what happened to Travis."

Renee swallowed. "What can't you keep quiet about?"

"Not on the phone. No telling who could be listening."

"Then I'll come into town." The library wouldn't open for another hour. "I can be there this morning." Just as soon as she found a way off Cain's property. "Ten o'clock, maybe?"

Lena Mae hesitated. "The church," she finally said. "Our Lady of Prompt Succor down on Cypress. Make like you're going to confession. I— I'll take care of the rest."

The shiver made no sense. Renee agreed anyway, and without another word, Lena Mae disconnected the call.

Fifteen minutes later, dressed and packed, acutely aware that she no longer had a choice, Renee opened the bedroom door and headed for the grand staircase. The luxury of time and objectivity had dissipated the second she'd let Cain touch her. The circumstantial evidence heaped against him was disturbing, the words that had haunted her for the past eighteen months chilling, but beyond a shadow of a doubt she knew Cain was not the one who'd wanted her dead.

In her heart, she'd known that all along.

Now she had to prove it. With only two days left, she'd come to realize the key lay with Adrian—and the missing Goose.

Downstairs she paused outside Cain's study, where the photograph of the old oak had illuminated a truth she'd never suspected. All this time she'd believed her brother and Cain had stood on opposite sides. That they'd distrusted each other. But now she knew she'd only seen what they'd wanted her to see. *To protect her.*

Playing with the pieces in her mind like a giant jigsaw puzzle, she followed the scent of coffee to the kitchen, took a deep breath and stepped into the magazine-worthy gourmet retreat. With Adrian's help, Cain's sister had commissioned a remodeling, discarding the old white Formica counters in favor of granite, replacing the chipped tile with marble, throwing out black-and-white appliances in favor of stainless steel. The bushy herbs that had once dominated the windowsill were gone. Only one African violet remained, and it was more dead than alive.

Biting down on her bottom lip, Renee glanced toward the intricately carved breakfast table Adrian had found in an old warehouse with a pedigree back to the 1850s, where Saura sat clicking away at her laptop.

"He's waiting for you," she said without looking up. "Down by the old plantation ruins."

Renee's heart surged at the words, but the smug undertone to Saura's voice gave her pause. "Why?"

Saura kept right on clicking. "That's between the two of you."

Renee opened the middle cabinet and reached for one of the Country Roses cups, felt a hot surge the second her fingers touched the china—china she should not automatically know where to find. She glanced at Saura, found her still glued to her computer.

Renee closed the cabinet and tried to forget how badly she wanted coffee. "Is there a way to reach him? I've got an appointment in town and really can't—"

Saura looked up. "Trust me, sweetie. Whatever's in town can wait. Cain can't."

SHE FOUND HIM exactly where Saura said he would be. For a moment she just stood at the edge of the clearing and watched him. Dressed in dark jeans and a soft gray pullover, he stood in the drizzle at the far end of the columns. The headwinds of the nearing storm swirled around him. Yellowed leaves fluttered and the tall grass rustled, but he didn't move. There was an absolute stillness to him, like the last mourner at a graveside service, unable to bring himself to leave.

Her heart caught on the sight, and she couldn't help but wonder what he saw. What he remembered.

She knew what she remembered. The only other time she'd been here. With Cain. Just weeks before the end. He'd told her the legend of the Robichauds and the mystical stained-glass window, then as the sun slipped beneath the treetops, they'd come together against the very column where he now stood, and made love.

He turned to her then, and across the clearing, his eyes sought out hers.

Run. That was her first thought. But as with so many other times since her return to Bayou de Foi, when logic told her to leave as fast as she could, she went straight for Cain.

Like the first night they made love, he didn't meet her halfway. He tracked her movements with a predatory air. The broken man from the night before was gone. The man waiting for her was completely whole, and fully in charge.

Adrenaline took over. She drew in a deep breath, let it out slowly, but the technique did nothing to calm the uncertainty ricocheting through her like a swarm of trapped bees.

And she couldn't stand it one second longer, not the stillness, not the silence. "Cain, Saura said—"

"Shh," he murmured in that dark and drugging way of his. Apprehension tangled with excitement. Without another sound he took her wrist and led her through the thigh-high grass to the steps that led to a nonexistent verandah, then, releasing her arm, gestured for her to mount them.

Almost hypnotically, she did.

The drizzle kept falling right along with the temperature. Elevated a few feet off the ground, Renee tried not to shiver, but the damp chill seeped through her flesh and into her blood, and the wind granted no reprieve. Swallowing hard, she glanced at Cain and found him studying her with the intensity of a searchlight, and though she was dressed from head to toe, she'd never felt more naked in her life.

The photographer, she realized. That's who was looking at her. Not the man, not the cop, but the talented artist, the one who erotically bridged the no-man's land between the living and the dead. He'd posed her on the truncated staircase against a world a thousand shades of gray, and with her long dark hair wet and plastered against her face, she knew once he snapped the shot, it would be impossible to tell if she was real, or imagined. Alive, or dead.

Stepping back from her, he crossed himself. *"Mon Dieu."*

Everything inside of her went ominously still. "Cain?"

He lifted the camera and adjusted the aperture setting.

Panic exploded through her. On blind instinct she turned from him and scrambled down the steps.

"You think that will change anything?" he asked, and her heart slammed hard against her ribs. He moved toward her, lifted a hand to her face and touched with excruciating gentleness.

'   She tried to turn from him, couldn't.

Tried to deny.

Couldn't.

"Sweet Mary have mercy on my soul," he murmured, but the words sounded more curse than prayerful. "I never knew a dead woman could look so beautiful."

CHAPTER TWENTY-FOUR

NOTHING HAD prepared her. Nothing could have. Not the lies or the truth, the betrayal or the fidelity. Not the clock that had been steadily winding down since the moment she'd stepped back into her old life. Not the dreams that had been surging to life.

In some barely functioning corner of her mind, Renee knew the drizzle still fell and the blackbirds still swarmed and cawed, knew the skeletal branches of the cypress trees still swayed against the cold gray sky, but shock dulled her senses. Nothing registered. Nothing touched her. Nothing seemed real. Except Cain, the hot sheen of condemnation in his eyes, and the horrible truth spilling between them like blood at a crime scene.

She tried to breathe. Couldn't.

Tried to move. Couldn't.

Inevitability wound deeper, tighter. No lie lasted forever, she knew that. No truth stay buried. She'd known this moment would arrive, had forced herself to imagine it, to walk through every possibility and live every nuance—the hatred in Cain's eyes and the acid in his voice, the sting of disgust.

Now she looked up at Cain standing against an ashen sky and felt the twist deep in her heart. This was where he belonged, here at the ruins of the home his ancestors had built over a century before. It was fitting that everything would crash down around her here. She drank in the sight of him, his dark hair plastered to his face, the whiskers crowding his jaw, the uncompromising line of his mouth and the glitter in his eyes, and knew that no matter how much he hated her, she could not regret the choices she'd made, not when they'd brought her back to this man and the life they'd once planned. Even if it was fleeting. She couldn't call it closure, but in coming home she'd learned to listen to her heart. And in listening to her heart, she had the ability to free Cain from hell.

"You know." Her throat closed on the words. Relief came anyway, sweet and burning and eighteen months too late.

"From the first moment I saw you." The cop's voice, cold and clinical and detached. "Before then even. I felt you before I stepped from the clearing, someone on my land, someone who didn't belong." He yanked his hand from her face, stabbed it into the pocket of his jeans and pulled something out. "I should have run you off then and there."

"But you didn't." And to her that said it all. He could have gotten rid of her if he'd wanted to. The Robichauds owned the parish. What they didn't own, they controlled. If a Robichaud wanted a person gone, that person would leave. Sometimes by their own will. Other times...other times help may be needed. But one way or another, what a Robichaud wanted, a Robichaud got.

Cain had not wanted her gone. *Because he'd known.*

Deep down inside he'd recognized the essence she'd been unable to scrub away, and he'd wanted. "You couldn't."

A hard sound broke from his throat, and before he even spoke, Renee knew the hot emotions of the man were fighting with the detachment of the cop. "For eighteen months I didn't give a bloody damn. I walked through a perpetual glass tunnel, able to see, but never to touch or feel or want. And then there you were," he said, glaring down at his hands. "So goddamn beautiful."

She didn't want to look. She didn't want to see what he held in his big hands, the ones as capable of violence as they were finesse. But she could no more have stopped herself from lowering her gaze than she could have prevented the collision of the past and the present.

It was a picture. Of her. Taken in black and white that very first day in the clearing. The sight jarred her, the long dark hair that once had been shoulder-length and blond, the stark suit where she'd once worn snug-fitting tops and jeans, the faraway look on her face as she stared at the cabin where they'd loved and laughed and dreamed.

Cain put his hand to the picture and dragged his index finger along the curve of her body, and she felt the shiver clear down to her bones.

"So lost," he said, and though there was a reflective tone to his voice, it was more disgusted than contemplative, as though he was trying to fit the pieces together. "I think that's what got me. I knew you were trouble and I knew you were lying, but I also knew there was something very wrong in your world." He dropped the picture, let it fall to the damp grass and stomped his boot over the image. Then he lifted his eyes to hers. "There was a desperation to you. A vulnerability you did a damn good job of hiding. But I saw it, and fool that I am, it sucked me in."

He'd wanted to save her. Like he hadn't saved Savannah.

She stepped back from him, from the truth, but everything inside kept right on shattering, and no matter how desperately she grabbed for the pieces, they slipped and slashed through her fingers like the porcelain swan her grandmother had given her for her tenth birthday, and smashed into something without form or substance. She'd stood for a long time staring at the shards of something that had once been beautiful, knowing that some things could never be glued back together.

"What's the matter?" he asked, closing the distance she'd just opened between them. "Did it finally occur to you that you're alone in the swamp with an alleged killer? That virtually no one knows you're here, and those who do know don't care?"

She took another step back. "You're not going to hurt me."

"I'm not?" he asked, tracking her movements. "Are you sure?"

Her heart pounded hard in her chest. "Yes," she said, angling her chin. But then he moved toward her again, and sheer blind instinct had her taking another step away—and straight into one of the columns.

She realized it then, what he'd been doing, that he'd maneuvered her exactly where he wanted her. He towered over her now, using his height as he had during his days with the force, as one of his most potent weapons for intimidation.

"Do you think she screamed?" he asked.

Her legs almost went out from under her. "Wh-what?"

"Savannah," he said, and his voice was cold and quiet and lethal. "Do you think she screamed?"

Everything stopped. Just…stopped. The question hovered there between them like a grenade, then exploded. Renee staggered from the impact, used the column to brace her, but after the debris cleared she saw and felt everything in sharp, crystalline focus, the birds and the rain and the wind, and most especially, the truth.

Whatever truth he'd found, he still didn't know who she was.

"I think she did," he went on, but from one heartbeat to the next his voice changed, went rough and broken. "I still hear her sometimes, when I'm alone in the swamp. I hear her cry my name, and I run, and I run, and I call out to her, promise her that I'm coming, but when I break through the underbrush she's never there."

Renee sagged against the column, tried to breathe.

"Is that what you wanted to hear?" He leaned closer, shrank the world to the two of them. "Is that why you dragged Savannah between us? You thought in resurrecting her you would soften me for the kill?"

The magnitude of her mistake stole her breath. She'd been seeing everything through her lens, that of the truth that only she and her grandmother knew. But now she viewed everything through Cain's filter and saw what she'd not allowed herself to see before. The look in his eyes, the anger and the contempt, but not the bone-deep betrayal of discovering the woman he thought was dead, the woman most people believed he'd killed, the woman he still dreamed about, was not only alive, but parading around town as someone else, earning his trust and seducing his heart, while all along he grieved. There was no recognition in his eyes, no white-hot fury like she knew he would feel the second he learned the truth.

She didn't know whether to laugh or cry. How in God's name had she actually thought Cain would clinically discuss her strategy and tactics if he knew the full truth? He was a man of hot driving passion. He'd be much more likely to—

She didn't want to think about what he'd be more likely to do. But she knew it wouldn't be pretty. Or soft. Or even clinical. It would be hard and brutal and... final.

"You're good," he murmured, lifting a hand to her face. But he did not touch. "You knew just how to play me, what to say and what to leave out, how to look at me and how to look away." His mouth twisted into a contorted smile. "But I hired a private investigator anyway, knew something wasn't right."

"I wasn't playing you."

"Your initial story held up," he said as though she'd never spoken. "Your Web site with your credentials. Your credit cards and bank account. Even the producer at *True Crime* backed you up."

She'd had to do some fast talking to secure that. "But you kept looking." Just like she'd known he would.

"Deeper," he said, and with the word brought his body closer. "Way back," he said. "And guess what? There you were. A classmate of Savannah's, just like you claimed." With his body pinning hers to the column, he reached behind him and pulled a packet of papers from his back pocket, opened them to reveal a faded class photo. "In the fifth grade."

The gap-toothed little girl who'd lived down the street beamed up at her from the page.

"But Renee Fox never made it to middle school," Cain said. "That little girl drowned during the summer in a friend's swimming pool."

Renee closed her eyes to the memory, but still saw her friend as she'd been that hot sticky afternoon, when she'd waited until everyone went inside for lemonade before venturing into the pool. They'd found her floating facedown ten minutes later. No one had known she couldn't swim.

"What's the matter?" Cain's voice came to her through the darkness, low and mocking. "You can't look at me? You're too scared of what you'll see?"

She opened her eyes, lifted her chin.

"Men are dead, damn it. Good men. Because of you."

"Don't say that!" she shouted against the wind that wouldn't stop blowing.

"Why not?" Cain bit out. "It's the truth. If you hadn't started poking around, Travis and Lem would never have opened their mouths." His eyes went even darker. "I knew, damn it. I knew there was something wrong about you, knew better than to let myself trust you. You've made me uncomfortable from the very first, and now I know why. You're a fraud. But even when my gut insisted something wasn't right, I wanted you anyway. Told myself the unease was because of Savannah, because in wanting you, I felt like I was betraying her."

"Cain—"

"Don't." He yanked away from her, severed the

contact between their bodies. "Don't say my name, not ever again."

She swallowed hard, pushed forward. "You didn't kill Savannah! I *know* that."

"Non?" he asked, and reached for the knife sheathed to his ankle, the one he always carried. He turned it over in his hand and ran the blunt side along his palm, straight through his lifeline. "You don't think I'm capable of murder?"

His pain blasted her. "I—I never meant to hurt you."

"Then what did you mean to do?" he snarled, and for the first time she heard his ironclad grip on control slipping. "What could you possibly want from me? It's been eighteen months, damn it. What in God's name possessed you to come here and start digging? What was your angle? Your end game? To distract me? Discredit me? Do you work for *Oncle,* is that it? Is that why you're so interested in Adrian Trahan? *Oncle* found out Adrian and I were friends, wants to use me to get to what Adrian stole from him. Is that it?"

"No!" The denial shot out of her. "You have to believe me—" Before she realized her intent, she was reaching for him, needing to touch him, feel him, to reestablish the connection he was trying so hard to destroy.

He stepped back from her, lifted a hand in warning. "You don't want to touch me right now." His voice was quiet, controlled. "It'd be a mistake."

She froze, everything inside of her going horribly still.

"And I don't have to believe a damn word you say," he went on. Droplets of mist gathered on his forehead. "Sweet Mary, I don't even know who you are."

She'd done this to him, she thought in some agonized corner of her mind. Her blind search for the truth had taken this strong, proud man and eviscerated him.

"Yes," she countered slowly, "you do."

"It's *over*," he ground out. "The games, the lies. You think it was bad when you first got here? Well, hang on for the ride, darlin', it's about to get a whole lot worse. I want you gone." He raked his gaze over her, then clenched his jaw and turned from her, took three steps before turning back. "You'll follow me to the house, where someone will arrive to take you to New Orleans. You'll be on the next plane out, and if you so much as think about coming back, trust me, you will be sorry… *Renee.*"

He turned from her and started walking again, and she knew he expected her to follow him. And she wanted to. That's why she'd come back to Louisiana. That's why she'd stepped back into his world. Because she'd never been able to expunge him from her system. Because she'd needed to see him, *needed him,* with an intensity that had strengthened with every day spent apart.

But she remained there with her back to the column and watched him walk away from her, knew the time had come. "You know who I am," she said again, this time louder, stronger. She let the Midwestern accent she'd forced into her cadence drop, let the rhythm of the South flow back in. "You've always known…" she said, then added the killing blow, *"Robi."*

Cain stopped dead in his tracks. His body, so big and tall and dampened by the mist, went rigid, his chest arching and his shoulders bowing back, as though an arrow had just pierced his back.

Because in a very real way, it had.

The black birds cawed and the wind whispered, but she would have sworn she heard the broken rasp of his breath, the violent slam of his heart. Then he turned to her. Very. Slowly.

His eyes, they were on fire. And in them, she saw what she hadn't seen when he'd first confronted her— the shock and the fury, the disbelief and the rage. "What—did—you—call—me?"

Robi. Short for Robichaud. A private nickname only Savannah had ever used, one shared between lovers in the heat of passion.

Numbly, Renee looked down at her hand for the non-existent gun that had just gone off, saw only the deep crescent gouges from her nails in her palms. The shaking started then, ripping through her in a violent tide. In the isolation of her mind, she'd rehearsed this moment countless times, how she would tell him, the look that would come into his eyes, what he would say in response. In her dreams joy flooded his eyes and he opened his arms to her, pulled her to him and held her tight. In her nightmares it was contempt and hatred burning from his gaze, and he turned and walked away.

Reality hovered much closer to nightmare than to dream.

Cain moved toward her with the precision of a predator. One. Slow. Deliberate. Step. At. A. Time. The survivor she'd become demanded that she turn and run, but she knew the time for that had come and gone. She'd made her choices. Now it was time for consequences. With her back to the column, she just stood there like a woman condemned and watched her executioner approach.

For so long she'd lived with the darkness, craving the light. Now it blazed before her, ready to consume her. And she welcomed it. Even as he moved, there was a stillness to him. And when he stopped, it was as if everything around him stopped, too. His eyes were dark and concentrated on hers, and for a moment he just stared at her. Then he lifted a hand to her blouse and released the buttons one at a time.

And she let him.

When her shirt hung open he unfastened her pants and pulled down the zipper, eased the fabric back to reveal her right hipbone, and the three freckles nestled just below, the ones he'd discovered while exploring her body with his mouth.

"Have mercy." The words were raw and rough and ripped from somewhere deep and agonized.

Renee's mouth went dry. Her skin exposed to the cold and the mist, she felt only his scrutiny and the hot rush of awareness. She swallowed against the quickening, channeling everything she was, everything she would ever be, into the one fragile moment that would define everything. "I can explain."

Betrayal flashed hotly in his eyes, the contempt she'd known she would see. The contempt she deserved.

"No, Savannah," he said in that dead quiet voice of his. "You can't." Then he turned and walked toward the emaciated trees, stepping into the wooded area and vanishing from her line of sight. Not once did he hesitate or falter or look back.

Renee stood there with the cool wind cutting against her abdomen and watched him go. Finally, at last, it was done.

CHAPTER TWENTY-FIVE

New Orleans
Eighteen months earlier

THE BREEZE BLOWING off the river is warm, carrying with it the somber strains of Leroy's sax. The young man stands outside Café du Monde as he does every night, sharing his music and hoping for a few coins in his cup.

It's late, close to midnight. Cain is on duty tonight. He won't tell me where or why. He's been different since we became lovers, quieter. More secretive. I can tell something is eating at him, but even when I straddle his back and rub his shoulders, I can't get him to open up to me. When I ask him about *Oncle,* he tenses. When I press him, he promises me everything will be over soon—and asks me to trust him.

I want to. Sometimes I think I do. But I know he wants me to drop my investigation into the crime syndicate and my brother's murder, and that I cannot do.

"Savannah Trahan?" The voice comes from my right. Glancing up, I see a skinny kid approaching the Jackson Square psychic's table where I'm sitting.

"Bender?" I ask.

The kid, in reality a rookie cop, nods. "I wasn't sure you'd come," he says, yanking his cap lower.

I gesture for him to sit. "Give me your palm," I say as I always do when using Magdalene's table to meet with informants. "You said you had information for me."

He extends his hand toward me, palm up. "I was the one who found your brother," he says. "I was with him when he died."

The jolt is immediate. I bank it, lift the flashlight to his palm and pretend to study his fate line. "The report says Adrian died alone."

"Because *he* wrote the report."

Another jolt, this one deeper. Sharper. "Who?"

"I know you're sleeping with him." Bender's voice is harder now. Almost desperate. "Everyone knows. But you shouldn't be. He's just using you."

The words slither through me, weaving their way around insecurities I'm not proud of. I've been in love before, but never with a man who blinds me to the world around me the way Cain does—and never with a man my brother, whom I trusted with all my heart, begged me to steer clear of.

"Somehow I don't think you suggested we meet to discuss my love life."

Bender winces as I drag my nail along his lifeline. "Don't you get it? Robichaud is playing us like puppets. He arranges the murders then writes the reports. Who in their right mind is going to come forward with evidence, when they know doing so is like signing their own death certificate?"

My heart slams hard against my chest. "Why are you coming to me then, if you know I'm his lover?"

"Because you were your brother's sister longer than you've been Robichaud's lover, and you need to know."

"Need to know *what?*"

In a lightning-quick move he yanks his hand from mine and pulls an envelope from his pocket, shoves it toward me. "Your brother named his killer before he died."

I feel the blood drain from my face.

Bender stands and leans toward me, braces his palms against the table. "'*Cain,*' he said. '*Evan. Lynn.*'"

Everything inside of me goes horrifyingly cold. "No…"

"I was there," Bender says again. "I found him dragging his finger in the dirt, saw the *C* and the *A* and the *I*."

"No," I say again.

Bender straightens. "My daddy was a cop and his daddy before him. They taught me right from wrong, that if a man doesn't have his honor, he doesn't have anything. But the force is dirtier now, filled with people like your lover who use their badge to further their own agenda. But I won't be part of that. I can't live with myself knowing your brother used his last breath to name his killer, only to have me sit on the information because I don't know who I can trust and who I can't. But you were his sister and you have a voice. You can do with the information whatever you want. My hands are clean."

I watch Bender walk away, but can't move. Can barely think. He's lying. That's my first thought. He has to be. But then I tear open the envelope and pull out a stack of black-and-white crime-scene photographs, and deep inside, my heart starts to bleed.

Ten hours later I'm sitting dry-eyed at my kitchen table with a cup of untouched coffee in front of me when Cain puts the key I gave him into the back door and lets himself in. He's been gone all night. He never called.

"Cain," I say. "We need to talk."

He looks at me through eyes completely devoid of emotion. "Not now," he says. "It's been a long night and I need a shower."

There's a weariness to his voice, and it reaches inside and touches me, despite everything. "Then after," I say, but then I see the blood on his shirt and feel my own run cold. "What's that?"

"Cop bit it last night," he says.

No, I pray. No, no, no! "Anyone I know?"

He pulls a glass from the cabinet and goes to the sink, turns on the water. "Don't think so. He was a rookie. Good kid. Smart, dedicated—Bender. He was the one who found your brother."

CHAPTER TWENTY-SIX

New Orleans
Present day

"*BARBADOS.*" Just saying the word brought a smile to Val's heart. Images formed immediately, of sun-drenched beaches and dazzling bays, warm breezes and frothy piña coladas. "Can you believe it? Maybe as soon as next week."

"Sounds lovely," Tara Prejean said from her bed-and-breakfast across town. "If you're not careful you might find me stashed in your suitcase."

Putting away a stack of burgundy towels, Val winced, chastising herself for being so insensitive. For a moment, she'd been so high on the prospect of getting away with Gabe she'd forgotten what Tara had just been through. "You know you're always welcome."

Tara laughed. "Thanks, but I think this is a case where three would definitely be a crowd."

Val turned to leave the bathroom, saw the pill bottle lying on the counter. Phone tucked between her shoulder and her ear, she picked it up and took off the lid, counted the painkillers inside, and frowned. "Don't rule it out," she said with a breeziness she no longer felt.

Yesterday there had been nine. Now there were only four. "You know we love being with you."

"I know, thanks," Tara said. "I'm guessing this trip means things are…better?"

"Gabe's under a lot of pressure." Was getting his headaches more frequently, staying up late and waking up early, closing the door when he spoke on the phone. "But I think the end's in sight."

Tara hesitated. "Any word on…Alec?"

Val slipped the prescription bottle back into the medicine cabinet and left the bathroom. Tara always wanted to know—but Val never knew how much to say, and how much to keep to herself. "Nothing definitive."

Just last night she'd slipped from the bedroom and stood barefoot outside the closed door to Gabe's office, and listened. He'd been on the phone, and agitated. Something about a shipment, about Prejean needing to be stopped. "He doesn't like to talk about work when he comes home."

"Alec never did, either," Tara said, and despite her resolution to be tough, she sounded sad. "He'd come home late and leave early, promise me everything would be okay but lie about where he was going, plan a romantic evening but come home too tired to do anything but fall straight into bed."

"But you loved him anyway." Val glanced at the black teddy abandoned on the damask rug by the bed. It had taken a couple of hours, but eventually Gabe had come to bed, and they'd made love.

Tentatively, she put a hand to her stomach, and wondered. In thirteen days, she'd know.

"I did," Tara said. "That's what makes this so hard.

The man I loved, the man I wanted to start a family with, is not a murderer. He cared about Savannah. There's no way he could have killed her."

Val sat down on the bed, saw no point in shattering Tara's illusion with what she'd overheard Gabe saying the night before. Everyone wore masks. Everyone kept secrets. It was impossible to fully know someone, no matter how many promises they made, how much you loved them. Sometimes, if you really wanted a future with someone, it was better to just not ask the questions. "I take it you haven't heard from him, either?"

"Not a word."

Fighting a wave of unease, Val pulled open the night-stand drawer and lifted the guidebook she'd picked up for Barbados. "How long has it—" she started, but then went very still.

"Val?"

She blinked, felt the room tilt. "Yeah, I'm here," she said.

But Gabe's .9 mm was not.

"DAMN IT, Cain, where the hell are you?" From his position on the second story of an old warehouse, Gabe glanced out the grimy window and scanned the deserted building across from him. He'd been trying to reach Cain since before sunrise. "The pieces are falling together, cuz. I think we've finally got our man."

Jabbing the call-end button, he narrowed his eyes and stared out at the dreary November day. For eighteen months he'd been looking for a way to lift the suspicion from his cousin's shoulders. Now the means had been practically gift wrapped and dropped into his lap. Back during the dark days when the grand jury had convened to determine Cain's fate, he'd never imagined it would be Alec Prejean who would ultimately take the fall.

Time dragged. He kept his gaze on the warehouse, looking for the slightest movement, kept his hand stabbed into the pocket of his trench coat, curled around the butt of his .9 mm.

When his phone vibrated sometime later, he checked the caller ID box and frowned when he saw Val's name.

She'd looked so peaceful when he'd left her that morning, lying on her side with her hair spilling against her face. For a long moment he'd stayed, watching her. Then he'd allowed himself a touch. He'd let his fingers drift against her cheek, and her lips had curved into a soft smile.

He hated keeping secrets from her, knew how much she valued honesty. So did he. Lies and deception were not commodities he enjoyed. But this was not something she would understand. Sometimes, the truth really was more dangerous than deception.

After thirty seconds, the phone went quiet, and guilt did a cruel last stand through his chest. Soon, he promised himself. Soon this mess would be over and it would be safe to leave town without fear of something blowing up in his absence.

Another vibration, and this time the caller ID box showed a different name. Evangeline. They'd hardly spoken since the awkward scene in his office, but that morning she'd suggested they do lunch. Scowling he checked his watch, realized more time had elapsed than he'd realized. But he did not answer the phone.

Movement then, only a few minutes later, the quick

blur of a shadow against the side of the warehouse. Gabe lifted a pair of binoculars and scanned the area, zeroed in on a man dressed in all black easing along the shadows.

Recognition came swiftly. "Son of a bitch."

D'Ambrosia wasn't supposed to be here. After waiting for a rendezvous the evening before that had never come, the two men agreed the information they'd received had likely been a setup. They'd parted with sundown, had not mentioned one word about returning with sunrise.

Not liking the direction of his thoughts, Gabe turned from the window and moved through the shadowy warehouse. He drew his gun and stepped into the drizzle, edged along the side of the wet bricks. Adrenaline boiled through him, but he kept his movement deliberate, cautious. The element of surprise was critical. He would find D'Ambrosia, and stop him.

The sound of a car engine changed everything. He stopped and turned, crowded himself against the side of the building and saw the bloodred Porsche. The door opened, and Alec Prejean emerged. The sight brought an acrid taste to the back of his throat. Justice or not, he could find no glory in what was about to go down.

With a furtive glance around the deserted parking area, Alec shut the car door and headed for the warehouse.

Only then did Gabe see the semiautomatic in the other man's hand. He took off after him anyway.

Cain had told him about raids before, how everything goes still and quiet, reducing the world to a vacuum devoid of activity and sound. That one moment could stretch forever, and no matter how hard his heart pumped or how fast his legs moved, it was like moving through molasses. But they'd always been mere stories for Gabe. He was a lawyer, not a cop. His world was an office and a courtroom, not a dilapidated warehouse district where snipers could exist behind darkened windows.

But now he knew, and now he felt. And it was too late for turning back. The dread was intense, tightening through him like some horrific tonic that turned his muscles to rock. He pushed through the haze anyway, even when he saw the second car idling at the end of the driveway, even when he heard a voice he recognized shout for him to stop.

Alec reached the entrance and slid something into a slot, then pushed open the door.

"Get down!" was the only warning Gabe got. The warehouse blew out toward him, metal and glass and fire raining down like blistering shrapnel. The force of another body hit him from behind and he went down.

Then…nothing.

"THAT TRAVIS, I know he came across a bit reckless, but me…he was my first crush. He lived across the street from me. Our mamas were friends. When we were little, they used to fancy we'd get married and give them beautiful grandbabies. For a while there, I thought so, too. He gave me my first kiss. It wasn't anything special, not at all like Ed—"

Lena Mae Lamont stopped and looked away, but not before pain flashed through her eyes. She stared toward the church's vestibule for a long heartbeat before lifting a hand to her face and resuming her story. "We were just kids then, but there's truth in childhood, *mais oui?*

Honesty. We're born who we are. We don't become someone different from that little babe who draws its first breath and lets out its first squawk. Oh, we can mask it for a time, but the seeds, they're always there."

Renee drew her leather jacket tighter and wrapped her arms around her middle, resisted the urge to rock. Like venom, the chill oozed deeper with every beat of her heart. Numbness wouldn't come. She felt everything. Vividly. The acidic sting of each breath moving through her body. The pressure in her chest. The strangling grip of reality curling around her throat.

It had been four hours since Cain had walked away from her.

"Well put," she said with a forced smile. "Is this why you think you know something about why Travis was killed?"

The librarian frowned. "Back when we were kids we didn't have all these TV shows and video games like they have today. We had books, and our imaginations. Travis and I used to play out in the swamp. One day he found a billfold stashed in some Spanish moss. There was no ID, no way of tracing it back to its owner. I told Travis he should just toss it, but he became obsessed with trying to find out who the wallet belonged to and how it came to be lying empty by the knee of an old tree."

Renee rubbed a hand along her arm. Blind obsession was something she knew well. "Did he figure it out?"

"Never did," Lena Mae said with a quick glance toward the altar draped in white. "But the stories he came up with were amazing."

"I'll bet."

"And he never stopped. Time went on but there was always a new mystery. For a while it was that blasted stained-glass window. He was determined to find it, thought he could use its healing powers to save his mama from cancer."

The church started to spin. Renee fought the dizziness, but the stained glass and pews whirred and blurred and merged. She tried to focus, knew she had to let go of what could not be changed and concentrate on what could. But letting go had always been a weakness of hers. She just didn't know how.

"So when that reporter disappeared—"

Renee blinked. "Savannah?"

"The Trahan woman," Lena Mae clarified. "When she went missing, Travis jumped on the case like he was Sherlock Holmes."

That first night came back to Renee, the warning in the other man's eyes. She'd taken it as ramblings. Now she had to wonder. "Did he find anything?"

Again, Lena Mae's gaze darted around the vestibule. "People didn't pay him any attention, you know? They thought he was a drunk and a clown... but that was the way Travis wanted it. He pretty much used it as a smoke screen. If anyone had taken him seriously, he wouldn't have been able to learn the secrets he did. And as long as the real bad guy thought Travis believed Cain was guilty, then Travis never had to worry about anyone finding out what he was up to."

It was all Renee could do to keep herself from lunging across the confessional. "Did he find anything?"

Lena Mae frowned. "He swore me to secrecy, but I—I…I'm scared he might have been right."

Renee reached for the librarian's hands, found them clammy. "About what?"

Lena Mae looked down at her hands tightly clasped in her lap, then let out a slow breath and met Renee's eyes. "He was sure Cain didn't do it, said he loved her too much. He thought…" She hesitated, lowered her voice. "He said the only way Cain could have taken the fall like that was if someone close to him set everything up."

Renee's heart gave a cruel lurch, and her mind started to race. Cain was a cautious man. He didn't trust easily. "That's not possible."

"But it's the only explanation that makes sense," Lena Mae said, and her voice was sad. "The only way Cain could have looked as guilty as he did is if someone close to him framed him, someone who knew his secrets and his weaknesses, his comings and his goings. Someone who could manipulate the seemingly innocuous into something dark and sinister and condemning. Someone he and Savannah both trusted. Someone who could have tricked them both, who had access to his files and his calendar and even his car—"

"Someone he called friend."

"Or partner," Lena Mae added nervously. "Or cousin, or—"

The librarian's stricken expression sent a jolt through Renee. Lena Mae's face went pale, her eyes dark. "Or who?" Renee urged, but the second she followed the other woman's gaze, she knew no more answers would be forthcoming.

Sheriff Edouard Robichaud stood at the back of the church with his hands on his hips and a cold glitter in his eyes.

"DAMN IT, Lena, what in tarnation did you tell her?"

Her chin came up at a sharp angle. "There's no law that says I can't talk to folks I run into while praying."

Edouard prided himself on control, despite the hot blood of his Cajun ancestors that ran through his veins. Like his brothers, he'd listened to his daddy's lectures about making your own fate, your own life. In 'Nam, those lessons had crystallized. The only way to stay alive was to keep your eye on the prize. Contrary to what sports pundits said, the best offense was, in fact, a strong offense.

Defense was for cowards.

He'd come home from war to a world he no longer recognized. Folks he'd once laughed with turned from him. Sweet Cassie Blankwell, the second girl he'd ever kissed, had turned from him on the street as if he was a baby killer. Only Millie and Lena Mae Lamont—the *first* girl he'd ever kissed—had treated him the same.

But he'd seen the pity in their eyes, and he'd felt like a goddamn charity case.

That was Lena Mae to the core. She wouldn't have turned down a starving, mange-ridden dog if it showed up on her doorstep, even if she knew that in taking the creature in, she was also taking her life into her own hands.

Edouard had refused to be that dog.

But he looked at her now, standing in the dappled light of the vestibule with her jaw at a fierce angle and defiance in her eyes, and realized he was dangerously close to barking.

He wanted to be angry with her, damn it. He wanted to blame her foolishness on that hot little number who'd blinded Cain to reality. But deep inside he knew the change had occurred before the woman who claimed to be Renee Fox ever stepped foot in Bayou de Foi.

And the only real emotion he could find was fear.

"It's not about laws." He tried to strip the emotion from his voice. Letting it shake would get them nowhere. "It's not about talking to whoever you please, either. It's about common sense. Safety. Travis is dead, Lena. *Murdered*. Because he talked to that reporter. Don't you get it? If you keep doing what I tell you not to, there's a damn fine chance you could end up just like him."

She didn't move, not physically, but something cold and hard moved into her eyes. "Are you *threatening* me?"

"Threatening you?" He strode toward her, stopped when he saw her step back. "I'm going to pretend you didn't say that."

She held his gaze, didn't back down. "You should go now, Edouard."

Edouard. She never called him Edouard.

But she was right. He should leave. Turn, walk away. Leave the church, go back to the station and read his most recent surveillance report on the Lambert brothers. But he looked at her standing next to the statue of the Virgin Mary, with strands of black and gray hair falling from the twist and whispering against her face, at the mutinous line of her mouth and the hot demand in her eyes, and something inside of him pinched. He wasn't sure he'd ever seen her look more provocative, not even when he was seventeen and she was sixteen and he'd picked her up for the school dance.

"I'll go," he growled. But instead of turning away, he charged across the wood floor and took her shoulders in his hands, her mouth with his own. The kiss was hot and greedy and surprisingly desperate, and even though she stood rigid in his arms, he pulled her closer, fisted his hands in her hair and damn near drowned in the scent of antique roses and sorrow.

He pulled back abruptly, brought his hands to her face, refused to let himself feel the sting of rejection— or the cold finality of goodbye.

"This wasn't how it was supposed to be," he ground out, and despite the hot emotion churning through him, his voice was soft, rough. Realizing he was damn close to making a fool of himself, he dropped his hands and turned, walked out of the church.

It was only when he reached for his ringing mobile phone a few minutes later that he noticed the moisture on his fingertips.

News of the explosion stopped him in his tracks. "Is he dead?"

"Yeah."

"Does Cain know yet?"

"Haven't been able to reach him."

Edouard swore softly. Saura had called with first light wanting advice about how to tell Cain what she'd learned. Then, she'd called a few hours later after Cain had grabbed a bottle of scotch and stormed out without saying one word. She'd been scared. Worried. Said she hadn't seen him like that in months, not since Savannah had gone missing. There'd been something in his eyes, she said. More than simple anger or betrayal, but something sharp and volatile and it had frightened her.

His niece didn't frighten easily.

"I'll find him," Edouard said on a hot rush. The need to locate his nephew before someone else did burned like a hot poker to the gut. The press would be all over this. They'd want a statement. They'd want to make connections, to make the easy, obvious link between yet another suspicious death and the man many still wanted behind bars.

Edouard wasn't about to let that happen, because finally, at last, he had the means necessary to clear Cain's name once and for all.

Dead men could neither talk nor deny.

SOMEONE CLOSE TO him framed him...

Renee clicked off the microcassette recorder and stared into the darkness beyond the window, knew in her heart that Lena Mae was right. Someone close to Cain, someone he trusted, had framed him. It was the only way he could have looked so guilty.

Closing her eyes, she saw the rookie cop as he'd been that night in Jackson Square, but no longer knew if he'd spoken the truth. Maybe his story was just another lie.

The pieces were falling together faster now, painting the picture she'd spent eighteen months dreaming of: Cain's innocence. No matter the price, coming back had been the right thing to do, the only way to find the answers that would clear his name. She was the only one who knew what had happened to her that night, what she'd seen and heard.

Restless, she stood and lifted her flashlight, let the beam run along the interior of the small room. Little had changed in the eighteen months since she'd last been in the remote cottage tucked away on Robichaud land, where she and Cain had come to escape the chaos of New Orleans, where they'd made love to the tune of crickets and cicadas and the occasional family of toads.

She had commanded herself from that first afternoon not to return here. But that was before. That was when she was trying to pretend she wasn't Savannah, when she was exerting every ounce of strength she had to not feel anything. Not remember.

But the truth was out now, and the need to feel again, to remember everything, yammered within her. Outside the rain of the day had passed, leaving a stillness in its wake. Out here in the middle of bayou country, without the glaring intrusion of city lights, the stars shone brighter, endless almost, beaming down from a brilliant black sky and flirting with the land. Their light filtered through the dust-coated window and blended with the flashlight, illuminating everything she'd tried to forget.

The intensity of it knotted in her throat. Memories lived in the cottage, lingering in that hazy place between life and death. They shimmered off the wooden walls and streamed through the open spaces, making it difficult for Renee to move without bumping into the ghosts she no longer wanted to avoid.

Crossing the small space, she ran her hand along a bottle of merlot on an old Formica counter. It was as though the room stood suspended in time, a door back to the life she'd lost. With a twist to her heart she closed her eyes and remembered the weekend when heavy spring rains had drenched the land and flooded the roads, trapping them. It had been the most bizarre, romantic encounter of her life, stranded without radio or television, with no idea of what was happening in the outside world, other than the rumble of thunder and slash of lightning, the rain and the wind. She'd been too consumed with Cain to care about anything else. It was as though the rest of the world had stood still, granting the two of them their own private time-out.

Then the storm had cleared and they'd returned to reality.

Two weeks later her world had crashed down around her.

Now she put a hand to her chest and took a deep breath, wondered how it was possible for her heart to beat on, when everything inside of her bled.

She felt the change immediately, the way the land goes quiet and still before a hurricane storms ashore. Tension wound through her chest and squeezed, and even before the door slammed open and the cool gust swept against her back, she knew.

The time for reckoning had come.

CHAPTER TWENTY-SEVEN

New Orleans
Eighteen months earlier

THE WATER IS COOL. It started out scalding hot, but that was twenty minutes ago, and my water heater can't handle more than a fifteen-minute shower without running cold. That's how I know the water is cool. But I don't feel the discomfort like I usually do. I don't feel anything. Except shock. And horror. Those I feel in abundance.

Three hundred and thirty-eight. That's how many little white tiles are on the far side of my shower, tiles that I splayed my hands against while Cain made love to me in this very place only the morning before. It had been the first time we'd come together without facing each other, and the intensity of the sensation had prompted me to cry out long before I came.

Now I want to slam my fists against those cruel white tiles, smear them with black and make them go away. Make the memories go away. They're obscuring everything, seducing me into thinking with my heart, rather than objectively facing the new pieces of the puzzle, necessary no matter how unwanted they are.

Stay away from Robichaud, my brother warned. *He can't be trusted.*

Be careful, my editor instructed. *Deception comes in all shapes and sizes.*

He scares me, my friend Val confided. *This thing between you two is happening too fast. Have you ever stopped to wonder why?*

The memories lash like a thin leather strip, and my body convulses. Wincing, I reach for the shampoo and squeeze a blob into my palm, then lift my hands to build a lather. Only then do I feel the silkiness of my hair and realize I've already applied shampoo and conditioner. Twice.

It's time to quit stalling.

Cain wants to meet at the cottage this evening. He says we need some quiet time, to get away. He says he has something special for me….

The chill is sudden and intense, starting in my chest and shooting out like venom to my arms and my legs. Trying not to shake, I step from the shower and reach for one of the oversize towels I bought to accommodate Cain's large frame, and wrap the soft material around me.

I shouldn't go, I realize as I step into a pair of pants and slip on a blouse. I know that. I'd be a fool to meet Cain alone in an isolated spot after learning that with his dying breath, my brother whispered my lover's name—and certainly not after the rookie cop who'd risked everything to give me that information had been found shot execution-style only hours later.

It doesn't mean anything I tell myself as I step into

the bedroom. None of it. It could all be a coincidence or some elaborate frame-up—

The scent stops me. I stand there and breathe deeply of leather and patchouli, feel my heart strum low and deep and longingly. I love that scent, would know it anywhere. My sheets even smelled of it—but I washed them this morning as soon as he left my house.

Swallowing hard, I slip from my bedroom and head down the hall, expect to find him in the kitchen making a po'boy or sprawled on the sofa watching SportsCenter—those are the only two things I can imagine him doing besides joining me in the shower.

But the kitchen is empty, and the TV is off.

I want to call out to him, but the incessant voices of my brother and my editor and my friend warn me not to. Hating the direction of my thoughts, I turn and move quietly to my office.

He's not there. The room is small and he is big, so his absence is easy to see. But I see something else. My microcassette recorder, the one I used to tape my conversation with Bender, is sitting on my desk.

I left it locked in a drawer.

Alarmed, I run across the room and grab it, find the tape gone. And my files, the ones I'd also locked away, are on the floor. Empty. My laptop is turned on—critical files deleted.

The sense of violation is swift and complete. Reeling, I reach under the rug and grab the key I keep stashed there, cram it into a lock and yank open another drawer—but my .22 is gone. My heart kicks hard and my mind starts to race, this time in concert with my imagination.

For the first time in my life, I'm scared in my own home.

Shakily, I reach for the phone, but before I can hit the nine key, I realize there's no dial tone.

The feel of something brushing against my legs brings a scream to my throat and I scramble around, only to find Esmy staring inquisitively at me. My heart slams hard. "It's okay," I whisper, and pray that it is.

My mobile phone is in my purse in the kitchen. If I can get to it, I can call—

Who? Who can I call? Who can I trust?

The realization that I can't answer that question freezes the breath in my lungs. I stand anyway and make my way across the office and back toward the kitchen.

Max. I can trust—

The keys stop me cold. Three of them. On a New Orleans Saints keychain. Sitting on the back of my grandpappy's recliner.

Cain's keys.

Swallowing hard, I know I have no choice. I can't let him see me like this, unraveling at the seams. I can't let him see the horror and doubt slicing through me like daggers. I have to pretend everything is fine and normal. I have to do whatever it takes. Whatever. It. Takes.

"Cain?" My voice is thin and strained, so I try again. "*Cher,* I was hoping you'd stop by…"

"*Vannah.*"

Just my name, that's all I hear, whispered in that black-magic way of his, and my heart starts to bleed. Forcing a smile like I usually give him, I turn toward him.

And see the candlestick.

There's no time to scream or twist away.

I raise my arms in pure reflex, but the big iron fleur-de-lis smashes down on me with stunning force.

Pain blasts me.

Vaguely I'm aware of falling.

Of everything spinning.

Swirling.

Fading.

No, I scream, but know it's only in my mind. No, no, no!

CHAPTER TWENTY-EIGHT

Bayou de Foi
Present day

THE WEEK AFTER Cain's mother died, his sister went missing. His uncles and the sheriff had mounted a search party, ordering a seven-year-old Cain to stay behind. But he'd been no more capable of sitting idle than he was of bringing his parents back to life.

He'd gone in search of her, wandering deep into the swampy territory at the back of the Robichaud estate. That's when the storm struck. The wind and rain had come on him so fast and violently there'd been no chance of finding the main path in time. With night the storm waned, but the darkness had been complete, trapping Cain where he stood beneath a massive red cypress.

He'd waited. Night sounds had rustled around him, and his imagination had wandered. He'd envisioned alligators sneaking up on him. Snakes slithering by. Maybe even a panther, even though his uncles swore the cats no longer inhabited the swamp.

He'd hated being alone in the dark, unable to see. He'd despised not being in control. But when he heard his sister's cry, he'd struck out anyway, and found her.

The two of them, wet and cold and frightened, had huddled together until sunrise, when he'd led her back to the main house.

And the two of them had gotten spanked within an inch of their lives.

In the ensuing years he'd pushed hard to develop the ability to see when others could not. He'd forced himself to spend countless nights in the swamp, to learn how to discern shadows from ghosts, reality from imagination. That's why he'd become both cop and photographer. The skills he'd developed had served him well, helped him see truth where others saw lies, danger where others saw only beauty.

Until Savannah Trahan walked into his life.

He'd known she was trouble the moment he set eyes on her, but for one of the few times in his life, he hadn't given a sweet damn. She'd been like a wild lily flourishing unabashedly and against all odds in the swamp, and his need for her, his desire, had blinded him to the instinct and caution that normally guided his every move. After they became lovers, he'd felt his focus slip even more. Suddenly the cop with the legendary concentration could hardly keep his mind on the biggest case of his career—because he'd been so flat damn terrified something would blow up in his face and he would lose Savannah.

And then he had.

Too late, his mistakes had glared, taunting him with the insidious fact that when it mattered most, he'd failed. He'd vowed to never again allow himself to be blinded, not by determination or deception or even by desire. He would see with his mind, like he'd always done.

He would never again see with his heart.

And he hadn't—until the afternoon he'd found a woman standing in the clearing by the cottage. It shouldn't have been possible, but just like the wild lily he'd once compared Savannah to, blooming irreverently at the base of a bald cypress, she'd looked completely out of place, and stunningly at home.

Mind versus heart, he knew now. His mind had decreed that this intruder didn't belong on his land, in his life, while his heart had immediately and automatically known that she had.

He looked at her now, standing so unnaturally and painfully still, like glass spun too thin. Not ten feet separated them. It would be easy to destroy the distance and go to her, do what he'd wanted from the moment he'd first seen her—in the distant past, and the recent past. To take.

But he didn't trust himself to move. Didn't trust himself to touch. Knew once he started, he'd never be able to stop.

He'd told himself to stay away. He'd spent the day with his camera and a bottle of scotch in the swamp, with his mobile phone turned off. He hadn't spoken to a soul since he'd walked away from her that morning. He didn't want to, either. That's why he'd told himself he was coming here, to the cottage. To spend the night by himself.

But as his eyes adjusted to the darkness, he knew that for the lie it was. Somewhere deep inside, on some primal, destructive level he'd known she would be here. And he'd wanted.

With the cool breeze whispering around him, he slammed the full liquor bottle onto a counter and drank in the sight of her—bathed in the mercurial light of the moon and drenched in uncertainty—and knew he'd never seen a more beautiful sight in his life.

With his foot he kicked the door shut, and the sound of it slamming against the frame rattled the cottage. But Renee—*Savannah*—didn't move. She just watched. And waited.

"I dreamed of you." The words were low and hoarse and torn from that dark place, and on them he saw her eyes flare.

"Cain—"

His sharply raised hand stopped her cold. He didn't want her to talk. He didn't want her to explain. He just wanted her to listen. And feel. And...want. "It didn't matter how long I'd gone without sleep or how much whiskey I drank, you were always there, waiting."

With the words, he crossed toward her.

"Sometimes you were smiling." His hand wanted to shake, but he lifted it anyway, let his fingers settle along her hair. Long now. Dark. Sleek. No longer wavy and blond as it used to be.

But it felt the same.

"You'd gaze at me like you were drunk on a secret no one else knew, but if I played my cards right, you would share it with me."

Through the hazy light, pain glimmered in her eyes. Dark now. Haunted. No longer vibrant and daring and blue.

"Other times you were frowning, thoughtful." His fingers threaded through her hair, closed into a fist. "Like you were that last morning, when I came home whipped and you looked at me like I'd just stepped on your grave."

She winced.

"Sometimes you were crying." The need to feel her closer, feel all of her pressed against him, lashed at him like the wind through the trees. There was something edgy and violent growing inside of him, something pulsing and relentless, that he understood too well.

"Screaming." That had been the worst, the cruelest of tortures, a broken sound that echoed insidiously through the night. "Calling for me." He swallowed the acrid taste at the back of his throat, the fog of memory and nightmare all roiled together. "Begging."

Her eyes were huge now, dark. "No," she whispered against his fingers.

"That's when I would run." The way he'd done that night a lifetime ago. "I would shout your name and promise you everything would be okay, that I was coming—"

"Don't do this." The words were barely more than a rasp.

"Then I would wake up." Hot and sweating and out of breath, crashing hard from too much adrenaline. "And I'd go outside, awake now, and run some more." Usually ending up at the plantation ruins. "But no matter how far I went, the questions were always there. Had you suffered? Had you hurt?"

Her eyes filled. Her hands lifted. She brought them to his face and cradled, let her fingertips sear into his flesh.

The sensation of her touch, familiar yet foreign, almost sent him to his knees. "I knew you'd bled," he forced himself to continue as his thumb eased along her lower lip. "I had your blood on my hands."

A broken sound slipped from her throat. Wincing, she slid her hand higher, skimmed a finger beneath his eyes.

For ten hours he'd been holding on tight, trying to make sense of the nonsensical. But his grip slipped now, and need shoved against restraint. "That's how they found me."

There was something in her eyes, something vulnerable, and it coiled through his chest, and squeezed.

"Savannah," he rasped, and God help him, the reality of it sang through his blood. She was here, and she was real, and he knew—*he knew*—that this time when he put his mouth to hers, she would not dissolve into the shadows.

But he didn't move, couldn't stop looking at her. Couldn't stop seeing what he'd not let himself see before. Feeling what he hadn't wanted to feel. "Savannah."

She'd always been a woman of passion and conviction. She'd never hesitated, rarely faltered. But there was a stabbing vulnerability to her now, a fragility that stirred something within him—and had from the moment he'd found her in the clearing. The way she was looking at him—sweet merciful God in heaven, no one had ever looked at him like that, as though she didn't know whether he was going to crush her in his arms or put a knife through her heart…and didn't care.

Questions pushed closer, harder. The need for answers coiled deep. But it was the need for something else—*the need for her*—that obliterated everything he'd ever taught himself, everything he'd ever believed about honor and survival and loyalty.

"Five seconds," he said. "That's how long I'm giving you to leave."

The flicker in her eyes was so brief he wasn't sure if it was real—or imagined. Her lips curved, though. That was real. And she pushed up on her toes. "I'm not going anywhere."

"I don't issue warnings twice."

"I know."

In his dreams, this was when he would wake up. When he would always, always wake up.

Swallowing against the burn, he slid his hand from her mouth to her throat, the sobering red streak left by the knife in the alley. He let his fingers slide around her neck, saw her eyes flare.

The unguarded reaction brutalized the detachment he wanted to feel.

"Do it," she challenged, and he felt her throat work against his palm. "I dare you."

Somewhere along the line the night had fallen silent. Not even the toads or the owl that nested nearby dared to make a sound. He felt his fingers tense, felt them hesitate, felt the truth pulse through him. There was no fear, he realized. No fear in her eyes. Only inevitability.

He refused to analyze why. "Be careful what you wish for."

"Why start now?" The words were low, quiet.

He let his hand slide lower, to the neckline of her blouse. Her skin was soft, abnormally warm, and beneath his fingertips he felt the steady thrum of her pulse. He wanted to hate her. He wanted to chase her away, tell her he never wanted to see her again. But even more he wanted to touch and taste and possess, to be inside her again, to feel the way she would welcome him as she had in his dreams.

"Cain," she whispered, and for the first time, her voice broke on his name. "There's so much I need to tell you."

"I didn't come here to talk."

Beneath his hand, the beat of her heart turned erratic. He watched her a long moment, just watched her, loving the play of shadows across a face so perfectly foreign to him, yet an expression of desire and defiance that had flourished in his memory long after he should have said goodbye.

His hand drifted lower, to the column of buttons, and slowly, expertly, his fingers began to work. She didn't move as he bared first her black lace bra, then her midriff, then, finally the curve of her waist.

The scars sent him to his knees. He hadn't seen them before, when he'd torn at her clothes to see the freckles he'd loved to kiss. He'd been too blinded by shock and the need to confirm what he'd been denying from the start.

But now—God. Now they glared at him, angry, contorted stretches of skin beneath the right side of her rib cage and just above the left side of her groin. She'd been stitched, but the flesh so obviously torn by a knife hadn't healed smoothly.

The need to punish ground through him, but he pushed it aside and brought his face to her abdomen, pressed his mouth to the first scar. Lifting his arms to curve around her waist, he held her like that, face to her stomach, mouth to the lingering evidence of a violent attack. Her hands fisted in his hair. And her breathing, the rise and fall of her abdomen against his cheek, quickened.

So did his own.

He fumbled with the snap of dark jeans riding low

on her hips. Then he released the zipper. More flesh came to him, fully exposing the second scar. With his tongue he traced the jagged length. With his mouth he wanted to absorb the pain that stood between them. With his body, already hard and straining, he wanted to reclaim what they'd lost.

Eighteen months was a long time to want. He'd caged the need away, tried to pretend it didn't exist, but it tore through him now, more volatile and punishing with each beat of his heart. The otherworldly light slipping through the windows dimmed. The cottage he'd come obscenely close to torching in the months following Savannah's disappearance pushed in around him. Everything else faded. There was only her. Always her.

"You'd come to me like this, too," he said, then demonstrated by easing the fabric over her hips and down her legs, letting it pool at her feet. He rocked back on his heels and looked at her, drank in the sight of her standing there in her unbuttoned shirt and panties. "I could love you then." In the deceptive safety of his own dreams. Where no one could take her from him. "And you could love me."

Her eyes went even darker, and for a moment she just stood there like that, staring down at him as if someone had just put a gun in her hand and ordered her to finish him off. Then, slowly, she extended an arm and held out her hand. "Please." Her voice was quiet, hesitant.

Because he didn't trust himself to do anything else, he put his palm to hers and stood. She had to tilt her head to meet his gaze, and in doing so she let her dark hair spill around her neck and shoulders. He reacted on sheer blind instinct, reaching for her, but she stiffened and stepped back.

"No," she said, then tortured him with a slow, easy smile. "It's my turn."

Before he realized her intent she was stepping into him, lifting her hands to his chest and working at the buttons of his shirt. She released them one at a time, her fingers teasing flesh as she did so. He wanted to yank open his shirt and be done with it, back her across the room to the bed and give them what they both wanted, feel her close around him. But even more he wanted to enjoy every agonizing touch and taste and sound. Every nuance.

"You came to me in my dreams, too," she whispered as she eased the wrinkled cotton over his shoulders and down his arms. She reversed the path with her hands, running up his biceps and over his shoulders, down to his chest, where she skimmed her thumbs over his nipples. He felt them pucker, felt them beg for the moist warmth of her mouth.

"Sometimes you would just take me," she said, teasing him with soft little kisses to his chest. When her tongue flicked across the flatness of his nipple, he wasn't sure where he found the strength to let her lead. He wasn't that kind of man. Taking charge ran like hot blood through his veins. When he knew what he wanted, he took. It was as simple as that.

Her hands moving to play with the fly of his jeans, she tilted her head and ambushed him with a glow in her eyes. "And sometimes I would take you."

There were tears in her eyes, he saw, pain that he felt. Her words were of seduction, but beneath them ran a current of uncertainty that squeezed like a vise around his chest. Savannah Trahan had always been a risk taker, never shied away from a challenge. She'd humbled herself to nothing or no one.

But now here she was, nearly naked and on her knees, handing him the very ammunition to destroy her. And in that instant he realized his mistake. It wasn't vulnerability he saw in her eyes and felt in her touch, heard in her voice, but a courage so raw he'd almost failed to recognize it.

She smiled as she glanced down at her hands. He both watched and felt her release the zipper, both watched and felt his heavy erection spring free. She cupped him, stroked him, molded her fingers to his length and his width—

And he couldn't take it one second longer, couldn't just observe, no matter how excruciating the pleasure. On a low moan he pulled her to her feet and took her mouth with his own. The kiss was rougher than he'd intended, but she didn't resist. She opened to him, twined her arms around him and pressed against his body, slanting her mouth restlessly against his own, tangling her tongue with his, taking and giving and demanding, until he couldn't distinguish one from the other.

The past eighteen months fell away, the horror and unanswered questions, the darkness, the cold emptiness that had him jerking awake with the embers of her name burning in his throat. There was only the sweet feel of her hand fisted in his hair and her breasts pressed to his chest, the warmth of her mouth clashing with his, and sweet cruel mercy, the taste of wintergreen.

"Vannah," he breathed into the kiss, then lifted her

against his body. Immediately she curled her legs around his, and he walked her toward the bed he'd once laid rose petals on—rose petals she'd never gotten a chance to see.

Need born of endurance and denial shoved everything else aside. Yanking back the blanket, he climbed onto the mattress and lowered her to the sheets, hovered over her like that, his body primed and ready and straddling hers. He wanted to go slow, be gentle. He told himself to. She deserved that.

But there was nothing slow or gentle inside him.

"I'm sorry," he rasped on his last breath of restraint, but wasn't sure whether he spoke in English or French. Wasn't sure what he was sorry for, either. The past, or what was yet to come.

Then his mouth found hers, and it was too late for apologies.

CHAPTER TWENTY-NINE

THIS, RENEE THOUGHT in some hazy corner of her mind, as the weight of Cain's body pressed down on her. This was what she'd dreamed of. What she'd imagined. What she'd wanted and craved and longed for. What she'd needed. To be back in his arms. To feel his mouth moving greedily against hers, the soft scratch of his whiskers against her jaw. To feel the heat of his flesh beneath her hands as she ran them along the hard planes of his body. To feel the ridge of his erection pressing into her abdomen.

But she always woke up to the harsh realization that even though her body still lived, dreams didn't come true. They glimmered and bolstered and promised, teased and seduced. But in the end, they also destroyed. She knew that. The life she'd led was over. She could never go back. Never pick up the pieces. Never hear Cain whisper her name or see him look at her as if he wanted to simply inhale her.

Except, he'd just done both.

Shock swam through her, but she refused to let it numb her to the feel of his mouth, taking and giving and demanding. He kissed her with a searing, almost violent hunger that scorched her soul and repaired that dark and shattered place deep inside, the one that had mourned him, missed him, loved him even as she read the devastating accusations against him; wanted him even as she forced herself to consider the heinous possibility that he'd been the one to betray her.

With her hands she mapped the hard lines of his back, loved the feel of his skin, so hot and vital. So real. Lower she found the waistband of his jeans, and tugged. She wanted to feel all of him. Taste all of him. She wanted him naked, to feel all of him hard and hot and rough against her. She wanted to give him all she'd dreamed of during the months they'd spent apart, to show him with her body what words would never express.

They'd made love before. Many times. Many ways. But this blind urgency was new, and it frightened. She'd never needed anything or anyone like this before, like that first greedy gulp of oxygen after being held underwater. She'd never let herself crave like that, had refused to let herself become that vulnerable. Ever.

Until she'd walked back into the life she'd left behind, and found Cain broken, and waiting.

I dreamed of you...

His hands, so big and scarred and yet capable of infinite gentleness, ran along the curve of her waist and up the swell of her breasts. She cried out when his thumb skimmed the lacy fabric covering her nipples, gloried when his mouth left hers and seared a hot path down her throat, lingering on the collarbone that, like so much else, had been shattered that brutal night. The feel of his whiskers against sensitive flesh stunned her, fed her. Thrilled her. The ache was immediate, intense. All-consuming. Her body begged. Her heart—craved.

He obliged her by releasing the front clasp of the bra she'd worn the first night they made love, then kissed his way down to her breast. But he didn't put his mouth to her like she wanted. He used his tongue first, long, moist flicks that sent longing pooling in her groin. She felt the rush of moisture between her legs and clenched against it, felt herself dig her fingers into the muscles of his back and arch into him.

What her mind had tried to block, her body remembered. Time and distance evaporated, and there in the shadows of the small cottage, she was Savannah again, and he was Cain, driving her to the brink with his hands and his mouth. He knew how to love a woman. How to love *her*. He knew how to tease and tempt, how to take and how to give.

The assault was the sweetest of agonies, the feel of his lips moving against her breast, his tongue swirling circles around her nipple, flicking against the automatic pucker. Everything inside of her flashed white, then dark with need.

"Yes," she rasped when he pulled her into his mouth and suckled. *"Yes."* Need streaked from her chest down between her legs, and pooled there, throbbed. She gave over to it, thrashed her head as he lavished equal attention on both breasts, kissing and licking, sucking. All the while she could feel his erection straining against her thigh.

His hand slipped down her stomach to her panties. There he made quick work of the lacy fabric, pushing her underwear down her hips. She wriggled them lower, kicked them from her legs. He wasted no time finding her, cupping her, working her first with his palm, then with his finger.

Pleasure assaulted her. She let out a broken breath and felt her head loll against the pillow, felt a thousand sighs float through her body as he explored the dampness, touching and stroking, tracing a remembered path, building a familiar rhythm. Instinctively she writhed into him and against him, demanded more even as she felt herself begin to come apart.

Lost in the silent wanting, it was a second before she realized he'd spoken. Another second before she realized the words had been in French. She opened her eyes and found him poised over her, his finger buried deep, his eyes glowing like black diamonds lit from the inside out. "You're wet."

The hoarse satisfaction in his voice sent pleasure rolling through her. But it was the awe, the wonder, that brought emotion into her throat. "For you."

Holding her gaze, he slipped a second finger inside and drove them up, thrust against her. The sensation almost blinded her. Her body convulsed around him, clutched him, welcomed him when he did it again. She rode the mindless wave of sensation, let it curl through every nerve ending.

"Don't," she forced herself to say, but barely recognized her own voice. She opened her eyes and met his. "Not with your fingers."

The low rumble was the only warning she got. Before she could catch her breath, before she could so much as breathe, he was on her again, flesh to flesh. His mouth was on hers, his lips moving against hers. She opened for him, mind, body, soul and heart, let him in. He kissed her with a carnal urgency that fired her blood, a rough sweetness that blanked her mind.

Pulling him to her, she wrapped her legs around him and ran her hand along his body, loving the feel of him, the strength and the need. She could feel him hot and hard against her abdomen, all of him, driven by the same urgency that consumed her. All that mattered was having him inside her, feeling him move against her, touching her in ways and places no other man ever had, the power of each deep, mind-numbing thrust.

And then he was there, guided by her hand and memory, nudging at the slick warmth of her opening, pushing inside and going deep. She arched into him and felt the breath gathered in her throat, felt her heart slam against her chest and her blood sing. All those dreams she'd tucked away and denied, convinced herself would never, could never come true, came pouring out of hiding, streaming through her, driving her.

"Look at me." The words were devastatingly quiet.

Floating toward ecstasy, she dragged herself back and opened her eyes, stared up into his and felt something deep inside her completely give way.

He didn't say anything else. He didn't need to. With his gaze holding hers, he slid an arm along her inner thigh and tucked it beneath her knee, drew her leg up beside her and thrust again, touched her even deeper, carried her beyond the point of return.

THE FEEL OF HER, all hot and slick and welcoming, almost sent Cain over the edge. She was real. She wasn't a figment of his imagination. She wasn't a ghost. She was a flesh-and-blood woman, and she was Savannah, and she was beneath him, around him. He wanted to go slow and savor, to draw each moment until the exquisite agony threatened to break him, but other needs pulverized him. The need to claim. To possess. To take. The need to bury himself as deeply as possible, to feel her clench and squeeze around him, feel her writhe beneath him, hear her cry out his name, make her fall apart.

"Yours," she whispered, and any trace of restraint he'd managed crumbled away. He moved within her, pulling out and pushing back in, drowning in the excruciating pleasure, his slow pace building with each thrust. She accepted him, took him deeper, kept her eyes glued on his.

And he couldn't take it. Couldn't take the raw trust he saw glowing there. The hope and the promise and the vulnerability. But he forced himself to look, to watch, even as he took her hand and dragged it over her head, linked his fingers with hers and held her like that as the past fell away. Bodies slick and entwined, hearts pounding, they moved as one, just as they always had, her hips arching to meet each of his thrusts. Deeper. Somewhere in the haze he was aware of her tensing, bracing in both surrender and invitation, and he found himself thrusting harder. Need blinded him to the lethal burn of lies and betrayal. There was only the need to bury himself as deeply as possible, to lose himself in her, forget everything but her and this moment.

And then she was crying out, her body tightening against his, the fingers of her free hand digging into his back, and no matter how much he tried to hold on, how much he tried to deny and delay, he went in deep and hard and heard himself shout out her name, felt the rush of pleasure pound through him and pour from him, spill into her.

He collapsed against her and fought to steady his breathing, absorbed the sweet scent of her, the combination of vanilla and musk that had tortured him long after she left his life.

He felt himself twist deep inside, heard the voice of the man who'd been betrayed, the voice that ordered him to roll from her and walk away. But the man who'd loved her couldn't do that, not when the feel of their bodies hot and slick and joined fed the place he'd written off as dead. He felt himself pulsing inside her, loved the way she embraced him, her limbs wrapped around him, holding him as closely as possible. Beneath his chest he could feel the thrumming of her heart, could hear it echo through his blood.

She shifted then, slid her hand up to his neck, threaded her fingers into his hair. *"Mon Dieu,"* she whispered, slipping into the cadence of the woman she'd once been for the first time since she'd revealed herself to him. "I missed you."

Her voice was ragged, and it damn near slayed him. "Shh." He didn't want words, damn it, no matter how sweetly they shimmied against his heart. He didn't want to talk or remember or analyze. There in the dead of night, in the bed where he'd once rehearsed the most important words of his life, he wanted only to savor the feel of her in his arms and the sound of her breathing. Because God have mercy on his soul, he'd missed her, too, as deeply and completely as though the oxygen had been extracted from his blood.

The burn at the back of his eyes surprised him. So did the tightness in his throat. He blinked against the moisture and squeezed his eyes shut, drew their joined hands to his mouth and brushed a kiss along her knuckles.

Losing her had shredded not just his heart, but his faith and his humanity.

He'd never imagined finding her could be worse.

SHE'D TAUGHT HERSELF not to imagine. She knew the danger. No matter how seductive the temptation to close her eyes and let herself be with Cain, to feel his arms close around her and hear the pounding of his heart, taste the saltiness of his skin, doing so was tantamount to taking a knife to her heart.

Because when she opened her eyes, he would be gone.

Against the far wall of the cabin, Renee watched the shadows dance. They moved slowly, erratically, sinuous and sensuous, brushing and merging, an erotic tango courtesy of the moon and the pecan trees beyond the window. All the while she held herself very still, not wanting to break the moment. She could feel him beneath her, his skin so slick and hot and vital, warming her despite the cool wind rushing against the outside wall. With her head resting against his chest she could hear the strum of his heart, knew that somewhere along the line the rhythm of her breathing had adjusted to keep cadence with his.

Silence wove between them, broken only by the fading song of the night. Neither of them had spoken since he'd shouted her name and she'd whispered his. Words had been unnecessary, unwanted intruders to the fusion found only in the absence of sound.

Closing her eyes, Renee concentrated on the feel of his hands, so talented. One rested against the small of her back, while the other played with her hair. It had always been like this in the aftermath, she remembered. He'd never had much use for words, but nor had he been a man to roll over and go to sleep, or worse, go shower. Unless the shower had been with her. He'd preferred to keep touching, subtle after-play that kept her body purring—and wanting more.

Safe, she realized as she opened her eyes. For the first time in almost two years, she felt safe, as though nothing could touch her, hurt her. There were still miles to climb, a killer to find, but the dark shadow was gone from her soul, and her heart hummed with a contentment she'd never imagined she would feel again.

"I think they were protecting me," she whispered, and felt him stiffen. "My dreams. If they'd been like this, there's no way I could have survived."

"Non." His hand slid to her mouth, where he ran his index finger along her lips. "No words."

She shifted to look at him, found him staring up at the ceiling. There was sorrow in his eyes, a pain that scraped at her heart. She'd done this to him, she knew. Her secrets. Her lies.

"We haven't talked about it yet," she whispered, and the contentment in her blood wobbled. "I know you have questions, that there are things you want to know—*need* to know."

The hand at the base of her back slid to frame her face. "I know what I need to, *cher.*" The words were low, hoarse, and they wrapped around her heart, and squeezed. He urged her closer and she went willingly, turning so that she straddled him. "You're here," he said as her mouth found his and the calm shattered. *"You're alive."*

And as they came together again, this time slower, more deliberately, that was all that mattered.

THE SONG OF THE warblers woke her. Renee lay still for a moment, listening to the lilting call of the migratory birds that flooded Louisiana in the fall. She'd missed the sound, she realized. She'd missed so much. The kiss of humidity. The grace of the oaks and the cypress. The birds and the flowers and—

Cain.

She knew he was gone before she opened her eyes. The bed was too cool. With a hard kick to her heart, she sat up and shoved at the sheets, swung toward the front of the cottage—and saw him.

He stood not fifteen feet away, at the window with his back to her. He'd pulled on the jeans she'd so fever-ishly shoved from his body, but his feet and his chest remained bare. His hands were shoved into his front pockets.

She watched him, the rigidity of his posture, the slow rise and fall of his shoulders, and felt something cold and uncomfortable slide through her. He was a man of action, of hot driving passion and relentless energy. He was capable of great patience, as well. She knew that. He could exert nearly inhuman control when staking out a suspect, whether it be a criminal who belonged behind bars or a shy heron he wanted to capture on film. And when he made love. Then the combination of action and patience could make a woman forget her own name.

But this stillness was wrong. He wasn't staking anything out. And he wasn't making love. He was just standing there, as motionless as the old cypress just beyond the window. She'd seen that kind of stillness from him only once before—on the day they'd buried her brother. He'd stood at the edge of the cemetery, present yet apart, just watching.

The need to go to him, to put a hand to his back and reestablish the connection they'd forged in bed, swelled through her like a warm tide. She stood and reached for his shirt, slid her arms through the big sleeves as she crossed to him.

Through the window she saw the sun beginning its slow boil up from the horizon, bathing the swampy land in a faded palette of crimson and saffron. She'd forgotten how red a Louisiana sunrise could be, how pure and still and haunting. The trees stretched like shadowy silhouettes against a sky on fire.

Fragile wasn't a word she liked, but as she neared him, this man she'd spent the better part of the night loving with her hands and her mouth and her body, she found herself fumbling with the buttons of his shirt. So much still stood between them. Secrets could hide in the darkness, but the light of dawn always brought exposure. She knew that, felt the fissure of truth deep inside.

For a moment she just stood there, absorbing the heat from his body and staring at the streaks and gouges in his back, marks she'd not been aware of making. Slowly she lifted her hand to trace a finger along the path—

"Don't."

The one word stopped her cold.

"Whatever it is you hoped to find," he added in that deceptively quiet voice of his, "doesn't exist anymore."

The slice of pain was quick and brutal, exactly what she'd been expecting the moment he'd walked through the door. Slowly, she let her hand fall.

"You know that's not true," she whispered. He wasn't a man to play lightly with forgiveness. She knew that. But then he'd touched her. Cradled her to his heart as if he never wanted to let her go. She'd felt the moisture beneath his eyes, tears neither of them had moved to swipe away. "Last night proved that."

"Life goes forward, Savannah, not backward."

"Maybe for you," she said, and didn't even try to stop her voice from tightening on the words. "But not for me. I can't just stroll on with my life as if nothing ever happened, as if I hadn't loved and lost and bled. As if I didn't know things, wants things. As if my heart didn't still cry every night."

He turned to her then, exposed her to the most scorched earth eyes she'd ever seen. "As if your killer wasn't a free man."

There it was, heaped right out between them. "Yes."

"Say it then," he added flatly. "*Me.* That's why you came back, isn't it? That's what you mean. You couldn't go on with your life while I got away with murder."

The words hit hard. Shame hit harder. She wanted to deny the ugly accusation, tell him he had it all wrong. But the words, the lie, wouldn't form. "That's—"

"I lost everything, damn you! *Everything.* My job, my integrity, my honor and self-respect. But none of that mattered." His eyes took on a dark glitter. "Because I lost you, too."

Renee wasn't sure how she stayed standing. She felt herself sway, felt her hand blindly reach for the back of an old chair. She curled her fingers around the wood smoothed by time and held on tight, refused to allow herself to remember another time she'd gripped the very same chair, not in agony, but in ecstasy.

"But I didn't, did I?" he bit out, and his voice betrayed the dark twist of emotion she knew he was trying to deny. "While I grieved you, you were God knows where, believing I'd tried to kill you and plotting your revenge." He picked up the folder she'd left open on the table, yanked out a page of her notes. "So now here you are," he said, and his eyes were on hers again, dark and damning, "with a new name and a new face, ready to crucify me for my sins."

The walls of the cabin started to close in on her. "That's not how it was."

His mouth went flat. "No?"

"No." She looked at him in the hazy morning light, at the hard lines of his face and the thickening shadow of whiskers along his jaw, the mouth as capable of pleasure as it was punishment, and felt something deep inside tear. She'd rehearsed this moment so many times, had forced herself to imagine the cold wash of hatred. But God, she'd never imagined she'd face him while her body still hummed from his touch, wearing only his big shirt, mere feet from the bed where they'd come together with a desperation that had stripped away the darkness and seduced her into believing the passion they felt for each other was strong enough to overcome the unforgivable.

That illusion crumbled now, leaving her naked in the only way that mattered.

"Everything was hazy," she said, and suddenly she

was in the small narrow bed again, squinting against the harsh glare of light and blinking at the gritty dryness to her eyes. "I didn't know what had happened to me at first, only that I hurt, and that I was scared." She wrapped her arms around her middle and squeezed, remembered the pitying glances of the nurses when she'd called out for Cain, the hushed whisper of the doctor when she'd demanded to know what had happened to her. The tears in her grandmother's eyes when she'd held her hands and told her the truth.

"I was broken," she whispered, and with each breath she drew, her ribs and her lungs screamed, just as they had eighteen months before. "Weak." From the loss of blood, they'd told her. "I couldn't walk, could barely talk." The memories had come to her in garish snippets, fragments of memory out of place and time. "They wouldn't tell me anything at first, told me all that mattered was getting my strength together for the surgeries. But then I started remembering things on my own, fractured images that made no sense." The smell of an achingly familiar cologne. The sight of keys on the back of her grandpappy's old recliner. The sound of her name on a dark and drugging voice. And words, horrible, chilling words that echoed mercilessly through the silence…

Your brother named his killer before he died.
Cain…Evan…Lynn.

The chill sliced in all over again, this time for entirely different reasons. She hesitated, waiting for Cain to say something. Anything.

He didn't. He just stared down at her, his eyes hard and detached, yielding no trace of the lover who'd

carried her through the darkness. There was only the
fallen cop, and the man betrayed.

"I was in Nova Scotia," she told him, shoving the hair
from her face. Beyond him, she watched the sun rise
higher in the sky, bright slashes of light cutting through
the thick cluster of oak and cypress and pine. "After my
car went into the swamp I managed to escape, walked
for hours before collapsing in an old shack. When I
woke up next, my grandmother was there. She'd
arranged to get me out of the country. The doctor said
I'd been unconscious for almost a week, feverish from
an infection and the loss of blood, that he hadn't known
if I was going to make it, but that in my delirium I'd
murmured one name over and over." Her heart pounded
hard at the memory. "Yours."

His mouth twisted, but he said nothing. In his hand
he still held a page of her notes, but somewhere along
the line his fingers had balled into a fist. "It was another
week before my grandmother told me why."

Now his face went even darker. And now he spoke.
"Because I was the one who'd attacked you."

"They showed me newspapers." Blindly she reached
for the file on the table and opened it, rummaged
through the pages until she saw the ugly headlines and
chilling pictures, the grainy image of Cain being led
away with his hands cuffed behind his back and murder
in his eyes.

The accompanying stories had been worse. He'd
been found with her blood on his hands. His prints on
the assumed murder weapon. He had no alibi. And he'd
refused to defend himself. "Gran told me you'd confessed, that a close friend had gone to the police

claiming she'd heard you crying, muttering over and over that you'd killed me."

A hard sound broke from his throat. "And like a good little girl you believed everything they told you."

She winced. "I had to consider the possibility."

He swore harshly and looked away, as though he didn't trust himself to look at her one second longer.

"It was the bad place!" she said, and God help her, she couldn't stand there one second longer, not without touching, without doing something to make him understand. She reached for him, grabbed his forearms and curled her fingers deep. "The one you taught me to visit. That's how you stay alive, you always said. By forcing yourself to the bad place, to see it and feel it and live it."

And she had. It had almost killed her, but to stay alive, she'd had no choice.

"Nothing made sense. In my heart I couldn't believe you'd ever try to hurt me, but no matter how badly I wanted to, I couldn't let myself think with my heart. I couldn't take that chance."

The muscle in the hollow of his cheek began to thump. With cold precision he uncurled her fingers from his forearms, then his eyes met hers. "Two days before you disappeared, Gabe took you jewelry shopping."

She stilled at the memory. "For a ring. For Val."

Cain shoved his hand into the front pocket of his jeans and pulled something out, looked down at his upturned fist and uncurled his fingers. "Not for Val."

Everything went white for one blinding, horrifying second. She stared down at his square palm, at the emerald-cut diamond surrounded by baguettes and set in platinum that she'd picked out, and felt what little remained of her heart shatter with a violence that stunned her.

Because God help her, she knew.

He hadn't come to the cottage to tear down the wall between them or offer forgiveness and love.

"I loved you, goddamn it," he said, but the words were empty now. Cruel. "I loved you so much it hurt just to breathe. I would have died myself before I let anything happen to you."

The words, the brutal truth of them, destroyed. "Let—"

"Don't." His eyes flashed and his nostrils flared, his mouth flattened into a hard line. Tilting his hand, he let the ring fall to the scarred wood of the floor. "Don't."

Then he turned and walked into the blood-washed morning.

CAIN TORE THROUGH the underbrush and hacked at a dangling vine, swiped away a clump of Spanish moss and reached for his mobile phone, turned it on. He'd been out of contact for almost twenty-four hours.

The small screen lit immediately, and the second he saw the message there, he stopped. Twenty-seven missed calls. Swearing softly, he thumbed through the menu and saw numbers belonging to his uncle and his cousin, his sister and D'Ambrosia. On a cruel rush he called his voice mailbox, swore when he heard the mechanical voice announce fourteen new messages.

Saura's was first. She was worried about him. Wanted to talk. Hoped he was okay.

Cain deleted it and started walking, felt his blood run

cold at the hesitation in his uncle's voice. "Where the hell are you?" Edouard roared. "We need to talk. It's about Alec."

Then Cain started to run.

CHAPTER THIRTY

"I WANT TO SEE THE forensics report the second it hits my desk." Edouard glared into the mirror and fumbled with his tie, worked the knot for the third time. "You're to find me, you understand?" he called to his secretary.

"I've already checked with the lab," Becca said from the other side of the door. "They expect it this afternoon."

Edouard frowned. He already knew what the report would show—absolutely nothing. Lem and Travis had been shot at point-blank range, execution style. Casings at the scene indicated a semiautomatic. There'd been no footprints, no fingerprints. The place had been wiped clean. Other than the blood—and the scrap of paper with a phone number scrawled on it.

Nothing linked to Nathan Lambert.

Reaching into the pocket of his suit jacket, Edouard ran his hand along the CD-ROM that had been delivered anonymously that morning, then pulled open his office door—and saw her.

She looked nervous. That was his first thought. Pretty, he quickly amended. He was used to seeing her in conservative suits and sensible shoes, her hair twisted behind her face. But now the salt-and-pepper streaks flowed well beyond her shoulders and made his hands itch to touch. Her blouse was soft and gauzy and the same pink as the azaleas that bloomed outside her house every spring, loose fitting like that of a gypsy.

The stab of regret was immediate. So was the twist of longing. They hadn't spoken since he'd stormed out of the church. But he'd been watching her. Constantly. Making dog-damn sure she didn't pay for her mistake.

"Lena." He hated the way his voice thinned on her name. Scowling, he cleared his throat. "I'm on my way out."

"I know." There was a wariness in her eyes, and it punished. "I won't be long."

He glanced at his watch. "I have to be in New Orleans in—"

"I came to say goodbye."

The words were soft, but they dropped around him like a heavy net. "Goodbye?"

She shifted her purse higher on her arm. "I—I've been interviewing for a job outside of Denver. A small town. Highlands Ranch. They made an offer." Her halting smile threw him back over a quarter of a century to the day he saw her for the very first time. She'd been wearing braids, he remembered. She'd lowered her eyes and looked away the second she caught him staring at her. But not before he'd seen her smile, so soft and tentative.

The pounding started then, a loud roar through his ears. "Colorado?"

"There's nothing for me here," she said, and the words, so matter-of-fact and true, sliced through him. "My friend Nini and her sister Jodie live out there. They're going to help me get settled."

He grabbed for his tie and jerked the noose from his throat. Still couldn't breathe. "When?"

She stepped toward him and lifted her hands to the collar of his shirt, yanked them back before touching the silk tie she'd helped him pick out years before. "My plane leaves in the morning."

His chest tightened on the words. "I hear it's real pretty out there," he said. But that was it. He would allow himself no other words. No other feelings.

With a curt nod, he turned and walked away, refusing to think about the fact there would be no more Monday-morning cookies.

THE LORD IS MY shepherd; I shall not want.

Gabe stared at the mahogany casket poised outside the ornate crypt where Prejeans had been laid to rest for over a century. Not even his sunglasses muted the glow of the white marble against a sky insanely blue for this time of year.

He restoreth my soul...

The slice of regret was immediate. He clenched his jaw and swallowed hard, tried to concentrate on the priest's baritone booming through the silent oaks of the old Metairie cemetery. But his thoughts kept traveling back seventy-two hours to the warehouse. The scene played through his mind in excruciating slow motion, unearthing more doubts with each showing.

What if he'd run faster? What if he'd shouted out?

What if he'd been wrong?

Thou preparest a table before me in the presence of mine enemies...

From the back of the canopied area, he looked at Tara

standing so rigid and alone. A widow now, instead of
the divorced woman she'd been about to become. He'd
spoken to her earlier, had no idea what he'd said. Words
of comfort, he hoped as Val leaned into him and put her
head to his shoulder.

Alec's death had shaken her more than he'd
expected. They'd walked around the house like zombies
for three days. He'd seen the travel books stacked on
the coffee table, but neither of them had brought up the
trip.

*Yea, though I walk through the valley of the shadow
of death, I will fear no evil…*

Overhead a formation of geese soared toward the
gulf. Gabe tracked them, then found his cousin standing
next to his uncle near the front of the small crowd of
mourners. In his black suit, Cain stood hard and unyielding, and though he stared straight ahead, Gabe saw the
readiness to his stance. He also saw the bulge beneath
his suit coat and knew Cain had come prepared. For
anything.

Except the secret he'd confided the night before.

*Surely goodness and mercy shall follow me all the days
of my life, and I will dwell in the house of the Lord for ever.*

Savannah. Frowning, Gabe glanced around for the
woman who'd deceived them all, stilled when he saw
a solitary figure standing in the distance beside one of
the graceful old oaks. Not Savannah, he realized instantly, but despite the black veil that concealed her
face there was something disturbingly familiar to the
way she was watching…not the priest or the casket,
but…him.

Adrenaline surged on the realization, but then he

blinked and just like so many other times over the past few days, she was gone, and he realized she'd never been there to begin with. It was his own mind playing tricks on him, imagining he was being watched when he wasn't, that he was being followed when no one, not even Val, knew where he was.

Holding Val tighter, he realized the priest had finished the psalm and returned his attention to the casket, where the man he'd once called friend lay inside. Whatever secrets Alec had known, whatever truths he'd refused to disclose, lay inside with him, lost forever.

Guilty or innocent, Gabe thought and felt his mouth go flat.

No one would ever know.

IN SURE AND CERTAIN hope of the resurrection to eternal life through our Lord Jesus Christ, we commend to Almighty God our brother, Alec Michael Prejean...

Cain stared beyond the coffin to the stretch of brown grass between crypts where the bagpipers should have stood. A stream of police cars should have been parked along the winding road that snaked into the cemetery. Men and women of uniform from throughout southern Louisiana should have been standing behind him, paying their respects to a fallen officer.

But Alec had walked away from the force, and his death was not one of honor.

...earth to earth; ashes to ashes; dust to dust.

Vindication, Cain had heard whispered at the sparsely attended wake. He'd felt the stares the second he'd walked into the funeral home, heard the whispers even as he stared at the picture of Alec, smiling and alive and in uniform, placed atop the casket. One of the detectives had actually thumped him on his back, asked if he'd come to enjoy the last laugh.

The Lord bless him and keep him, the Lord make his face to shine upon him and be gracious unto him and give him peace.

Closing his eyes, he saw Alec as he'd been eighteen months before, when he'd found Cain kneeling with Savannah's blood on his hands. His partner had been among his staunchest defenders. He'd stood beside him when very few had. He'd dragged Cain out of bars and poured coffee down his throat, driven him into the swamp and pressed his camera into his hands, stood in the cold while Cain had stared out at the mist rising from the water, and silently wept.

But now Alec was dead and Savannah was alive, and sweet Mary have mercy on his twisted soul, Cain could make claim to neither.

Amen.

"Someone thinks they've gotten away with murder," he said to his uncle as the small crowd broke fifteen minutes later. He glanced at each of them, Alec's grief-stricken parents and Tara's sister, a childhood friend Alec had introduced Cain to a few years before, Gabe and Val, five members of the New Orleans police department who'd come not to pay respects but to gawk at the spectacle of burying a dirty cop, two men, one woman and a little girl he'd never seen before. Two reporters and a photographer hung farther back.

Cain would stake his life that at some point during the past twelve hours, he'd come into contact with not just Alec's killer, but the bastard who'd framed Cain for attacking Savannah.

Edouard slipped his hand into his suit coat and pulled out a CD. "You need to see this."

Cain took the disk and turned it over, saw his partner's name scrawled in bold black marker. "That's Alec's handwriting."

"Came this morning. There's two files on it, one word processing, the other encrypted."

The buzz started low, spread fast. Dirty cops didn't leave messages in case they were taken out.

Cain turned toward the dispersing crowd and spotted his cousin and Val, waiting to talk to Tara. "Gabe knows someone," he said. "Let me get—"

"No." Edouard's voice was urgent, his eyes grim. "The Word file had instructions, said to make sure no one in the district attorney's office finds out about the disk until it's decoded."

The implication sickened. "Gabe's blood," Cain ground out. "One of us."

"I'm not taking chances."

"There's no way in hell—" His protest died the second he saw her step from behind a marble crypt. Dressed in a slim-fitting black suit and dark sunglasses, with her long dark hair pulled behind her head, she walked with a disturbing combination of grace and apprehension. He watched her move toward him, watched her skim a hand along a statue of the Virgin Mary, and felt something sharp and ragged shift through him.

His heart pounded hard, a brutally familiar rhythm as though not a day had passed since he'd stood inside the small French Quarter jewelry shop and fingered the ring she'd unknowingly picked out. He could still see the shock in her eyes when he'd shown it to her three days before. Still hear the broken edge to her breathing. Still feel the cold moment of truth when he dropped the ring to the floor and walked out the door.

But Christ have mercy, if he let himself, he could still see and hear and feel other things, unwanted reminders that intruded during the long hours of the night—the glow of passion in her eyes when they'd made love and the sound of his name on her lips when they'd come together, the hope and promise and hunger in her kiss. The way she'd touched him and held him, the way she'd given herself to him with such unabashed abandon that it had almost killed him to roll from the bed.

He stood there now and watched her approach, using each step she took to shove aside everything that made him weak and made him want, still, after everything, baring the impervious edges that allowed him to feel nothing.

"What the hell is she doing here?" his uncle asked.

Cain slipped the disk into an inside pocket. "What she does best," he drawled. What she'd always done best. *Messing with my mind.* But he didn't say that, wasn't about to let his uncle think she'd crawled under his skin. Wasn't ready for him to know the truth. Wasn't ready for anyone. Except Gabe. Half a bottle of scotch and Cain had told him everything.

He glanced at his cousin now, found him standing quietly as Val and Tara embraced, but his eyes, hard and implacable, tracked Renee. *Savannah.*

"That woman doesn't belong here," his uncle said. "She's like one of those storms that blows up from the

Gulf and catches you off guard. Mark my words, she's up to something."

Cain watched her approach, didn't allow himself to move. Didn't trust himself to. For seventy-two hours he'd been maintaining a death grip on the hot boil inside of him. The sight of her now, walking toward him through a labyrinth of crumbling statues and weathered monuments to the dead threatened to undermine everything he'd taught himself about survival.

"Leave her to me," he said. "I know what she's about."

His uncle snorted. "I've seen the way you look at her—"

Cain lifted a hand in silent warning. "Leave her to me."

She hesitated when she neared Val and Gabe and Tara. Sunglasses concealed her eyes, but the uncertainty, the longing, was obvious. Gabe and Val had been her friends. They'd cared for her, mourned her. But their lives had moved on. They stood together in a small intimate circle, with Renee—Savannah—on the outside. She was a stranger to them. A passing acquaintance. Someone they didn't know, didn't trust.

What must it be like? he started to wonder, but killed the thought as soon as it started to form.

"For now." Despite the concession, suspicion remained in Edouard's voice. He pulled his mobile phone from his pocket and pushed a few buttons, swore softly. "Call, damn it," he said, then shot Cain a loaded glance before turning away.

The breeze sent loose strands of dark hair against Renee's face. She shoved them back and stepped around the paltry three sprays of gladiolas and roses.

And then she was there, standing so close he could

smell the subtle scent of roses and vanilla, and it punished. "You don't belong here."

In a gesture that threw him back in time, she angled her chin and squared her shoulders. "He was my friend, too."

"He was Savannah's friend," Cain corrected, "and despite your little fantasy that the past can be rewritten, she doesn't exist anymore."

His words were deliberately harsh, but typical Savannah, she didn't wince or flinch, didn't back down. "You know that's not true," she said with a quiet strength to her voice. But there was sorrow there, too, compassion, and the combination landed like a punch to the gut.

He looked from her to Alec's casket, where Tara stood with a single hand pressed to the mahogany.

"There was no funeral, was there?" she asked quietly, and the memory spilled through him like poison. "Without a body—"

He spun toward her. "Without a body hope tries to survive." He stepped toward her and lowered his voice, couldn't stop himself from touching. His hands found her arms and his fingers curled, not rough like all the edges inside of him, but with a softness he despised. "Without a body you never stop looking, wanting. You never know if the woman who makes love to you in your sleep is dead or alive, if she comes to you as a dream or a nightmare. You never know if she's hurt or scared or if she's beyond feeling anything at all, if she needs you, wants you, if you let her down somehow, if you should have held on tighter, looked harder, done something, anything—"

He broke off and tore his hands from her, sucked in a

harsh breath and looked toward a statue of the blessed mother standing in silent prayer over the grave of a child.

"Cain." Just his name, that's all she said, but the sound of it on her voice—*Savannah's voice*—lacerated something deep inside.

Her hands then, soft and gentle, settling against his forearm. "Don't you want to know who did this to us?"

His jaw went tight. He looked down at her and lifted his hand, slid the sunglasses from her face. The crystalline blue stunned him. It was Savannah's color, so pure and unfathomable it almost gutted him.

"Maybe you can just walk away from the past," she said, "but I can't. I won't. Not until I find out who took away my life and destroyed yours, and make them pay." She paused, slid the hair from her face. "But I can't do it alone."

HE SHOULD GO HOME. Gabe knew that. Val would be waiting. She'd been upset when he told her he had to go out. Worried. She'd asked him to stay. Told him she would cook dinner.

He'd picked up his keys and pressed a kiss to her forehead, walked out the door.

He hadn't turned around to see if she'd been watching through the window.

Restlessness twisted through him. He needed to do something, damn it. But didn't know what. Go somewhere. But had nowhere to go. He'd driven around for hours, sat outside the remains of the warehouse while the sun set, waiting for a bottle of whiskey to kill the slow burn of guilt.

It hadn't happened.

He'd failed him. Alec. His friend. No matter how many ways he tried to twist and spin what had happened, he couldn't get past that one dominating fact. He'd failed Alec.

Scowling at the bookcase full of law books that mocked him, Gabe took another long swallow from the bottle and tried to kill another certainty—the insidious reality that Alec's death had not been an accident.

"Thought I might find you here."

The smoky voice came to him through the darkness of his office and had him slowly turning to see Evangeline standing just inside his door.

He knew he should have closed it.

"Evie." Her name scraped on the way out. She looked better than she had any right to standing there with a soft smile on her face. As always she wore her long leather jacket, but it was open now, revealing a red blouse, and blue jeans.

He'd never seen her in jeans.

"You don't want to be around me right now," he practically growled. Because God, the sight of her fed something dark and needy he'd been trying like hell to deny.

"Leave that to me to decide," she said, crossing to where he stood on the far side of the office, near a small sofa and table where he conducted meetings.

He watched her approach, forced himself not to move.

"Gabe—"

"It was all a setup," he ground out. "There never was a goddamned shipment."

"You don't know that," she said.

But he did. "Someone used you to lure Alec into the open—"

A dark curtain of hair fell against her face. "But that doesn't make any sense. Alec wasn't a cop anymore. How could telling the D.A.'s office—"

"Then why was he there?" Gabe wasn't sure what he was getting at, knew that he made no sense. But something wasn't adding up. "There's no other reason for him to have been there, damn it."

She lifted a hand to his arm, stilled him with her touch. "You have to stop torturing yourself like this."

"It was a trap." Through the stillness of the office, he stared down at her hand splayed across his forearm. "No one was meant to leave there alive." Slowly, he lifted his eyes to hers. "And whoever set that trap, Alec's blood is on their hands."

The light in her eyes went dark. "I—I'm so sorry."

He should have turned away. He knew that. He should have broken the contact and walked out of the office, like he'd done when she'd first put her hands to his body.

But this time he didn't. He moved so fast neither of them had a chance to react. He lifted a hand and stabbed it into her soft, soft hair, pulled her to him and crushed her mouth to his. The kiss was hard and dark and desperate, and it made him feel more alive than he had in days.

Longer than that.

He waited for her to struggle. She didn't. She lifted a hand and touched his face with devastating gentleness, pushed up on her toes and opened to him in ways that damn near drove him to his knees.

Walking her backward, he guided her toward the sofa and urged her down onto the cushions, went down with her and felt her legs fall open in greeting.

She was so damn soft and so damn sweet, offering herself to him like—

Offering herself to him.

And he was damn near about to take.

Room spinning, he pulled back and stared down at her lying there on the sofa, hair spilling around her face and eyes heavy lidded, lips parted and swollen, shirt yanked from her jeans, and realized he really was a son of a bitch.

Not trusting himself to look at her one second longer, he turned and walked away.

CHAPTER THIRTY-ONE

THE BARKING PENETRATED his shower. On a growl of his own, Edouard turned off the water and grabbed a towel, strode toward the front of the house where Hanoi, the scrawny fleabag of a hound who'd moved in on him years before, paced anxiously at the screen door.

"Something out there you want?"

Soulful eyes darker than melted chocolate met his.

"Go ahead then," he said, pushing open the door.

Hanoi bounded into the early morning, where he would no doubt reunite with the other mutts who thought a filled food bowl every morning made a place home.

Hanoi kept barking, an agitated sound quickly joined by a chorus of half-breeds.

Scowling, Edouard dried off and dropped the towel, strolled to the fridge. He wanted a beer. Maybe a whiskey. But it wasn't yet 8:00 a.m., and he needed to be at the station in thirty. Never mind that he hadn't gotten home until sometime after one, then had spent another hour trying to find a link between the Lambert brothers and Renee's appearance and Alec's death.

Settling for orange juice, he grabbed a handful of chocolate-chip cookies—only four remained on the plate—and headed into the main room, sprawled out in his big easy chair. The dogs were still barking—

Edouard flipped on the TV, but he barely heard a word the news reporter was saying.

My plane leaves in the morning.

The uneasiness oozed deeper, forcing Edouard to confront a truth he preferred to deny. To make sure he never became that mangy dog that Lena had no choice but to bring in from the rain—*to flat out survive in a world in which he no longer fit*—Edouard had done the only thing he could. He turned off all those emotions his daddy had insisted made a man weak. His once-proud, booming father had never recovered from the death of his wife from an infection that set in after giving birth to her fifth son.

They'd buried him just a short time later.

His oldest brother Jacques had fallen, too, marrying young and immediately fathering two children, only to drop dead of a sudden heart attack. His young wife, fragile even before she'd lost her husband and became the single mother of a one-month-old and a one-year-old, had joined him seven weeks later, courtesy of a pre-scription for sleeping pills and a bottle of schnapps.

Faced with the task of helping raise his brother's children, Edouard had vowed to never do anything that might leave him weak in any way. After his sister lost her husband and left two more children, Gabe and little Camille, fatherless, Edouard's need for control morphed into a monster.

Becoming sheriff had been the logical progression.

Caring for Lena Mae was not part of the plan. He'd had no choice but to secure a tight grip on their relationship and set the parameters, make sure it never slid too far toward commitment.

And for a while, she'd gone along with it.

Until the baby.

Even now, almost twenty years later, the memory of learning he was going to be a father had the power to shake him.

The memory of finding Lena Mae slumped on the bathroom floor in her own blood had the power to destroy.

Grabbing the remote, Edouard changed the channel. Again. And again. But nothing appealed. Nothing held his interest.

Nothing killed the thoughts.

Hanoi was howling now. So loud Edouard almost didn't hear the phone ring. Almost.

On a growl of his own he rolled to his feet and found his cell phone on the kitchen table. "Robichaud."

"Eddy." The voice was soft and sweet and…wrong.

"Lena?" Something inside him started to shake.

"Someone's in my house," she whispered. "My bedroom."

He was running before she'd finished speaking.

PLACES CARRIED memories every bit as real and powerful as those recorded in a diary. A house absorbed what transpired in its walls. Trees stood silent witness to the beauty that blossomed at their trunks—and the depravity that bled at their roots. Rivers flowed, the current concealing evidence that sank to the murky bottom.

Time moved on, but the essence of all that had once transpired remained. Love lingered. So did hate.

Pulling a cluster of vines aside and stepping into the circle of massive oaks, Renee knew without Cain saying a word that they'd reached the place where her brother had drawn his final breath. She felt the chill, an icy slap to her body, and stopped.

Sensations blasted her, vivid slashes cutting like lightning through the thick canopy. The unease was as primal as it was immediate, a nauseating awareness, un-invited and unwanted. Completely unvindicated.

Her brother had died here, miles away from those who loved him and any hope of medical attention. Looking at the carpet of decaying leaves and sticks covering the ground, she felt her throat tighten in renewed horror.

The urge to turn to Cain was strong, to feel his arms close around her like the day in the cemetery when he'd found her at her brother's grave, when he'd held her and rocked her, and made promises without saying a word. She wanted that now, needed it with an intensity that shook her.

But he just stood there in the cool damp hollow, and so did she.

They'd barely spoken since he'd picked her up at the hotel, where he'd paid someone to deliver her things. Barely looked at each other. Yet the awareness remained, humming strong and violently like a danger-ous song neither wanted to sing. She could feel him, just as she always felt him, standing beside her without touching, condemning through absolute silence.

Once, the barricade had worked. Eighteen months before, she'd not let herself see beyond the hard exterior to the man inside, the man driven by deep passion and a relentless need to protect. They'd come together too fast. She'd convinced herself it was just sex, because just sex she understood. Just sex she could handle.

It hadn't been just sex.

And now the barricade no longer worked. She saw the struggle for control in every rigid line of his body, saw the residue of hurt and betrayal in the dark glitter of his eyes. They could never go back. Maybe they couldn't go forward. But they weren't strangers, and she refused to pretend otherwise.

"What was he doing out here?" she asked.

Cain stepped forward and reached up, grabbed a scrap of yellow police tape still speared by a small branch. "The forensics team believes he came out here on his own, that he was followed."

In the city someone might have noticed a stranger who didn't belong, noises that didn't make sense. But here in the swamp, where even during the day little light leaked through the vegetation, there'd been no one. He could have run, Renee knew. He had run. But knowing that only made it worse. "He never had a chance."

"The hunted usually doesn't."

The chill came hard and fast. It was a familiar sensation, the same she'd experienced at an old Civil War battlefield. Adrian had felt it, too. "I don't like this place," she whispered. "It's cold." Like death.

Something dark and volatile shifted through Cain's gaze. He yanked off his camouflage jacket and stepped toward her, draped it around her shoulders.

The warmth stunned her. The scent of leather and patchouli seduced. Instinctively she slipped her arms into the sleeves and hugged the jacket, refused to analyze why he'd given it to her.

"It's been more than eighteen months," he said, and the ragged edge to his voice surprised her. "There's nothing left."

Maybe he meant of their relationship. Maybe he meant the crime. She chose to go with the latter. "Where was his body?" she asked, turning back toward the clearing.

Cain swore under his breath, but he stepped forward anyway and pointed beneath the largest tree.

Renee thought she was prepared. She herself had asked to come here. She knew what had happened. But seeing the spot where her brother had died peeled scabs off old wounds, and the horror and the grief came pouring back. She stepped forward and went to her knees, put her hands onto the bed of decaying leaves—and found it soft.

The tears surprised her. She thought she'd cried all of them she had to cry. But they gathered and stung, and through their blurry haze, she envisioned her brother lying in the leaves, just like they had as children.

Bender's words came back to her, and with a hand she fought to steady, she put her finger to the ground and began to trace. First a *C*. Then an *A*. An *I*…

Cain's foot stomped down on the letters. "Christ Jesus, Renee, what the hell—"

It was the first unchained emotion she'd heard in his voice since she'd called him Robi. Bracing herself she looked up, almost gasped at the disbelief twisting his features, as though instead of scribbling letters in the leaves she'd shoved a knife into his gut and twisted.

"Bender," she said with a hard thrum to her heart. "Bender said Adrian wrote the first three letters of your name in the mud before he died."

He tensed. "Bender?"

"The rookie cop who found him."

"I know who Bender was," he said darkly. "What I don't know is what the hell you're talking about. I was here, damn it. I wrote the report. There was nothing written in the dirt."

She pushed to her feet and stood, wrapped her arms around her middle. "Bender said your report was a lie."

The lines of Cain's face hardened. "Then Bender was lying."

Maybe. Or maybe they'd both been played. "He sounded scared, Cain. He was shaking."

Eyes narrow, he glanced around the clearing. There was a stillness to him, a readiness, and instinctively her gaze looked to the leather holster strapped around his shoulder, the Glock he could have in his hands before she could blink. His hands were open, ready.

But it was the memories that chilled her, the holo-caust of them darkening his gaze. He was there, she realized, back in time to the evening he'd crouched near her brother's body.

A long moment passed before he turned back to her, but even when he did, she wasn't sure what he saw. "When did you talk with Bender?"

She swallowed hard. "The night he was murdered. He contacted me, arranged to meet me in the Quarter. Said he couldn't live with the lie, that I deserved to know Adrian's dying words…two names I'd never heard before—and yours."

SHE WASN'T THERE.

Edouard threw the cruiser into Park and grabbed his

service revolver, ran toward the house. Six and a half minutes had passed since her phone call.

He'd wanted her to be there, damn it. He'd wanted her to slip from the bushes or bolt from across the street, run to him the second she saw his car. That would mean she was safe. That she'd gotten away—

The old Creole house was too damn still. Too damn dark. Ungodly quiet. No sound came from within. There was only the unwanted soundtrack of warblers and robins.

Training told him to go slow. Case the house. Scope out the scene. Exercise caution.

The cold fist in his stomach demanded that he kick in the front door.

The fist won. "Lena!" he wanted to shout. But that was one mistake he did not allow himself to make. He couldn't risk giving the perp even one second to get crazy on him.

So he ran. Quietly. From box-filled room to box-filled room. They were all empty. And they all seemed to breathe with him. The parlor. The dining room. The kitchen. At the end of the hall he swung open the door and found the big bedroom, saw stacks of clothes on the bed, a half-packed suitcase on the floor.

Everything inside of him was roaring and screaming, shredding the cold precision of the cop he'd been for the majority of his life. He saw the room through the eyes of a man, who now stared at broken glass and a knocked-over chair, the phone lying on the floor.

"Lena?" He barely recognized his own voice. His body convulsed as he moved to the bed and dropped to his knees, pulled up the bed skirt and looked underneath.

The rush was so intense he went light-headed. For a
fraction of a second. Then he was back on his feet and
swinging around the room—

The old black-and-white cat damn near got shot.

Shiloh, his name was. She'd had him for at least
fifteen years. And he was standing with narrowed eyes
at the entrance to the hall.

Slowly Edouard approached him, followed when
Shiloh turned and slunk toward the other side of the
house. That's when he saw the broken lamp.

And the butcher knife.

And the blood.

Training went out the window. Because God Christ
have mercy on his soul, he knew what was behind the
closed door.

"No!" The roar wobbled in his ears. "Lena!" He ran
toward the door and kicked it open, saw the dark form
writhing on the floor—and Lena Mae pressed against
the wall in a corner, with some kind of metal container
in her hands.

Relief almost felled him. "Jesus," he roared, and was
by her side before his heart could so much as beat. "Are
you all right?"

She didn't answer, didn't move, didn't so much as
blink. Her eyes were huge and dark and swollen. Her
cheek was bleeding. Her lip was split.

He wanted to hold her in the worst kind of way.
Instead, he lifted the canister from her hands and read
the label. Paint thinner.

The moaning perp would not be going anywhere
soon.

"Eddy."

Her voice was so damn soft, filled with a kind of emotion that should have been destroyed years ago. "You came."

She sounded surprised. That was his fault. His and his only. "Of course I came," he growled, easing her into his arms and burying his face into her hair. The hot moisture stinging his eyes surprised him. Fisting a hand in her hair, he pressed a kiss to her forehead and stared over her head—saw the portrait.

The room. It wasn't a spare room as he'd initially thought. It was her studio, where she did her painting. Canvases leaned everywhere, some painted on, others bare. Many of the faces he recognized. Others he did not.

The portrait at the back of the room embodied a combination of both. He recognized the features, the mane of silver hair and the intense, hawkish eyes, the wide cheekbones and strong jaw. But underlying the features was a kindness, a gentleness, he'd not seen in the mirror since before he left for Vietnam.

"Eddy," she whispered, but before he could look down, her body went limp in his arms.

That's when he saw the blood.

HIS NAME. *His goddamn name.* Cain stared down at Renee, at the cold horror in her eyes, the sorrow and the contrition, and saw memories he didn't want to see. *Her* memories. Through *her* eyes. The sight chilled him, the way she was dwarfed by his big jacket. She looked small somehow, fragile. Vulnerable. Once he'd wanted nothing more than to protect her from the world—and herself. The urge was still there, to reach out and pull her into his arms, promise her everything would be okay. That he would make it okay.

So he crushed it.

"What others?" he asked with deliberate precision.

The breeze kept blowing hair into her face. She pushed at it, shoved the tangled strands behind her ears. "Evan," she said, and her voice was strong. "And Lynn. I've been looking for them since I returned, but no one's heard of them and there's no mention in any police report."

The names meant nothing to him. "Did it ever occur to you?" he asked in a voice she'd once said made her skin crawl, "that Bender was lying just like that prostitute you told me about? That you were being set up?"

"Hindsight is easy," she said, and her voice lashed. "But that morning you came to me with blood on your shirt." She paused and closed her eyes, opened them a heartbeat later. "You didn't want to talk."

Streaks of sunlight cut through the oaks and fell on her face, returning him to that morning in her kitchen, when he'd found her sitting at the table staring at a cup of coffee. Her eyes. Christ, he would never forget the revulsion he'd seen in her eyes. "So you decided I must have killed him."

"*No.*" Her voice was soft, but the word echoed through the stillness like a cry for mercy. "We were going to meet that evening," she said, "at the cottage. You said it was important."

The memory twisted through him, the ring and the wine and the rose petals, the foolishly romantic words he'd rehearsed all afternoon. Gabe had said he was loco to propose after such a short time and in the middle of the biggest case of his career, and maybe Gabe had been right. But there'd been so much darkness. And she'd been such a bright light.

"When I got out of the shower that afternoon I smelled you," she said, and the words were coming faster now, harder. Darker. "But you didn't answer when I called."

Cain's jaw went tight and he looked away, toward a clump of Spanish moss. But sweet Mary the image wouldn't fade, the picture of her wrapped in a towel and realizing someone was in her house.

"I went into my office and found my laptop on, critical files deleted. My case folder was empty." She paused, swallowed. "I tried to call the police, but there was no dial tone. I ran for my mobile phone, but stopped when I saw your keys on the back of Grandpappy's recliner."

Where he always put them. "My keys were stolen that morning. So was my car."

Her eyes met his, showed him a hell he'd never imagined. "Then I heard you whisper my name."

And the setup had been complete.

"I spun around," she said, never looking away, never blinking, just staring into his eyes as if he could make the memory and the aftermath go away, as if he could make it all better, like he'd once promised he would. "But it was too late."

His imagination seized on what she didn't say, assaulted him with all the ways it could have been too late. "Did you see a face?"

"No, just a candlestick."

Something inside of him went cold and dark. He told himself not to do it, to keep his distance and continue taking her statement like a jaded cop so far removed from decency and humanity that nothing fazed him. But he stepped toward her anyway, felt his hands lift and his fingers settle against the side of her face, the way he'd once touched that butterfly in what seemed like a different lifetime. The butterfly he'd killed.

"It was dark when I came to," she whispered. "I was alone in an old shack. It was dirty and smelled like death."

And he'd been throwing back a beer because she'd stood him up.

"My ankles and wrists were bound, but I was able to work the rope, get free."

Like he'd taught her during one of the many self-defense lessons he'd insisted upon.

"I saw the keys on a table and lunged for them, made it out the door before someone tackled me from behind. We struggled. He had a knife and he was big. Strong."

The truth glinted there in her eyes, the devastation of what had been running through her mind as she'd struggled for her life. "Like me."

"He wore a ski mask and just kept slashing at me," she said in a robotic voice that sickened him. "I kicked and thrashed, got my elbow into his nose hard enough that he let go of me long enough for me to get my feet and run to my car." A single tear spilled over. "Your car was parked beside it."

Against the side of her face, his hand stilled. "Jesus, God—"

She backed away and wrapped her arms around her middle, ran her hands along the bulky sleeves of his jacket. "I made it onto the highway, but he was right behind me. It was so dark that night, foggy. I could barely see two feet in front of me."

He could take it from here. "You went off the road."

"Hit a tree at full speed then slammed into the bayou."

"Your car was found two weeks later." Submerged in the water.

"I was thrown, came to sometime later and started wandering. That's all I remember until I woke up in a clinic. I'd been found with nothing, no purse or ID. They had no idea who I was, only that I'd said one name over and over, and begged them not to call the police."

His eyes met hers. "Because *I* was the police."

Somewhere in the swamp a heron cried, and another answered. "I was scared," she said. "There wasn't a single part of me that didn't hurt. I didn't know what to think or who to trust."

Not even herself.

"It killed me," she whispered. This time it was she who moved, she who curled her hands around his upper arms. "Because despite everything, the newspaper articles and your arrest, my own hazy memories, I still loved you. Still wanted you."

Just as he still wanted her. He staggered away from her and curled his hands into tight fists, recoiled from the stricken look on her face—and from the truth. It ripped through him anyway, with a violence that charred everything inside him.

For eighteen months he'd lived without her. There'd been only memories and nightmares, the chilling questions that followed him everywhere, the even more chilling knowledge that he'd failed her. That because of him she'd hurt and she'd suffered. That when she'd needed him, he hadn't been there.

But sweet God, for the past four days everywhere he turned, the truth stared back at him, and laughed. Because all that time she'd been alive.

"That's why I came back," she whispered, and her voice broke on the words. "I made myself go to the bad place, told myself it was the only way I could protect myself. But the first chance I got, I ran straight back to you."

He went still. He should hate her. He knew that. But when he looked at her now, at her huge dark eyes and pale soft skin, the strand of tangled dark hair caught against her mouth, like some idiotic masochist all he wanted to do was touch. And taste. And take.

And heal.

CHAPTER THIRTY-TWO

EDOUARD BALLED his hands into tight fists. They wanted him to sit. To wait patiently. These things take time, the attending doctor had told him. He'd known Martin Guidry for more than half his life and trusted him with all of it, knew the man could and had worked miracles, but the pale green walls shrank with every excruciating minute that crawled by.

And the silence. God, the pulsing silence was worse than the cage they wanted him to wait in. It pounded in his ears, snickered and sneered and reminded. No way could he just hunker down on one of those little sofas like Laurelee Bertrand whose husband was having hemorrhoid surgery, and wait. The adrenaline rushed too hot and hard, like the full force of the floodwaters through the spillway.

Lena. Sweet God have mercy, not Lena. She was going to be okay. He knew that. She had to be. Anything else—

Swearing softly, he strode to the nurse's station for the fiftieth time. And for the fiftieth time little Lucy McGregor, who should still be in diapers, damn it, flashed him a smile so tight with pity he wanted to slam his fist into something.

"I'm sorry, Sheriff, Dr. Guidry is still in with her. We'll let you know just as soon as—"

The double doors swung open then and a somber-looking Dr. Guidry stepped into the hall, walked toward Edouard.

He broke toward him. "Martin, thank God. How is she?"

"Let's go somewhere we can talk," the doctor said, and Edouard's heart damn near stopped.

"Mon Dieu, non—"

Martin took him by the arm and led him toward the emergency exit. "She's going to be okay," he said in a low but reassuring voice. "Her vitals are strong."

"The blood—"

"Puncture wound to the abdomen…a few inches from her liver. She's lucky. A few cracked ribs and marks on her arms. Whatever happened, Miss Lena Mae put up one hell of a fight."

The swell of pride was ridiculous. But damn it, he had been the one to teach her self-defense, all those years ago. For her own good, he'd told her. But there'd been plenty of good for him, too. When he let himself, he could still remember how she felt in his arms when he positioned her at the shooting range.

"You can see her now," Martin said. "She's a little groggy from the pain meds, but she's been asking for you."

His chest tightened. His heart slammed much the way it had the day a lifetime ago when he and Jesse had dared the girls to spend the night in the swamp. They had, but not without a close encounter with a moccasin. He could still see Lena's terrified face the morning after. He'd wanted to hold her so damn bad. And she, she'd slapped him across the face and walked away.

She'd always been a smart one, his Lena.

"Millie's on the way," he bit out, grabbing the pack of cigarettes from his shirt pocket. "I—I've got to go."

Martin frowned. "Ed, are you—"

"I'll be in touch." With one last glance toward the double doors, Edouard turned and walked away. A report at the station required his attention.

Lena did not.

THE GLITTER IN Cain's eyes stole Renee's breath. It was dark and it was volatile, but it was vulnerable, too, the irreconcilable combination she'd seen so many times in the dizzying days before the bottom fell out of her world. When he looked at her like that, everything else fell away. There were no trees or vines, no ferns, no birds squawking. No flowers fading.

No past ripping them apart.

No future that would never happen.

There was only Cain and the devastatingly familiar rhythm of her heart.

"Part of me wanted to die when you didn't recognize me," she whispered, because this was what she'd needed. What she'd craved. Like a torch in a cave, she'd needed to see the dark light in his eyes, to feel the slow burn all the way down to her soul. Now she inhaled deeply and stepped toward him, again lifted her hand and feathered her fingers against his jaw. "Then I looked into your eyes," she whispered, "and realized that you did."

Sunlight sneaked through the branches of the old

oaks, casting his face in an odd combination of shadow and light. But he didn't move, didn't say a word. Just stood there looking at her as if she was skinning him alive.

"That's the collision course you kept warning me about," she added quickly. "Why you couldn't stay away from me. Because somewhere deep inside you recognized me." He'd all but told her so the night she'd woken him from the nightmare. "You're just so used to isolating yourself and ignoring your feelings, that you wouldn't let yourself accept what was happening."

Slowly, his hand came to the side of her face, and cradled. "Wintergreen," he said, and his voice was raw. "You still taste like goddamn wintergreen."

The flood of warmth was immediate. She wanted to step closer and curve her arm around him, put her head to his chest and hear the thrumming of his heart, but the truth wouldn't let her move.

"But you were right yesterday." She took a deep breath, let it out slowly. "The Savannah you knew did die that night. I couldn't stay that person and survive. I had to shut myself off from everything and find a strength I never knew I had. It was like living without a soul."

She realized her mistake the second she felt his fingers tense against her face. His eyes went hard as his hand fell away. "Don't talk to me about living without a soul," he said in a voice devoid of any and all emotion. Then he turned and walked away.

Renee stood there a long moment and tried to breathe. She'd been wrong, she realized. Dead wrong. She'd seen the look in his eyes and let her heart take over, stepped onto hallowed ground not only as if she had some right to be there, but as if he wanted her there. The naïveté of her mistake twisted deep.

She hated that she had to go after him, hated that she needed him when he so brutally did not need her. But he knew his way around the swamp, and she did not.

Even on the edge of winter, green dominated the land. For so long she'd thought of fall as a season of death and decay, but as she pushed through a cluster of vines, she found it impossible not to see the primal beauty. Here, so far from the intrusion of man, there was a simplicity to the order of life. Trees grew, and trees died, trees fell into decay and started the cycle anew. Families and generations surrounded her, young saplings and those in their prime, tired, weary oaks and cypress that had seen war and drought and disease, but still stood, solid proof that no matter how grim the circumstances, life did go on.

Cain was just ahead of her, and as she pushed aside a clump of moss, she found him down on one knee, angling his camera up at a sprawling oak. Sunlight glinted through the branches and fell in fickle puddles around the knobby roots jutting out from the leafy carpet. Moss made the shadows dance.

Renee stopped as recognition hit. She'd been here before, stood in this very spot. She'd sat with her back to the massive trunk, engrossed in one of the historical romances her mother kept stashed between her mattresses, while nearby her brother worked on a duck blind.

This was *his* tree, the one he'd said reminded him of the poem "Evangeline"—the one immortalized through the photograph in Cain's gallery, next to the picture of the butterfly she'd taken the week before the attack.

"He was coming here." She felt that truth in her bones.

Adrian had always been drawn to this remote corner of the swamp, said he could think here, clear his mind.

Heart pounding, she turned to Cain, found that he'd shifted the lens of his camera to her. "Maybe part of him always knew this was where he would die."

Cain lowered the camera, confronted her with his eyes. "If that's true it doesn't bode well for us."

Because it hurt to look at him, she turned and moved toward the tree, lifted her hand to the trunk. Adrian had been coming here. Maybe he'd come alone. Or maybe—

...someone close to him set everything up...

Lena Mae's theory roared through her. Maybe Adrian had brought someone here with him. Someone he knew—someone he trusted.

Someone Cain trusted.

"You haven't told anyone about me," she said, spinning toward him, "have you?"

He slung his camera over his shoulder. "Just Gabe."

Someone he trusted—someone her brother had trusted. She felt the chill immediately, the truth she'd known all along, the reason she'd chosen to hide her identity, even from those she loved. Someone had wanted her dead—if they were to learn she still lived, it would be they who got the second chance, not her.

"What?" Cain asked, moving toward her.

She frowned. "Travis had a theory that whoever framed you was someone close. Someone you trusted, someone you'd never suspect."

"Travis was a drunk."

"He knew you were innocent," she shot back. "He just pretended otherwise to protect himself."

Cain narrowed his eyes and looked off into the swamp. She could see the wheels of his mind working, see the denial hardening the lines of his face.

"Who else could have done this to us? Who else would have had access to your keys and your car, your cologne, your voice?"

His eyes went hard. "There's no way Gabe—"

The name drilled through her. She grabbed his arm, felt everything inside of her go horribly still. "Who said anything about Gabe?"

"WHAT DO YOU think? The black one or the leopard one?"

Gabe looked up from his Blackberry and squinted toward the doorway. "I'm sorry, hon, what was that?"

Val sauntered into his study and struck a pose, tilting her head and giving him a slow smile, making it impossible for him to look at anything but the bikini that barely covered her breasts and hips. Two strings for the top, two strings for the bottom.

"Is the black too harsh? I could always take the leopard—"

He glanced at his watch and stood, didn't know how to tell her that their trip would have to wait two more weeks.

If they went at all.

"You could always take both," he said as she strolled toward him and pushed up on her toes, skimmed a kiss along his lips.

"How about neither?" she asked, running her hands down toward the fly of his khakis.

He caught her hand and brought it to his mouth, pressed a soft kiss to the inside of her wrist. "Val, honey," was all he got out before the light in her eyes drained.

"Gabe—"

"I'm sorry," he said, but no longer had a choice. "Uncle Ed called, wants me to meet with him. Said it was important."

Her sigh damn near broke his heart. "All these late nights and secrets are starting to scare me. Are you sure everything's okay?"

He took her face in his hands and looked into her eyes, brushed a kiss across her mouth. "They will be."

VAL STARED OUT THE window a long time after Gabe's car vanished into the dreary fall day. The days were shorter now. The holidays were close. The stores had already hauled out their Christmas merchandise even though Thanksgiving was still two weeks away.

The soft light of a lamp cast her reflection against the windowpane, and she frowned. There was a buzz inside her, a low, frenetic roaring, and no matter how many times Gabe promised everything was okay, it grew louder with each passing day. He was keeping secrets from her. She knew that. And it made her uneasy.

The gun was back. It had returned mere hours after she'd found it missing—and mere hours after Alec had died.

Gabe was involved. He denied it, but Val knew. He'd been there when the warehouse blew. She'd seen the cuts and bruises he'd tried to hide. Heard the hushed phone calls late into the night. When he'd finally come to bed, she'd felt the tension in his body and had worked for a long time on his shoulders, but her hands had not done the trick.

It was like living with a stranger.

They'd been together for three years. It hadn't always been smooth sailing, but during that time she'd learned what made Gabe tick. Or at least she thought she had.

Fighting a chill that had nothing to do with the temperature, she turned from the window and went to his study, carefully flipped through the neatly stacked files. It was the calendar that made her heart beat harder, the thick dark circle drawn around one of the days they were supposed to be in Barbados.

Then she noticed the folded sheet of paper wedged under his laptop and pulled it free.

GABE SWERVED INTO his reserved spot and slammed on the brakes, shoved the gear into Park. He stared at concrete blocks surrounding him, but barely saw them.

Everything inside of him shook. Roared. His uncle's words played through him over and over and over, more insidiously with each second that ripped by.

He wanted them to be lies. He wanted Edouard to be wrong.

But he knew that his uncle rarely was. He would not have come to Gabe unless he was sure. Edouard had been rattled, not because of the information he'd delivered, but because Lena Mae Lamont had almost been killed.

The insanity had to stop.

On a vicious rush he pushed open the car door and strode toward the elevators, his Bruno Maglis echoing furiously through the quiet garage.

The elevator came quickly. He stepped in, jabbed the button, then waited.

Her door was open. That was the first thing he

noticed as he strode down the hall. Her door was open whereas she frequently kept it shut.

He didn't knock. He didn't hesitate. He walked straight in and around her desk, refused to allow himself to remember the last time he'd seen her, how she'd tasted and felt and—

"Gabe." She minimized the document open on her laptop and stood. "Is something—"

"You set me up." The words were quiet.

They didn't need to be loud.

Something dark and dangerous flared in her eyes. "Gabe, what are you talking about?"

He just barely resisted the urge to take her shoulders in her hands. He knew better than to touch her, had no idea what would happen if he did. "Don't play games with me, damn it!"

Dark hair fell into her face. "What are you—"

"*I know.*" He could still hear Edouard's words, see the report one of his contacts had faxed him detailing the theory that the leak they'd all been searching for did not originate from the police department—but from the district attorney's office. "Every time you looked at me, all those seemingly casual conversations, little comments here, a touch there…" She'd played him perfectly, and like an idiot, he hadn't just fallen for it, he'd come back for more. "All a setup."

Her eyes went even darker. "It wasn't like that—"

"Is that why you went to law school?" he pressed. "To hang fellow attorneys out to dry?"

"Gabe, please, you have to listen to me."

Once, the desperation thinning her voice would have

disturbed him. Now he ignored it. "There never was a shipment, was there?"

"Gabe—" she said again, but this time she made the mistake of touching him. She lifted a hand to his forearm, like she'd done so many other times.

Everything inside of him went stone cold. "Alec died because of your game," he said, looking first at her hand, then into her eyes. "He *died.* And his blood—" He took the hand she'd put to his arm and turned it over, exposed her palm. "It's right here."

"No." It was barely more than a whisper.

"I saw you!" he realized. "At the warehouse, just before it blew. I saw your car…just didn't realize whose it was until today."

"It wasn't about you," she said. Hand still turned over and exposed in his, she looked up at him. "We had to find the leak."

He dropped her hand. "It's not me."

"I know that." Her voice was sad. "But someone close to you is."

He didn't want to hear anymore. Didn't trust himself to look at her one second longer. Knew better than to analyze the twisted mess boiling inside him.

"Go to hell," he whispered, ignoring the fact that her stricken gaze said she was already there.

VAL LOOKED NERVOUS.

Renee set down a cup of hot black tea and shifted on the formal sofa, felt a dull pang of guilt. Val had been a gracious hostess from the moment she'd arrived, welcoming her into her home and offering refreshments, but her smile had been strained and her eyes guarded.

The two women now sat across from each other, and though the conversation was casual, Val's posture in the lovely antique wing chair was stiff.

She was uncomfortable, Renee realized. She also knew why. The two women had been friends once. They'd shared martinis and manicures, shopping trips and secrets. Renee knew Val was a smart woman. She no doubt realized Renee had not invited herself over to discuss the weather in Barbados. Renee was a reporter. Val knew that. It didn't take great deductive powers to realize Renee wanted something from her.

Renee uncrossed her legs then recrossed them, searched for the right words. She couldn't just blurt out the real reason she'd come. Val would be as defensive as Cain had been.

Cain. *God*. He'd told her to let it go, that there was no way Gabe was involved in the attempt on her life. But Renee couldn't do that. The idea had settled under her skin like an invisible splinter, and until she found a way to extract it, there was no way to ignore it.

All this time they'd been looking for a dirty cop, someone who'd sabotaged the investigation into organized crime by feeding critical information to *Oncle*. Informants had been executed. Sources of information had dried up like creek beds during a drought. Her brother, quietly cooperating with the police, had been murdered.

And an innocent man had taken a long, hard fall.

Now Renee had to wonder. She knew Cain was innocent, and deep in her bones she believed Alec was, too, despite the rumors to the contrary. Travis had believed the real culprit could be found closer to home.

Gabe was an assistant district attorney—and Cain's cousin. He had access to everything his cousin did…

"Where's Gabe?" It was a Saturday. Two suitcases sat across the room. "He's not working is he?"

Val's cup clanked as she set it down. "I'm afraid so."

"That's too bad," Renee said as casually as she could. "I was hoping to see him. Something big going on at the D.A.'s office?"

Val bit down on her lip and stared at Renee, glanced nervously at the door. "Have you heard something?" she asked, and this time she sounded scared. "Is that why you're here?"

Renee uncrossed her legs and leaned closer, hoped Val couldn't hear the frenetic pounding of her heart. The rush of adrenaline almost made her sway. "What would I have heard?"

"Nothing," Val said. Agitated, she stood. "I just…" She hesitated, looked at Renee with the same searing intensity she'd once looked at Savannah. "Ever since you showed up, strange things have started happening. I mean, Alec is dead and now Gabe is—"

Very slowly, Renee came to her feet. This time she did sway. "Gabe is what?"

"You should never have come here," Val said. Renee watched her fiddle with a silk floral arrangement, and knew her instincts had been right. Val knew more than she was saying.

"But I'm so glad you did," Val said, looking up. That's when Renee saw the gun—and felt the room start to spin. "Savannah."

CHAPTER THIRTY-THREE

"THAT'S IT, *mon chou.* That's it." Crouched beside an old duck blind with his camera angled toward a cypress, Cain watched a female anhinga dry her wings. The brown-and-white bird stood on a decaying tree trunk and flapped her wings, spraying off water that quickly dissipated into the gray fall mist.

He adjusted his aperture setting and snapped. The graceful bird froze, glanced his way, took flight.

Cain pushed to his feet and watched the bird soar, knew that she had the potential to become Miss November in his next calendar. Lifting his camera, he snapped a shot of her silhouetted against the hazy sun. Then he swore viciously. Because no matter how many pictures he took, he couldn't stop seeing Renee as she'd been that morning, kneeling at the spot where her brother had died. Her quiet words haunted.

She'd suffered. Her body, yes, but more than just the physical, it was the emotional scars he'd seen that morning, the same shell-shocked look he'd seen count-less times as a cop from women whose only mistake was falling in love with the wrong man. He'd taken their statements, urged them to think with their heads and not their hearts, knelt beside their lifeless bodies while behind him their children cried.

Sometimes there were no warnings. Other times there were. It was those situations that had always incensed him, made him wonder how a woman could stay with a man she didn't trust. But God help him, now he knew. Uncertainty and love didn't cancel each other out. They could live side by side, scraping and twisting, tangling, until it was impossible to discern one from the other. Just like love and hurt could.

In the end, it was the dichotomy that destroyed.

Frowning, he lifted his camera and searched for another target, but there was only Renee as she'd been that morning, gazing at him with through eyes huge and dark and bruised, as though *he* was the one who'd driven the knife into *her* back. Every time he saw her, the woman who'd betrayed him faded further, replaced by the woman who'd walked through hell and back to reclaim her life. The shadows in her eyes offered chilling testimony to the nightmare she'd endured, the heinous tug-of-war between faith and doubt that had shattered the woman she'd once been. But there was strength, too, and courage, more raw and gut-twisting than he'd seen from the majority of his brothers on the force.

On a cruel rush of adrenaline he turned from the increasingly bloodred sky and slung his camera strap over his shoulder, heard his boot crunch down on a pile of twigs. His heart pounded with an urgency he hadn't felt since the night he'd run through the swamp searching for Savannah. Because God help him, she'd more than just endured. More than just survived. She'd come back to him. Against all odds and every scrap of cold logic, she'd defied the conventional wisdom that would have granted her the chance to start over fresh. She'd ignored the cesspool of evidence against him, which had given her the power to make sure he was locked away for a long, long time, and she'd come back to him.

He, in turn, had walked away.

Behind him the cry of the anhinga echoed through the swamp, but he no longer cared. There was only Renee, and the insidious knowledge of what he'd done to her.

AWARENESS CAME slowly. First there was peace. Her body was relaxed, her mind drifting like clouds on a lazy summer day. But then came the pulses of confusion. She didn't remember going to sleep, couldn't place whether it was day or night.

Alarm flickered next, bringing with it the realization that her body wasn't relaxed. It was heavy. And her mind wasn't drifting. It was racing—reeling.

Memory slashed in last, and on a horrific rush she squinted against the shadows. The room wasn't small and dark and dirty, and the scent wasn't of death and decay. The surface on which she lay wasn't hard and damp. And her head didn't throb like it always, always did when sleep took her back to the night she'd almost lost her life.

There were shadows in this room, but only because of the plantation shutters closed to all but a few streaks of sunlight. The scent was of apricots. Beneath her was a soft bed.

Renee swallowed against a cottony throat and blinked against the haze, brought the room into focus. And the woman. She sat in a straight-backed chair near the bed. In her hands was a gun.

"Feel better now?" she asked.

Renee pushed against the lethargy, but the bindings at her wrists and ankles impeded movement. "V-Val…"

The woman she'd considered a friend stood. "It's been a long time," she said, moving to the side of the bed. There was a gleam in her eyes Renee had never seen before, a malevolent light that made her blood run even colder. "It was so nice of you to stop by this afternoon. You saved me a bit of trouble."

"I don't understand."

Val lowered a hand to the side of Renee's face and gently stroked the hair from her eyes. Her touch was obscenely soft. "I always wondered what happened to you," she said in an odd singsong voice. "Why your body wasn't found." Her fingers stilled against Renee's cheekbone. "Sometimes I would dream of you. You would rise from the swamp, dripping and decaying, and come toward me, staring at me through vacant eyes."

"It was you," Renee whispered, and the realization punished. She'd been blind to Val. They all had. She'd been like wallpaper in Gabe's life, something that was there but that no one ever paid much attention to. "All this time it was you."

"And no one suspected a thing," Val said, clearly pleased. "It's the curse of being a woman, always overlooked and underestimated. But it's also the gift."

Renee struggled to connect all the dots with lines that didn't make sense. All the seemingly innocuous conversations, little choices that shouldn't have impacted so many lives, the little lies. Val had always seemed clingy, almost desperate to hang on to Gabe. Renee had always thought it a little pathetic.

Now she realized her friend's cover was downright brilliant.

"Gabe loves you," she whispered, and her heart hurt for him. Thinking he might be responsible for all the deception had been hard, because she'd always thought of him as a stand-up guy, with a core of integrity that ran a mile deep.

"Yes," Val agreed. "I worked hard to make sure that he does."

"This will kill him."

Val smiled. "Only if he finds out."

Which Val had no intention of happening. Which meant she had no intention of letting Renee live to tell him.

"You weren't supposed to die, you know," she said with a wistful smile. "At least not that night anyway."

Renee's mind raced. She was in Gabe's house. He had to come home at some point. If she could keep Val talking— "What *was* supposed to happen?"

"Your brother took something from me. Something important."

"The Goose…" She'd heard the rumors, the whispers Cain had refused to verify that her brother managed to steal one of the small electronic devices that had brought the gaming industry to its knees.

Val's expression turned dead serious. "I want it back."

Renee's heart kicked hard. From the look in Val's eyes, she more than wanted it back. She *needed* it back. "That's why you abducted me. You think I know where it is."

"I know you do," Val said. "You're his sister."

Renee stared at the woman who'd fooled them all, tried not to see her as she'd been almost two years before, when she and Cain and Gabe and Val had shared drinks at the Golden Pelican. Adrian had come over to them. He'd flirted with Val, told her that if he wasn't already in love and if Gabe wasn't her almost fiancé, he'd make a play for her himself.

Only a few weeks later she'd had him executed.

The rage built like a vicious force within her. "My brother would never have said anything that would endanger me."

Val ran her hand along the barrel of her semiautomatic…silencer already in place. "That remains to be seen. He was quite proud of the fact he'd hidden what he stole from me someplace where no one would ever think to look."

"Then what makes you think I know?"

"We gave him a choice. He could return what he stole, or you and Saura would die."

Renee cringed.

"So he relented. He said he'd return it, we just had to let him retrieve it." Val's eyes went hard. "He went, but I had someone follow him. He drove to a wooded area that bordered a swamp. Then he started to walk."

Lying there on the bed, Renee went very still. Cain had been right after all. Adrian had gone to his death alone and of his own volition. "I don't understand. Why would you kill him before he could return the Goose?"

Val's expression twisted. "Adrian got foolish, thought he could outmaneuver his tail. He circled back, tried to take him from behind. But my man was faster, took him out before your brother could so much as blink."

Renee closed her eyes, saw the soft bed of leaves where her brother had fallen—and died.

"We searched the area," Val added. "But came up with nothing."

With his final breaths Adrian had tried to communicate something—not the name of his assailant, Renee now realized. But something else. Something more important.

Cain...Evan...Lynn.

"...checked it out," Val was saying. "According to some of his friends, Adrian used to go duck hunting in that same area. He and your dad." Her smile was slow, confident. "You're his sister. If anyone would know what he was doing out there, where he was going, it would be you."

Heart hammering, Renee could see it all, the dense undergrowth and the knobby cypress knees, the ethereal Spanish moss and the sun cutting through the branches—and the tree.

Not names, she realized on a hard surge of adrenaline. There was no Evan or Lynn. But there was an Evangeline—the old oak with the massive branch that swooped like a bench to the ground, the one he'd always loved, the one he'd called the Evangeline tree—the one Cain had photographed.

"My God," she said because it was all so clear now. She'd had a few pieces all along, but Cain had had others, and Val had possessed the rest. They were all needed to see the truth. "The tree."

Val stilled. "What tree?"

"In the swamp," Renee said, and her heart pounded hard on the revelation. "Where he died."

"There are thousands of trees in the swamp."

"But not like this one. It was special to him."

Val's eyes lit. "Then take me there."

And surrender what Adrian had given his life to protect? *Never,* Renee wanted to shout, but she saw the gleam in Val's eyes and realized how desperate she was to find what Adrian had hidden. Maybe it was more than just the Goose. Maybe his investigation had yielded other fruit—fruit that terrified Val.

The reporter Renee had once been screamed that there was more going on here than the mere search for an electronic device. And the survival instincts Cain had helped her hone went off like a string of firecrackers.

"I can't," Renee said, pleased by the despondency she injected into her voice. "I don't know where it is." Val didn't need to know Renee had been there just that morning.

"That's not a problem. I know where the area is."

"But like you said, there are thousands of trees."

Val's gaze hardened. "Then I guess you're not so useful after all, are you?" she asked returning the gun to point at Renee's chest. "Looks like this time there will be a body."

"Wait." Adrenaline raced harder, faster. She'd risked everything to come back and reclaim her life. She wasn't going to let Val steal it without a fight. "There is a way," she said. "I know how to find the tree."

"DID SHE SAY WHERE she was going?" Cain asked over the roaring in his ears. Vaguely he was aware of the edge to his voice, the way the assistant hotel manager's eyes widened, but he was beyond the point of caring.

"I'm afraid not," she said, coming around the hotel's reception counter. "Should she have? Is something wrong?"

No one had seen her in almost three hours. No one had heard from her. No one knew where she'd gone. "I want you to call me, you hear?" he instructed. "The second she shows up, the second you hear from her, you're to call me."

She nodded, but Cain was already turning from her. He'd just stepped outside when his mobile phone rang. He grabbed it without breaking pace, glanced at the caller ID box and saw the words *wireless caller,* stopped dead in his tracks.

"Vannah?" he roared, fumbling with the buttons.

"Cain."

Her voice. Sweet God have mercy, it was her voice. "Where the hell are you?"

"I'm where you told me to be," she said, and her voice was oddly calm, almost cold. "On my way out of town."

His hand tightened around the phone. "What the hell—"

"Because you were right," she said in that same monochromatic tone. "I never should have come back."

His heart pounded harder. "Where are you, *cher?* Let me come get you—"

"It's too late for that," she said. "I thought I could walk back into my life, but I can't. People change. Life goes on. It took coming back to realize that I was better off away from here. That I was happier."

His gut twisted on her words.

"But I'm hoping you'll do me a favor," she said blandly. "For old times' sakes."

Coming from anyone else, the request might have made sense. But not from Savannah. She didn't ask favors, especially not from someone who'd slammed the door in her face.

"What kind of favor?" he asked in the same deadly quiet voice he'd relied on to coerce information from informants.

"Two things really," she said after a brief hesitation. "First I was hoping you could tell me how to get to Adrian's tree, the one that's in the picture hanging in your gallery. I'd love to see it one last time."

Everything inside of him went brutally still. *"And the second?"*

If she heard the silent understanding in his voice, she gave no indication. "I know I told you I wanted her back," she said, and finally, finally, a trace of emotion leaked through. "But I was hoping you'd keep feeding my dog."

CHAPTER THIRTY-FOUR

THE SUN SLIPPED low on the horizon, bathing the swamp in a crimson glow. Shadows fell from the trees and dripped from the gnarled undergrowth, while a cool breeze flirted with the Spanish moss. The air was damp and heavy, expectant. So were the birds. They cawed from all directions, unseen from their perches high atop the cypress and the oaks, but Renee felt them watching every step she took.

Every step Val took.

They'd been walking single file for almost thirty minutes. The tree lay just ahead. The gun jabbed into her neck served a constant reminder that time was almost out.

Her heart twisted on the realization. She'd been so sure, so completely, totally sure that Cain would recognize the silent alarm she'd tried to trip.

But now doubt crept in, and with it came the sobering realization that there was no guarantee he remembered the brief exchange at her brother's grave. Time had passed. Lives had moved on. Deception had marred what they'd once shared. His voice, normally rich and dark and drugging, had been calm and detached, clinical almost, as he'd given her directions. There'd been a brutal note of finality to his goodbye.

This time there will *be a body.*

The memory lashed through Renee as she shoved at a tangle of vines and neared the hollow where Adrian's tree had sprawled for over a century. Untouched. Unmarred. A strong solid reminder of beauty and sanctity, innocence. The place where Val planned to kill her—and frame Cain.

"This way," Renee said, deliberately steering Val in the wrong direction. The second she led her to the tree, her usefulness was over. If she could mislead her until the sun went down…the darkness could once again be her friend.

"What was that?" Val asked, and only then did Renee realize that she'd stopped.

She turned toward her, saw the semiautomatic pointed at her heart. "What was what?"

"That noise." Val's eyes were narrow, suspicious. "It sounded like twigs breaking."

Renee heard it then, a soft crunch from the direction of Adrian's tree. "Probably just an animal."

"Or a man," Val snapped, and Renee's heart kicked hard. "Check it out," she instructed, motioning with her gun. "And so help me God, if you try anything, you know who will pay the price."

She did. Cain—and her grandmother.

Renee turned toward the clearing and tore at a clump of moss, moved silently toward the gorgeous old oak. Adrenaline streamed frenetically, bringing a hot rush to her blood. She felt it swirl through her as she stepped from the dense undergrowth, and instinctively knew that she was not alone.

"Adrian," she whispered, and her throat closed on

the words. The moisture came next, warm, salty, burning her eyes.

"*Non.*" The soft word boomed through her like a shout. "*C'est moi.*" He emerged from behind the tree and stepped toward her, all tall and strong and dark, but battered somehow. Mud streaked his camouflage pants and beneath the holster strapped around his shoulders, his long-sleeved T-shirt was torn. She recognized the gun immediately, the one he'd once put into her hands and taught her to use. But it was the shadows to his face that stopped her breath, the strong set to his jaw and the glitter in his eyes.

"*Cain.*" Her heart pounded so hard she barely heard the agitated squawk of the birds. He'd heard. He'd understood. And despite the terrible things she'd done to him, he'd come. "You shouldn't be here," she whispered.

Like a violent wind he destroyed the distance between them and crossed to her, took her hands in his arms. "The hell I shouldn't," he said hoarsely, then stunned her by crushing his mouth to hers. The kiss was hard and possessive and completely unexpected, and in it Renee knew she could drown.

His lips moved against hers with shattering hunger, nibbling and claiming, whispering words that made her heart slam cruelly against her ribs.

"No!" she rasped, pushing against his arms and ripping away, making herself breathe. Making herself think. Val was not fifteen feet away. She could see everything. Hear everything.

If Renee couldn't get rid of Cain—

"I know I hurt you," he was saying, but his words barely registered. A cool calm came over her as she looked at him standing there, at the steady rise and fall of his shoulders and the bulk of his chest, and she knew what she had to do.

"No words," she whispered, stepping toward him and lifting her face to his, letting her hands settle against his stomach. Then as her eyes met his, she grabbed his gun and pushed away from him, curled her hands around the butt and lifted it between them. "Not another step, either."

Shock flared in his gaze. "Vannah—"

She forced a laugh. "My, my, Detective, you really have lost your touch, haven't you?"

He stood there so horribly still, staring at her with a combination of dread and horror that broke her heart. *"What the hell are you talking about?"*

Around them even the birds fell silent as the shadows kept slipping and merging, squeezing out the last vestiges of bloodred light. "Sorry, *cher,* but denouements aren't my thing." With a calm she didn't come close to feeling, she curled her finger around the trigger. "But I will thank you for making this so easy."

Then she pulled the trigger.

The force of the blast knocked her backward. She staggered and grabbed a low-hanging branch, held on as she watched Cain's face contort. The primal sound that ripped from his body echoed hideously through the swamp. "Y-yo-u…" he gasped, bringing his hands to his gut. Then he doubled over and went to his knees. "You…sh-ot m-me."

Horror coiled in her throat. She crossed to him and stared down at him curled in fetal position, made herself smile. "When I was hired to impersonate Savannah and find the Goose, I thought you would be my biggest obstacle—guess I was wrong."

A strangled sound broke through the silence and Renee knew she couldn't wait one second longer. She started to run just as Val broke through the underbrush.

"Not so fast," commanded a harsh, authoritative voice, but Renee kept running. She slapped at the low-hanging vines and tore at the dense underbrush, stumbled on a Cypress knee.

The second voice, so horribly familiar, stopped her cold.

"THERE'S NO WAY OUT." Gabe watched her back stiffen, watched her twist toward him as she kept the semiautomatic trained on D'Ambrosia. He'd recognized the outfit. He'd bought it for her. He'd recognized the swingy dark hair—he'd encouraged her to try the style. But God help him, even when he saw her shadow-drenched face, denial hammered through him.

The eyes were wrong. They were hard and cold, not bright and vibrant. Merciless, not insecure. Even her mouth was different, a tight line instead of the soft fullness he'd tasted so many times.

"*Gabe,*" she whispered, and the sound of his name exploded through him like a grenade. Because it was…right. He'd heard the unsure tone so many times—when he'd told her he loved her for the first time, when he'd proposed after only a month and she'd touched her fingers to his mouth and told him no, when they'd found each other again, when she'd held him after Savannah disappeared and his cousin faced a life behind bars—and just like every other time his heart surged on the unspoken need, the fierce desire to protect.

"Put down the gun," he said, and even as he felt himself step toward her, none of it felt real. It couldn't be. This was Val, and he was Gabe. They'd been together for three years. The night before she'd cried in his arms, told him how much she needed him.

Now she stood in the hazy crimson light in the middle of the swamp, with a semiautomatic trained on a cop.

You need to get out here, Cain had instructed less than an hour before. Savannah had slipped him a silent alarm, and he'd been in the process of laying a trap. *I'm afraid we're going to need your help.*

He looked at his cousin now, crumpled on the leafy carpet beneath an old oak, and felt the rage coil through him anew.

"I'm here," he said to Val, careful to keep his voice low and reassuring. "I'm not going to let anything happen to you."

She shook her head, sent her hair swaying. "I told you to stay away from Cain," she whispered. "I *begged.*"

His eyes met D'Ambrosia's in silent understanding. Somewhere in the brush, his uncle waited.

"I know you did, honey, but we can't change what's already happened. I'm here now. That's all that matters." He stepped closer. Out of the corner of his eye saw Savannah slip between two young saplings. "I want to help you. Just put down the gun—"

"I can't," she said, and her eyes went even darker. "It's too late for that."

"It's never too late." To prove his words, he lowered

his own gun and let it fall to the ground, kicked it toward the underbrush even as he saw D'Ambrosia fiercely shaking his head no. "See? All you have to do is put down your gun and let me help you."

She gestured toward D'Ambrosia. "Tell him to put his gun down."

"You know he can't do that."

"It's the only way," she said, but D'Ambrosia didn't move a muscle.

"Watch out!" Savannah shouted, but it was already too late. The gunshot ripped in from behind him and D'Ambrosia went down. Val swung around and lifted her gun, looked him dead in the eye.

"I'm sorry," she said in an emotionally devoid voice he'd never heard before, "but *this* is the only way." Curving her finger around the trigger, she pulled.

CAIN LOWERED HIS GUN and watched Val slump against Gabe, watched his cousin drop to his knees and cradle to his chest the woman who'd betrayed them all. There was a roaring in his ears, a violent pounding that drowned out all the sounds of the swamp which had shrieked so loudly seconds before.

Renee. He swung around and saw her, kneeling not ten feet away. Her eyes, dark and stunned, were on his. In her hands, Gabe's gun dangled from her fingers.

"Cher," he breathed, then was on his feet and running, dropping to his knees and pulling her against him. She curved her arms around him and held on tight, pressed her hands into his back.

"Couldn't let her do it," she muttered into his chest. "Couldn't let her hurt anyone else."

The pain in her voice wrapped around his heart and squeezed. He glanced beyond her to D'Ambrosia, propped up against a big rock while Edouard tended to him and called for air support. Then he saw his cousin, methodically rocking the lifeless body of the woman who'd been on the verge of executing him. His eyes were dark and vacant, completely dry.

"It was my shot," Cain said, pulling back to cup his hands to Renee's face. "I got it off first."

She put her own hands to his face, strummed her fingers along his jaw. "You don't know that."

Her raw courage slayed him. She'd played her part flawlessly, following the instructions he'd whispered while kissing her as though she'd been in on the plot to lure Val into the open from the very beginning. Pretending to shoot him had been the only way.

"Yes," he said. "I do."

Gratitude glistened in her eyes. "You remembered."

"Toujours," he murmured, feeling the tight surge all over again, the cold horror of Renee's disguised call for help. He tucked her head against his chest and buried his hands in her hair, savored the feel of her body curled into his. "Always."

THE RUMORS WERE TRUE. The Goose was a small electronic device, no bigger than a quarter. It looked innocuous enough, like a trinket a child might find in a gumball machine and lose interest in only a few minutes later. Left on the floor or a counter, no one would look twice at it.

Adrian *had* stolen it. And he had hidden it. Ultimately, he'd died for it.

Val had died to get it back.

The FBI could hardly wait to get their hands on it.

Chest tight, Renee watched Cain hand the plastic bag containing the black magnetized device to his uncle. She and Cain had found it concealed in a small carved-out compartment on the underside of the large branch that swooped toward the ground. Adrian had hidden a computer disk in the little vault, as well, its files encoded.

An electronic forensics specialist was already en route—Tara Prejean. Renee smiled at the thought of the delicate-looking innkeeper, who used her bed and breakfast to cover her true passion. She was the FBI's go-to person for decryption, which was, Cain told her, how she'd met Alec in the first place. Tara felt confident that within twenty-four hours, forty-eight tops, she'd break the sophisticated code.

"There was a second shooter," she heard Cain tell Edouard. "We caught up with him a quarter of a mile away."

But not before he'd taken down the tall, dark-haired man Renee recognized from the casino. Shortly after arriving at the hospital she'd learned that Cain's uncle had asked the detective to keep an eye on her, make sure she didn't cause trouble for Cain. "Any word on D'Ambrosia?"

"More of a flesh word than anything else. Bullet grazed his thigh. Doc Guidry says he might have a limp, but that's it."

Relief washed through her. "Thank God." There'd been enough lives lost, too many destroyed. "And Gabe?" she asked, feeling cold inside at the memory of him kneeling in the mud with Val's lifeless body in his arms. She had no idea how a man got past that kind of betrayal.

"Father Voissin is with him," Edouard said, frowning. "So is Saura. I'm gonna get down there just as soon as I check on Lena."

She blinked. "Lena Mae? Is everything okay?"

The change came over Edouard so fast she had to blink to be sure it was real. He was a big bear of a man, always grim faced and on the prowl. But the second she'd asked about Lena Mae Lamont, something incredibly soft had filled his eyes, taking ten years off him. "She will be," he said, sliding a hand into his pocket. "We all will be."

THE ROOM WAS EMPTY.

Edouard stared at the bare hospital bed for a long quiet moment before closing the door. This was what he'd wanted, he reminded himself. Lena. Gone.

According to the nurse, she'd checked herself out of the hospital an hour before, said she had a plane to catch. Dr. Guidry had tried to talk her out of it, but Lena, being Lena, had been determined. There was very little the woman couldn't achieve when she put her mind to it.

Life would go on. Lena would make a new home for herself. She would be happy. He would continue to protect his family and his town, would be ready for the day Nathan Lambert finally messed up.

It still galled him that he'd been so consumed by his belief that the Lambert brothers were behind all the ill that had befallen his family that he'd failed to see the threat right under his nose. Val. She'd always made him a bit uneasy, but he'd attributed it to her being shy. Not cold-blooded.

He looked forward to going through her files.

"Eddy?"

He looked up to see Millie hurrying toward him without a scrap of makeup on. "Honey, what are you doing—"

"I just heard." Breathless, she took his hands and squeezed. Hers were much too cold. "Is it true about Gabe's gal?"

A disturbing combination of hope and grief hollowed out her eyes, reminding him entirely too much of her cousin. "It is," he told her in as reassuring a voice as he could. He'd known her forever. It was damn hard to envision her as a widow. She wasn't that old. None of them were.

But age didn't seem to discriminate.

"Lord have mercy, he was right," she breathed, and her eyes filled.

"Who was?"

"Travis. He always said it was someone close to Cain that set him up. Maybe Gabe or Eti or—"

"Me?" Edouard finished for her.

She had the grace to flush. "He mighta mentioned your name," she admitted. "But Lena Mae always said…"

The words dangled there between them for a long moment, then they started to wind around him, twisting, constricting… "Lena always said what?"

Millie pulled her hands back and looked up at him with a pained smile. "That she couldn't imagine you killing anyone."

Edouard sucked in a sharp breath, would have

sworn he smelled fresh-baked cookies. "But she didn't know for sure."

Millie's expression gentled. "She's gone, Eddy. Said to tell you there's no need to keep mowing her grass. The real-estate agent has someone who can do that until the house sells."

He nodded, reached for the pack of cigarettes.

"I—I've got your portrait," Millie added. "It's in my back seat. I thought you might want to see it before—"

"I've already seen it."

"She really captured you, don't you think?"

The sight of the missing cigarette shamed him. "Honey," he said, shaking out a second. This one he wouldn't light, he told himself. This one he would force himself to merely taste. "I hate to leave you, but I need to get back—"

"Of course you do." Millie's smile was fleeting, reminding him for a flash of the girl she'd been before marriage to Travis had replaced smiles with frowns. "Wait," she blurted out, reaching into her satchel. "Here. These are for you."

Not wanting to hurt her feelings, he glanced down at her offering, felt everything inside of him go very still.

Because in her hands she held a pie plate, covered with tinfoil. A small tear revealed the cookies.

Chocolate chip.

THE BUTTERFLY HOVERED over the honeysuckle blossom, a splash of yellow forever suspended against the shadowy outline of a woman. *Her* shadow. *Savannah's.* Cain had taken her deep into the swamp, said he wanted to share something with her. At first she'd thought he meant the land, but as the day progressed and shadows stretched longer, she'd realized what he wanted to share was himself—the man who took pleasure in simple things, the photographer who found beauty where others found only decay.

Until that afternoon over a year and a half before, she'd known only the hard-edged detective everyone warned her to steer clear of. Because of his photography, she'd suspected the still waters he presented to the world were just a facade, but until she'd watched him go down on a knee and frame a delicate dogwood blossom, she'd never imagined how breathtakingly deep and beautiful still water could be.

Renee lifted a hand to one of the old church windows of Cain's gallery. A light glowed from within, but with the hour pushing toward ten, the doors were locked. She'd left the hospital almost an hour before, after the FBI had hustled Cain and his uncle into a private meeting, something about Val and additional evidence they'd seized from the home she'd shared with Gabe.

Renee had tried waiting, but the walls of the hospital had started to close in on her, and before she even realized her intent, she'd slipped out the emergency room exit and into the night. Now the darkness whispered around her, cool and damp and primal, carrying with it the sounds of the toads and the crickets, the earthy scent of the bayou flowing nearby. She inhaled deeply and closed her eyes, found it impossible to believe less than two weeks had passed since she'd stood in this exact same spot with Cain on her first night back.

Hasn't anyone told you it's not smart to be alone with me in the dark?

One week. That's what she'd given herself. One week to find the truth. One week to secure justice. But in truth, she'd only needed a day. A moment. A heartbeat. Because the second she'd seen Cain, all the walls she'd hammered into place had come tumbling down, leaving her with the devastating truth that had been slowly and softly killing her from that moment forward.

She should go, she knew. Move on. Her time here had come and gone. She'd accomplished what she'd come to accomplish.

The hum started deep inside, low and fierce like the echo of thunder somewhere in the distance. Her heart kicked in recognition, her breath caught in anticipation. She knew without turning, felt without touching—wanted without defense.

"I used to come here," he said from the darkness, and the low cadence of his voice sent her heart strumming against her ribs. "Late at night." To her right, the steps leading up to the porch creaked. "I'd stand just where you are," he said, coming up behind her but stopping before he touched. "Put my hand to the window, and remember."

The image formed before she could stop it—Cain, so big and brutal and allegedly untouchable, without remorse or conscience, alone in the darkness, staring at a delicate butterfly hovering against her shadow—and it devastated. "Why didn't you burn it?" The question was oddly unemotional. "Like you did all the others."

His breath feathered against her neck, bringing both warmth and a chill. "I couldn't," he said, and then his hand was on the window, slowly tracing the curve of her shadow. "It would have been like destroying you."

Her heart kicked hard. She was acutely aware of him standing behind her, of every line of his body, every beat of his heart, every breath.

All she had to do was turn and she would be in his arms.

On a broken breath she pivoted to her left and crossed the porch, curled her hands around the old rail and tried to breathe.

The cool air rushed against her face and sent her hair flying, but she made no move to push it back. "I used to dream of what it would be like to come back to you," she whispered, staring at the statue of the woman waiting for a lover who never returned. "To see you again. Sometimes I would wake up out of breath with the sheets damp and tangled around me—" her body burning, begging "—with your name burning in my throat." And confusion clawing at her heart. "I'd look for you." First in the bed next to her, then in the room, sometimes she'd even run through the small house. "Because I knew you'd been there with me."

"You came to my dreams, too," he said quietly.

More than anything she wanted to turn to him, to see him, to touch. More than anything she wanted to believe the promise she'd seen glittering in his eyes that afternoon, when he'd kissed her hard and asked her to trust him—to shoot him. It had taken several long, dizzy seconds before she'd realized the beauty of his plan.

Still, lifting the gun to his chest had been one of the hardest things she'd ever done.

"For so long the need to reclaim my life consumed me." Like a living entity it had grown within her, driven her. "Coming home, seeing you, finding the truth and making sure someone paid…it's all I thought about. All

I wanted." Her chest tightened on the memory, the reality. "I never imagined success could feel so empty."

Behind her the porch creaked and she knew that he'd moved, but she didn't trust herself to look. Didn't trust herself to see.

"I thought I could just step back into my life and move on," she said, watching the way the big oaks loomed like giant shadows against the night sky, swaying and swishing. "Like a book I'd set down for a while, that it would be waiting in exactly the same spot when I was ready to pick it up again." She'd never let herself consider anything else. "But that life doesn't exist anymore. Time moves forward, not backward."

"It still exists," he said from behind her, and then his hands were on her shoulders, gentle but firm, turning her from the night. Her heart slammed hard at the sight of him, so big and tall, but battered somehow, a man not afraid of violence but capable of excruciating tenderness.

They'd been lovers. They knew each other's bodies intimately. They knew each other's secrets and dreams, passions and fears. But as she looked up at him, at his wide cheekbones and the dark glitter in his eyes, she felt as though she stood before him naked for the first time.

"TIME DOES MOVE forward," Cain said, drinking in the sight of her standing there in the mercurial light of the moon. The crystalline blue of her eyes fed some place deep inside of him. "But that doesn't mean the past goes away."

The meeting with the feds had been near torture, hashing through details and theory when all he wanted to do was find Savannah. If she hadn't called him— If he hadn't understood— If he'd been a few minutes later—

The possibilities chilled, but he also knew they didn't matter. Because she had called, and he had understood. He'd gotten there in time. Because of her tenacity, they'd finally learned what really happened that night, a seeming lifetime before.

"Not a day went by when I didn't relive everything," he said, needing to say the words almost as badly as he needed her to hear them. The truth. It was all they had left. "The first time I saw you—the first time we made love—and the last." He saw her eyes widen and couldn't resist the need to slide a hand to her face and touch, to feather his thumb along her cheek. "If you think for one second," he rasped, stepping closer and bringing his thighs up against her hips, sliding his arms around her waist and spreading his hands against her lower back, "I'm going to let you get away from me again, you don't know me as well as I think you do."

The light in her eyes dimmed. "I hurt you—"

And he couldn't let her do it, couldn't let her continue to berate herself for the decisions she'd had no choice but to make. "I was a cop," he reminded. "I know the statistics." The percentage of women killed by someone they knew and trusted, compared to those killed by a complete stranger, was chilling. "I'd have to be blind to not see what this has done to you."

But she'd come back to him anyway.

"Don't paint me as the victim," he said, loving the feel of her pressed up against him. "You're the one who went through hell and back. You're the one who kept fighting when most people would have rolled over and surrendered. Don't you think I know what it cost you to come back? Don't you think I know the risk you took?"

Long dark strands of hair blew into her face, but she made no move to brush it away. "I had no choice."

"Yes, you did." He slid the strands behind her ears, needed to see her eyes as he said the words. "You could have taken the evidence at face value and gone straight to the D.A. You could have crucified me. You could have had me locked away before I even knew what had happened. But you didn't do that."

"I couldn't—"

"You came back to me, Savannah." When every scrap of logic had demanded that she stay away. "You risked your life to come back to me."

And God help him, he was going to spend the rest of his life making sure she never hurt again.

"I never really left," she whispered. Holding his gaze, she took his free hand and drew it to her chest, where her heart beat hard and fast. "Not here."

Her smile, slow and daring and pure vintage Savannah, slayed him. "Do you remember what I told you at the cottage?" he asked. "That I loved you so much it hurt to breathe?"

Her eyes went slumberous. "Cain—"

"I still do," he practically growled, and with the words his restraint shattered, and he lowered his face to hers, needed to taste, to take back what he would never relinquish again. "Your life, *cher.* It *is* waiting." His mouth hovered just above hers. "And so am I."

EPILOGUE

CAIN PUSHED aside a stringy clump of moss, but even as he neared the clearing, he knew he would find no trace of the woman to whom he'd made love less than forty-eight hours before.

After almost two years away from the force, he remained intimately familiar with the taste and feel and texture of deception. But he'd become equally familiar with the taste and feel of deliverance. He knew what words to use, which to leave out. He'd learned to work illusion to his advantage, how to take something ugly and turn it into beauty. And no matter what had transpired in the past, this time the promise would be honored.

Come alone, the cryptic note had instructed. To the old, burned-out ruins. At midnight. Leave your cell phone at home.

A quick glance at his watch showed that ten minutes remained. With an early spring breeze rustling through the land, he stepped into the clearing and found the abandoned columns rising against the night sky, proud placeholders of the once-grand plantation. No longer pristine white, but ivory, the Corinthian pillars had persevered through time and the fire that claimed the manor they once embraced. Nature had done its best to enhance the remnants, making the columns look as at home among the sprawling oaks and towering cypress as Savannah felt in his arms.

It still awed him that she'd come back to him, that she'd found the courage to listen to her heart and not the malicious lies orchestrated by Val. If he let himself, he could still see the shell-shocked look in Savannah's eyes the morning before the attack, when he'd told her Bender was dead. Now he knew why. Now he understood. He could only imagine the devastation she must have felt when Bender had implicated Cain in Adrian's death. But now they knew Bender had been the dirty one, arriving at the scene before Cain and destroying the message Adrian had tried to leave for him. The prostitute Angel had been found, as well, and had confessed that she'd been hired to spew lies to further incriminate Cain.

But Savannah hadn't believed them. She'd trusted her heart, and she'd trusted Cain. Ironically, the same horror that had ripped them apart had ultimately brought them back together—and exposed the depth of Val's deception. If Savannah had stayed away, Val's lies would never have been exposed. The files the feds had seized from her real-estate office had contained a gold mine of information, names and dates, places and plans, all leading to several major arrests.

Both Adrian and Alec had died trying to expose her. The CDs they'd left behind, decoded by Tara, had proved that. On them she'd found a name that made his uncle very happy—an old nemesis of his.

The ruthlessness with which Val had infiltrated Gabe's life staggered. She'd targeted him, moved in on him, played him like a song, all the while using her guise as the insecure lover to keep a pulse on the investigation into the criminal activities she herself was carrying out. The revelation had rocked Gabe, exposed him to ugly shades of gray he'd never imagined possible. But he was a strong man, and Cain knew his cousin would recover.

Lena Mae had recovered from the attack ordered by Val, as well. She'd moved on to Denver. Millie said her cousin was in love with the mountains. The town didn't seem the same without her. Neither did his uncle.

He saw her then, Savannah, drenched in moonlight as she stepped from the mob of cypress and oak. The sight of her fed that restless place deep inside him, and one by one all the pieces fell into place. Her hair was back to its original blond color, and even though he couldn't see them yet, he knew her eyes were as daring and crystalline blue as the day they'd met. His body tightened at the sight of her in black jeans and a soft olive sweater—and the anticipation of the little black dress that waited at the cottage. She didn't even have it on yet, and already his hands itched to take it off.

But this was her night, not his. She wanted her life back, and he was going to give it to her. Everything. Starting exactly where they'd left off, with the rendezvous at the cottage that had never happened. Rose petals once again lay strewn on the floor and the bedspread. A bottle of merlot once again sat waiting on the counter. And in his pocket—

But first he had one more gift to offer.

From across the clearing, their gazes met, and she started toward him.

For eighteen months he'd been a man of sunsets. But

for weeks now he'd been leaving her bed before dawn and trudging through the wetlands, waiting with the land for the sun to boil over the swamp. He'd shot endless rolls of film until he'd preserved the perfect image.

That was his gift to her—a photograph of a sunrise, a palette of vivid reds and oranges and yellows chasing away the darkness. Just like she'd done by coming back to him. Against every feasible odd she'd picked up the threads of her life, not as though she'd never been gone, but as though she'd finally, finally found where she belonged.

Savannah was home.

Everything you love about romance...
and more!

Please turn the page for Signature Select™
Bonus Features.

Killing me
SOFTLY

BONUS
FEATURES
INSIDE

Author Interview:
A conversation with
Jenna Mills

Where did the idea for *Killing Me Softly* come from?

As strange as it may sound, I've always been fascinated with "back from the dead" stories, both real and fictitious: soldiers who go off to war and are presumed dead, only to return at some point in the future; people who mysteriously vanish into thin air, only to reappear years later, sometimes with no memory of who they once were; women or children who are abducted and feared lost, only to be found after all hope has been lost. The Elizabeth Smart case out of Utah still makes me cry happy tears.

What would it be like, I always wondered, to lose the one you love, only to find them again? Life goes on, after all. People change. Would your feelings be the same? Could they?

What would it be like to *be* the individual who was lost? To suddenly find yourself home. Could you walk back into the life you left behind? Would you want to?

These are the questions I sought to answer in *Killing Me Softly*. From the very beginning I had a vivid impression of Cain, a strong, passionate cop who lost everything: the woman he loved and the career that defined him. A man who faced a firestorm and came out on the other side. A man who has shut himself off from the world—and himself. And then comes along a woman, a woman who makes him feel things, remember things, he does not want to feel or remember. He finds himself falling for her, only to feel like he's betraying the woman he lost, and himself. The paradox in that obsessed me as Cain and Renee pulled me through their story.

And then there were the other questions that drove the story, those that dealt with the essence of love, and the power of the heart. Typically we think of recognizing a friend or lover by sight or hearing their voice. But what if you faced a complete stranger, someone whose face you did not recognize and whose voice you had never heard before, and yet deep inside, you felt a rhythm or a hum that felt...familiar. Does someone have to look or sound the same, to be the same? Can you recognize someone you love without use of the five traditional senses? Against all logic and conventional wisdom? And just

where does love come from? Is it something
that develops slowly over time, or is it something
that is just...there, which can be neither created
nor destroyed...?

Ah, poor Cain. He sure did go through the
wringer to find his happy ending!

Did you need to do research for this story?
Yes! While the location of the story—southern
Louisiana—is near and dear to my heart, crime
and police procedure are not! To keep the story
accurate, I consulted with a police detective
friend on all the criminal aspects.

Why did you become a writer?
I'm not sure anyone ever *becomes* a writer. I
think you're born that way (either that or it's a
psychological disorder!). I know I was. From the
time I was a little girl, I've adored stories and
enjoyed creating my own. And if I didn't like the
way a story I read or saw ended? Well, I'd just
change the ending in my mind. In high school I
was the girl who wrote the sappy love poems
about the angst of being a teenager in love. I was
also the freak who *enjoyed* writing research
papers! So when it came time to go to college
and earn a degree, journalism was a natural
choice. By that time I had many notebooks full of
poems and song lyrics and stories. However, it

wasn't until many years later when I was married and settled in my life that I began writing seriously for publication. As to why I write...honestly, I think it's because I'd go nuts if I didn't. There are so many stories and scenarios and characters moseying around in my mind. I've got to get them out!

What matters most in life?
Family and friends, hands down. Everything else is transient. Jobs and houses and cars and vacations, they all come and go. But those individuals with whom we share intimate relationships define and drive us. I was blessed to have all four of my grandparents in my life for over thirty years, and I treasure the love and memories they gave me, the lessons they taught and examples they set. And now there's a new generation of my family coming on, children of my own, nieces and nephews! It's an utter joy to shower them with love and support, see them grow and develop, watch them reach for their own dreams. The circle of life is truly amazing.

Do you believe in the supernatural?
Yes! I'm a big believer in things that cannot be seen, but rather felt (as is evidenced by some of Cain's challenges). I'm notorious for thinking of a friend, only to have that friend call within the next

day or so, even if the friend and I have not spoken in quite some time. I frequently log on to e-mail to contact someone, only to find a note from them in my box. Just recently I couldn't stop thinking of a friend serving in Iraq. I e-mailed him to ask him when he was coming home, only to have him e-mail me back with the news that he had arrived home just that day!

Those are only small examples from my own life...and perhaps they could be chalked up to coincidence. But I do not believe in coincidence. Instead I believe in connections and in energy, and that there is far, far more to this world (and ourselves) than we are aware of. Tapping into it, I believe, is a matter of opening yourself up to possibility and seeing where it takes you. Thoughts are things, I firmly believe, which is why I work hard to keep mine positive, and open.

When you're not writing, what do you enjoy doing?
Simple things. My daughter is my greatest joy. My husband is a pretty close second! I love puttering around in my yard and working on my flower beds, music, reading, movies and watching TV. And no day would be complete without a cat sprawled in my lap (such as the one there right now!).

Do you believe in love at first sight?
Absolutely. I believe there's an awareness right
from the beginning, whether it be positive or
negative, romantic love or fondness. I've met
people whom I've felt like I've known forever, just
as I've met people who immediately put me on
guard for no apparent reason. I believe there are
connections between and among people, and
that if you're open to it, you can and will feel
these connections from the very first meeting.
I still remember the first time I saw my husband.
It was a work function. He was across the room.
I remember looking up and seeing him. He was
laughing, and it was like a ripple straight through
me. I felt warmth, even though we lived in cities
1,000 miles apart and had never met. Would I call
it love? I didn't think so at that moment, but I
knew I needed to go over and meet him!

Is there one book that changed your life somehow?
There are many books that have changed my life.
An easy answer is Judith McNaught's *Paradise*,
which unlocked something inside of me. My
imagination soared and my love for romance
took over, leaving me no choice but to begin
writing my own stories and pursuing publication.
On a different note, another book that really
changed my life was *Conquering Infertility* by
Alice Domar...for obvious reasons!

What are your top three favorite books?
That's a hard one! *Island of the Blue Dolphins*
by Scott O'Dell (a children's book). *The Stand* by
Stephen King. And...yes, *Paradise* by
Judith McNaught.

What are you working on right now?
I'm transitioning, actually! I just finished writing
Veiled Legacy, book six in an exciting new series
(MADONNA KEY) that will be published by
Silhouette Bombshell starting next summer. The
series features the descendants of ancient
priestesses on a race against time to reassemble
the lost pieces of a powerful mosaic...and stop
the bad guys from unleashing their own insidious
brand of terror on the world.

Now I return to southern Louisiana, where I
will be continuing the stories of several characters
introduced in *Killing Me Softly*. First up is Cain's
sister Saura and the mysterious police detective
John D'Ambrosia, two solo operators forced to
join forces to find out who killed their mutual
friend Alec Prejean, and why. Next up is Cain's
cousin Gabe Fontenot. Gabe's been having a
tough time since *Killing Me Softly*, and even
though Evangeline Rousseau knows she should
leave him alone, she can't. Evie has very personal
reasons for working her way into Gabe's life!
And, finally, in the third book we'll meet

Camille Fontenot, Gabe's younger sister who has been missing for over a decade. We'll learn what she really saw the night her father allegedly committed suicide, why she left town and, more importantly, why she's back! I hope you'll enjoy reading about the Robichauds as much as I enjoy writing about them!

Recipes from the Robichaud Family Cookbook
by Jenna Mills

ROBICHAUD FAMILY GUMBO

Cajuns know how to cook, and the Robichauds are no different. Like most long-standing families, recipes are handed down through the generations, but rarely committed to paper. And you're every bit as likely to find a man in the kitchen, as a woman!

While the rest of the country is feasting on turkey at Thanksgiving and roast beef for Christmas, the Robichauds are more likely to be indulging in a gumbo. Every good Cajun knows there are almost endless possibilities to a good gumbo, from chicken and sausage, to seafood, to venison, etc. But to start you out, here's a peek at how the Robichauds make shrimp and crab gumbo!

2 lb whole shrimp
10 cups water
2 tsp salt

1/4 lb shortening
1/2 cup flour
1 large white onion, chopped
1/2 cup celery, chopped
1 cup chopped okra
1 tbsp minced parsley
1 lb crabmeat
1 tsp black pepper
1/2 tsp cayenne pepper
Salt to taste
1 tbsp filé powder
4 cups hot, cooked rice

Peel and head the shrimp, put the meat aside. Put the water, salt and shrimp peels into a large soup pot and bring to a boil. Keep boiling for approximately 30 minutes, or until the water has been reduced to about 4 cups. Strain out the shells and reserve the liquid. Set aside.

Add the shortening to a large soup pot and melt. Add the flour and cook, stirring constantly until the mixture, called a "roux" is a dark nutty-brown color. (The darker the color, the richer the roux. But don't burn.) Add the chopped white onion, celery and okra. Cook until they brown.

Add the parsley and cook for another 5 minutes. Blend the reserved shrimp liquid into the ingredients. Bring to a boil, reduce to a

simmer and continue cooking for another 30
or so minutes. Add the shrimp and cook for
2 minutes more. Blend in the filé powder.
Put 1/2 cup hot, cooked rice into a large bowl,
and ladle the gumbo on top. Hunker down, and
enjoy. Serves 6-8.

TARA PREJEAN'S PAIN PERDU

There's nothing like a plantation breakfast. When
establishing her bed-and-breakfast, Tara Prejean
knew one of the ways she could make sure her
guests came back for more was to give them
something special for breakfast...and hence her
Pain Perdu was born.

In the old days, money was tight and Creoles
couldn't afford to throw away food. Stale bread,
they learned, could actually be quite useful—
bread crumbs, croutons, bread pudding
and...French toast (lost bread/pain perdu).
Baked fresh daily, French bread only maintains
its freshness for a short amount of time. But slice
it up and dip the pieces in a sugary batter, then
fry them up...oh, la, la!

Here's what you need:
3 eggs
1/4 cup sugar
1 tbsp vanilla extract
1 tbsp cinnamon
1/2 tbsp nutmeg
1 cup milk
2 sticks butter
1 loaf stale French bread
(or 10 slices of regular bread)
Powdered sugar
Cane syrup

Here's what you do: Beat the eggs and sugar together until the sugar is dissolved. Blend in the vanilla, cinnamon and nutmeg. Whisk in milk. If using French bread, cut the bread crosswise into 1-inch slices (otherwise use presliced bread). Melt the butter in a heavy skillet. When butter is hot, begin cooking the bread by dipping each slice into the egg and milk mixture, then placing it in the hot butter. Brown the bread on both sides. Remove to serving platter. Spread with margarine, if you like. Add a dusting of powdered sugar and a dribble of syrup. Enjoy! Serves 6.

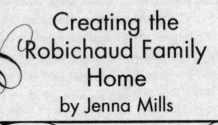

Creating the Robichaud Family Home
by Jenna Mills

I've always been fascinated by old places. There's a feel to them, a texture, as if the echoes and memories of all those who lived there before linger somehow, inviting and seducing. If you close your eyes, you can almost see everything as it once was.

As a little girl, I loved visiting the old antebellum plantations of Louisiana. I would walk through the grand entry halls and walk up the sweeping staircases, run my hand along the banisters and let my imagination soar.

Somewhere along the time Cain and Renee's story was first starting to form in my mind, I was home visiting my parents. Now my father, he's an avid amateur photographer, and visits home always include viewing the photographs he's taken since our last visit. He travels a great deal, so I'm always in for a treat. This time was no different. This time I was flipping through his photo album when I ran across one of the most haunting photographs I'd ever seen. Columns. That was all. Beautiful, ornate, weathered columns standing by themselves in a heavily wooded area. Clearly they'd once embraced a home. But the columns were all that remained, rising like placeholders against a steely gray sky.

And just like that, Cain and Renee's story had a home—a home that no longer stood. Suddenly I could see everything. I could see Cain standing among those columns, waiting for his lover to emerge from the woods. I could hear the echoes of her voice, and feel the whisper of the wind. I could feel his anguish. His horror. His guilt. And then I could see them there many months later, when she came back to him—and he walked away. And I could see him standing there again another night, ready to put the past to rest and embrace the future.

A photograph...that's all it was. But for me, those columns provided the soul to the story, and the rest, as they say, was history.

Why Romance Matters
by Jenna Mills

Sometimes it's hard to watch the evening news. We turn on the TV and hear about flood and famine, hurricanes and tsunamis and earthquakes, wars and discord. It's impossible not to look in the mirror and wonder what really matters. What's important. What cannot be replaced. Many of life's small pleasures suddenly seem trivial, even insignificant. How can we sing when there is so much strife in the world? How can we dance when there is so much turmoil? How can we smile when so many others hurt?

How can we curl up with a book when there are cities and countries to rebuild, and a war to win?

So many questions...too few answers. Can we ever go back to *before?* Can hope fill our hearts? Can we find a way to believe in happy endings again, in peace and harmony and security, in dreams that once upon a time we believed unequivocally could and would come true?

Should we even want to?

Yes. Absolutely, positively, without a doubt *yes*.

History is populated by events, horrific and wonderful, that changed the course of the world. One instant can change one life, ten lives, thousands of lives. But it's important to use this heightened awareness to celebrate all that is good. Because still, there is so much good. It's everywhere, all around us. It's the laughter of a child. The warmth in a friend's smile. The gentleness of a lover's touch.

Romance.

But what is romance, really? Is it red roses and expensive chocolates, sexy lingerie and champagne and silk sheets? Maybe. Sometimes. However, more often than not it's a celebration of the power of human relationships, of communication and values and principles, of honor, loyalty and commitment. Growth. Respect. Making the hard choice, because it's the *right* choice.

Romance is as old as time itself. Romance is love. Romance is the belief that dreams can come true, good can defeat evil and happy endings really can happen.

Recently, my husband I celebrated our fourteen-year anniversary. Now, maybe this isn't all that long, but considering over half of all marriages end in divorce, we considered the event a significant milestone. It also prompted us to evaluate how we've stayed together, when so many of our friends and relatives have suffered the heartache of broken marriages.

The answer?

Romance.

No, I don't mean flowers and expensive jewelry, candles and fine wine, though sure, each of those has a time and place. Romance in real life is much like romance in movies and novels— not the clichés everyone thinks of, the bodice rippers from another era, but the honest representations of life as we live it. The struggles and challenges and compromises, the tears and triumphs. The joy. Stakes may be higher in fiction (hopefully!), the drama more intense, the characters larger than life, but at the core of each story are the same touchstones we all encounter—the hard choices, desires that conflict with responsibility, the compromise and growth that make life so rewarding.

In fiction (just as in reality), romances offer a glowing affirmation of the best of the best, a world where good conquers evil and dreams come true. Where multifaceted men and women face challenges and grow to overcome them. Where insecurities and pettiness are put aside for a common good.

A librarian's daughter, books have always filled my hands, stories my heart. I can't imagine anything different. Shortly after 9/11, I picked up a book by a friend of mine, Kylie Brant. Now, one thing you need to remember: a book goes into production approximately nine months before it hits the shelf. That means the author puts words to paper a good twelve to eighteen months before. Well, in Kylie's book, her protagonists were hunting terrorists threatening to release the anthrax virus in the United States. Wow. Does art imitate life, life imitate art, or are the two really mirror images? Many would say my friend had terrible luck to have this work of fiction released during such a tumultuous time. And her sales may well prove this to be true.

But let me tell you something. In her book, the good guys won. And at that moment in time, there was nothing I needed to read more than a story of a man and a woman with the courage to face down an evil challenge and not only survive, but win. Because I need to believe that's possible. I need the faith that comes from believing art and life *are* mirror images, that anything is possible, that good can win in real life, so long as the values promoted in romance are the values we live by—honor and integrity, compassion, dedication and loyalty, courage. Faith.

Because romance isn't all roses and flowery vows of love. It can be as simple as putting gas in your significant other's car because you know they're busy and won't have time to do so. Romance can be taking a loved one's hand and holding on tight, because you know they desperately need the warmth of human touch. Romance can be walking your dog through a park or doing the dishes. Because when it comes down to it, romance is not about sex, but rather, the glue that makes our world a place where we want to live.

Romance is about *love*, and romance matters *now more than ever*. Romance is a mirror of the world in which we live, the world where hope still fills our hearts, where happy endings happen, where dreams can and do come true.

COMING NEXT MONTH

Signature Select Collection
A FARE TO REMEMBER by Vicki Lewis Thompson, Julie Elizabeth Leto, Kate Hoffmann
A matchmaking New York City taxi driver must convince three women he's found their life matches...but it's hardly a smooth ride.

Signature Select Saga
YOU MADE ME LOVE YOU by C.J. Carmichael
For six friends, childhood summers on a British Columbian island forged lifelong friendships that shaped their futures for the better... and the worst. Years later, death brings tragedy, mystery and love to two of them as they explore what really happened.

Signature Select Miniseries
SEDUCING McCOY by Tori Carrington
Law-enforcement brothers David and Connor McCoy find that upholding the law can get in the way of love as they try to convince two women not to settle for less than the *real* McCoy!

Signature Select Spotlight
CONFESSIONS OF A PARTY CRASHER by Holly Jacobs
Though her friends agree that it's a great way to meet men, Morgan Miller isn't comfortable crashing a posh wedding reception. Then again, it's better than not going at all...especially when wedding photographer Conner Danning enters the picture!

Signature Select Showcase
LOVE SONG FOR A RAVEN by Elizabeth Lowell
A ferocious storm plunged Janna Morgan into the icy water of the frigid sea—until untamed and enigmatic Carlson Raven saves her. Stranded together in a deserted paradise, Raven is powerless to resist his attraction to Janna. But, could he believe her feelings were love and not merely gratitude?

Silhouette®
BOMBSHELL™

THE GIFTED.
MAGIC IS THEIR DESTINY.

DAUGHTER OF THE FLAMES
by Nancy Holder

June 2006

When a mysterious stranger helped her discover her family's legacy of fighting evil, things began to make sense in Isabella DeMarco's life. But could she marshal her newfound supernatural powers to fend off the formidable vampire hell-bent on bringing Izzy down in flames?

More dark secrets will be revealed as
The Gifted continues in

Daughter of the Blood
December 2006

SPECIAL PRICE!

This riveting new saga begins with

In the Dark

by national bestselling author

JUDITH ARNOLD

The party at Hotel Marchand is in full swing when the lights suddenly go out. What does head of security Mac Jensen do first? He's torn between two jobs—protecting the guests at the hotel and keeping the woman he loves safe.

A woman to protect. A hotel to secure. And no idea who's determined to harm them.

On Sale June 2006

HOTEL MARCHAND

**Four sisters.
A family legacy.
And someone is out to destroy it.**

_____

**A captivating new limited
continuity, launching June 2006**

_____

The most beautiful hotel in New Orleans,
and someone is out to destroy it. But mystery,
danger and some surprising family revelations
and discoveries won't stop the Marchand sisters
from protecting their birthright…
and finding love along the way.

If you enjoyed what you just read,
then we've got an offer you can't resist!

Take 2 bestselling
love stories FREE!
Plus get a FREE surprise gift!

Clip this page and mail it to Harlequin Reader Service®

IN U.S.A.	IN CANADA
3010 Walden Ave.	P.O. Box 609
P.O. Box 1867	Fort Erie, Ontario
Buffalo, N.Y. 14240-1867	L2A 5X3

YES! Please send me 2 free Harlequin Romance® novels and my free surprise gift. After receiving them, if I don't wish to receive anymore, I can return the shipping statement marked cancel. If I don't cancel, I will receive 6 brand-new novels every month, before they're available in stores! In the U.S.A., bill me at the bargain price of $3.57 plus 25¢ shipping & handling per book and applicable sales tax, if any*. In Canada, bill me at the bargain price of $4.05 plus 25¢ shipping & handling per book and applicable taxes**. That's the complete price and a savings of 10% off the cover prices—what a great deal! I understand that accepting the 2 free books and gift places me under no obligation ever to buy any books. I can always return a shipment and cancel at any time. Even if I never buy another book from Harlequin, the 2 free books and gift are mine to keep forever.

186 HDN DZ72
386 HDN DZ73

Name	(PLEASE PRINT)	
Address	Apt.#	
City	State/Prov.	Zip/Postal Code

Not valid to current Harlequin Romance® subscribers.
Want to try another series? Call 1-800-873-8635
or visit www.morefreebooks.com.

* Terms and prices subject to change without notice. Sales tax applicable in N.Y.
** Canadian residents will be charged applicable provincial taxes and GST.
  All orders subject to approval. Offer limited to one per household.
  ® are registered trademarks owned and used by the trademark owner and or its licensee.

HROM04R   ©2004 Harlequin Enterprises Limited

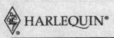